The Saint

FROM BIG SCREEN TO SMALL SCREEN AND BACK AGAIN

PAUL SIMPER

CHAMELEON

In memory of Georgie

All those years of happy viewing at Harepath

First published in Great Britain in 1997 by
Chameleon Books, an imprint of André Deutsch Ltd
106 Great Russell Street
London WC1B 3LJ
André Deutsch is a subsidiary of VCI plc

CIP data for this title is available from the British Library

ISBN 0 233 99102 6

Book and jacket design by Sarah Habershon

Printed and bound in Great Britain by
Butler & Tanner Ltd, Frome and London

Contents

UNICEF

[signature] Roger Moore
8th March 1997.

Acknowledgements

Without the extraordinarily generous help of the following, this book would simply not have been possible: Roger Moore, Doris Spriggs, John Kruse, Freddie Francis, Roy Ward Baker, Sylvia Syms, Shirley Eaton, Annette André, Tony Arnell, Johnny Goodman, Malcolm Christopher, Terry Cole, Burl Barer, Dave Crowe, Deanne Pearson (for overcoming all production difficulties, including an armed robbery!), Meg Simmons at Eon, Jane Shaw at the NFT, Mike Jones, Ian Dickerson (for cutting the Episode Guide), Dan Bodenheimer, Kevin Higgins and Mark Corby (sorry your copy was cut), Johanna Hargreaves, Steve Furst ('You put your clothes on and I'll buy you an ice-cream'), Mike 'Giddy Up!' Leigh, Paul Marcus, Audrey Charteris, Kate Whitaker, Teresa O'Hehir, David Johnson, Steve Turney, Jon Keeble, Maria and Andrew Panos, Mark Booker, Steven Brand, Anthony Way and Mrs W, Patrice Ferviér at Polygram UK, Maggie Nuttall, Radio Days, Mrs Simper and, perhaps most vitally, Robert S. Baker for giving such kind encouragement and support and Sarah Habershon for her beautiful design and patience with all the excess copy.

Excerpts and background material from the following invaluable publications reproduced with permission:
The Saint: A Complete History in Print, Radio, Film and Television by Burl Barer (McFarland Press)
The Roger Moore Action Adventure Annual (Panther Books)
The Epistle

Saint memorabilia property of Mike Jones. Used with kind permission.

<u>Recommended Reading</u>
The Saint: A novelisation by Burl Barer (Pocket Books)
The Saintly Bible on the Internet by Dan Bodenheimer (saint @ saint. org)
Roger Moore as James Bond 007 by Roger Moore (Pan)
The Epistle, official newsletter to The Saint Club by Ian Dickerson (The Saint Club c/o Arbour Youth Centre, Shandy Street, Stepney, London E1 4ST, England)

Front cover photo: Shirley Eaton and Roger Moore partake of tiffin in *The Talented Husband* (Popperfoto)

An introduction

There's a scene in *Pulp Fiction* where we see Bruce Willis' character, Butch, when he was a kid. Butch is sat on the floor in the front room watching TV. Except he's not just watching it, his nose is practically glued to the screen. If he were any closer he would be behind it. Actor/director Steve Buscemi quotes this as his idea of the young Quentin Tarantino – a kid who saw the TV as his friend. Quentin was not alone...

Growing up with television in the 1960s was an all-consuming experience for many children both here and in America (and no doubt other parts of the globe where parents stomped their feet with frustration at the apparent sudden inactivity of their young ones). There was nothing like the choice we now enjoy in the 1990s – that child with her toys, balloon and blackboard on the test card seemed an almost permanent fixture – but what series there were, were perhaps all the more priceless for it. And as the TV experience grew, so we grew with it.

For me, a good credit sequence and signature tune were the key. *Captain Scarlett* had both. So, in their own way, did the *Banana Splits*. But it was only when my roving radar locked in on the ATV/ABC stable of action series that I really hit paydirt. *The Champions* with their lustrous theme and fountain. *The Avengers* – Diana Rigg of course – with their surreal mix of Old England and sexy judo moves. *The Persuaders* rolled two irresistibly glamorous success stories past your eyes while your heart quickened at that John Barry bass line. *Randall & Hopkirk (deceased)* told a more macabre tale with an appropriately haunting tune. And *The Saint?* Well, *The Saint*'s beginning was just perfect...

Each week we would be primed – as we were in the *Bond* series – with a taste of his forthcoming adventure. Each week some probing soul would question or reveal his identity. And each week we would wait for Roger Moore to nonchalantly roll his eyes to the heavens, as that trademark halo appeared above his immaculately coiffed bonce and Edwin Astley's sprightly theme tune kicked in...

Thirty five years on, and it seems the power of that formula has barely diminished. Simon Templar is once again on our TV screens in the reassuring shape of Roger Moore, despatching merry quips and lethal right hooks with equal aplomb. There are video releases from ITC of the two double-length *Saint* episodes, *The Fiction-Makers* and *Vendetta for the Saint*, and for those who feel so inclined there is Paramount's Val Kilmer offering (though Saint aficionado Burl Barer's novelisation is more likely to please Charteris fans).

And what is the purpose of this volume? Simply, dear reader, to take a fresh look at a favourite series. Hopefully the collection of new interviews, generously agreed to by a number of key contributors to the show, will throw some new perspective on a particularly bountiful period of British television. Personally I like the old press clippings where the showbiz journos still respectfully refer to Rog as 'Mr Moore'.

Whatever, enjoy...

1: THE SAINT COMES TO TELEVISION

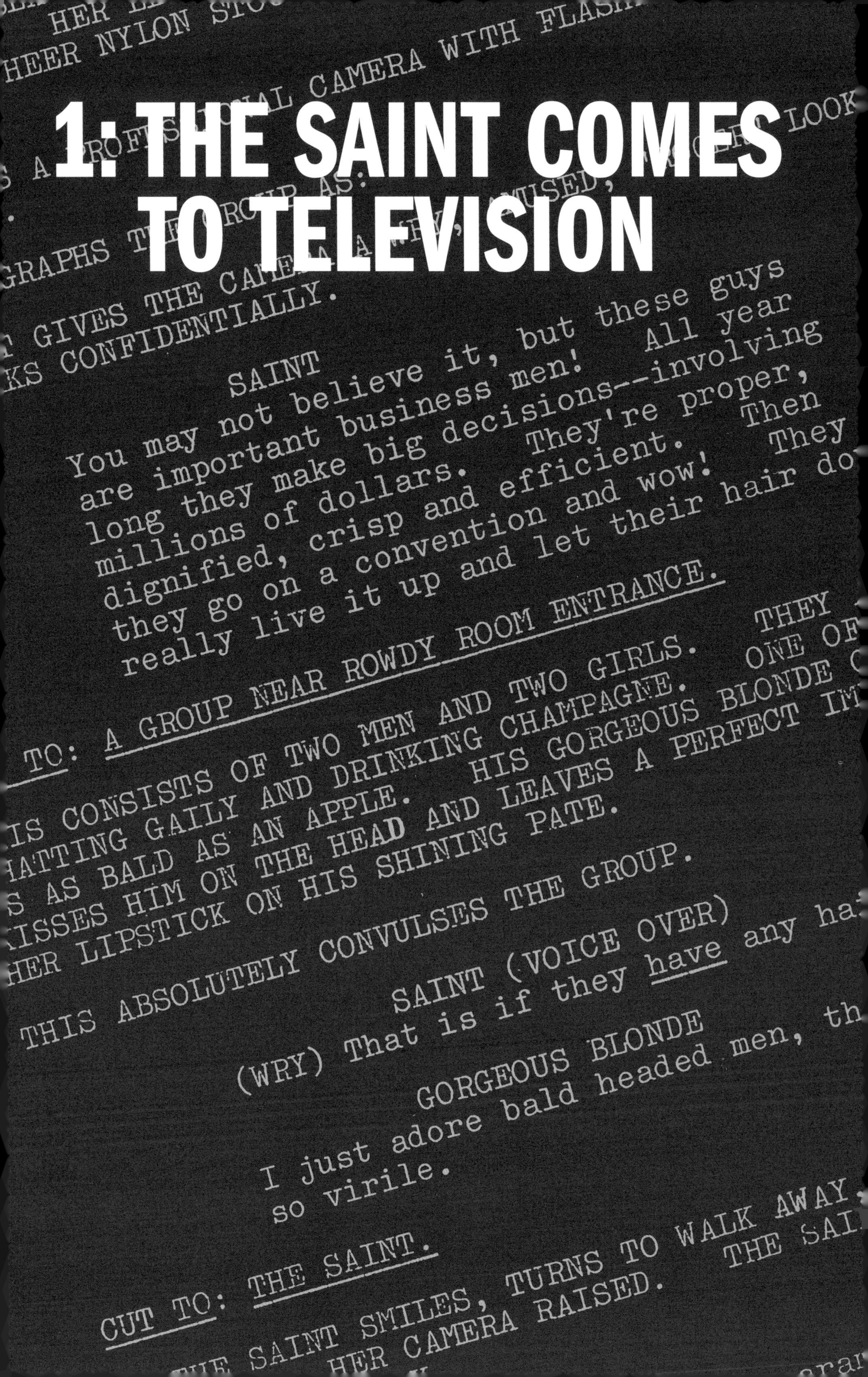

HER LI...
HEER NYLON STO...
S A PROFESSIONAL CAMERA WITH FLASH...
GRAPHS THE GROUP AS: ...AMUSED, ...ER LOOK...
T GIVES THE CAMERA...
KS CONFIDENTIALLY.

SAINT

You may not believe it, but these guys are important business men! All year long they make big decisions--involving millions of dollars. They're proper, dignified, crisp and efficient. Then they go on a convention and wow! They really live it up and let their hair do-

_TO:_ _A GROUP NEAR ROWDY ROOM ENTRANCE._

IS CONSISTS OF TWO MEN AND TWO GIRLS. THEY
HATTING GAILY AND DRINKING CHAMPAGNE. ONE OF
S AS BALD AS AN APPLE. HIS GORGEOUS BLONDE
ISSES HIM ON THE HEAD AND LEAVES A PERFECT IM
HER LIPSTICK ON HIS SHINING PATE.

THIS ABSOLUTELY CONVULSES THE GROUP.

SAINT (VOICE OVER)

(WRY) That is if they _have_ any hai

GORGEOUS BLONDE

I just adore bald headed men, th
so virile.

CUT TO: THE SAINT.

SAINT SMILES, TURNS TO WALK AWAY.
HER CAMERA RAISED.   THE SAI

'Things are beginning to liven up'

Dennis Potter reviews the first *Saint* episode for the television page of the *Daily Herald, 1 October 1962. (*the popular left-wing daily that would later become your caring, sharing *Sun*).**

A review of *The Talented Husband* by Dennis Potter in the *Daily Herald*, 1 October 1962

'THINGS ARE BEGINNING TO LIVEN UP'

Last night the new offering was *The Saint*, a delightfuly sleek and promising series featuring Leslie Charteris' famous sleuth, the handsome hero figure with a portable halo and a fast sports car.

I have been a fan of the Saint ever since discovering that he was not, in fact, the prig his name suggested that he might be.

Roger Moore played the Saint with just the right well-tailored dash. His good deed last night was to prevent a wastrel of a husband from murdering his third wife.

The plot was wildly improbable, with the wicked husband stirring rat poison into the lamb stew with all the gleeful viciousness of an army cook feeding new recruits. (*Potter then watched Perry Mason on the BBC.*)

IT IS HARD NOW to imagine the impact of *The Saint* on the great British viewing public of the early – and far from swinging – 1960s. Along with that other ATV action/adventure series *Danger Man* (starring Patrick McGoohan) it instigated a whole new era of television.

Until the BBC's 20-year broadcasting monopoly was broken on 22 September 1955, there had been a rather nannying feeling that television was something only to be enjoyed in the most moderate and austere of doses. A chance for the middle classes to exercise the old brain cells for a few hours, before popping off to bed.

Commercial television changed all that.

All of a sudden education was out and Entertainment was in. With a brash new style that owed plenty to the more vigorous (and in terms of pacing and production values more sophisticated) fare from across the pond the head of ATV, Lew Grade, (once Sir, now Lord Grade) showed folk what a good time they really could be having when they turned on the box.

Lew brought us game shows (*Beat The Clock*), variety shows (*Sunday Night at the London Palladium*), comedies (sassy imports like *I Love Lucy*), swashbucklers (*The Adventures of Robin Hood, William Tell*) and finally fast-moving, stylised action/adventure. At the same time that two Americans, Harry Saltzman and Albert R. Broccoli, were introducing cinema audiences to a new, sexy, cosmopolitan version of that famous British agent 007, Lew and two British producers were making in-roads into a similar small screen transformation – the updating of another hero of British fiction, Leslie Charteris' Saint.

It was a package that seemed as attractive to producers Robert S. Baker and Monty Berman as it did to Lew Grade when they brought it to him. Almost unbelievably Leslie Charteris – a zealous guardian of his hero – was making the rights available for Baker and Berman to adapt his best-selling stories into hour-long TV adventures. A tried and tested character, with enough original Charteris tales to keep their modern-day Robin Hood in business for a very long time, seemed as close to a racing cert as you could possibly hope to get.

After a week of intense haggling in Florida (which Charteris and his American wife, Audrey, had made their home at that time) Bob Baker returned with the deal. With typical aplomb, Lew Grade announcd that not only would he commission an initial run of 26 *Saint* episodes (starring

Roger Moore and Jane Merrow imagine the impact in The Happy Suicide

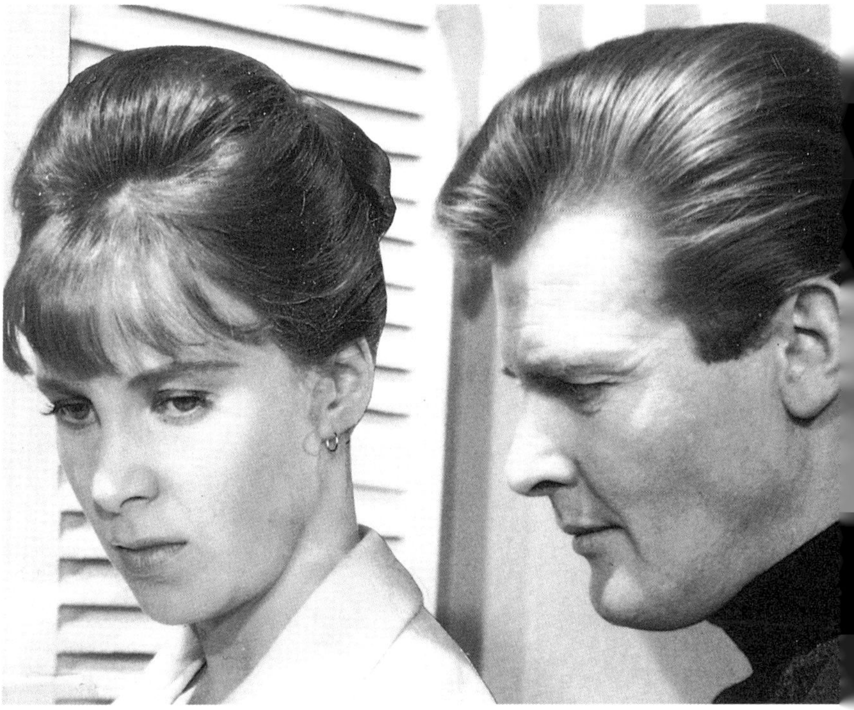
POPPERFOTO

REVIEWS FROM THE *DAILY MIRROR* AND *DAILY TELEGRAPH*

The Talented Husband, reviewed by Clifford Davis in the *Daily Mirror*, 1 October 1962

Roger Moore made a big impact in the first of ITV's new *Saint* series last night. He isn't exactly my idea of the tough, hard-hitting adventurer created by Leslie Charteris – but all the same, he made a very likeable hero.

He had the right touch of charm and devil-may-care approach. In the past Mr Moore has never quite made it as a TV hero – obviously he's never been given the chance. This series should put him right at the top.

The Talented Husband, reviewed by J.F.W. in the *Daily Telegraph*, 1 October 1962

'A QUEER ACCENT AT COOKHAM'

The furrowed brow, the righteously moved expression, on the face of Roger Moore, playing Simon Templar: that is doubtless what we shall be getting at the end of each of the 39 episodes of *The Saint*, which Associated Television began last night. The first story was about a man's thwarted attempt to poison his third rich wife. No criticism on production: it was all presented in the slick and easily digestible way we have come to expect from television.

But the stated setting of the old-world village of Cookham caused annoying distraction throughout.

Everyone, with possible minor exceptions, had that semi-American accent often denigrated as mid-Atlantic, which is known to help sell TV series in America. J.F.W.

2.

CONTD.

STOUT MAN

Hey Pete..smell!

PETE OBEDIENTLY BENDS OVER THE FLOWER, SNIFFS AT IT. HE GETS A STREAM OF WATER IN HIS FACE.

THE GROUP IS ABSOLUTELY CONVULSED WITH THE HUMOUR OF THIS.

DURING THIS NORMA UPTON WALKS INTO THE SHOT. NORMA IS ABOUT TWENTY FIVE, BEAUTIFULLY BUILT. SHE WEARS VERY SKIMPY BLACK SATIN SHORTS AND SOME SORT OF TIGHT FITTING TOP. HER LEGS, WHICH SEEM ENDLESS, ARE ENCASED IN SHEER NYLON STOCKINGS AND VERY HIGH HEELED SHOES.

SHE CARRIES A PROFESSIONAL CAMERA WITH FLASHBULB ATTACHMENT.

SHE PHOTOGRAPHS THE GROUP AS:

THE SAINT GIVES THE CAMERA A WRY, AMUSED, "ROGER" LOOK AND SPEAKS CONFIDENTIALLY.

SAINT

You may not believe it, but these guys are important business men! All year long they make big decisions--involving millions of dollars. They're proper, dignified, crisp and efficient. Then they go on a convention and wow! They really live it up and let their hair down.

CUT TO: A GROUP NEAR ROWDY ROOM ENTRANCE.

THIS CONSISTS OF TWO MEN AND TWO GIRLS. THEY ARE CHATTING GAILY AND DRINKING CHAMPAGNE. ONE OF THE MEN IS AS BALD AS AN APPLE. HIS GORGEOUS BLONDE COMPANION KISSES HIM ON THE HEAD AND LEAVES A PERFECT IMPRINT OF HER LIPSTICK ON HIS SHINING PATE.

THIS ABSOLUTELY CONVULSES THE GROUP.

SAINT (VOICE OVER)

(WRY) That is if they have any hair.

GORGEOUS BLONDE

I just adore bald headed men, they're so virile.

CUT TO: THE SAINT.

AS THE SAINT SMILES, TURNS TO WALK AWAY, NORMA UPTON STOPS HIM, HER CAMERA RAISED. THE SAINT PUTS UP HIS HAND DEFENSIVELY.

SAINT

No thanks. I'm not a caramel cooker.

NORMA

I know. Let me take one anyway. For myself.

CONT'

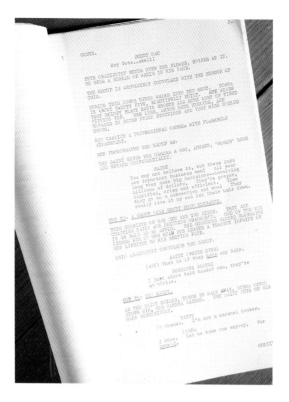

The script is the thing. A page from The Ever-Loving Spouse

young ATV favourite Roger Moore), but he would also do so at a cost that was twice the originally proposed budget.

Where another competitor, Brian Tesler at Rediffusion, had balked at a fee of £15,000 an episode (Baker and Berman had approached him first), Lew decided on £30,000 and to hell with the expense. He was prepared to gamble on its greatness with a confidence that was self-fulfilling. He was also aware that by shooting these features on film, rather than the inferior but cheaper telecine, he would have a much better chance of selling them to the American market. And Lew liked to sell.

Like the swashbucklers that he had so boldly staked almost the whole of his initial budget on, (£390,000 out of £500,000), when first commissioning programmes for ATV, *The Saint* would lead the way with its high production values, its dazzling stars and its New Era brand of excitement. It was given the prime slot – 7.25pm on a Sunday night, right before the channel's showpiece, *Sunday Night at the London Palladium*.

The first week it was number three in the ratings, by the New Year it had made it all the way to number one. Roger Moore's career, which had briefly stalled after a series of none too satisfying brushes with American television, was suddenly sniffing the rarefied air of the internationally famous. The series – or rather the six series – were sold to 63 countries for a figure in excess of £370 million. For Lew Grade and ATV (the first company in the entertainment business ever to win the Queen's Award to Industry), there was even the crowning achievement of selling back to the Americans a genre which they were under the impression they had invented themselves.

POPPERFOTO

Manning Wilson, as Inspector Quercy, goes hunting for pearl necklaces in Jeannine *while the guilty party, Sylvia Syms, looks on*

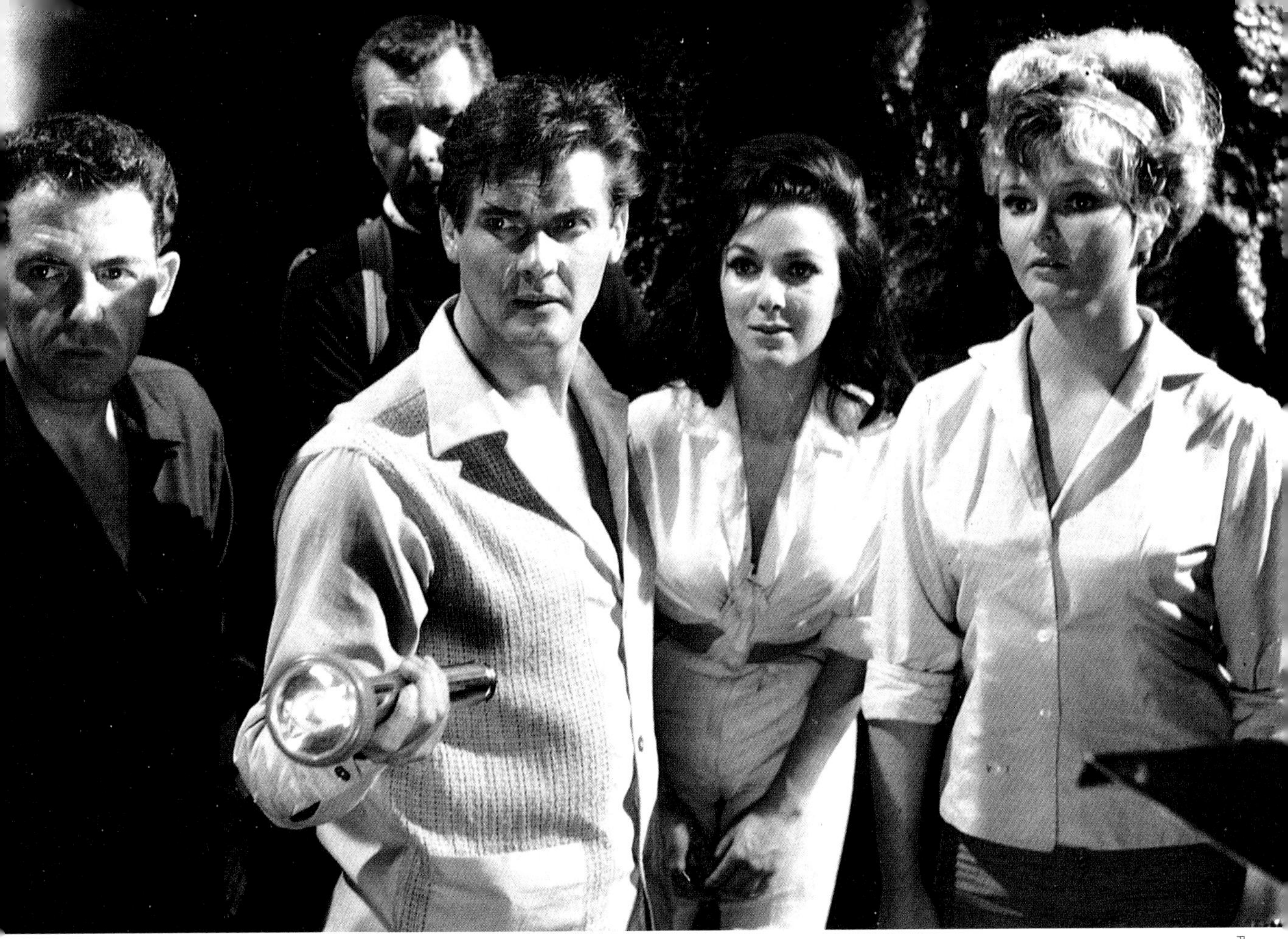

POPPERFOTO

Roger demonstrates his dazzling torch technique in The Old Treasure Story *with (l-r) Jack Hedley, Robert Hutton, Jill Curzon and Erica Rogers*

As success breeds success, more series followed. Monty Berman left *The Saint* to create *The Baron, Department S, The Champions* and *Randall & Hopkirk (deceased)*. While Bob Baker found a willing new co-producer in Roger Moore (they formed BAMORE) with whom he produced the last 47 episodes, including the two double-length features *The Fiction-Makers* and *Vendetta for the Saint*, which were both released theatrically in Europe (in Spain *El Santo* was as hot as hot could be!)

In fact, the last 47 episodes were a success story in themselves. In 1966, *The Saint* was still languishing in the no-man's land that is syndicated TV in America. In other words, different parts of the country would get to see it at different times. But there was no regular slot. Just as here viewers have had to chase the random transmissions of imported series like *Seinfeld* and *The Larry Sanders Show*, so in America you would stumble across *The Saint* if you were lucky. Not the way you make a hit.

All this changed when a programme was needed to fill the slot left by *The Dean Martin Show* through the summer months. At that time the rival network, CBS, was doing first runs of classic Hollywood movies and trouncing NBC hands down. Lew Grade, who was on good enough terms with the US executives that he often used to sit in on their board meetings, suggested *The Saint* be given a shot. Episodes were tested, first on the east coast then the west, and much to the surprise of at least one NBC executive, who had earlier said of the show, 'I've never seen so much crap in all my life,' their success rocketed overnight. Suitably encouraged NBC ordered up 47 more – this time in colour – and the greatest deal of *The Saint*'s (and Lew Grade's, Bob Baker's and Roger Moore's) career had been done.

The only soul who was less than ecstatic through all the celebrations was Leslie Charteris. Delighted though he was with the tidy sums of money he was pocketing (and it was back to the haggle table for him and Bob Baker for the US colour series deal), he was much less satisfied with television's interpretation of his devil-may-care doer of derring.

Forced to adhere to the stringent morality codes of American TV, he saw his ingenious buccaneer reduced, in his eyes at least, to 'a conventional cliched TV-formula figure so busy rushing about and brawling that his own character has been submerged'.

It is a matter of critical debate that has raged between fans of the books and fans of the series (by no means two mutually inclusive factions) ever since...

A *Daily Express* review by Laurence Marks, 15 December 1962

'IT'S TIME FOR THIS SAINT'S HALO TO SLIP'

Leslie Charteris's (*sic*) hero spent a large part of my boyhood keeping humanity safe from the machinations of international gangsters.

He was tough and ruthless. But Mr Moore looks like a thoroughly scrupulous member of society.

Is this the man who stood by while Ivar Nordsten, one of the richest men in Europe, was killed by his own black panther?

No, sir. Mr Moore with his simple, honest, Li'l Abner face and open smile wouldn't have lasted one chapter among the gangsters.

And last Sunday's episode (*The Man Who Was Lucky*), I'm afraid, was just about as exciting as a shipping forecast.

It needed more incident and better dialogue to sustain a full hour's television.

The basic rules of this kind of entertainment are simple enough: you shouldn't know what is going to happen next, but you should definitely want to find out.

CLASSIC SAINT EPISODES

THE TALENTED HUSBAND **4 October 1962 (black & white)**
Cross-dressing and deadly lamb casseroles in this *Tales of the Unexpected*-style first outing for Mr Moore and his halo. Shirley Eaton makes her first of three appearances in the series, there's a deceptively dubbed cleaning woman, a sly Dirk Bogarde-style charmer from Derek Farr and S.T.'s entertaining theories on method acting and flat British beer, ('warm and nourishing').
With Derek Farr as John Clarron and Shirley Eaton as Adrienne Halberd.
Scr: Jack Sanders. Dir: Michael Truman.
From the 1954 Leslie Charteris short story, first published in The Saint Detective Magazine. *Included in* The Saint Around the World.

THE PEARLS OF PEACE **8 November 1962 (black & white)**
A fantastic Hemingway-style quest for mythical pearls, ('somewhere in the depths of the sea a grain of sand invaded the shell of an oyster), set in Mexico and featuring the first appearance of *Saint* regular Erica Rogers as an ambitious and wholly mercenary young lady. Only unnerving moment is a truly surreal bit of back-projection of Brad and Harry as they drive down to Mexico. They seem to be floating magically above the ground, while there is no sign of the luggage or spare tyre (most noticeable in the next scene) behind them!
With Dina Paisner as Consuelo and Erica Rogers as Joss Hendry.
Scr: Richard Harris. Dir: David Greene.
From the 1954 short story first published in The Saint Detective Magazine. *Included in* Senor Saint.

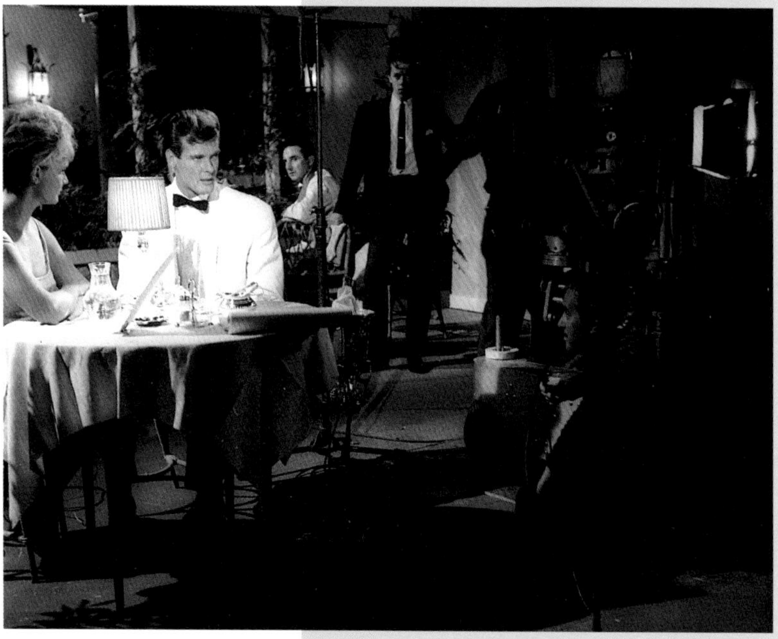

ROBERT S. BAKER. PRIVATE COLLECTION

'Alright Roger, you've got one take – and don't forget this is meant to be a classic.' Robert S. Baker directs The Golden Journey

THE GOLDEN JOURNEY **6 December 1962 (black & white)**
Essentially a two-hander, as Simon decides to do a friend a big favour by taking his spoilt, wealthy fiancée (Erica Rogers in feisty form) for an extended hike along the Costa Brava, pre-nuptials. Pretty much violence-free – unless you count a sound spanking of the brat by the Saint – but the banter and chemistry between Rog and La Rogers is great as the young lady is subjected to all sorts of indignities in the wild and given a quick lesson in better grammar. Belinda to Mr Templar: 'Oh no! I pick the best man and you are not it!' The Saint (oh so patiently): 'Not he.'
With Erica Rogers as Belinda Dean and Stella Bonheur as Aunt Joan West.
Scr: Lewis Davidson. Dir: Robert S. Baker.
From the 1934 short story. Included in The Saint in Europe.

THE SAINT PLAYS WITH FIRE **28 November 1963 (black & white)**
'People who forget the past are sometimes condemned to relive it.' Originally written by Charteris as the Nazis threatened to engulf Europe, this John Kruse update responded to uneasy rumblings of a Second Coming in the early 1960s.

It's a terrific episode, with bold use of close-ups and dramatic compositions by director Bob Baker and cameraman Lionel Banes. There's a great inquest scene, with smoke practically coming out of Rog's ears as he listens to a whitewash covering up the death of a young reporter by the neo-Nazis. Justine Lord sinks her teeth into the wholly unsympathetic role of gold-digging socialite Lady Valerie, attacking her 'h's and snapping each syllable, ('What a dis-gust-ing suggestion!'), while Joseph Furst moves with scary precision as the Nazi industrialist. Going to the wire there is even a protracted scene where you see the damage done to hands if you try that old movie trick of burning the ropes that bind you with a lighter.

This would have made a great theatrical release.
With Joseph Furst as Kane Luker, Justine Lord as Lady Valerie, Ivor Dean as Inspector Teal and Joe Robinson as Austin.
Scr: John Kruse. Dir: Robert S. Baker.
Adapted from the 1938 novel Prelude for War.

THE SCORPION 29 October 1964 (black & white)

From its atmospheric opening of Dudley Sutton, clad in motorcycle leathers and goggles, terrorising a victim round Bayswater at night, this is one of the very best of the series. Simon Templar discovers a friend of his is being blackmailed by a ruthless mastermind with the moniker The Scorpion. On the way he encounters cheap, blonde extortionist Nyree Dawn 'Avenues and Alleyways' Porter, ('Just a plain, simple girl trying to get along'), and yes, that prince of sleazy henchmen Dudley Sutton. On the small screen in the 1960s and 1970s, if something truly unpleasant had to be done to you Dudley, with his baby-gone-bad looks, would gleefully do it. 'Man is an animal and should behave like one,' he cheerfully philosophises to a petrified Nyree. T'would be a long time before he'd mellow into *Lovejoy*'s Tinker. One final thing for thrill seekers – at the very end of the story we get a shot of Roger himself dressed as a 'skid kid', goggles on forehead. Not quite *The Wild One*, but diverting all the same.

With Catherine Woodville as Karen Bates; Nyree Dawn Porter as Patsy Butler; Dudley Sutton as Eddy; Geoffrey Bayldon as Wilfred Garniman and Ivor Dean as Inspector Teal. Scr: Paul Erickson. Dir: Roy Baker.

Adapted from the 1931 short story The Inland Revenue, *first published in* Thriller. *Included in* The Saint versus Scotland Yard.

THE QUEEN'S RANSOM 30 September 1966 (colour)

High on the banter-factor, this sees Mr Templar slugging it out in the verbals department with Dawn Addams, whose haughty demeanour as Queen of Fadeera belies her roots as the daughter of a London bus driver. 'We find you arrogant, smug, self-important and impertinent,' she declares. And as they go to retrieve some stately jewels the Saint delights in winding her up every step of the way. 'Mem Sahib, permission to speak. May we have our lighter back, please?' he innocently requests. Before the life lesson is over Her Highness is intimidated by a cow and dropped on her Royal sit-upon by her reluctant courier. Watch out also for some grand old scene-stealing by Nora Nicholson as a deceptively benevolent widow. 'Willoughby was always able to raise the ede in me right to the end.'

With George Pastell as King Fallouda; Dawn Addams as Queen Adana; Nora Nicholson as Hortense; Peter Madden as Colonel Faied and John Woodvine as the pilot. Original screenplay: Leigh Vance. Dir: Roy Baker.

THE GADGET LOVERS 21 April 1967 (colour)

Bond-meets-*Ninotchka* in this tale of Russian secret agents being killed by their own gadgets. There's a great opening shot of a bunny girl carrying a flaming skewer of meat across a Berlin nightclub, to the sound of Swingin' Sixties music – a skewer which the Saint is quick to make good use of as he deals with a Russian assassin. Main focus of the story is an uneasy alliance between Simon Templar and Mary Peach's Russian Colonel – who could very well be the love child of a tryst between Tatiana Romanova and Rosa Klebb – as they try to uncover the source of all this mischief-making (Burt Kwouk's name in the cast list may give you a clue). Anoraks ahoy, as we're treated to an appearance by Glynn *Minder* Edwards as a close-cropped Russian bodyguard called Igor. It's the little things.

Leslie Charteris didn't give his favourite scriptwriter full marks for this one, but still thought it 'better than almost anyone else's'. One improbability he felt couldn't go unremarked on: 'How could a large bunch of Chinese take over, and inhabit, a Swiss monastery without being noticed by any of the villagers?' Especially if they were led by Cato.

With Mary Peach as Colonel Smolenko; Campbell Singer as Fenton; Glynn Edwards as Igor; Burt Kwouk as Colonel Wing and Vernon Dobtcheff as Vogel. Original screenplay: John Kruse. Dir: Jim O'Connolly.

THE HOUSE ON DRAGON'S ROCK 24 November 1968 (colour)

To Wales this time, for another legendary duel betwixt man and beast (or, er, insect). This time it's the Saint vs a giant ant. In probably the most outrageous entry in the whole series, Simon Templar has to do battle with a mad scientist, ('The Human race is doomed... I plan for the ants to take over), with only Annette André and her big black lashes to help him. Points of interest along the way are Glyn Houston as the publican and *Dad's Army*'s Taff – Talfyn Thomas – as a gibbering victim of the antenna-ed thing. 'Absolute first class script and very good treatment of my story,' was Leslie Charteris' surprisingly fulsome verdict on Mr Junkin.

With Anthony Bate as Dr Sardon; Annette André as Carmen; Glyn Houston as Dylan Williams and Talfyn Thomas as Owen Thomas. Scr: Harry W. Junkin. Dir: Roger Moore (trying to contain his mirth).

Based on the 1939 short story The Man Who Liked Ants. *Included in* The Happy Highwayman.

> ‘We find you arrogant, smug, self-important and impertinent,’
>
> Dawn Addams as Queen Adana in *The Queen's Ransom*

2: THE MOGULS

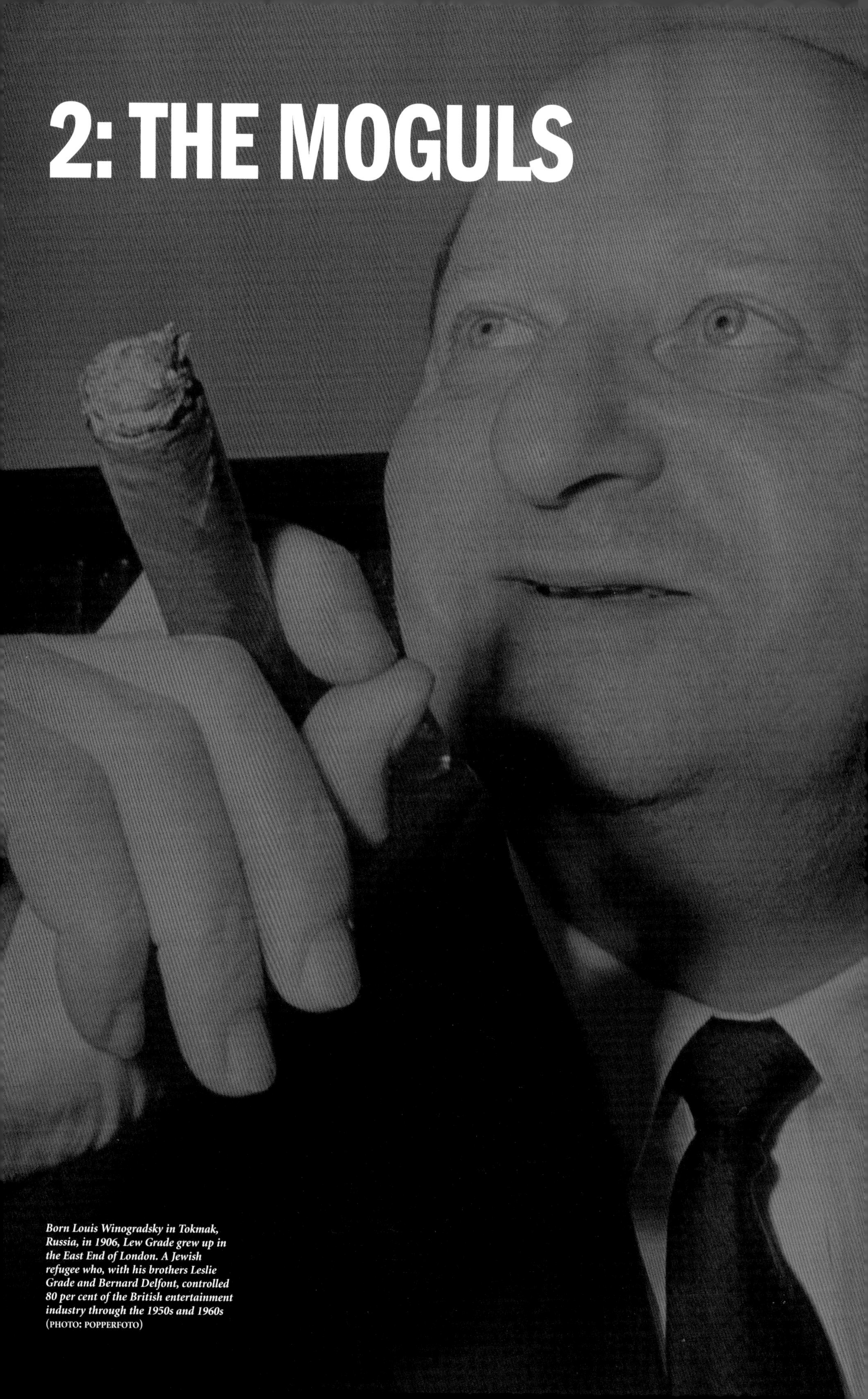

Born Louis Winogradsky in Tokmak, Russia, in 1906, Lew Grade grew up in the East End of London. A Jewish refugee who, with his brothers Leslie Grade and Bernard Delfont, controlled 80 per cent of the British entertainment industry through the 1950s and 1960s (PHOTO: POPPERFOTO)

'It's not that I'm such a good salesman – it's the <u>product</u>'

Lord Grade interviewed by nephew Michael Grade, 1995

From the tip of his seven-and-three-quarter inch Monte Cristo cigar to his World Champion charleston dancing tootsies, Lord Grade is a legend of British television. As plain old Lew Grade, managing director of ATV, he brought us *Danger Man, The Baron, The Champions, The Persuaders, Randall & Hopkirk (deceased), The Prisoner, The Protectors, Jason King* and of course *The Saint.*

In an age when American executives laughed at the idea of even buying one British television show, he sold them 40 series.

By 1969, when the Roger Moore Saints came to an end, his company had worldwide programme sales of over $100 million. All this he achieved on the strength of his word or a handshake – with a sales pitch that would indeed sell igloos to Eskimos.

Now 90, Lord Grade has five movie projects on the go, is already making his first deal of the day from his office at 7am and can boast a marriage to Lady Grade which celebrates 55 years this June (1997).

'The last of the great showmen', producer Robert S. Baker calls him. Here is what some others have said about the man and a collection of gems to have emanated from his own mouth, between puffs on that legendary cigar...

LEW GRADE ON:

HEADLINING AT THE MOULIN ROUGE IN THE 1920s 'It was a wonderful experience, but I was a little innocent. I remember being shown my dressing room and thinking how big it was. After my act, I went to towel myself down and found it full of naked chorus girls. I ran out and told the manager that there must be some mistake. He said, "It's no mistake. This is Paris".'

THE AMERICAN MARKET 'None but a fool makes television films for the British market alone. Without the guarantee of an American outlet he will lose his shirt.' – *23 January 1958*

THE VALUE OF A GOOD SCRIPT 'To hold our viewers we will aim to spend more money on scripts and production values. Stars are important, but not as important as a good scriptwriter. A good scriptwriter is the most wonderful thing. There is the person I always like to meet.' – *23 January 1958*

AN EARLY START 'At 5.30am I'm up. At 6am I've had my cup of tea with biscuits – currant biscuits. At 6.30am I've lit a cigar and I'm thinking of the day's problems. At 7am I'm on my way to the office and if I get held up in traffic I nearly go mad.'

THE SAINT AROUND THE WORLD

Lord Grade sold the Roger Moore series of *The Saint* to the following countries ...

Aden	Lebanon
Argentina	Liberia
Austria	Luxembourg
Australia	Malta
Belgium	Malaya
Bermuda	Mexico
Brazil	New Zealand
Chile	Nicaragua
Colombia	Nigeria
Canada	Norway
Costa Rica	Panama
Cyprus	Philippines
Denmark	Puerto Rico
Dominican Republic	Peru
El Salvador	Poland
Ethiopia	Portugal
Finland	Rhodesia
Formosa	Romania
France	Sierra Leone
Ghana	Singapore
Gibraltar	Spain
Guatemala	Sweden
Holland	Switzerland
Honduras	Thailand
Hong Kong	U.A.R.
Hungary	USA (syndication and network)
Iceland	
Iran	Uruguay
Italy	Venezuela
Japan	West Germany
Kenya	Yugoslavia
Kuwait	Zambia

CULTURE 'I'm not very fond of cultural things, but I don't dislike them. I enjoy good culture... and Westerns.' – *8 March 1959*

HIS RECIPE FOR SUCCESS 'Find a business that you like so that it doesn't seem like work. Then stick at it without thought of the clock or the money you will make.' – *14 July 1959*

SEALING A DEAL 'A hand-clasp is all that's needed. That or a note. I always trust people until they let me down.'

QUALITY, QUALITY, QUALITY 'When you decide to do a production of major significance, it's the quality and the idea of the project that counts – not what it's going to cost. That you face afterwards.'

ENTERTAINING POLITICIANS Lew once found himself sitting next to the Minister of Education at a formal dinner. Making polite conversation he asked the Minister if he saw much commercial TV.

'No, Mr Grade. I've too many demands on my time,' came the reply.

'Pity,' said Lew, 'because we have some cultural shows. Only last night there was one with eight politicians.'

The Minister laughed. 'But you can't call that cultural...'

'Maybe not,' said Lew, 'but you can't say it's entertainment either.'

THE OLYMPICS At an ATV programming conference the sports chief proudly announced he could get film of the Olympic Games.

'So what?' said Lew. 'Who's interested?'

'But these are the greatest amateurs in the world,' said the shocked sportsman.

'Amateurs!' snorted Lew, 'We're only interested in professionals.'

STEPTOE AND SON 'I will not allow my boy to hear such things as "Where the bleeding hell have you been?" and "Cobblers to you". There is no need to use such language in a so-called comedy series. It's just filth, sheer vulgarity.' – *12 February 1963, on the first broadcasts of the BBC series*

THE DEPTHS OF HIS DESPAIR 'I can get depressed. For an hour or two at a time.'

THE SUCCESS OF *DANGER MAN* AND *THE SAINT* 'There was a period of about six years when nobody wanted to know British TV programmes. It was really *Danger Man* that broke the bad run. We sold it to America in 1964 – and since then we have never looked back. Both that and *The Saint* are seen in almost every country that has a television. *The Baron* is doing fine in Poland and Nicaragua. Sir Kenneth Clark's art programmes are going down well in Egypt. Zambia likes *The Power Game* and Thailand's bought *The Adventures of Sir Francis Drake*.' – *12 October 1966*

THE PRISONER 'The President of CBS came over to England to see me about *The Prisoner*. He had watched four episodes and still didn't understand what it was about. After spending two days in Wales, at my suggestion, watching them filming he returned and said, "I don't understand that Patrick McGoohan. Do you have problems with him?" I said, "I never have any problem at all with Patrick McGoohan. He's wonderful." He said, "Well, how do you do it?" I said, "Always give in to what he wants."'

BUDGETING 'Well, a normal hour's TV drama would cost about £15,000 to produce. The ones I make, like *Danger Man* and *The Saint*, work out more like £40,000 each. They are quality films, and it costs me around £5 million to make four series of 26 programmes a year. For that, I get two hours of TV a week on our home station. Two-thirds of the money has to be recouped overseas or we just couldn't afford to give the British public shows of this quality. We all gain by the export market – the country, the Treasury and the viewer.'

ATV RECEIVING THE QUEEN'S AWARD TO INDUSTRY 'It is a wonderful acknowledgment, not only to our sales efforts, but it pays tribute to all the elements concerned with the production of programmes – the producers, directors, writers, artists and technicians.'

THE NEED FOR COLOUR TV 'There is no hope of getting anybody to pay £250 for a colour

THE GRADE COMPANY

'Why not go out and sell something, Lew?' Lady Grade joins her husband and Roger for another showbiz gala

receiver while there is only four hours of transmission a week. ATV alone, apart from the other Independent Television companies, could put out 20 hours as soon as the transmitters and channels are made available.' (*This on 9 March 1966, when Harold Wilson's government was proposing only four hours of colour TV a week by the autumn of 1967!*)

'At the time, Lew really was Mr Television'

Roger Moore on the Mogul of Moguls

HIS ENEMIES 'I have hundreds of rivals, but no real enemies.' – *22 March 1968*

FALLING PREY TO ROGER MOORE'S ANTICS 'On a trip to Rome I was met at the airport and taken to a chauffeur-driven car. In the front was a driver with his collar turned up, hat pulled down over his eyes. I didn't like the look of him at all and said as much to my host. I was told to hush up because this man was an influential member of the Communist Party. I was very relieved when we arrived safely at the hotel to discover that our driver was really Roger Moore.'

HIS MANY GREAT SHOWS 'All my shows are great. Some of them are bad – but they are all great.'

THE POPE 'The Pope's got great charisma. He could play any part and dominate any scene on television. I'd love to sign him up.' – *After meeting His Holiness*

HIS PRIVATE LIFE 'I have no private life. I have a wife who understands. When the phone doesn't ring at home, I get depressed. So my wife says, "Why not go out and sell something, Lew?" And that always cheers me up.'

TELEVISION TODAY 'When you see those old *Saint* and *Persuaders* shows, there was no real violence, they were relaxing. If you missed three minutes, you still knew what was going on. Now it's all so gloomy . You hear accents even I don't understand.' – *30 October 1996*

ON RETIREMENT 'I used to say I'd retire in the year 2001. But I already know it won't happen.'

LORD LEW – GRADED BY HIS PEERS

'Lew's larger than life, although I doubt if he's more than five foot nine. He never eats butter, he gets up before the rest of the world, he smokes cigars bigger than himself. He's a mogul, and at the time he really was Mr Television.' – Roger Moore

'Dancing's how he broke into showbusiness. He enjoyed it and became a champion. Then he worked himself up into London's leading theatrical agent. He brought to the English music halls such stars as Bob Hope, Jack Benny, Johnnie Ray, Lena Horne, Frankie Laine and Dorothy Lamour. Now he will not be content unless Associated TeleVision presents the best programmes.' – *Wife Kathie Grade, 'Mrs Television', from a 1963* Modern Woman *profile*

'I once booked Lew and his brother Bernard (Delfont) as dancers in a chain of clubs. I thought they were awful, but Lew came across as the most charming of men; you knew it was a straight deal with him, however bad the consequences might be.In fact, I had to fire them.' – Harry Saltzman, co-creator of the *James Bond* series

'Those early days (when Lew was making the ITC swashbucklers *Robin Hood, William Tell* and *The Buccaneers*) were quite extraordinary. No programme ambition seemed unattainable. Budgets were simply unheard of. It seems extraordinary to say that. But there was a time when all this was true.' – *Brian Tesler, who passed on* The Saint *but became an ATV producer and later Deputy Chairman of LWT*

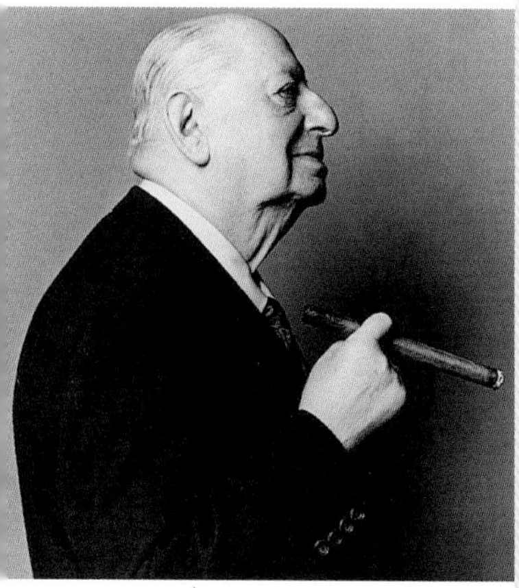
THE GRADE COMPANY

'Let's see what Uncle Lew has prescribed for us on ATV this week...' MP Jeremy Thorpe, 1960, in the News of the World.

'Let's see what Uncle Lew has prescribed for us on ATV this week. Today, at tea-time, we can see desperadoes stealing arms intended for partisans, or, if that interrupts your Sunday sleep, half-an-hour later you can view settlers at the mercy of scouts in Indian territory.' – M.P. Jeremy Thorpe sarcastically asking, 'Does he really know what we want?' in the *News of the World*, 1960

'Lew must get his rest as he only has about five hours. Fortunately, he drops off as soon as his head's on the pillow and sleeps the sleep of the just.' – *Mrs Grade in 1963*

'Lew Grade's belief that Britain is a cultural appendage of the United States is one that most Britons might disagree with... This policy of Lew's embodies one of the biggest threats menacing TV. The differences of nationality and custom that make life interesting will be ironed out in the cause of international sales.' – *Daily Mail* critic Peter Black, in 1967

'I have to say about Lew Grade – rightfully Sir Lew Grade, rightfully thereafter Lord Grade – from the very moment that he said, "Go," and shook my hand – we never had a contract – he never interfered in anything that I did. It was marvellous. I can't conceive of anybody else in the world – then or now – giving me that amount of freedom with a subject which in many respects was, you might say, outrageous.' – *Patrick McGoohan on* The Prisoner, *in the 1995 BBC documentary,* The Persuader: The TV Times of Lord Lew Grade

'Lew Grade wants to reduce ITN's News At Ten *from 30 minutes to 20 minutes. He says that's all the public wants to hear of current affairs each night. But ITN will have none of it, and so far has survived.'* – *Sunday Times* profile by Nicholas Tomalin, from December 1968

'One day Lew Grade called me to write *Zoo Gang*. This was a series with a whole bunch of oldsters in it, set in the South of France. It had John Mills and a couple of white-haired, overweight Americans whose names I can't remember now. He asked me to work on an outline for the story. So he set me up in an office, personally making quite sure I had enough pencils and pens and paper. When I was settled he tiptoed out, closing the door behind him. After I'd been working for about 20 minutes, the door opened very, very quietly and in he came with his big fat tummy and his big fat cigar carrying a little cup of coffee, in a saucer. This he placed on my desk in dead silence, then tiptoed out again!' – *John Kruse, scriptwriter on* The Saint

'Lew Grade, the best man perhaps I ever worked with... He said to me "Franco, remember you are a movie director, but this is television. How many people can you put in a television screen? You better cut down the numbers." He almost wanted me to cut down the number of the apostles' – Franco Zefirelli, director of the ATV series *Jesus of Nazareth*

'Lew wanted me to direct a film about Livingstone in Africa. He wrote a cheque for half a million pounds for me and when I refused, tried to stuff it in my pocket. I fended him off and we sparred for a moment. Then he deftly stuffed the cheque between my backside and the chair.

'I tried to ignore it. But I felt at a distinct disadvantage with half a million pounds of Lew's money sticking up my bum.' – *Director John Boorman*

'On a bright day, a boat's a boat and the sea's the sea...'

Bob Baker on not-so-exotic British locations doubling for the Bahamas

When Robert S. Baker and Monty Berman first approached Lew Grade with the idea of turning *The Saint* into a TV series, Lew instinctively knew it was a winner. All that remained was for him to do the deal and check the credentials of his producers...

Bob Baker recalls those early meetings and the day-to-day problems of being co-producer, and sometimes director, on a series where the budget for your supposedly exotic locations would just about get you to Portsmouth.

How did you first come to work with Monty Berman?

I met Monty Berman during the Second World War when I was working in the Army Film and Photographic Unit as a combat cameraman, making PR films for the army.

Monty was already a well-established cameraman, and we decided that after the war we'd try and set up our own film company and make our own pictures. About 18 months later we financed our first picture, *Date with a Dream* with Norman Wisdom, Jean Carson and Terry-Thomas. Of course they were all unknown then. I think we paid Terry-Thomas £50.

The film wasn't a financial success – we made some deals we shouldn't have – but a distributor saw it and liked it and with their backing we made 49 feature films up until 1960 (including horror Bs like *The Trollenberg Terror, Blood of the Vampire, The Siege of Sidney Street, Flesh and the Fiend*, a horror spoof *What a Carve Up* featuring soon-to-be *Saint* guest star Shirley Eaton and a war epic with Dickie Attenborough, *Sea of Sand* – 'our best picture').

And then the director, John Paddy Carstairs, suggested to you the idea of *The Saint* as a TV series?

Well, John was very friendly with Leslie Charteris (Carstairs had actually directed the earlier film *The Saint in London*). I'd been speaking to Paddy one day in our offices and he introduced us. I persuaded Leslie Charteris – and I must have been very good then – to give us a totally free option on *The Saint* for a period of time. He protected *The Saint* like a bulldog – and many offers had fallen flat on their face.

What were the main stumbling blocks doing the deal with Charteris, after Lew Grade had given you the okay?

Money! I spent a rather unpleasant week in Florida with Leslie but in the end he got what he wanted and I went back to Lew. He then very wisely recommended a Canadian story editor Harry Junkin, who had worked for many years in New York on a soap opera called *Love of Life*. He was a very good writer and we got on well. So we set up a *Saint* bible together – what you could and couldn't do on the show – and then got in other writers.

ROBERT S. BAKER FILMOGRAPHY

AS DIRECTOR UP UNTIL THE SAINT

1950 **Blackout**
1952 **13 East Street**
1953 **The Steel Key**
1956 **Passport to Treason**
1959 **Jack The Ripper**
1960 **The Siege of Sidney Street, The Hellfire Club**
1961 **The Treasure of Monte Cristo**

SAINT EPISODES AS DIRECTOR

The Golden Journey
The Saint Sees It Through
The Saint Plays With Fire
The Wonderful War

The sea's the sea, a step's a step. Roger, still on the back-lot in The Pearls of Peace

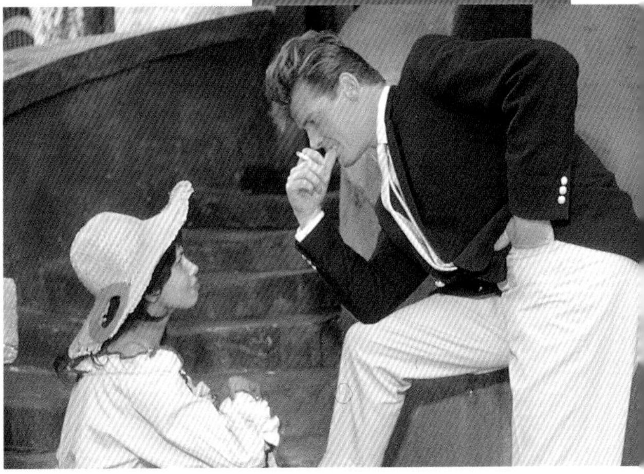

POPPERFOTO

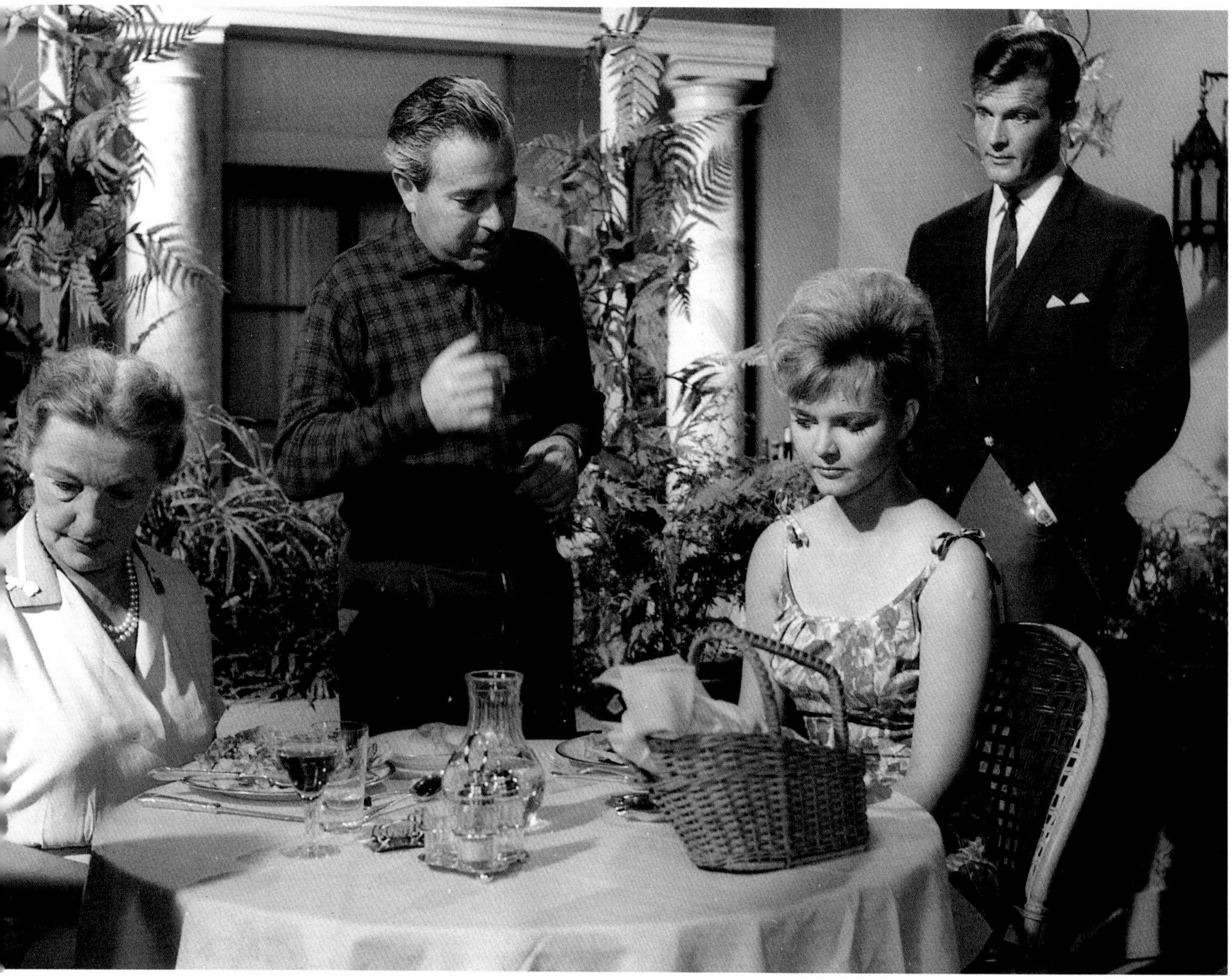

ROBERT S. BAKER. PRIVATE COLLECTION

'Nice girls rarely hitch hike in Spain.' Director Robert S. Baker gives Erica Rogers some advice before she sets off on The Golden Journey. *Roger Moore and Stella Bonheur, as Aunt Joan, contemplate the studio floor*

Could you talk a little more about this bible?

In those days violence was a big no-no. Television here was pretty strict and it was also strict in America. So in all the fights the Saint would play by the Marquess of Queensberry rules – he wouldn't kick you in the balls as he could do now. In the books the Saint wasn't that much of a gentleman – it was just the code. Violence had to be very minimal.

And yet there is violence there. In *The King of the Beggars*, Warren Mitchell threatens to stick corks in a hood's ears and nose and blow his head up with a tyre pump till it explodes.

I don't remember that, but I guess it wasn't deemed so bad if they were just talking about it. You certainly couldn't show it.

The other thing the bible dealt with was the First Act, Second Act and Third Act.

Throughout the series the scripts are remarkably tightly plotted with usually a good twist in the Third Act. How much of this came from the source material?

Well, the first 70-odd black and white pictures were all based on Leslie Charteris' books, so you had the basic material there. However, most of Leslie's stories were short stories, so we found that when it came to transferring them to the screen for an hour show we only had about 30 minutes of material we could use.

His stories were constructed like this – you set the problem up with which the Saint becomes involved, First Act. Then they went straight from there to his resolution of the problem, which is basically half of the Third Act. So what we were short of was the middle act and a little bit of the Third Act. What that meant was we had to invent something in the First Act that would complicate and further develop the plot to get us to a stage where the Saint could then unravel it again.

Quite often we would have to alter the structure of the First Act, which was where most of our confrontations with Leslie came from. We would create new situations which he would object to and sometimes – and this really got up his nose – we'd even invent new characters.

Leslie wanted to have a veto on the stories which we couldn't, and wouldn't, agree to. It's alright to do that if you're doing a one-off, but when you're making a television series you're shooting for two weeks then you're going straight on to the next show. There's no question of anyone vetoing your show – you've got to carry straight on.

I think he eventually saw this point, but we agreed that the scripts would be sent to him for his comments and consultation. We used to get these very abusive replies from Leslie, and if we could accommodate his suggestions we would, but a lot of the time it was down to structure which we couldn't change simply because of that bloody Second Act he was missing.

Anyway, after the 71 black and whites we stopped for six months. Then I approached Lew again about doing some colour episodes – colour had very much come in in America – and it was back to negotiating with Leslie.

I explained that I didn't think there were many more of his stories which were suitable to transfer for TV so I asked him if we could invent a few more. That brought us back to the whole veto thing, but in the end it worked out well. Suddenly we were relieved of the confines of the written word and we could do stories which were much more suitable for one-hour television slots.

How did Lew Grade tend to involve himself with the day-to-day workings of *The Saint*?
He wasn't hands-on. Lew deals with people. He knows your reputation. He knows you can do the job and from that point on he doesn't interfere. Once you've set the deal, you know what the budget price is, he just lets you get on with it. He relied entirely on his producers. That said, he'd made plenty of enquiries about Monty and me with people we'd worked with in the past. We had a pretty good reputation of producing inexpensive, commercial pictures.

Lew is the greatest deal-maker in the world. He hasn't really stopped being an agent – that's what he is. It's ingrained in him. He has to do a deal – no matter what – and it works. He's the last of the great showmen. There's no-one left. Not in this country at any rate.

What's the story of Patrick McGoohan's near involvement?
Patrick McGoohan had done *Danger Man* – *Secret Agent* they called it in America – and Lew suggested we use him. We had a meeting with Patrick McGoohan... (*pauses*)...McGoohan's a rather *aggressive* person, amongst other things. He was being a little difficult in the meeting and we felt he did not have the lightness of touch. I think he's a great actor. He's good to watch and a good technician. But he did not quite have that laid-back sense of humour that we wanted for *The Saint*.

'The Saint wouldn't kick you in the balls, as he could do now'

Bob Baker on TV censorship in the 1960s

Didn't McGoohan also feel the character was too promiscuous?
Yes, oddly enough he had a thing about women – he never touched women in his shows. I presume McGoohan's a Catholic. I don't know whether he's a devout Catholic, but he had this thing about women.

Did you do a screen test with Roger?
No, we didn't need to. We'd seen enough of his work to know he was right. Lew did that actual deal with Roger – he wouldn't let anyone else do the deal if he was available himself. Then at the press conference to announce it all there came the famous moment when he said, 'And now, here's Roger Moore who will be starring in our hour-long series of *The Saint*...'

'Half hour,' said Roger.

'Hour,' said Lew.

Afterwards Roger told me he just thought the script had been well padded!

But *The Saint* made Roger. The second we saw the first day's rushes we knew straight away it was going to be a hit. It just gelled.

Was there much deliberation over which should be the first *Saint* episode filmed, to set the tone for the whole series, because *The Talented Husband* is quite dark – almost like a Roald Dahl story? In the last shot, after the wife has broken down on the stairs, Roger walks off looking slightly horrified by the whole sorry affair...
My memories of that are that there was one significant change we made from Leslie's original story. *The Talented Husband* is about this fictitious housekeeper, Mrs Jafferty, whom the husband has created to do his dirty work, poisoning his wife. And in the original story Roger would have disguised himself at the end as Mrs Jafferty.

I'm sure Roger would have loved doing that, wouldn't he!
Well, we didn't think in the first episode we could really have the Saint in drag. It wasn't on. So we cut it, which got up Leslie's nose a bit.

You'd worked with Shirley Eaton before and she was already very successful at that time. But were you often lucky in getting young actors and actresses before they'd really become established?
Yes, Julie Christie was a case in point (in *Judith*). It was an interesting thing with Christie. When she was playing her first scene she was very hesitant. She kept forgetting her lines and the director ended up breaking them down into small sections. Watching her on the set we weren't terribly impressed but when we saw the rushes the next day the whole thing lit up. Amazing. This was before *Darling*.

Was it policy to look for new names, rather than hiring established actors as the guest stars?
Well, we didn't have that much money to get big names in, so we really just started by finding anyone who was suitable for the part. We didn't worry about names. But of course when the show became established it became much easier to get guest stars.

Another great plus of the series is the variety of stories that Charteris provided...
Yes, one week we'd have a drama, the next week we had a chase story, the next something that was tongue-in-cheek and humorous – that variety kept the audience going. The trouble with American TV shows, in particular, in the 1960s, was that if you'd seen one you'd seen them all. They stuck rigidly to the formula, while with *The Saint* the viewer never quite knew what they were going to see. This was a good period in television series' development in Britain.

One of my favourites of the early episodes is *The Golden Journey,* which you directed. It's almost a two-hander between Roger Moore and Erica Rogers.
Yes, it's a road picture really. As a matter of fact Lew Grade wasn't very happy with *The Golden Journey,* essentially because there was no fighting in it. Lew always liked each show to have at least one battle. I could have altered the story, but in this case I decided to keep close to Leslie's original.

As an aside, it's also entertaining spotting Roger and Erica Rogers' doubles doing all the location work. One second there's a close-up of Roger splashing water on his face, the next it's this long shot from behind of him bathing. Did he ever get to go on location in the black and white episodes?
No, he was always in the studio. Those shots of the doubles climbing over the hills, which in *The Golden Journey* were meant to be Spain, were actually shot in Wales.

The Second Unit shots were always silent and they'd be carefully worked out beforehand so you knew specifically what was needed.

Apart from local scenes, we hardly ever went on location. Sometimes it was meant to be the Bahamas, but all it was was a palm tree with a girl in a bikini freezing in the middle of winter.

One of the locations was meant to be Bimini, but we just went down to Hamble and shot the boat stuff on the estuary there. On a bright day a boat's a boat and the sea's the sea. It may not be quite so blue here as it is in the Caribbean, but it was good enough. A lot can be concealed with skilfull lighting.

'We didn't think we could really have the Saint in drag in the first episode'

Bob Baker on story changes that riled Leslie Charteris

Was it enjoyable for you to put on the director's hat for a change?
The difference between films and television is that in television the producer is very much involved in the script. So it was simple for me to direct as I knew the script inside out before I even went on the floor. But the input of directors in television is minimum. They might ask for some alterations, but they really have no influence on where the story is going to go. That has already been decided. Television is the producer's medium.

Would that mean most shots would be got in one or two takes?
No, not necessarily. A director has to shoot about 4½ minutes of screen time a day. About 20 set-ups. So if a director is falling behind he will certainly settle for a take which is not perfect. But if it's an important master scene then he may take up to 15 takes.

Did you ever have major problems with a scene?
Not really. Roger has a photographic memory. How he learnt pages and pages of dialogue day after day I will never know. All he'd do in the evening was go home at the end of a day's work and read the next day's shooting script. He read it two or three times then forgot about it for the rest of the evening. Next day he'd be doing his own make-up – he never had anyone do his make-up – and just glancing at the scenes. Then we'd do the first run-through. He'd probably still have the script in his hand, then he'd dump the script and ad-lib his way through the scene. But though he altered dialogue it was always a natural alteration. He would never throw anyone else out of kilter with it. He was very professional in that way.

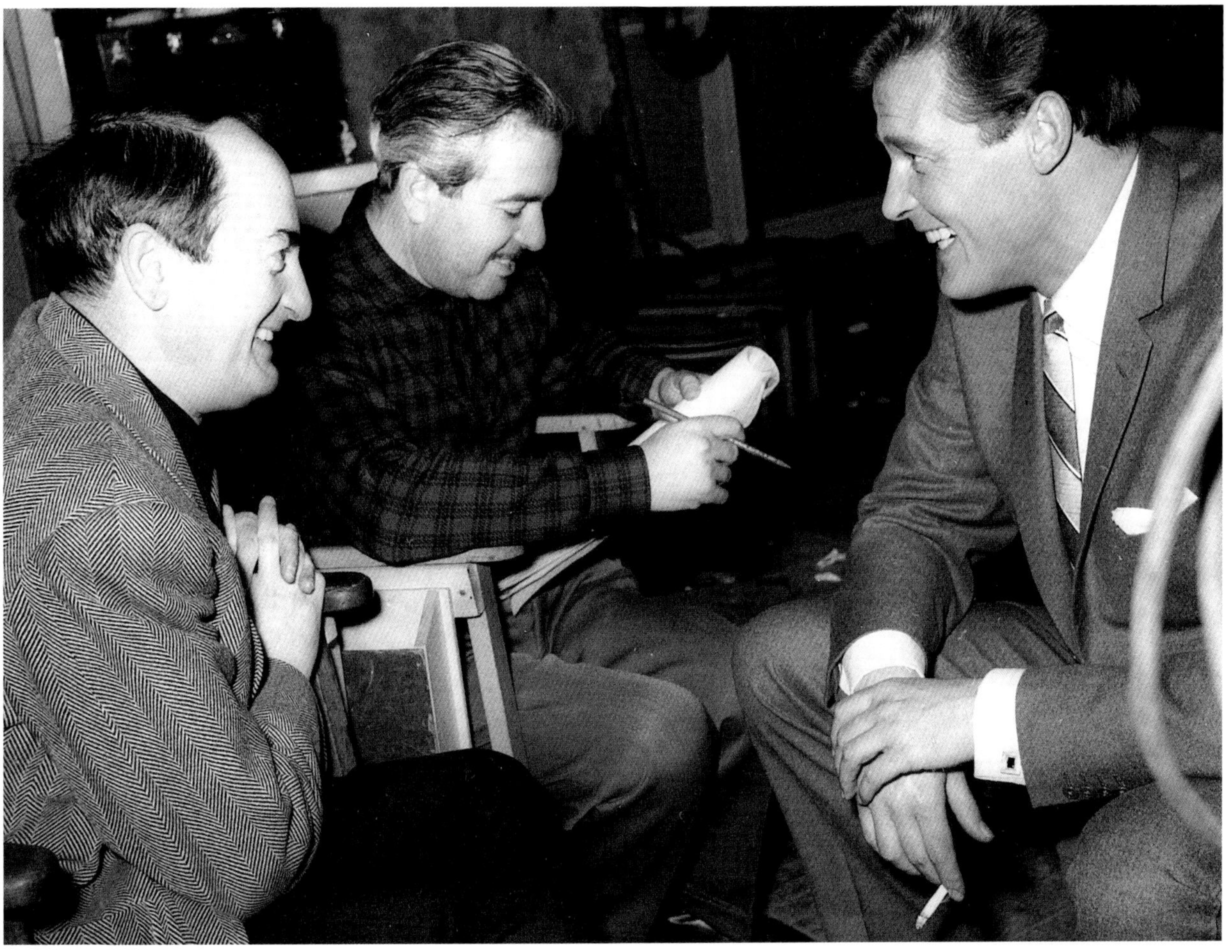

ROBERT S. BAKER. PRIVATE COLLECTION

'Television is the producers' medium.' Saint *producers Monty Berman, Robert S. Baker and Mr Moore chortle in anticipation of all the lovely lolly*

Did you ever come a cropper with any of his practical jokes?

Oh yes, he was always making practical jokes. And we'd always see the results on the rushes. Suddenly he'd pick the villain up and start dancing round the set with him. But that's a good thing because it kept the unit happy.

There's a story that's been documented before about Roger doing a car scene where he's driving in profile. For such a scene you could either use back projection, or if it's a night scene you had a big drum on which you would paint trees and bushes and so forth. You turned the drum and for a side-on shot it looked very effective.

Anyway, I was watching the rushes of this scene when suddenly one of the camera assistants appeared in the driving seat with Roger running alongside the car apparently trying to keep up. Roger held up this sign, 'Stop!' then kept on running. The assistant held up another sign, 'Why?' Roger kept on running. Then the final sign, 'Because my cock's caught in the door!' That was the sort of thing you could expect almost every day.

The thing was, Roger was liked by everybody – the electricians, the entire crew. And at that time in the 1960s the electricians' union was extremely militant – very left-wing – and at the slightest problem the brothers would all hold a meeting. There was a rule that if you were in the middle of a shot in the last 10 or 15 minutes of the working day, the unions would allow you an extra quarter of an hour to finish the shot. But they could be bloody-minded about it. But with Roger they'd say to me, 'Ok, you can do this shot. But we'd like you to know we're not doing this shot for management, we're doing it for Roger.'

Roger knew that if you were going to work in a long-running series you made things as simple and happy as possible. I'm pretty sure he'd picked that up from working in America.

How did you find Oliver Reed in the two episodes (*The King of the Beggars* and *Sophia*) he appeared in?

He was alright. He hadn't gone quite off the rails in those days. Now, of course, he's unbelievable. I ran into him once in the South of France and he was as drunk as a coot. He's a strange sort of guy when he's in his cups, I must say.

Was there much of a breather between each of the four series?

Well, just enough time to get the next scripts ready. We would usually start each series with six

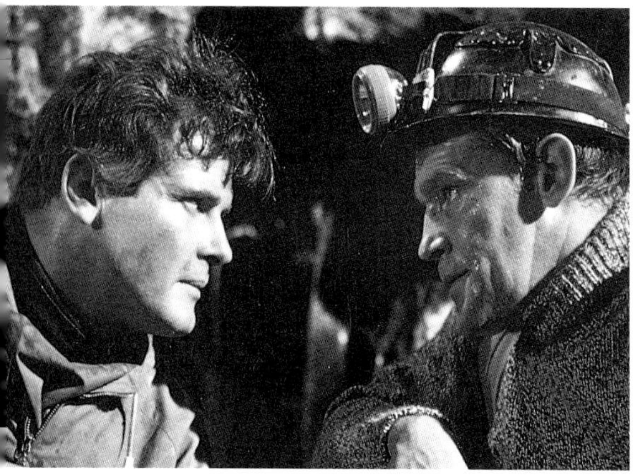

POPPERFOTO

completed scripts ready to go. But by the time we came to the end of the series we were often writing the scenes in the office and sending them straight down to the floor to shoot. You would keep losing ground all the way through.

One of the last episodes we did, *Island of Chance*, Harry was practically finishing off the script as they shot it downstairs. In the story the three characters were wandering through caves and one of them says, 'What's that I smell?' I wrote back, 'It's the script!' gave it to Harry and he fell about.

How would Monty and yourself divide duties as co-producers?
Monty would look after the business end of the operation. Although he was a cameraman he would totally run that end, while I would spend most of my time with the writers, the director and the editors. It worked very well.

The Saint meets The Man Who Could Not Die (Patrick Allen). According to Bob Baker and Leslie Charteris, neither could The Saint

How did it change when you and Roger became the show's producers?
Basically, I had more to do with the finance then and had no time left to direct. So in a way, Roger took over from me in the director's chair. But if you're a good technician, as he is – don't forget he'd been Hollywood-trained – then it's not a problem. I worked a lot with American actors and they would turn to the cameraman and ask him what lens he had on. Then they would adjust their performance according to the lens. If it was a wider angle lens they could make it a little bit bigger, if it was close they'd keep it in the eyes and no more – just think the thing.

That said, we didn't have that many American guest stars in the series. We got David Hedison because he was a friend of Roger's. He was over here and Roger offered him the part so he said sure, why not. Otherwise, if we'd had to negotiate with him through his agent, we couldn't have afforded him. They usually came in on the old chums basis.

Later, it was the same with Terry-Thomas when he appeared in *The Persuaders*. We could not have afforded Terry, but because he'd done those first two pictures with us, *Date with a Dream* and *Melody Club*, he came in and did it at a nominal salary. Just for old time's sake. He was very good in it actually. It was a shame the way he finished. He lost a lot of money. He and several other actors got swindled by a guy who was supposed to do pig farming. George Sanders lost a fortune on it and I think Terry lost money too.

The *Saint* episode *The Ex-King of Diamonds*, in which Templar falls in with a Texas oil baron/playboy in the South of France, is basically a pilot for *The Persuaders* isn't it?
Yes, it was a dry run. I just wanted to see how certain elements would work, so what we did in that episode was actually downplay the Saint a bit and give the American (*The Champions'* Stuart Damon) an equal share of the story – just to see the balance. So Roger played it ever so slightly differently.

Was there any thought that Stuart Damon could then have carried on the role?
No, we had to get a 'name' from America. That was essential. The first person we tried to get was Rock Hudson, so it would have been an Englishman and a Texan. But we couldn't get him and couldn't get Glenn Ford, who didn't want to leave America, but Tony Curtis was on the network's wish-list and Lew said, 'Leave it to me'. In the end it was the best thing that could have happened to the series, changing it to a guy from the Bronx, because it made it much more 'with it'. So much so that the actors used to ad-lib a lot of the dialogue. Tony's quite quick and Roger's very bright, so it worked great.

Former champ and part-time thespian Nosher Powell gives Southpaw Roger a few pointers in the fine art of on-screen pummelling, in The Crooked Ring

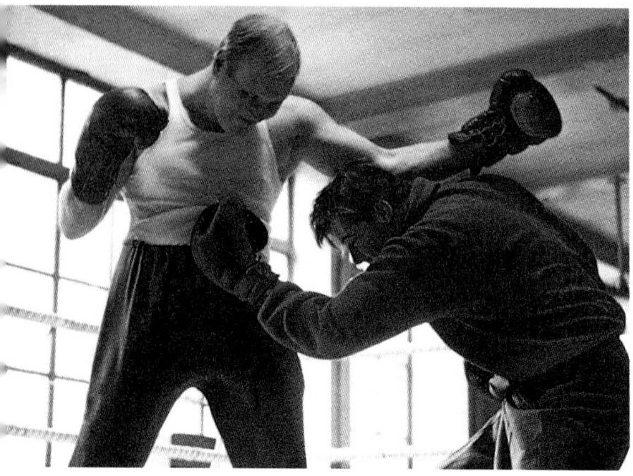

POPPERFOTO

Where did you find the composer of *The Saint* theme, Edwin Astley?
Edwin Astley had already done some music for ITV and he lived close by – a few hundred yards from me here in Stanmore (*north London*). He was very commercial and he had a library of his own music which we could call upon when we needed it.

So he provided all the great incidental music...
He recorded the incidental music, but on top of that he had his own library so we had the choice of using all of that as well. He was very competent, very good.

The Saint series also has a very defined, a very stylised look – as the _Bond_ series had at the cinema. Was there a similar style bible for the look of the show?
Yeah, glossy. And the same went for the photography. You could light a scene dark or you could light it glossy. A lot of back-lighting to give the characters a slight halo effect. It was particularly good for the women as it made their hair look alive. It was the opposite end of the spectrum to film noir.

The colours are almost Technicolor...
Yes, but by then the film stock had been replaced by Eastman colour. That was what was used on *The Saint*.

Was there ever a storyline considered that the Saint might marry?
Oh no. That was in Charteris' contract. He couldn't get married, he couldn't really get injured and he couldn't get venereal disease. We wouldn't have wanted him to get married anyway, as the idea of having a different girlfriend in every episode was very appealing.

Presumably, wearing your producer's hat, there was never any thought of killing him off either.
Hardly!

Do you have a favourite episode?
It's very hard to say, but probably *The Queen's Ransom* with Dawn Addams. I like it because it's very flippant. It's a little bit like those Hollywood comedy-thrillers they used to make. It's very American and Roger spends the whole episode sending Dawn Addams up. That amused me. That's what I liked best – the battle of the sexes. That was the buzz in the show. If the Saint thought a woman to be pompous, or think a lot of herself, he would love taking her down a peg or two. It was The Taming of the Shrew.

Were there not plans hatched between you and Roger to do a period film of _The Saint_?
Yes, I've actually got a couple of very good scripts. I wanted to do *The Saint* set in the 1930s when Leslie originally wrote them, which would have worked frightfully well, but the powers-that-be wouldn't go along with it. They wanted to update him. One of the scripts I have, by John Goldsmith, is set in Germany just before Hitler came into power against the background of the Brown Shirts. And the other is based on Leslie's *The Saint Plays with Fire*, which I directed in the TV series. I've gone back in time for that one and it's set against Oswald Mosley's Black Shirts movement. You have the Communists on one hand and the Fascists on the other. It all focuses on an attempt to assassinate the Prince of Wales, as he was then, before Mrs Simpson.

The Fascists were going to kill him and make it look like the Communists had done it.

And who would you have cast as the Saint?
Well, I had a meeting with him but I couldn't get him at the time that we were trying to put it all together. That was Pierce Brosnan. He's made a first class Bond and he'd have made a good Saint as well. There's a great similarity between the two roles, except one was working for the government and the other was a freelancer.

I'm an executive producer on *The Saint* film that's out now for Paramount. But I wasn't really active in the production of the thing.

Do you think we'll ever see a renaissance of action/adventure series like _The Saint_ and _The Persuaders_?
I don't know. One of the problems, I think, with television today is that a series is never given a chance to develop. They make six episodes then they stop. With *The Saint* we had started with 26 episodes, so you developed a pattern that people would watch. I suppose that pattern now has been taken over by soap operas.

Is that purely a financial consideration, do you think?
I think they're just frightened to take a chance. If you make a series of 26 and they flop you have problems...But the Americans still do it. They still take a gamble on shows.

Is that because there isn't someone else like Lew Grade around?
Yes, is the simple answer. The thing with Lew is he would back his own judgement. If he liked an idea – if it smelt right to him – he'd go ahead and do it. And there was no-one to argue with him – he was the guv'nor.

'I trust you will understand that I do not choose to sign myself as yours sincerely, truly or even faithfully; and the adverbs which come to mind... are not in conventional business usage'

Memo from Charteris to Bob Baker after a Harry W. Junkin adaptation had 'really got up his nose', re-told in the _Daily Mail_, 1965

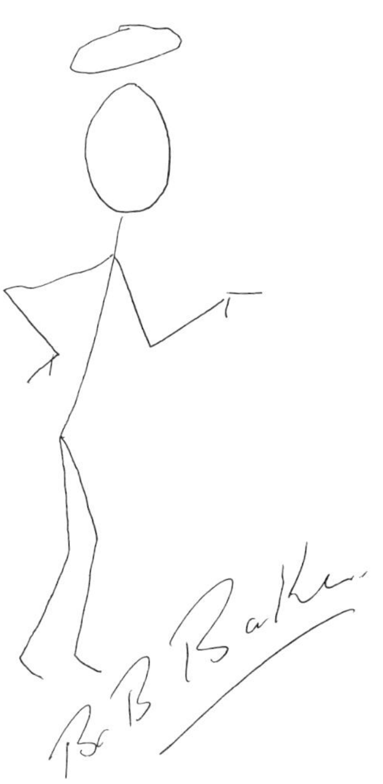
Bob Baker

MR MOORE

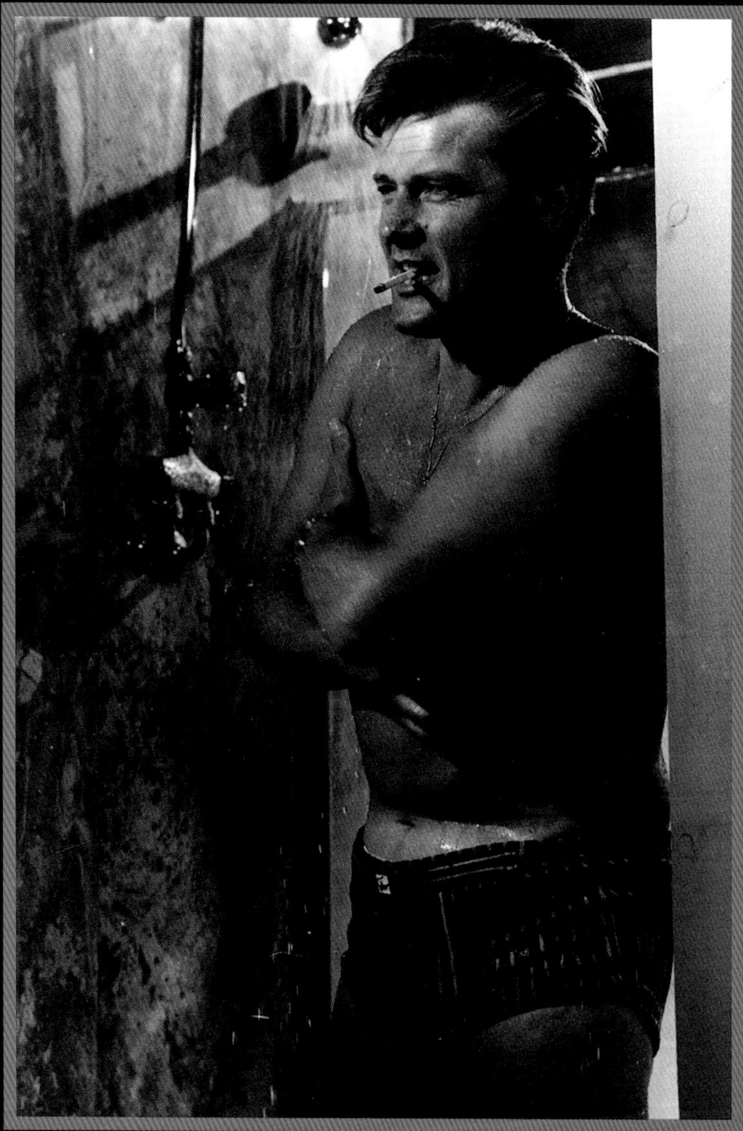

'I doubt if you'll find me in a TV studio again'

Roger Moore quoted in London's *Evening Standard*, 6 May 1961

A year later, almost to the day, Mr Lew Grade, deputy managing director of ATV, announced at a London press conference that Roger Moore was to play the Saint in a series of 26 hour-long films for television. To the 34-year-old ATV star it was just too good a part to pass up.

Seven years and 118 episodes later he emerged from Elstree Studios, blinking at the daylight and marvelling at his transformation into a bona fide international star. So what happened in between?

Flying in from his home in Switzerland to visit his father for a few days in February 1997, Roger recalls the series.

I wonder if we could start by contrasting your experience of work on *The Saint* with the American TV shows, *The Alaskans* and *Maverick*, that preceded it. I understand they were less than perfect conditions to work under.

The problem in American TV is they work much longer hours. Or they used to. When we were doing *Maverick* and *The Alaskans* we would work until 9pm or 10pm at night. In fact, we were the first actors at Warner Bros to go on strike. We started a revolt and that's when I started doing my own make-up. They had the audacity to put a clock-in machine for the actors in the make-up department. So to avoid it I bought myself my own make-up, went up to my room – they were all screaming that I hadn't come in of course – did my make-up and just walked onto the set, simple as that. We soon got rid of the time clock. The problem was, there were only three of us under contract at Warners – myself, Clint Walker (Roger's co-star in *The Gold of the Seven Saints*) and Jim Garner (the original TV *Maverick*) who were getting more than scale. It was everyone else who was suffering with the overtime. And it was worse for the girls as they had to be in hair and make-up for much longer than the men.

So after all of that it was quite pleasant to come to the civilised hours of doing *The Saint*, which was into the studio about 7.30-8am and finish at 5.30-6pm. That was unless the hour was called or the quarter was called to finish off a scene. In other words, 'Can we have another hour?' – in which case you had to go to the Shop Steward by 11am to ask permission. I mean, they were going to get paid anyway, but this was one of the reasons the British film industry fell into such disrepute with the Americans. The Union's working conditions were so prohibitive.

Bob Baker comments that you seemed to have a perfect grasp of the fact that you need a good atmosphere on set when working on a long TV series (hence all the practical jokes).

Well, we all worked with enthusiasm. *The Saint* was fun to do. And you cannot work under that constant pressure of having to get five or six minutes on the screen a day, if there is tension. I personally can't work unless it's a relaxed atmosphere. You get knotted up inside. So I'd make jokes and clown around which sometimes is annoying, I presume, to some people because they're trying to concentrate. For my part I could be telling a joke, be called on to set, do the scene then come back and finish telling the story.

Is that almost one of the jobs of the leading man – to set the tone and keep the tensions down?

I think it helps.

ROGER MOORE

BIOGRAPHY PRE-SAINT

Born: 14 October 1927, at the Annie McCall maternity hospital in Jeffrey's Road, London SW4.

Father: George Alfred Moore, a Bow Street police constable and Plan Drawer (the person who draws the plans of the scene of a crime or accident).

Mother: Lily Moore, born in India, the daughter of a Regimental Sergeant Major.

Family home: 4 Aldebert Terrace, London SW8.

School: An elementary school on Hackford Road, London SW9. In 1939 evacuated to a middle-class family in Worthing, Sussex where 'the perpetual, subtle implications that I was really rather common made me terribly homesick'. Conveniently, Roger caught impetigo and spent till 1940 up north in Chester, with Lily. When the Blitz began they were evacuated to Amersham, where he attended the 'distinguished' Dr Challoner's Grammar School.

A return to London meant time huddling in Anderson shelters and attendance at Vauxhall Central in Cowley Road, London SW9, where he was prone to annoy one girl classmate, Joan Norris, by perpetually thumping her on the head with a big green book.

Left school at 15 in 1943. Family moved to 16 Albert Square, London SW8, literally round the next corner and nowhere near Walford.

First job: Through a friend of his dad's he got work making animated films for the war effort at Publicity Picture Productions, D'Arblay Street, London W1, for £2 a week. Was later sacked when he forgot to deliver a can of film (instead he'd gone to get his first £5 suit, made 'with turn ups'). But as a junior technician in a film-making company he had acquired an ACTT card (Association of Cinematograph and Allied Technicians) which would later allow him to direct on *The Saint*.

FILMOGRAPHY

1944 Caesar and Cleopatra. Filmed at Denham by Gabriel Pascal, from the George Bernard Shaw play. The 16-year-old Rog got a part as an extra, standing proud with his spear, wearing a red toga. With Vivien Leigh and Claude Rains.

Most crucially, in the course of filming this, his father introduced Roger to co-director Brian Desmond Hurst (PC Moore had been on site after burglaries.

ROGER MOORE

at Hurst's house) saying his son wanted to be an actor. If Dad was happy to support his thesping young son while he attended RADA, Hurst said he'd see what he could do.

1954 The Last Time I Saw Paris. A melodrama adapted from F. Scott Fitzgerald's short story *Babylon Revisited*. Director Richard Brooks, with Liz Taylor, Van Johnson, Donna Reed, Walter Pidgeon.

Roger played a ne'er-do-well tennis bum who tried to seduce Liz. Roger recalled in a piece he wrote, 'Reaching For My Halo', in *Woman*, that La Taylor was 'at all times remotely beautiful and even more remotely gracious'.

1955 Interrupted Melody. The story of Marjorie Lawrence, an Australian opera singer stricken by polo. Director Curtis Bernhardt, with Eleanor Parker, Glenn Ford, Cecil Kellaway.

Rog played Eleanor Parker's brother and was well looked after by the star, who also warned him about Glenn Ford's habit of subtle scene-stealing: 'I noticed all his chalk marks were right in camera range. All of mine were slightly out.'

1955 The King's Thief. Costume thriller in which dastardly nobleman David Niven plans to steal the crown jewels. Director Robert Z. Leonard, with Edmund Purdom, Ann Blyth, David Niven.

1955 Diane. Costume drama with Rog in his first lead strapped into shiny armour as Henry II of France. Director David Miller, with Lana Turner and Pedro 'Kerim Bey' Armendariz.

1959 The Miracle. Melodrama, with Carroll Baker cast against type as a novice nun rebelling against God, from Max Reinhardt's play. Director Irving Rapper, with Carroll Baker and Walter Slezak.

Playing the Duke of Wellington's nephew, Roger's romantic clinches with Carroll Baker were made a little less comfortable due to the iron corset he was forced to wear under his scarlet tunic and white britches.

1961 The Sins of Rachel Cade. Angie Dickinson convincing as an American nurse doing missionary work in the Belgian Congo. Roger does an American accent. Director Gordon Douglas, with Angie Dickinson and Peter Finch.

When you were in Hollywood, acting with the likes of Lana Turner, Liz Taylor, Eleanor Parker and Glenn Ford, who did you look to for guidance, both on how to act and how to behave?
Well, I adored Eleanor Parker. She was one of the most professional actresses I ever worked with and a great help. I was very raw to film acting when we did *Interrupted Melody*. In one scene where I, as her brother, had to introduce her to the head of an opera house, I took up my position with my back to the cameras.

Quickly she grabbed my arm and whispered, 'This is your scene. If you take me by my right arm instead of my left, *you'll* be facing the cameras.' Very kind.

I discovered, again from Eleanor, that Glenn Ford was a bit of a scene stealer. But I did learn one very good tip from him. This will only make sense to an actor, but always point your downstage toe towards the middle of the audience or the middle of the camera – it brings your shoulders around which leaves you facing the camera.

What sort of help did David Niven proffer? You had first met the then Lieutenant Colonel Niven when you were working as an office boy at Publicity Picture Productions, hadn't you?
Oh, well he didn't even know I existed that first time. He was a Lieutenant Colonel, which was very grand. But when we filmed *The King's Thief* we chatted and I got to know him much better later. Niv was a wonderful character. In fact there was one series, *The Rogues*, he did with Charles Boyer which I was mooted to do but in the end the part went to Gig Young. *(Coincidentally, some ten years later, Leslie Charteris would say that he wished the TV Saint had been more of a buccaneer 'swindling some unlikeable character with ingenuity, charm and humour as David Niven, Charles Boyer and Gig Youg do in* The Rogues'.*)*

Was there much of a hierarchy working at Elstree? Would everyone eat together whether you were the Saint or the sparks?
Yeah, sure. But all studios usually have two dining rooms – an executive dining room and a general one. And if you're in a long-running series you want to eat in the most comfortable place – not because you don't want to be with the Herberts, just for comfort.

Whose dressing rooms were adjacent to yours?
You know, I have no idea. You see, there was no other regular member of the cast, so I suppose it was either the leading villain or the leading lady. I don't remember ever spending much time in my dressing room, unless I was actually rushing back to change.

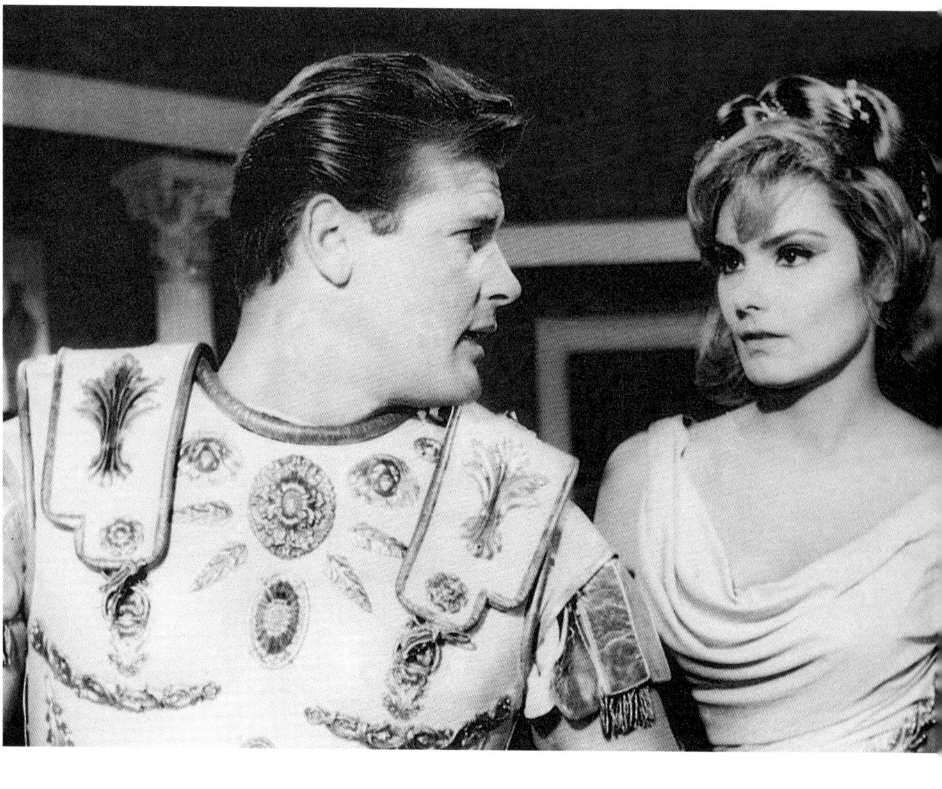

POPPERFOTO

The Sartorial Saint makes a guest appearance on Gladiators *with 'vibrant' Suzanne Lloyd. From* The Man Who Liked Lions

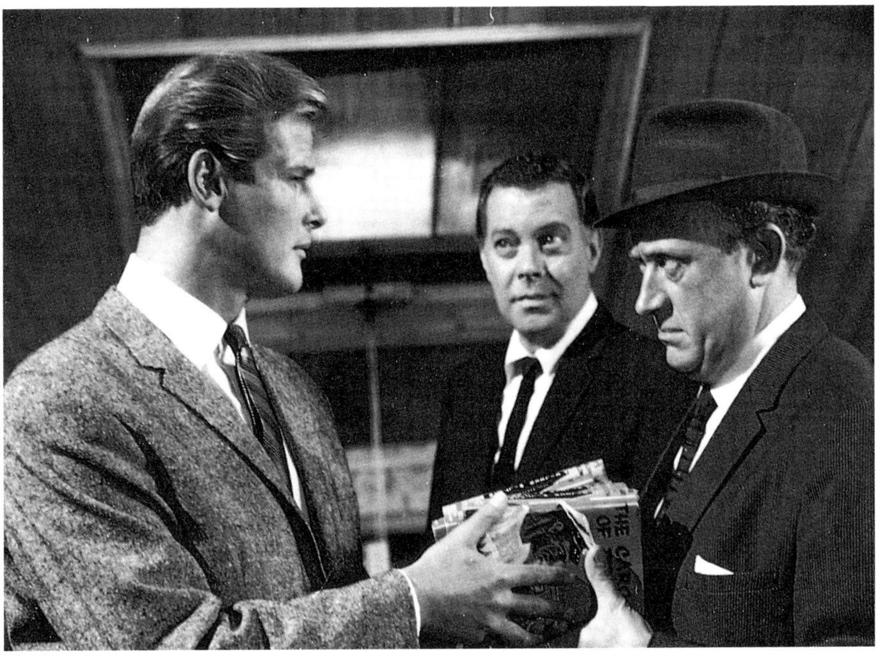
THE CA OF

POPPERFOTO

'Half hour.'
'Hour.' Roger continues to re-negogiate with Ivor Dean and Dick Haymes in The Contract

If you add the running times of all 118 episodes together, you essentially made 59 films in seven years, which is some workload. Was there a time when you thought, 'This is never going to end?'
Sometimes I look at them on television and I go, 'Oh my God, I didn't know I knew that actor!' I have absolutely no memory whatsoever of certain episodes, while there are others I look at and think, 'And now I'm going to say this, and she's going to say that.'

Did you get sick of looking up at that damn halo?
In the early episodes I never used to look up. Then I started to, through sheer boredom. It's rather like grinning for the camera – that terrible sickly smile you get. All I know is it (*the halo*) was nine feet from the camera on a 75mm lens. So for filming you framed the bottom of the shot on the top of my handkerchief pocket, and that gave you the right headroom for the halo to be put in later.

You warned Annette André, when she was going to take the lead in *Randall & Hopkirk (deceased)* only to lose her rather fiery temper when she really had to. Did you ever explode on set?
I've only twice lost my temper in all the years I've been filming, I think. One was during *The Persuaders,* when I lost it with an assistant who persisted in calling me down onto the set far too early. You know, I'm always ready. I don't need to be told 55 times to get ready – I'm ready! I walk on the set and I'm on time and that's the way it's always been. I don't believe you should waste other actors' and other technicians' time by being late. So having been called down and figured my time (*chuckles*) was being wasted I called him a twat or something. I felt so bad three minutes later that I gave him a solid gold Dupont lighter – which will teach me to lose my temper.

The other time was with an actress, who shall be nameless, on the *Bond* series, who was absolutely impossible. But otherwise I'm fine. I only lose my temper at breakfast time in hotel rooms when the eggs are hard boiled.

Did Lord Grade ever give you any advice when you were co-producer on the series?
To Lew everything was wonderful. 'You're wonderful – have a cigar.' He used to shove them in your mouth to stop you asking for more money!

Was it Lord Grade who first introduced you to the delights of Monte Cristo cigars?
Oh yes. Lew's a hell of a character.

From what Bob Baker says *The Saint* would never have got sold to America without him?
Lew was a master salesman. He really was quite brilliant. He could sell *Gideon's Bible* to a crowd of Muslims. Nothing was unattainable for Lew when he set his mind to it. Lew could always

ROGER MOORE

1961 The Gold of the Seven Saints. Western, with bands of outlaws chasing Roger as Shaun Garrett up hill and down dale through the Utah desert. Where a dehydrated Roger first developed his painful and recurring relationship with kidney stones. Director: Gordon Douglas, with Clint Walker, Chill Wills and Leticia Román.

Roger recalls Clint Walker not being a fan of the social events put on by the good folk of Utah in the evening. 'People sort of look at yah, an' poke yah, an' pinch yah - an' I don' like it,' said the former lifeguard and star of *Cheyenne*.

1961 The Rape of the Sabines. Franco-Italian gladiator pic about the founding of ancient Rome, filmed mainly in the former Yugoslavia. Never released in Britain and most notable for the appearance of 28-year-old Luisa Mattioli, seven years later to be the third Mrs Moore.

Roger played his part in English, Mylene Demongeot played hers in French, others played theirs in Italian and the whole soundtrack was finally dubbed. It was chaos.

1961 No Man's Land. Another Franco-Italian pic considered unreleasable in Britain. But conveniently again including Luisa in the cast.

TV SERIES

1958 Ivanhoe. In the title role. 'In that damned plumed helmet and armour I looked like a medieval fireman.'

1960 Robert Montgomery Presents. Opposite Diane Lynne. 'Then I got a part on Broadway in *A Pin to See the Peepshow*,' he confided to *Woman's Own* in September 1963. 'Ye Gods, what a flop that was! Then I made a movie test and the Hollywood contract arrived...')

1960 Maverick. As Beau Maverick, taking over in the series when James Garner got sick of the part and those lousy scripts.

1961 The Alaskans. As Silky Harris. A series most notable for the fake snow, which was wood shavings and grit, blown full-pelt into Rog's mush (and mush was all he said) by huge fans.

The huskies passed their own critical appraisal of the whole affair by weeing on every fake tree in sight.

THE SAINT IN THE PRESS

19 MAVERICKS WERE ENOUGH FOR BRITAIN'S MR MOORE… 'I DOUBT YOU'LL FIND ME IN A TV STUDIO AGAIN.'
Evening Standard, by Ramsden Greig, 6 May 1961

Having finished the Maverick series, Roger returns to England for a few days, finding time to speak to the splendidly monikered Mr Greig.

'Making television films in Hollywood would drive the most staunch teetotaller to the bottle,' he tells Greig.

'The pace is terrific and the studio space so limited that you find yourself acting back-to-back with some guy who is making an entirely different series.

'Apart from that I soon discovered that I was hating the director every bit as much as he was hating me.'

Cutting from the *Evening Standard*, 24 July 1961

Roger contemplates life on the big screen.

'…having given up TV and taken on the status of an independent actor, he is anxious to do more serious things. He is proposing to appear in a film of the life of the poet Shelley.'

ROGER MOORE (OF *IVANHOE*) WILL PLAY THE SAINT
Evening Standard, by Ramsden Greig, 1 May 1962

'Associated TV is to spend £800,000 putting Leslie Charteris' *The Saint* on to the TV screen.

This is the 'conservative' estimate Val Parnell gave me today.

The series will go into production later this month and will reach the screens in the autumn. Each episode – 26 in all – will run for an hour.

WHAT MAKES A TV HERO SIGN ON THE DOTTED LINE?
Daily Express Interview, 26 November 1962

On the set at Elstree, Roger begins his career as The Saint *in typically flippant mode, much to the horror, according to this interviewer, of the ATV PR.*

Why, I wanted to know, did he change his mind about tangling with a TV series?

'You know how it is, old boy,' drawled the one-time Ivanhoe in his carefully cultivated mid-Atlantic accent.

'They come along and dangle all sorts of splendid financial inducements – like luncheon vouchers and free milk for the ulcers you will undoubtedly acquire – and you break down and sign. Of course, I'm mad.'

And of course he signed.

POPPERFOTO

Roger menaces a villain with his new unkempt Man of Action look

find his way round any problem, and if that didn't work he'd get on the table and do a tap dance. He could do the fastest charleston in the world, and in fact he's probably still doing it. I'm getting ready to go to what is his 55th wedding anniversary in June (*1997*).

Is it true there was a knife fight that was cut from one episode? Did you have a lot of problems with the American TV censor?

At the time we made *The Saint* there were all sorts of restrictions in various countries, and as we were going to be sold throughout the world you couldn't make different versions for each place. I know we were not allowed to show a flick-knife opening. You were not allowed to hold a gun to somebody's head. Personally, I have two different thoughts on the matter of screen violence. One side of me says that children are going to be influenced by what they see, so you should not show certain things. But the other says, well, if they're going to be influenced by Simon Templar, who only throws punches to the jaw, then they're going to lose a lot of fights because people will come at you with a bottle, or their knee. My real advice is lie down on the floor, then nobody can punch you!

The only instance I can think of where you blow someone away with a gun is in the climax of *Vendetta for the Saint,* where you're armed with a double-barrelled shotgun.
That could be. I don't remember too much about *Vendetta,* except for the fact that we shot it in Malta.

Is it true you were the only member of the cast that actually got to go to Malta?
Yeah, I don't think we took anybody else. I think they had a few local people. The funny thing when you're shooting somewhere like that is that very few of the British audience know what that country looks like. They don't know the geography. So you can happily have cars going from left to right and right to left and it's all edited together and they're none the wiser. But when you then show that film in the country where it was made, it's obvious to the locals that you've just gone three times in the wrong direction and ended up in a completely different town.

We had a charity premiére in Malta for *Vendetta,* very kindly attended by Prince Philip, and at one such point the audience became completely hysterical. He didn't understand why they were laughing, but he was very gracious about it.

There's an early scene with Aimi Macdonald where she's driving you in her car and she's wearing this big pink headscarf and huge dark sunglasses. In the location shots you can quite clearly see it's you in the car, but of course it could have been any convenient double hidden away behind her props.
Yes, that was a very good way out!

Can you remember your first day of shooting on the very first episode, *The Talented Husband*?
Yes indeed. We were shooting in Cookham village and I was waiting round the corner in the Volvo – ST 1 on the number plates – waiting for a signal to come ahead in the car. Derek Farr was dressed up as Mrs Jafferty, waiting to cross the road, and all the action was meant to tie in together. So I'm sitting there when a police sergeant rolls up on his bicycle. He's got the bicycle clips and so on. He stops and looks at me. (*Adopts voice of a rustic country bobby.*) 'Thaat's a very int-er-esting looking car you've gaht there. ST1. ST1. Thaat's a nice numberr.'

I said, 'Actually, it's a false number plate. The real ST1 belongs to the Chief Constable of so and so.'

'What?' he said. 'Hall-lo...' So he started pulling out his notebook, and at that moment the wave came. I took off like Clapham out of Bournemouth, round the corner, did the take and when I came back (*laughs*) he was still standing there!

He had no idea what was going on, poor fellow.

What was your reaction when you saw the first rushes of yourself as the Saint?
I probably shut my eyes. I don't really like looking at myself on screen. These days, unfortunately, they have a video playback of everything they're doing so the actors all stand around at the end of each take thinking how wonderful they are. Terrible time-wasting.

I was taught in Hollywood never to look at rushes, just to listen to them. If they sounded right they were going to look right. Unfortunately, when I was directing *Saint* episodes you had to look at them as you were part of the production team. But you can do that quite dispassionately. The character playing Simon Templar or James Bond may look like you, may sound like you, but it's somebody else. It's a piece of meat up there.

In fact, what really happens with rushes is everyone goes to look at their own thing.

If you say to make-up, 'How were the rushes?' they'll say, 'Oh, the make-up looked great.' Say the same to the wardrobe, 'Oh the suit looked lovely!'

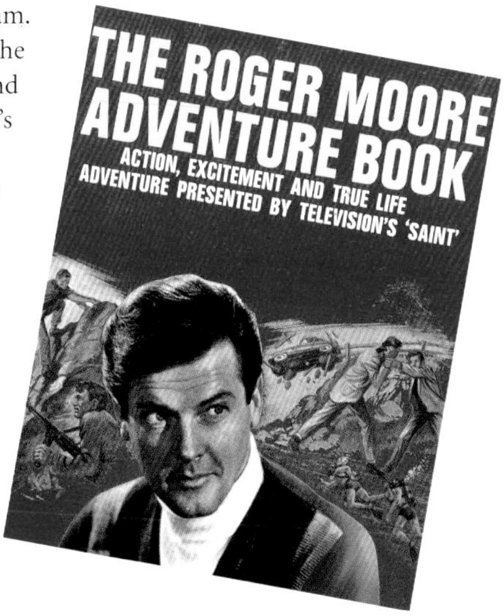
THE ROGER MOORE ADVENTURE BOOK
ACTION, EXCITEMENT AND TRUE LIFE ADVENTURE PRESENTED BY TELEVISION'S 'SAINT'

The Roger Moore Adventure Book. *Wholly unrelated stories of derring-do mixed with Saintly secrets*

THE SAINT IN THE PRESS

HE'S GOT EVERYTHING – HE'S THE SAINT
***TV Times*, by Max Wyman, 12 October 1962**

Apart from various compliments from co-star Shirley Eaton – 'He is very good looking indeed' – the highlight of this piece is a wee glimpse into Roger's personal life outside the studio.
He attends an occasional race meeting, one or two Twist parties. But most of the time he is travelling between his London house and the Elstree studios, sleeping, or learning the next day's lines.

DROPPING IN ON THE SAINT
***TV Times*, by Diana Lancaster, 25 October 1962**

Ms Lancaster enrols in the 100-strong Roger Moore Fan Club. Janet Lane, the 17-year-old president and founder of the club, from Worthing, Sussex, where she is a jeweller's assistant, addresses the six lucky club members present at Victoria Coach Station. They are about to head off for Elstree to watch the filming of The Wonderful War.

'Now – no screaming. And please, nobody faint. Be careful you don't ask him awkward questions. Lots of people have asked what toothpaste he uses, but I refuse to ask him that. Besides, if we knew it wouldn't be fair on the other manufacturers,' she said...

Apart from nearly losing 15-year-old Vida Dunster, from Lambeth, to a touch of the vapours – she's the first to lay eyes on Rog as she spots a 2-inch patch of his famed bonce through the studio throng – it all goes swimmingly well. As well as answering non-toothpaste-related questions, Roger tucks into some salmon and cucumber sarnies with them and even does a quick round of Win, Lose or Draw.

He even found time for a series of lightning cartoons on a handy blackboard. 'Give me a number,' he challenged. 'Thirty-seven? A subject? Horses.'

Within seconds a haughty mare with a seven for her neck, and a curly-nosed jockey made from the figure three, appeared on the board.

And with the Saintly One despatching a couple of arab cut-throats with his trusty sabre, it all ends splendidly for the gang.

There were swoons all round as we were treated to a rather enduring final image of Roger 'roaring with laughter, sweat streaming down his face and hair sticking out at unsaintly angles.'

All in a day's work. for our Saintly hero of course.

THE SAINT IN THE PRESS

THE SAINT SEEKS A REAL THIEF
***Daily Sketch*, 2 March 1963**
Roger finds art imitating life.
Roger Moore, who plays the Saint on TV, had a real case to tackle yesterday. Someone broke open his car outside his house at Mill Hill, London, and stole books, a track suit, a ten pin bowling ball and shoes.

NOW THE SAINT GOES RESPECTABLE
***Daily Mirror* interview, by David Lewin, 17 October 1963**
In a rare encounter at Elstree, Roger and Leslie Charteris compare notes on the character.
Roger Moore, the TV Saint, said: 'I can only look like me and take on part of the character I play. The Saint is a superman, out of the ordinary, and only made credible by the skill of the writers on this series in getting him into situations and showing how he deals with them.'

Charteris said: 'I don't quite follow this bit about Superman. I didn't plan him as that.'

Curiously, considering Swingin' London is just around the corner, it is the whole social climate that Charteris sees as being the downfall of his one-time rakish buccaneer.

Charteris: 'The trouble is the Saint has gone respectable. Not only on TV but even in some of the more recent stories I have written. The older *Saint* fans tell me so. It is a sign of the times, this respectability.'

And having established that he was neither a fan of Louis Hayward or George Sanders, Charteris praises the lad.

To Roger Moore he said: 'You're younger than I've made the Saint (Moore is 35), but your performance is better than any other actor in the part so far.'

THE SAINT GETS A £50,000 HALO
***Evening News*, by James Green, 7 December 1963**
Season 3 and 4 are confirmed.
Like a well-brought-up gent Mr Moore does not talk about money, but if the news isn't worth £50,000 to him I will eat his halo.

Roger goes on to confirm that he doesn't like to talk about money, and if you want to know who would win in a fight between Simon Templar and James Bond (a key Alan Partridge interview question in his not entirely successful An Audience with Roger Moore) the answer is, 'Tell me who the producers are and I'll give you the winner.'

Could you speak a bit about the many directors on the series? How did Leslie Norman, John Gilling and Roy Baker, say, differ from Bob Baker, Peter Yates and Freddie Francis?
We were lucky. We were very well served with directors. Most of them were very experienced. Les Norman was a lovely guy. Unfortunately, he always had a cigarette hanging from his lips and throat cancer got him. But he was good. He started off as an editor at Ealing. A very good technician. As was Roy Ward Baker. He had started as an assistant director with Hitchcock. John Gilling was another Hitchcock assistant. John and Roy were the two great technicians I worked with. Yatesy came to us straight from *Summer Holiday* with Cliff Richard. Then he went on to do *Robbery* with Stanley Baker and because of some very good car sequences in that he got to do that picture in San Francisco with Steve McQueen (*Bullitt*).

They were all very wise. Nobody ever said much to me except, 'Go there, then go there'. Because when you're playing the character, they know that you know the way you're going to play it. You had to be consistent. (*Smiles.*) Well, it always looked like me.

Annette André says she found John Gilling rather curt when dealing with actresses.
Yes. I think it was John who told me about working with Hitchcock. Hitchcock was working with this actress and he said, 'Action'. The scene started to play and he said, 'Cut'. Hitchcock turned to John and said, 'I wind her up, I put her down and she don't go. Bring me *Spotlight* (*the casting agency directory*) and we'll recast.' Which is terribly cruel!

I can remember working with one actress who was fairly bad. (*Chuckles.*) I said to John, 'Tell her the Hitchcock story!'

What was your own approach to directing *Saint* episodes?
I always used to bring along storyboards. I'd do the opening frame and the closing frame of each scene so that I knew how I wanted it to begin and finish. I liked to have a general, overall picture.

Val Guest, I remember, always had all the scenes on little bits of paper. He'd cut them out of the script, (*chuckles*), then he'd keep producing them out of his pocket, looking at the dialogue. But he had a storyboard as well.

Were there problems filming on location? You must have attracted a crowd whenever you went outside the studio.
Yeah, I remember I was directing one episode and we were shooting at Waterloo Station. All the scenes were tied in very precisely to the times of clocks and the arrival of trains because I was not, I'm afraid, able to have trains stop and start to my whim. I had actors coming from Vauxhall Bridge Station and I knew they'd be on a certain train so I had to be ready to shoot. During the morning I planned every scene to be shot that could be done without me in it. To this end I was wearing a disguise so I could just anonymously get on with being the director. I had an old hat, a moustache and glasses and I wore scruffy old clothes.

It was only a week later that my mother, who had come down to watch, told me that she overheard someone in the crowd point at me and say, 'Ooh, look at that Roger Moore. Isn't he scruffy? He don't look at all like he do on the telly, do he!'

What was Oliver Reed like to direct (in the episode *Sophia*, where he played a Greek villain)?
Oh he was fine, Ollie, in those days. He was just a young up-and-coming lad. I remember Donald Sutherland was in another one I directed, where we escaped from prison (*Escape Route*). And he asked me if he could show it to some producers as he was up for an important part. In fact we were still in the middle of editing it so I couldn't send a copy to America, as he had hoped, but they came to view a rough cut at the studio and he got *The Dirty Dozen*.

What are your memories of directing that giant marauding ant in *House on Dragon's Rock*?
Oh God. That frigging ant. I'm not sure

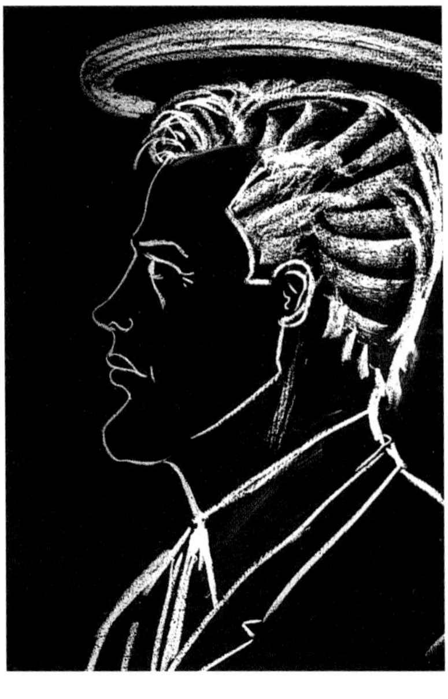

ROBERT S. BAKER. PRIVATE COLLECTION

'Well, it always looked *like me.' Roger Moore self-portrait*

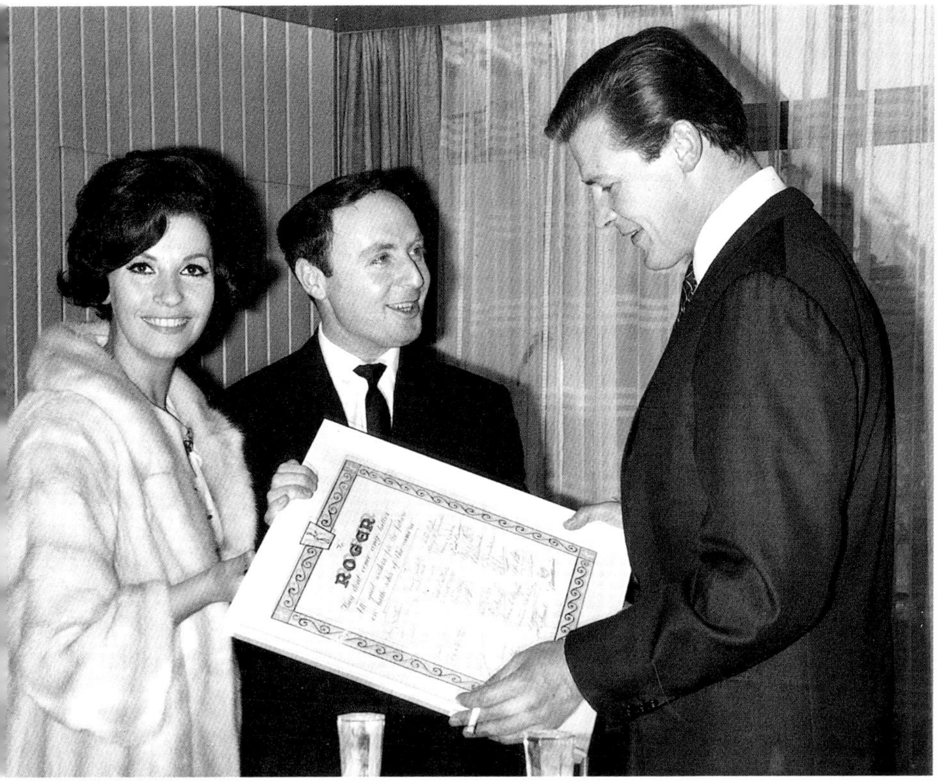

JOHNNY GOODMAN, PRIVATE COLLECTION

'Roger, they don't come any better.' Associate producer Johnny Goodman presents Roger with a certificate of thanks from the whole crew of The Saint, *for being such a swell guy. Luisa Mattioli ponders where to hang it*

whether this story means anything, as they don't do it with eggs today, but we had this scene with myself and Annette André where the ant's chasing us through the interior of this cave. What we had to do was find the ant's eggs and destroy them. You know, otherwise the place would soon be crawling with ants. (*Smiles.*) Giant ants. So we had the art department paint all these rugby balls white and cover them with spunk and cobwebs.

I said to Annette, 'Look, we haven't got time to rehearse. Whatever I say, you just say, 'How do you know?" She said, 'Fine, fine.' So we rushed in, I picked up an egg and said, "These are the ant's eggs alright.'

She said, 'How do you know?' I said, 'Because they haven't got fucking lions on them!' Do you remember, they used to stamp eggs with that lion's symbol?

Is there any trick to learning a lot of lines very quickly?

If I had a long speech I would sit down and learn it, but for the rest of it... I knew the way the character thought and what he was going to say. By the time you had had one rehearsal you knew it.

Is it true that at the end of a day's shooting you liked to go home and sing and strum a guitar? Apparently it soothed your ulcers.

Yeah, that was Jon Pertwee who taught me that. He taught me to play the ukelele when I was doing *Ivanhoe*. Then I graduated from that to a guitar. You just strum chords whenever you're feeling wound up. You'd be surprised. It just takes your mind off everything.

Having enjoyed both, what - if any - are the differences between being a TV star and a film star?

The beauty of film, for instance a *Bond*, was that a lot of money was spent on them and you had the luxury of much more time to get everything right. But the beauty of televison filming was you only had a limited number of days to get everything, so you had to be adaptable. You got used to doing things off the top of your head. Of the two I think I prefer television. I like the pressure and the challenge.

What are your memories of working with the great Finlay Currie on *Vendetta for the Saint*? He plays an ailing Mafia don, but he really does look like he's on his last legs.

Yes, I remember suggesting to Jim Connolly – who directed it – that we would probably have

THE SAINT IN THE PRESS

THE SAINT OPENS COOPER'S NEW WINE AND FOOD STORE
***Evening Standard*, 12 December 1963**

The Saint (actor Roger Moore) had an 'assignment' in Brompton Road, Kensington, today.

With a guard-of-honour of the Dagenham Girl Pipers massed band, he opened the newly enlarged and modernised food and wine store at Coopers.

Tinned and frozen food of every description and a large range of wine were featured in the new premises.

'SAINT' TO RESCUE
***Daily Express*, 16 December 1963**

Roger Moore - 'the Saint' of the ITV series - has saved the jobs of 100 film studio men because 25 *(sic)* more episodes are to be made at the Associated British Picture Corporation studios at Boreham Wood.

AIRLINE'S CHOICE - 'THE SAINT'
***Evening News*, 22 May 1964**

Roger was now discovering, to his delight, that there were many perks to being the increasingly famous Simon Templar.

British film and television star Roger Moore - 'the Saint' in the TV series - was chosen by Air France to be the airline's eight millionth Caravelle passenger. The airline chose him as representing the ideal British air traveller.

SECRETS OF THE SAINT
***Daily Sketch* interview, by Shaun Usher, 22 March 1965**

In this three-parter Roger talks about the perils of doing his own stunt work, such as running in and out of blazing garages.

'Hello, matey, somebody's going to get burned here if they don't get out in a hurry.' *Trading punches with former boxer Nosher Powell.*

He even recalls the change that got the ball rolling for him. Having spent years giving himself ulcers fretting about whether he would get such and such a part, Roger suddenly had a moment of illumination which meant he would no longer be surviving on fried egg sarnies.

'While waiting outside an agent's office in New York a few years ago I thought: To hell with it! I'm so nervous about making a good impression that the real me doesn't show through. From here on in I will be myself and see what happens.

'I banged on his door and barged in, aggressive and unworried. It worked.'

THE SAINT IN THE PRESS

WHY I SMASH UP THE HOME –
DAY TWO: SECRETS OF THE SAINT
Daily Sketch, 23 March 1965

Part two and Rog tells us how smashing an ornament at home relieves the tensions of the day (perhaps not for his other half, Luisa) and talks about his fat whack. Or not.

'I hear that I earn £2,000 a week – I do not. Or that I am the second highest paid British television star – and I am not. But I will not tell you how much I do earn. That just leads to envy – and a lot of disillusion for those who are new to television.

WHEN A HERO IS CHICKEN...
SECRETS OF THE SAINT – DAY THREE
Daily Sketch, 24 March 1965

Loud noises make him blink, which Rog was often happy to tell the press, but the secret we want to know is what does he watch on the telly when he's finished smashing ornaments for the evening...

'My favourite? The ITV thriller, *The Fugitive*. I watched TW3 (*That Was The Week That Was*) for 20 minutes. *Not So Much* for 20 seconds. Oh yes, and I have been known to watch *Coronation Street*.

Roger concludes this enlightening series, much of which would reappear in The Roger Moore Adventure Book, by revealing...

'I have just been reading a fan letter here on the film set, with a kidnapped scientist chained to a dungeon wall just a few feet away.'

SOUTHPAW SAINT WEIGHS IN WITH A K.O.
TV Weekly, 8 July 1965

For The Crooked Ring Rog spars with former heavyweight boxer Nosher Powell. Nosher, now 36 and working as a nightclub bouncer, approves of Rog's floating like a Saint and stinging like a real son of a b.

'Roger made great progress in just a week,' he added. 'He doesn't pack a particularly lethal punch, but he more than makes up for this with deftness and terrific reflexes.'

And in true Scorsese-style Nosher makes sure the details of the fight are as authentic as can be.

Says Nosher: 'Avid boxing fans so often scoff at ring set-ups in boxing films that we were determined to make the scenes true-to-life. Little things like not sealing the water bottles properly are glaring mistakes in the eyes of many fight followers.'

JOHNNY GOODMAN: PRIVATE COLLECTION

Andrea Goodman, with a gatecrasher, on her honeymoon. 'It was more or less an accident that Roger and Luisa were in Majorca at the same time,' recalls Johnny Goodman. 'Roger got me well and truly plastered one evening. I spent a terrible night throwing up, much to the disgust of my new bride!'

to re-voice Finlay Currie because he'd look up as Don Corleone or whatever and say, (*adopts thick Scottish brogue*), 'Simon Templar, what are yoo dooin' hee-ah in Pal-ermo?'

Jim said, 'He played the bloody Pope with that accent. He played Saint Peter with that accent. You'll go down in history as the man who had Finlay Currie dubbed. He's won an Academy Award for God's sake!'

Well, you got your way. It most definitely sounds dubbed.
Did I? Oh dear.

I remember going up to him on the first day of shooting. The assistant director said to me, 'Finlay Currie's arrived and he doesn't look well. I'm going to get rid of the canvas chair and get him an armchair!' (*In the final cut of the movie he actually does all his scenes propped up in bed.*) So I went over to introduce myself. Finlay Currie had this long, long, long hair which was going a bit yellow.

I said, 'Mr Currie, I'm Roger Moore and I play Simon Templar.'

'Aye, aye,' he said and looked at me.

I said, 'We're very happy that you are with us.'

'Aye, aye.' He said. 'I must apologise for the long hair.'

I said, 'That's perfectly alright, sir, you look like a Beatle.'

'Whaat?'

I said, 'You look like a Beatle.'

'WHAATT?!'

I said, 'You look-like-a-Beatle, sir.' I thought, Christ I'm in it this time, I might as well go on. I said, 'You look like a *Beatle*.'

He said, 'Aye. Saint Peter. I played him!'

I presume you must have had a ridiculous amount of fan mail over this period. Did it divide into very different types?
There was an awful lot of fan mail. We used to spend a fortune on stamps sending out pictures. And actually we still get a lot for *The Saint*. Doris (*Spriggs, Roger's Personal Assistant*) will tell me the show must have started up somewhere again, because I'm getting a lot of mail from Romania, or Pakistan.

Michael Caine has said he welcomed it when he was meant to be carrying a movie as the lead and some character actor stole a scene off him. It meant one less for him to have to worry about. Who were the best scene stealers on *The Saint*?
Everybody.

It's interesting the number of supporting actors who would then reappear with you in the *Bond* movies – people like David Hedison and, of course, Lois Maxwell. Was any of this down to you?
Oh yeah. (*Chuckles.*) I would always give casting directors a list of my friends when I was directing! That's what friends are for. Tony Doohan (*a snooper in Escape Route*), Charles Houston (*Al Vitale in* Invitation to Danger)... Hedison very nicely came and did an episode on his way back from Egypt. We couldn't pay him anything like his Hollywood fee

Could you talk a bit about your wardrobe? In time, of course, it would be billed as the Roger Moore Collection.
Yeaas. (*Smiles.*) But that was because I was on the board at Mills, who made all the material. It was something that we never developed. I thought it might be a handy little money-making machine to have, but who the hell gave a shit!

To a young lad it looked most impressive – The Roger Moore Collection. It seemed the very height of glamour, with your signature on the design.
Well, nothing was sold anyway!

Do you feel you achieved everything you wanted to with the character?
I would like to have gone back and really got it right. That was a line of John Huston's when he was asked if he would re-make *The Maltese Falcon*. He said, 'Why, boy, why? You should only re-make the ones you didn't get right!' (*Smiles.*) Maybe I would like to have gone back and spent some more time on it and not been so flippant. But who knows, it wouldn't have come out the way it did then.

And finally, who would make the perfect Saint now, would you say?
Mother Teresa. Well, I sincerely hope that Val Kilmer's going to be good. He's the new one wafting the halo over his head. Myself and Bob Baker watched some of the scoring going on the other day and the footage we saw looked good. And Graeme Revell's music is beautiful.

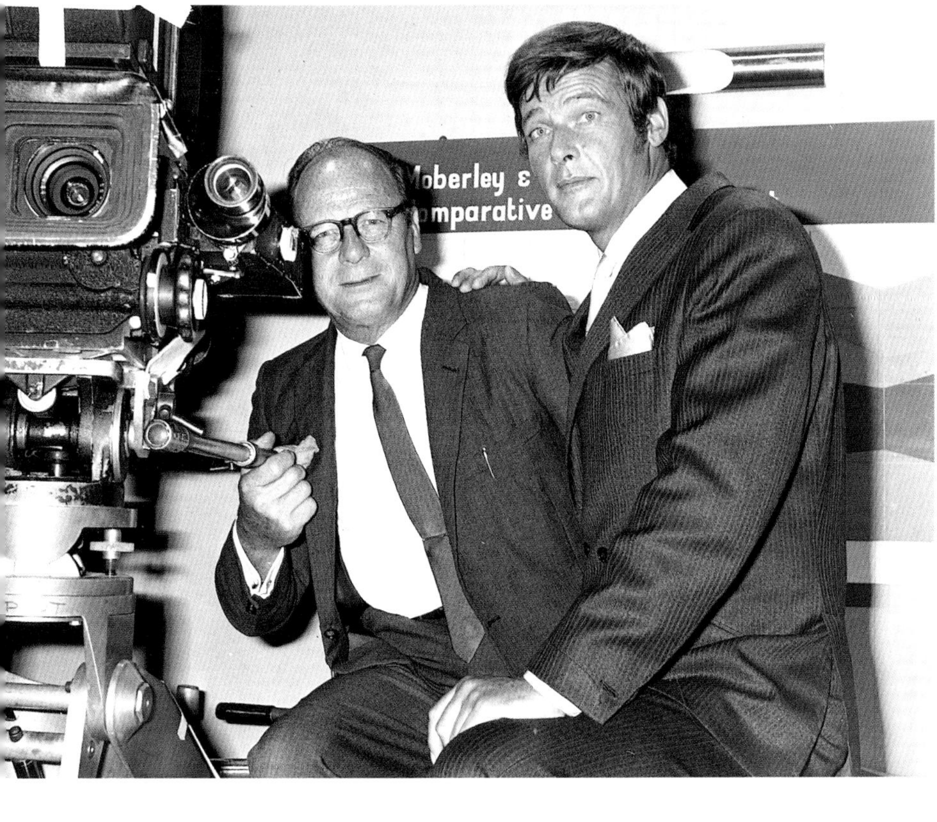

ROBERT S. BAKER, PRIVATE COLLECTION

*'Sure this isn't knock-off, son?' George Alfred Moore with his successful young lad on the post-*Saint *movie*, Crossplot

THE SAINT IN THE PRESS

THE TV SAINT GETS BOND FILM OFFER
***Daily Mirror*, by ace reporter Barry Norman, 27 June 1964**
Roger Moore, 36-year-old star of *The Saint* television series, is to be asked to play James Bond.

The film, based on Ian Fleming's book *Casino Royale*, would be a rival to the Harry Saltzman-Cubby Broccoli productions in which 007 is played by Sean Connery.

THE SAME OLD HALO WITH JUST A LITTLE MORE DIRT
***Sunday Mirror*, 23 August 1964**
A journo moans about the implausible Saint.
No matter what silly things Roger Moore is called to do in his new television *Saint* series he is not going to take the silly grin off his face.

It is the grin he puts on at the beginning, just before the little white saintly halo comes on over his head. 'I am stuck with it,' he said.

'That's the way we started and it is some sort of trademark now.'

Amongst the journalist's various beefs are the fact that Templar is never seen unshaven and that he manages to snag one bunch of villains who are making their getaway across a Canadian lake by casting off with a convenient trout rod. Roger agrees. 'That was a bit tall,' and promises a bit more grit in the new series.

'At least I will get a bit dirty this time... And I promise that at least my suit will be new.'

THE SAINT SAYS FAREWELL
***TV Weekly*, 21 August 1965**
It's the end of the television trail for Simon Templar. After 71 episodes in three years, all the Leslie Charteris stories suitable for TV have been adapted. So it's farewell to *The Saint* (tonight 8pm).

THE SAINT STAYS FOR BIG ITV DEAL
***Daily Sketch*, by Shaun Usher, 22 October 1965**
And just when you think it's all over...
Roger Moore who intended to quit as 'The Saint' on television, is staying on – because of multi-million pound deals with the US.

The new series will probably make him one of the world's highest paid TV actors.

Mr Moore said last night: 'I was quite happy with the idea of the series ending, but one really can't resist an opportunity like this...'

The Saint and I, by Roger Moore

Cometh the successful TV series, cometh the successful TV series tie-ins. In the 1960s there were annuals a-plenty. And who better to do a spot of guest writing than the star himself...

'STARS OF TV IN STORY, PICTURE AND COLOUR' was the cover line on one of the many ATV Television Star Books that the company released to eager fans throughout the 1960s. Bearing in mind the size of the ATV roster and the variety of the programmes, there was – in true *Sunday Night at the Palladium*-style – something for everyone.

Wrestling ('Hello, Grappling Fans!') with the likes of Jackie 'Mr TV' Pallo and 'the man they love to hate' Mick McManus; light entertainment (everyone from 'that versatile and talented young man' Roy Castle to Lonnie Donegan, Morecambe & Wise, Arthur Haynes, Bruce Forsyth – 'With Bruce there never is a dull moment' – and even Tony Hancock who had recently defected from the BBC); westerns ('Rowdy Yates – Clint Eastwood – finds time to share the company of a pretty girl in *Rawhide*'); The Golden Stars of Pop (a whole galaxy from Shirley Bassey and The Springfields – Dusty's family band – to Cliff Richard, The Beatles, Billy Fury, Joe Brown – 'with his effervescent Cockney wit' – and Tommy Steele, 'a man who has matured from a hip-wiggling, guitar-strumming boy to one of the most talented entertainers in show business'); and of course the action/adventure series (*Danger Man*, *77 Sunset Strip* -- 'the firm of Bailey and Spencer, Private Investigators find that their services are in great demand' – *Hawaiian Eye* with Connie Stevens and *The Saint*).

As fans of Roger's excellent 1973 book, *Roger Moore as James Bond 007* (a diary of the filming of *Live And Let Die*) will know, Mr Moore has always fancied himself as a bit of a scribbler. So while most of the features in these annuals are a trifle on the bland side – 'Some of those crazy things that happen on the show actually do happen!' says Dick Van Dyke – Roger's account of tackling *The Saint* in the 1963 piece *The Saint and I* provides a welcome insight into his characterisation.

More insider information from the 1966 Roger Moore Adventure Book. *An annual packed with curiously non-*Saint *action spreads of oceonauts, sharks and avalanches. Oh, and a bit about self defence, Rog-stylee*

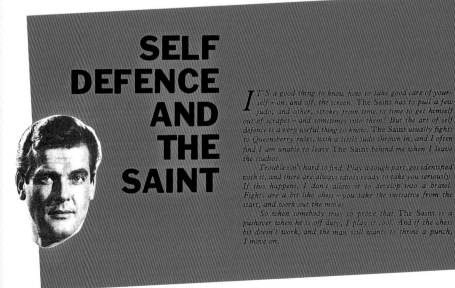

SELF DEFENCE AND THE SAINT

IT'S a good thing to know how to take good care of yourself – on, and off, the screen. The Saint *has to pull a few judo, and other, strokes from time to time to get himself out of scrapes – and sometimes into them! But the art of self defence is a very useful thing to know.* The Saint *usually fights to Queensberry rules, with a little judo thrown in, and I often find I am unable to leave* The Saint *behind me when I leave the studios.*

Trouble isn't hard to find. Play a tough part, get identified with it, and there are always idiots ready to take you seriously. If this happens, I don't allow it to develop into a brawl. Fights are a bit like chess – you take the initiative from the start, and work out the moves.

So when somebody tries to prove that The Saint *is a pushover when he is off duty, I play it cool. And if the chess bit doesn't work, and the man still wants to throw a punch, I move on.*

THE SAINT IN THE PRESS

SAINT'S SONG
***Daily Mail*, 10 November 1965**
Working pretty much on the basis that with a hit show you can have a crack at anything, Roger decides to add another string to his bow...
Roger Moore has recorded a song *Where Does Love Go?*, an old Charles Boyer number. He speaks it. Why not sing? Mr Moore said yesterday: 'I didn't want to inflict that on the public.'

SAINT ROGER'S HALO IS OF GOLD
***News of the World*, 23 October 1965**
Essentially more stuff about the forthcoming colour Saints with one interesting titbit about the demands that colour would make on the series...
Strange to relate, while making the past 72 (sic) black-and-white shows he (Rog) was unable, because of camera problems, to wear a white shirt. Usually it was blue. But going into colour means he can wear white in future.

NOT YET
***Daily Mail*, 29 April 1966**
Has Rog gone to meet his maker? In a Beatles-esque Is Paul Dead? story there have been reports of Roger's demise in a car. In actual fact he is very much alive and filming.
'I don't,' he says, 'mind the premature obituaries as long as they are nice.'

SAINTLY DEVOTION
***Daily Mirror*, 23 June 1966**
The Saint gets involved with affairs of State. An iron and steel conference in Romania is interrupted.
'Well, comrade,' said the official. 'It's *The Saint*. He's on at nine o'clock...'

***WeekEnd* magazine, 15 February 1967**
Here we get a wee peek into Roger's future, courtesy of WeekEnd*'s version of Mystic Meg.*
What of Roger himself, by 1977? He says: 'I hope to be well ahead with my own production company by then. I've got ambitious plans for feature films and television productions.'
So there it is - what the stars foretell... In actual fact, of course, he would be leaping off snowy precipices to the strains of Nobody Does It Better, *delighting audiences in his third 007 adventure,* The Spy Who Loved Me.

OLÉ - THE SAINT
***Daily Express*, 18 May 1967**
Roger Moore, 'The Saint' on TV, has been awarded Spain's Golden Don Quixote statue as the most popular foreign actor.

'One's conception of a fictional character is a very personal thing,' he writes. 'It doesn't matter how hard an author attempts to draw a word picture of his brain child, few readers will see it in exactly the same way. Similarly, no two actors will portray a character in an identical manner.'

Rejecting any thoughts of imitating previous screen Saints like George Sanders and Hugh Sinclair, Roger writes that he preferred to look for the Saint inside little old him.

'Self-identification is something readers of books very often experience, and I have always felt this way about the Saint. I've been reading him since I was so high. And I've always had a mental image of myself in his shoes.'

He was well aware though that his self-image might not correspond to that of three previous generations of *Saint* fans.

'There are so many *Saint*-lovers throughout the world that, from the moment it was announced that I was to become Simon Templar, there were protests from all directions. Every *Saint*-reader, with his own personal impression of what the Saint was like, had strong ideas on the casting, and in a lot of cases they reckoned I was just about as wide off the mark as Norman Wisdom would have been.

'Having come of tough stock...I pressed on regardless, and if my portrayal of the Saint is more like a portrayal of Roger Moore in some people's eyes, it's because I happen to be Roger Moore and because, in my own arrogant way, I've got this feeling that the Saint and I have a devil of a lot in common.'

Roger also clears up why Inspector Teal is in very few of the early episodes that were filmed. 'The stories themselves span so many years that if they were filmed in chronological order the Saint would certainly be growing into middle age. But we have deliberately avoided dating them in any way. They are all given contemporary settings. But in no case have any of the characters been changed and this is why, for instance, Inspector Teal crops up only very infrequently. The English policeman belonged to the period in Leslie Charteris' own life, before he took a home for himself in America and switched the Saint's background more and more to the United States. Inspector Teal, therefore, comes into only those earlier stories in which he was featured, and only a few of these happen to have been selected.'

The reasoning for the absence of his companion from the novels, Patricia Holm, is rather more totty-orientated: 'Her presence would be an encumbrance in a series which, to a large extent, exploits Simon Templar's penchant for chasing pretty faces'. While *Saint* fans who delighted in Simon Templar leaving his calling card stick figure, Raffles-style, at the scene of the crime were informed, 'The TV Saint does so only when described in the stories as doing so, and he dropped this habit some considerable time ago.'

Whether setting the record straight on these divergences from the books helped to alleviate his postbag, or merely fan the flames for further impassioned discussion, rather remains to be seen.

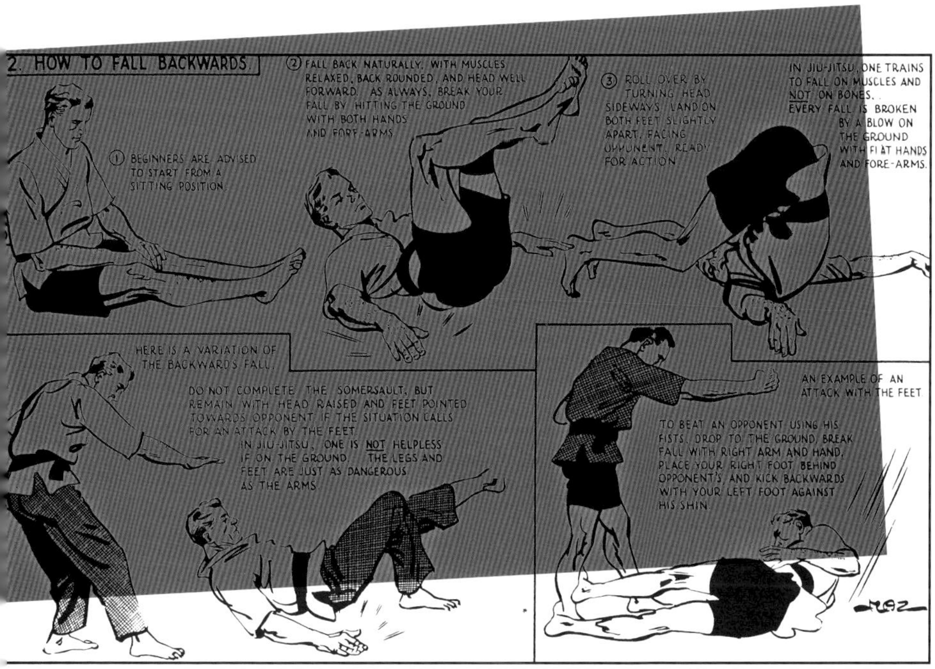
2. HOW TO FALL BACKWARDS.
① BEGINNERS ARE ADVISED TO START FROM A SITTING POSITION.
② FALL BACK NATURALLY, WITH MUSCLES RELAXED, BACK ROUNDED, AND HEAD WELL FORWARD. AS ALWAYS, BREAK YOUR FALL BY HITTING THE GROUND WITH BOTH HANDS AND FORE-ARMS.
③ ROLL OVER BY TURNING HEAD SIDEWAYS. LAND ON BOTH FEET SLIGHTLY APART, FACING OPPONENT, READY FOR ACTION.
IN JIU-JITSU, ONE TRAINS TO FALL ON MUSCLES AND NOT ON BONES.
EVERY FALL IS BROKEN BY A BLOW ON THE GROUND WITH FLAT HANDS AND FORE-ARMS.
HERE IS A VARIATION OF THE BACKWARDS FALL.
DO NOT COMPLETE THE SOMERSAULT, BUT REMAIN WITH HEAD RAISED AND FEET POINTED TOWARDS OPPONENT IF THE SITUATION CALLS FOR AN ATTACK BY THE FEET.
IN JIU-JITSU, ONE IS NOT HELPLESS IF ON THE GROUND. THE LEGS AND FEET ARE JUST AS DANGEROUS AS THE ARMS.
AN EXAMPLE OF AN ATTACK WITH THE FEET.
TO BEAT AN OPPONENT USING HIS FISTS, DROP TO THE GROUND, BREAK FALL WITH RIGHT ARM AND HAND, PLACE YOUR RIGHT FOOT BEHIND OPPONENT'S, AND KICK BACKWARDS WITH YOUR LEFT FOOT AGAINST HIS SHIN.

THE SAINT IN THE PRESS

WOULD YOU BELIEVE IT – SIMON TEMPLAR SCARED OF GIRLS!
***TV Weekly*, 7 September 1967**
As The Saint *comes to an end Rog reveals he's been duping us all along.*
'All my life I've lacked confidence. When I was a child I was disgustingly fat. I remember when I tried on a new coat, my father told me I looked like a sack of mud tied in the middle with a belt.

'Until my early teens I knew nothing about girls. I remember falling in love with a girl and never getting to hold her hand, let alone kiss her...'

ROGER MOORE WINS SPANISH TV AWARD
***Daily Telegraph*, 14 October 1967**
It's statue time for El Santo. Spain was one of The Saint's biggest fans.
Roger Moore, the Saint of the television series, was tonight awarded the 'Ondas' prize for the best international actor. The 14 radio and television 'Ondas' are awarded by a private broadcasting corporation founded by Radio Barcelona.

ACQUISITIVE SAINT
***Financial Times*, 30 March 1968**
Roger Moore, I.T.V.'s 'Saint', Mr Robert Baker, his producer, and Mr John Goodman, their associate producer, have taken over Television Reporters International, the independent documentary and current affairs company formed in 1962 by Ludovic Kennedy, Robert Kee, James Mossman and Lord Francis-Williams.

'THE SAINT' HANGS UP HIS HALO
***Sunday People*, 7 April 1968**
Time for fond farewells as Rog heads for the movie Crossplot *with Bob Baker producing.*

Anyone expecting a jaw-dropping shock in the final episode, The World Beater, *would be disappointed. Both Leslie Charteris and Bob Baker were too aware of the rewards of keeping their hero in one piece.*

Said Roger: 'Under the contract with author Leslie Charteris, the Saint cannot be killed off. The series could possibly return with someone else in the part.' *(Ahoy, Mr Ogilvy!)*

STYLE ROGER
***Financial News*, 2 May 1968**
Roger Moore is to be design consultant to a Bradford textile firm. One of the screen's best-dressed men, he will help the company select cloths from their range for classical English clothes.

4: THE FICTION-MAKER

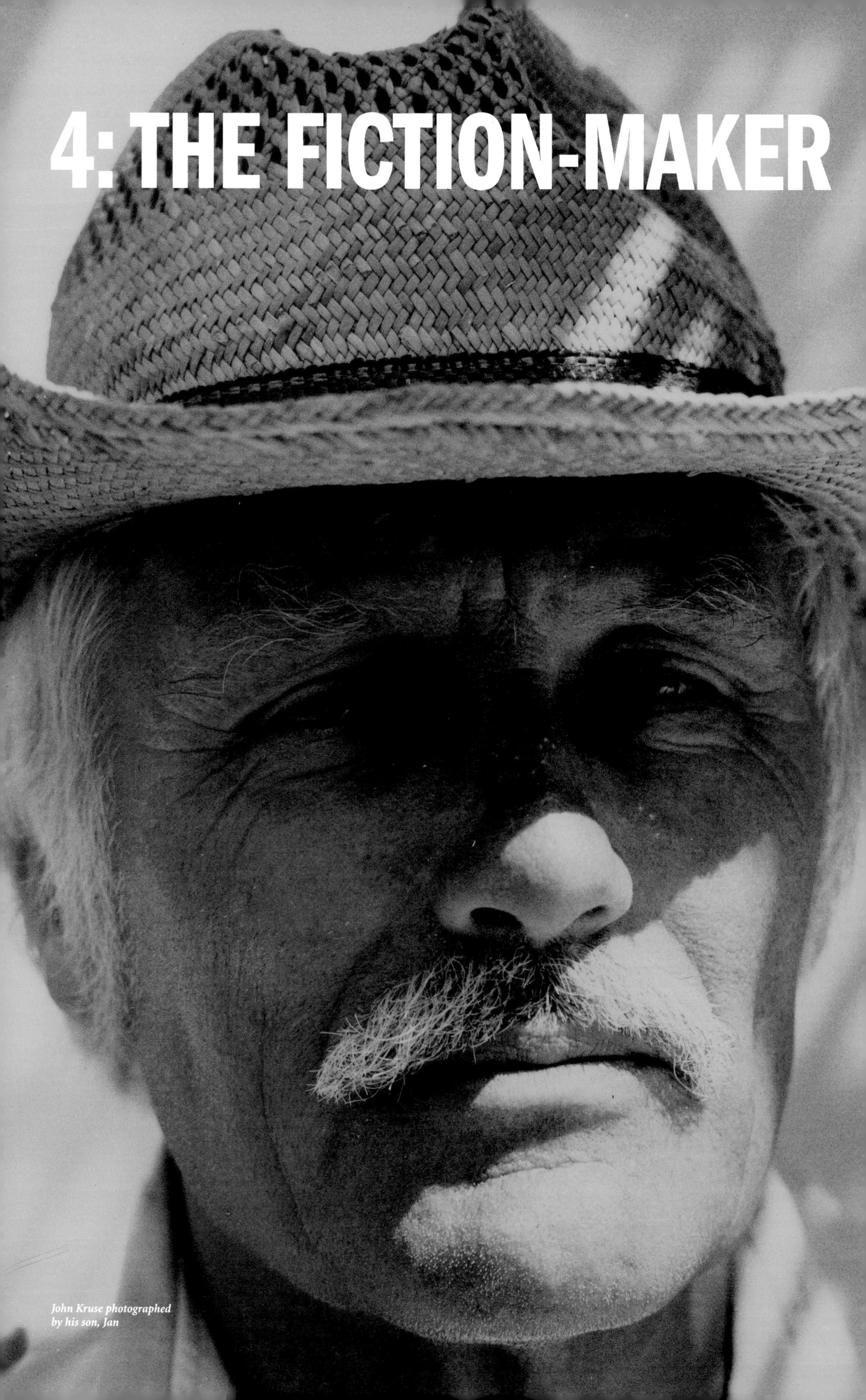

John Kruse photographed by his son, Jan

'This guy Kruse is really the find of the operation'

Memo from Leslie Charteris to Robert S. Baker, 26 July 1966

Over the seven years that *The Saint* TV series was being made, Leslie Charteris received most of the scripts with mounting displeasure as he saw his piratical wit and cavalier approach to justice neutered by the constraints of the sponsors. 'Plenty of action and no fun or surprises,' was his typical summation.

But one screenwriter proved to be a refreshing tonic. John Kruse's adaptations of the Charteris originals captured that mixture of playful wit and outrageous buccaneering quite perfectly, even on occasions adding a little extra venom to the piece. The two writers' styles blended seamlessly into a sophisticated whole that even today gives stories like *The Fiction-Makers* and *The Death Game* a pleasingly ironic and contemporary bite.

Now contentedly writing novels in Spain, John Kruse recalls the unique demands of adapting *The Saint* for television and reveals what became of his possible collaboration with Charteris on a new *Saint* novel.

How did you come to work on *The Saint* series back in 1963?

I think I'd written something for Bob Baker way back and I was in the thick of various TV series like *William Tell* (an early ATV hit). It was a very busy time. There were a lot of American entrepreneurs around who were picking up scripts to be made both here and in America. Many of them didn't happen, but I got paid anyway.

Can you remember your first meeting with Bob Baker, Monty Berman and Harry W. Junkin? Did they give you a very specific brief?

Yes, they put it to me that the scripts would have to conform to the (Charteris) stories that already existed. It was just a matter of converting them to screenplays really, but it was more work than it sounds because one had to lengthen them to incorporate a Second Act.

Did you physically share an office with Harry Junkin and write there?

No, I'd write the actual scripts at home. But what happened on the later episodes, when we were no longer working from Leslie's stories, was I'd sit down with Bob Baker and Harry Junkin and we would discuss the plot first. Harry would always be sat at his typewriter and I would throw something into the ring and we'd kick it around. The second Harry said, 'Hold it! That's it!' we'd stop and he'd go tip tap tap tap on his typewriter. Then it was, 'Ok, got that. Where do we go from there?' At the end of that we had what he considered a sort of outline – of course it never really was – which I'd then take away and work out properly. Then I'd come back with a full 10-page outline. Not every writer

JOHN KRUSE

SAINT SCREENPLAYS

Teresa
The Saint Plays With Fire
The Sporting Chance
The Saint Steps In
The Death Game (original story)
The Gadget Lovers
The Power Artists
The Double Take
The Fiction-Makers
Vendetta for The Saint
The Ex-King of Diamonds

John Kruse letter from Spain, January 1997

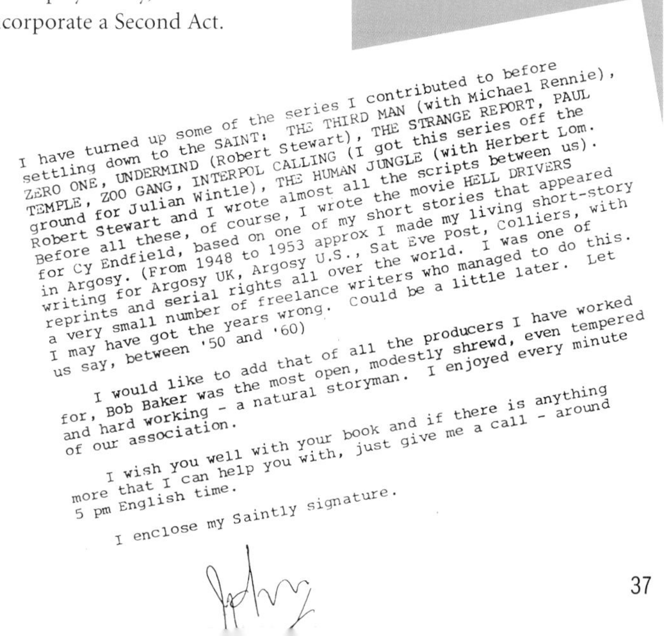

I have turned up some of the series I contributed to before settling down to the SAINT: THE THIRD MAN (with Michael Rennie), ZERO ONE, UNDERMIND (Robert Stewart), THE STRANGE REPORT, PAUL TEMPLE, ZOO GANG, INTERPOL CALLING (I got this series off the ground for Julian Wintle), THE HUMAN JUNGLE (with Herbert Lom. Robert Stewart and I wrote almost all the scripts between us). Before all these, of course, I wrote the movie HELL DRIVERS for Cy Endfield, based on one of my short stories that appeared in Argosy. (From 1948 to 1953 approx I made my living short-story writing for Argosy UK, Argosy U.S., Sat Eve Post, Colliers, with reprints and serial rights all over the world. I was one of a very small number of freelance writers who managed to do this. I may have got the years wrong. Could be a little later. Let us say, between '50 and '60)

I would like to add that of all the producers I have worked for, Bob Baker was the most open, modestly shrewd, even tempered and hard working - a natural storyman. I enjoyed every minute of our association.

I wish you well with your book and if there is anything more that I can help you with, just give me a call - around 5 pm English time.

I enclose my Saintly signature.

THE FICTION-MAKERS ON FICTION-MAKING

'I'm a capitalist. I'm through with publishing so-called important books. I don't want to educate people. I just want to be a millionaire.'
– Amos Klein's publisher, Finlay-Hugoson

'Was it a good fight?'
'No, they were more interested in getting away.'
'How did they?'
'Well, they beat me to the elevator.'
'You could have stopped them. You could have fused the elevator power circuit.'
'From *above* the car?'
'Mm. You just put a coin in behind the call button.'
'I never carry small change.'
– Amos reviews the Saint's villain-apprehending technique

'There's a tiny microphone in there. It was a present from the Turkish police. Sweet.'
– Amos chucks Simon a pair of handcuffs

'You see officer, I don't just make my stories up. I have to live them – every step of the way. I have to get *inside* my characters, don't I, darling? I know them as well as I know myself.'
– S.T. gets into the part of Amos Klein

'Of course, you know these gentlemen. After all, you created them. But to refresh your memory – The Bishop, Nero Jones, Frug and Simian Monk. Nice casting you'll admit.'
– Arch villain Warlock introduces S.T./Amos to his supporting cast

'I'm sure you'll write just as good a story this time. Telling how S.W.O.R.D. ransacked Hermetico, how, through brilliant thinking, we breached every defence, penetrated to the core of this invulnerable fortress and laid it bare. You will write it just like any other story, breaking down every problem detail by detail. You will write it and we, your characters, will live it.'
'And what if I refuse?'
'Oh, you yourself have provided me with far too many gruesome methods of torture to make such a refusal even thinkable.'
– Warlock lays out the plot for Simon/Amos

gave full outlines, but I must say I liked to otherwise one could never be sure that the script would actually work. (*Leslie Charteris admonished another writer, Michael Winder, on this very point concerning his outline for* Legacy for the Saint: '*Michael Winder is another of those writers who expects you to plug a lot of holes and develop a lot of brilliant stratagems, without telling you how he proposes to do it,' read the memo. 'I am left asking a lot of questions.'*)

I mean the outline is a con job in a way, because you're trying to get the commission to do the whole screenplay. But if you leave those kind of gaps you're going to be doing yourself a disfavour when you actually have to sit down and write the thing properly.

Did you like to incorporate some of Leslie Charteris' original dialogue where you could?
Yes, well you weren't *obliged* to use it. But occasionally it worked out. As Leslie was at that time reading every single script, you had to be fairly careful with your departures from his text. In those days he was quite stroppy, and he lived fairly close to me. He was only down the road in Egham. I must say, we didn't actually meet till fairly late in the series, but when we did it was very interesting. I never realised he was such a silent man. He had his American wife, Audrey, who was, as it were, his mouthpiece. If you asked him a question she would answer! I mean, he was just sitting there. It was very strange. I was told he was extremely old when I met him, but as he then went on for many more years I can only assume I was misinformed. He was ageless. But obviously he was impressed with my work because we thought the same way about the series.

What did you respond to about Charteris' writing?
Well, I originally read the books when I was about 16, which I should imagine is the age when they would most appeal to someone. I remember going off on adventures with The Saint somewhere in the back of my mind. In Sunningdale, where I lived then, I'd actually go creeping through other people's gardens, hiding behind bushes listening to their conversations, imagining there was some skulduggery afoot. I'm amazed I was never arrested.

But what I think I responded to, years later when I was adapting them, was a shared sense of humour. Leslie lived for a while in the States and I wrote there for television (*on* The Third Man *series with Michael Rennie*) and I think we both had a more American than British sense of humour.

How would you contrast the two types?
I would say American humour is slightly more cynical. More of a wisecrack than a gradually built-up joke. And as short as possible. Unfortunately, on *The Saint* they had a habit of rushing the story. You can rush at certain points but you can't rush the whole thing, otherwise the story is a garble. I'd learned on *The Third Man* how to write a really sharp, absolutely bare script. And with dialogue use only the words that were completely necessary. Somehow, after I'd handed them over, my *Saint* stories became more of a scramble. Still, a scriptwriter can't expect to have every word he writes adhered to.

Was this where Harry W. Junkin would have his say as story editor?
Yes. I don't think Harry Junkin tended to take much out, but he was inclined to put something extra in. (*Laughs.*) He had to do that because he was after a stake in the credits. I think when he owed a lot of bills he then nudged his way into the script!

With *The Death Game*, I wondered how it came about that you wrote the original story but Harry Junkin wrote the final script?
I think that must have been one of those weeks. I must admit it mystified me. It seemed to happen again on *Vendetta for the Saint* (*on which Junkin has a co-writing credit*). I never quite discovered what he was doing on that, or what the hell he added to *The Fiction-Makers* (*the credit is 'additional scenes and dialogue by Harry W. Junkin'*).

Leslie Charteris always described the Saint as a buccaneer, while Roger Moore talked of him around that time in terms more appropriate to a superman. Did you have your own interpretation of Simon Templar?
Not really, because one was not dealing with abstract figures. One was dealing with Roger Moore, so for that reason you just wrote for him. He could do it, although I think there have been some better Saints in the history of the movies. Louis Hayward was the one for me. I felt Roger Moore was physically a little bit big for the part. It needed someone a little more light-footed, a little more subtle. But Roger was fine and I'm sure he was a lot better than this guy who's just made the movie (*Val Kilmer*).

One of the early episodes you wrote, that I love, is *The Saint Plays with Fire*. It's quite unusual in that pretty much the whole of the Second Act takes place in a court room, at the inquest of Kennet, the murdered journalist.
Well, that came from the original book so that's why it survived. I don't think Bob Baker would have liked to have filled a whole act with such a scene unless it was very, very lively. I seem to remember we pretty much reproduced it as Charteris had originally conceived it – except for changes to the dialogue.

***The Saint Plays With Fire* seems to be one of the very few episodes where the Saint is actually badly hurt. Justine Lord accidentally burns his hands with a cigarette lighter as they try to free themselves. It's an unusually raw scene. Was there much debate about its suitability for Sunday night entertainment?**
Oh no, as far as I can recall I don't think the censor came into play much on that one. Although one certainly did try to give a more modern bite to the material, wherever it was possible.

In the opening scene of *The Saint Steps In* you have two young city types sat at the bar mocking the Saint's Casanova image. It's just occurred to me that the Saint never had to use any chat-up lines – women would just be attracted to him.
Yes, it's a kind of macho treatment of women. He was one of the boys. I can't help thinking that the 'real' Saint actually put himself out a bit more, was a bit more charming and more sensitive towards women. (*Laughs.*) That never came out in our series. The woman was always just The Girl. She was someone to get tied up and and kidnapped and rescued. But she was never really a person.

The only time it really changed from that – and this seemed to bring out some of the best writing – was when you had a girl who didn't actually like him and you'd get a lot of banter.
Yes, like the Russian woman in *The Gadget Lovers*.

'With Kruse's crackling dialogue this should be a great one'

Leslie Charteris memo to Robert S. Baker on *The Death Game* – before Harry W. Junkin took over the dialogue

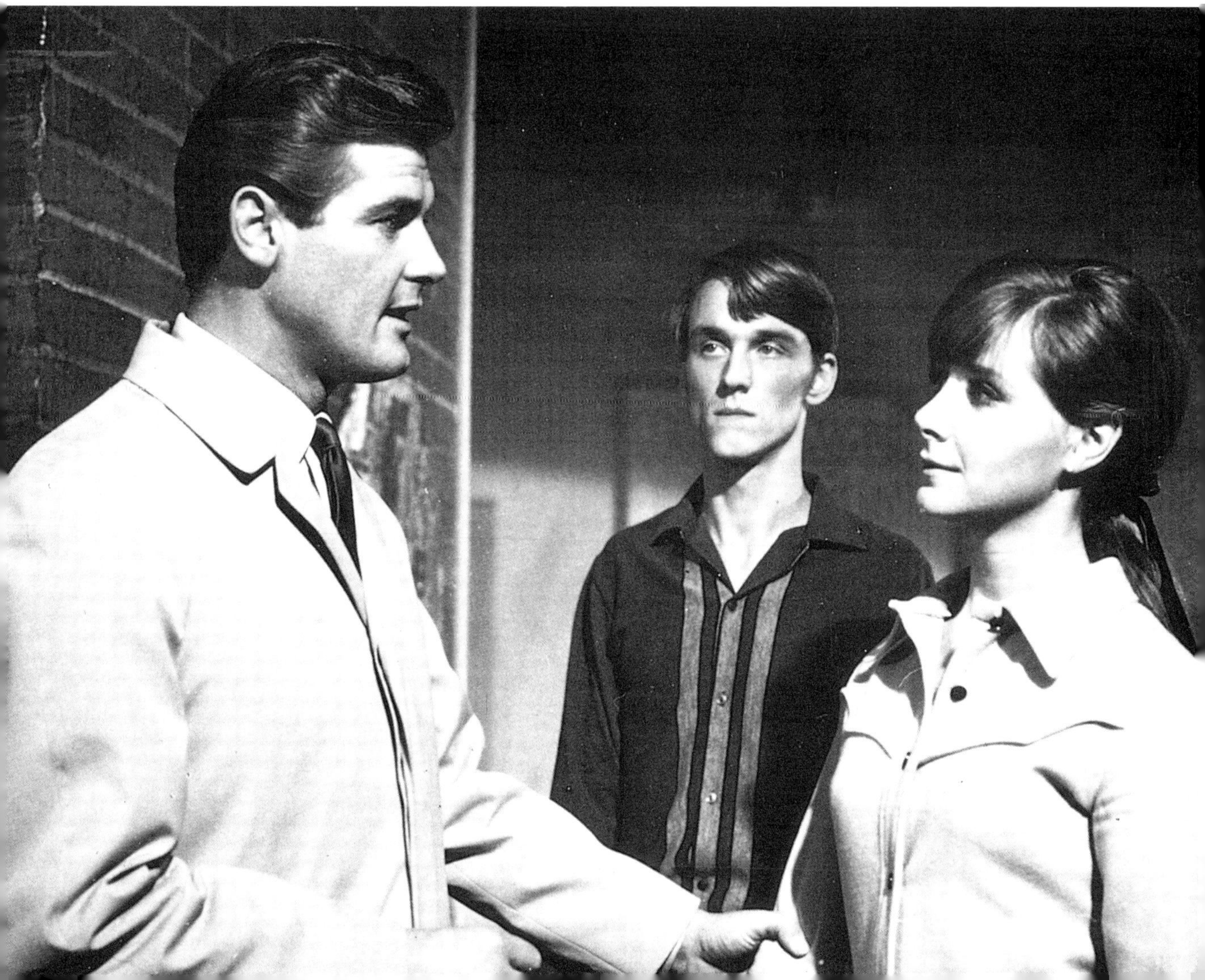

POPPERGOLD

'You are now the famous, but dead Simon Templar...' Simon Templar learns how to play The Death Game, *with Angela Douglas as Jenny Turner and John Steiner as nauseatingly smug student Greg Wyler*

THE FICTION-MAKERS ON FICTION-MAKING

'Don't look at me. In the books I never helped anybody to escape.'
- Galaxy Rose stays in character

'With a sad, sexy twist of her lissome body, Galaxy Rose turned away. "Farewell, fellow suckers!" she intoned as she left the room.'
- Galaxy makes her exit

'Alright, you invented S.W.O.R.D, now invent a way out of its clutches.'
'I did. For Charles Lake in *Hate Lover*.'
　'What happened?'
　'He was electrocuted.'
- Plot problems for Amos and the Saint

'In *Earthquake Four* Charles Lake escaped from the castle.'
　'How?'
　'Balloon!'
　'Where did he get it?'
　'Well, it was rolled up inside his umbrella and he inflated it with gas from his cigarette lighter.'
　'Oh boy.'
　'Well, it's just a simple structural problem after all.'
- Amos displays her ready grasp of the highly improbable

'You know, at this point I usually write in a helicopter.'
- Amos and S.T. stuck on the roof trying to make their escape

'It's no good, Simon, the car's hermetically sealed. The device is foolproof.'
　'The device may be. Not me.'
- Trapped in one of Amos' own fiendish devices, the Saint decides it's time for the characters to divert from the traditional storyline

'I insist on seeing Hermetico myself.'
　'I see. Well, gentlemen?'
　'It was in the book that they made two visits.'
　'And you can't diverge from the book.'
　'Yeah, stick to the book!'
- The Saint reiterates Charteris' philosophy, with the help of S.W.O.R.D.'s henchmen

That episode rather reminds me of Billy Wilder and Leigh Brackett's *Ninotchka*, a Russian general suddenly exposed to the bourgeois delights of Paris with the Saint as her guide and tempter.

Well, that was what triggered the idea really. It was a lot of fun writing that kind of dialogue, giving Roger the chance to make laconic remarks to her all the time. It gave it all a little more spice and was actually a sure-fire thing that you could repeat again and again with different nationalities. You need that conflict throughout the story. Of course, the pair of them may see eye-to-eye and be shoulder-to-shoulder by the end, but earlier the conflict of those two different personalities is absolutely vital.

Talking of conflict, the perfect example of that – where you take it to almost painful extremes – is *The Fiction-Makers*. You're forever getting Roger Moore and Sylvia Syms into deeper and deeper trouble. At one point the Saint slips a warning note into someone's pocket, only to see their potential saviour inadvertently discard it again when he pulls his hankie out to blow his nose. It's agonising. Did you delight in creating puzzles for yourself, and how would you go about it?

Aha! Well, I suppose the best way is to set yourself a goal and be the criminal in your mind (*which is exactly what the characters do in* The Fiction-Makers). You have to make the goal almost impossible, surrounded by all sorts of block elements, and then you have to think your way round those elements. The bit of paper has to fly away, the phone you're calling has to be engaged – this is the nature of suspense.

There is another way, which is to work out your climax first and then work back from that, but generally speaking I preferred the first method.

Have you got the sort of brain that enjoys unravelling puzzles?

(*Chuckles.*) No. I can't do crossword puzzles or anything! It's more of a physical thing. One has to go through all the moves oneself. For one episode of *The Return of The Saint* (*One Black September*) I set the climax at St Katharine's Dock and I actually went down there and walked the whole thing through with my wife. It was the only way I could be sure that it could be filmed the way I wanted it to be filmed. I wrote the whole damn thing there!

The Fiction-Makers must have been tremendous fun to write. It's basically an autobiography of your work?

But I was a little disappointed at the way it was filmed. I felt they made it too jokey. The Americans would have played the heavies straight while here they were trying to be funny – sort of buffoonery – and that took all the tension out of it and spoiled it.

Yes, Kenneth J. Warren doesn't play his megalomaniac like, say, Gert Frobe played Goldfinger, where he's a larger-than-life character but at the same time scary.

Absolutely. They've got to be a live threat. If they're not a threat then who cares? *The Fiction-Makers* was composed in the way that I most like to compose a story. I had two ideas – nothing whatsoever to do with each other – both of which I very much liked, and suddenly I saw a way to put them together. When that happens you have a very firm basis for a story.

There was an ex-mine in Wales at that time – it could exist to this day, I don't know – which was underground and absolutely inaccessible. It was used by all sorts of foreign dignitaries and governments for storing their wealth. So I began to imagine what the security arrangements for such a place would be. Then I doubled it and said, now find your way in!

The other idea was that somebody like Ian Fleming produces a character like Bond – what happens if a real life criminal were to imitate his methods of work?

I'm surprised you were never approached to write a *Bond* movie.

Yes, I would have been delighted to do one. I would also probably be a millionaire!

I was actually rather surprised by the writers who were coming up from left field to write the Bond films, like Roald Dahl (*You Only Live Twice*). But I was fascinated by the technique of their writing. It was so completely blatant. You'd never had a film before where somebody would come along, for instance, with a piece of information, the other person goes 'thank you very much' and shoots them dead. That was a first as far as film drama was concerned.

I was actually very good friends with Kevin McLory (*co-writer of* Thunderball *and producer of the rogue* Bond, Never Say Never Again, *now rumoured to be working on another 007 re-make*). He had been a boom swinger in the days when I was a focus puller for Freddie Francis (*who would later direct two* Saint *episodes*). When he was putting together *Thunderball* I was surprised that he didn't come to me and say, 'Rough us out a script'. Instead he got Jack Wittingham to do it, who I'd never heard of. Still, they got a good enough property together to sell to Saltzman and Broccoli.

POLYGRAM VIDEO

'You, skinny! Bulge under your armpit – get rid of it!' For once armed with a shotgun, Roger rounds up the Mafia in Vendetta for the Saint. *With Rosemary Dexter as Gina*

One *Saint* story of yours, which is rather different again, is *The Death Game*. It's black, surreal humour is more typical of *The Avengers*.
(*Laughs.*) I think I arrived at it in a bona fide fashion. The thing that triggered the idea, if I remember correctly, was those army games that people had started to play. That rather interested me.

What are the most tedious aspects of writing a thriller? Are there three or four elements that have to be in every story – the chase, the explosion?
Well, you have to work to climaxes, and there are small climaxes for each commercial break

In *The Fiction-Makers* you deal with one point that often bothers me about both *The Saint* and *James Bond* – the fact that on the screen people are often acknowledging them as 'the famous Simon Templar' or 'Meester Bond', and yet the baddies never seem to know what they look like. You nail this when one of the henchmen, Frug, finally rumbles Templar's true identity when he comes across a picture of the Saint in a celebrity magazine...
Yes, you could actually have got a whole script out of that. You'd have had it so everybody recognises him and he has to change his appearance the whole time!

Your final screenplay in the series, *The Ex-King of Diamonds*, was very much a dry run for *The Persuaders*. How did Bob Baker ask you to change your approach?
I don't think he did, really. If there's any difference in the tone of it, I think it's probably more in the way it's played than the way it was written. Bob did ask me to write some scripts for *The Persuaders*. I was paid to do three, which were to be used if they ever got to make a second series. Pleasingly, Bob remarked at the time that he thought they were much better than the scripts they'd been using. When the series wasn't picked up again in America – and quite rightly too in my opinion – I re-shaped them to then be used on *The Return of the Saint*.

'Stars are important, but not as important as a good scriptwriter. A good scripwriter is the most wonderful thing. There is the person I always like to meet'

Lew Grade, interviewed for *Television Outlook*, 23 January 1958

You weren't a fan of *The Persuaders* then?
No. I didn't think it was clever enough, it was too ham-handed, it was corny. The banter between Roger Moore and Tony Curtis was fun, but to get good ratings in America you've really got to know what your market is. Otherwise, with all those channels to choose from, people will just keep flicking till they find something just as good or better.

You do have one neat little touch during the baccarat game (in *Ex-King of Diamonds*) when a loud American woman who's ignorant of the game asks the professor the rules. Usually film-makers just assume we all spend half our lives sat in casinos and know exactly what's going on.
Whatever I detailed in that scene I must have researched, because I know nothing about gambling or cards whatsoever. Having researched it I expect I thought it was hardly fair not to share my new-found knowledge!

Though actually, you can get suspense out of gambling without knowing the rules. There are issues at stake, somebody needs to win, blah blah blah – you don't have to know that the cards have to add up to eight or nine.

Finally, can you tell us what happened to your proposed collaboration with Leslie Charteris in 1975 on a new *Saint* book?
Leslie had said to me previously that if I ever wanted to write a *Saint* story he'd okay it, then I could go ahead. At this stage I had stopped writing scripts and it occurred to me that to write an ordinary novel was a long and painful and difficult thing, but to write a book with the character of the Saint would be like second nature to me. So I dropped him a line saying I might do this – how much was he going to pay? He said, 'You will get £1000 but I will get the rights'. In other words I was writing the book and then selling it to him. I would have no copyright.

Well, at the time that seemed absolutely absurd. I would have got at least £2000-£3000 for an hour's *Saint* script. Then somebody told me later that there was actually a very small market for these books, that Hodder & Stoughton published them 'for old time's sake', and as soon as Leslie died (*in 1993*) they stopped.

Would you ever return to the character again?
Oh no way, no. I'm beyond all that now. I'm writing novels. First I did *Red Omega*, which was a bestseller in 1981 for Random House, just as we moved out to Spain. Then *The Hour of Lily* and *Long Live the Dead*, both published by Hutchinson. I'm now in the middle of what you might call a 'realistic fantasy'.

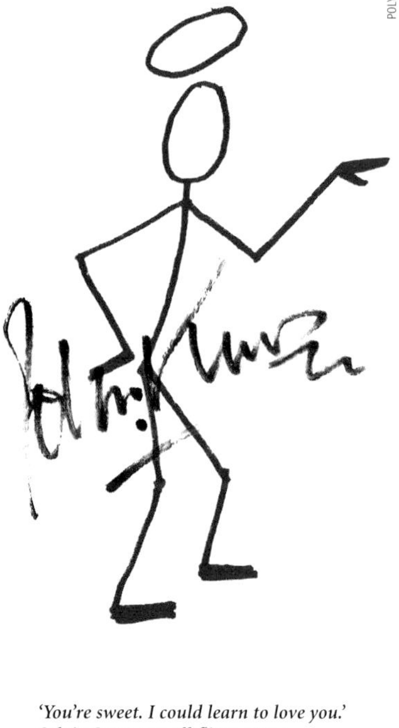

POLYGRAM VIDEO

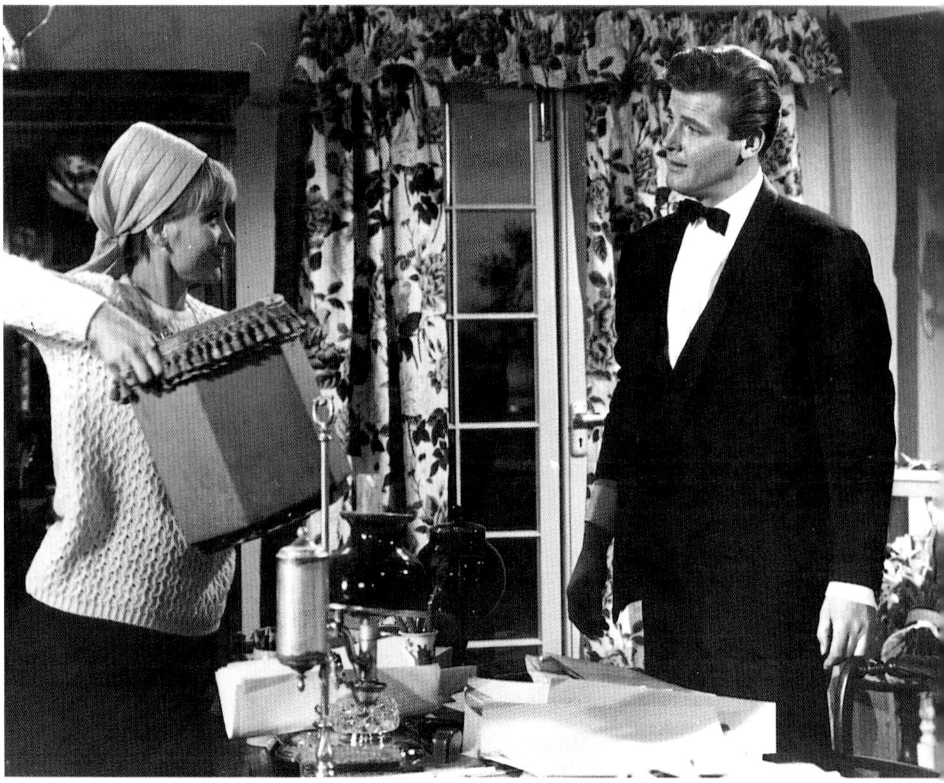

'You're sweet. I could learn to love you.' Sylvia Syms gets all flirty over a wastepaper basket in The Fiction-Makers

THE FICTION-MAKERS (1968)

CAST

The Saint	ROGER MOORE
Amos Klein	SYLVIA SYMS
Galaxy Rose	JUSTINE LORD
Warlock	KENNETH J. WARREN
Frug	PHILIP LOCKE
Monk	TOM CLEGG
Bishop	NICHOLAS SMITH
Nero Jones	ROY HANLON
Carol Henley	CARON GARDNER
Finlay-Hugoson	PETER ASHMORE
Rip Savage	FRANK MAHER
Carson	GRAHAM ARMITAGE
Ma	LILA KAYE
Pa	JOE GIBBONS
Morgan	ANTHONY BLACKSHAW
McCord	ROY BOYD
Guard,Gamekeeper	SHAUN CURRY
Ist Guard	VINCENT HARDING
2nd Guard	RALPH BALL
Reporter	OSWALD LAURENCE
Reporter	DAVID RENDALL
Reporter	RICHARD DAVIES
Reporter	IAN KINGLY

Directed by ROY BAKER

Produced by ROBERT S. BAKER

Story and Screenplay by JOHN KRUSE
Additional Scenes and Dialogue by HARRY W. JUNKIN

Music Composed by EDWIN ASTLEY
Original Saint Theme by LESLIE CHARTERIS

Director of Photography MICHAEL REED

Production Supervisor PETER MANLEY
Art Director ALLAN HARRIS
Editor BERT RULE

Casting Director G.B. WALKER
Assistant Director GORDON GILBERT

Camera Operators RAY STURGESS, TONY WHITE

Camera Assistant ARTHUR LEMMING
Set Dresser MICHAEL PITTEL

Post Production PHILIP AIZLEWOOD
Recording Director A.W.LUMKIN
Dubbing Editor JIM SIBLEY
Recordists CECIL MASON, LEN SHILTON
Continuity JUNE RANDALL

Make-Up Supervisor GEORGE BLACKLER
Wardrobe Supervisor CHARLES GUERIN
Hairdressing ELSIE ALDER
Construction Manager BILL GREENE

Titles by CHAMBERS + PARTNERS

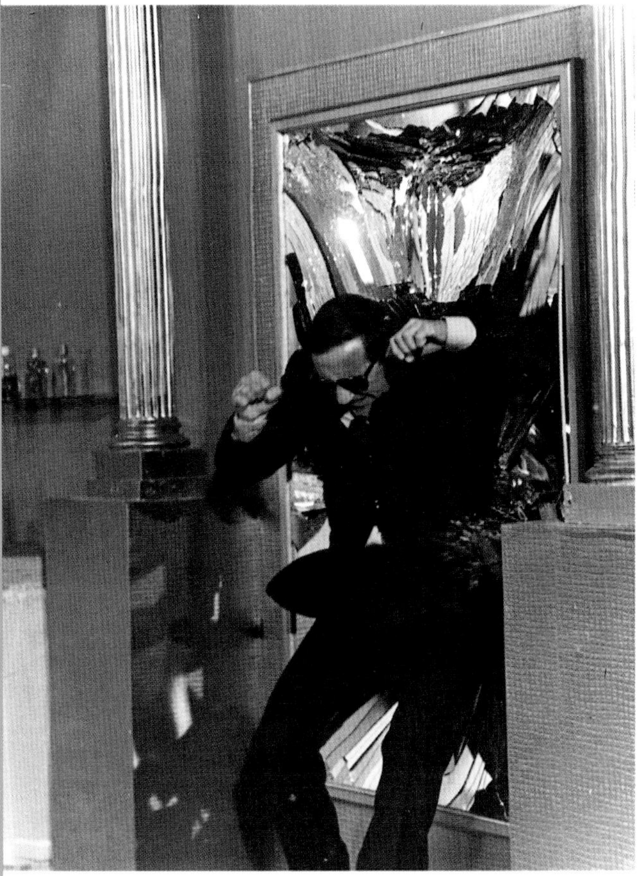

POLYGRAM VIDEO

'Screen fights are all the same and not difficult to out-guess. Now let's see – a couple of hay-makers followed up by a flying hip throw. Now a karate chop to the neck, to the midriff, another to the neck and into the bath. Turn on the shower – back into the bath. The mechanical horse, mm-hm, that must be there for some reason... Which leaves us with the mirror. Plus the groping hand bit. Dialogue...'

SO BEGINS ***THE FICTION-MAKERS***, the first and most ambitious of the two John Kruse-scripted feature length *Saint* episodes. First shown on British television in the Christmas 1968 season, it then enjoyed theatrical releases throughout Europe the following year.

Considering the general restrictions of the genre at this time it's a remarkable script. A beautifully constructed thriller that also serves as a wry essay on the whole TV action/adventure

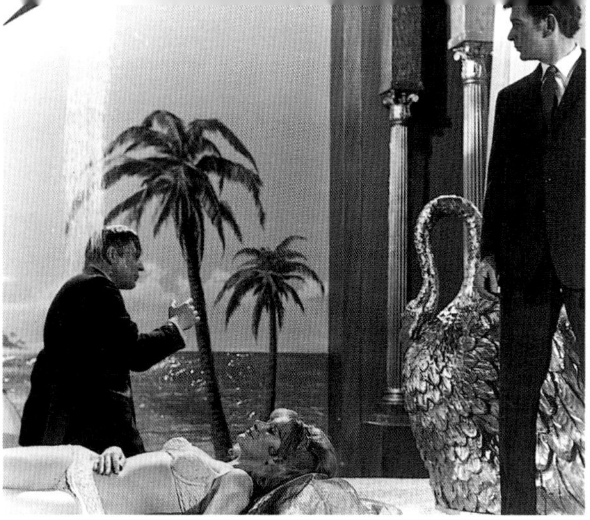

POLYGRAM VIDEO

Caron Gardner ignores the mayhem around her in Sunburst Five, *the film-within-the-film in* The Fiction-Makers

stable, which Kruse had been tied to for over a decade. Pre-dating Tarantino's *Pulp Fiction* by almost 30 years, it shows a master of his field playfully stretching to the limit the conventions with which he was so familiar.

The Fiction-Maker of the story is one Amos Klein, a writer of best-selling thrillers, creator of Charles Lake ('the greatest hero of modern times') and a living enigma who has never been seen by the general public. All of which is about to change when the flat of Klein's publisher is broken into and the author's carefully guarded identity revealed. Reluctantly, the Saint agrees to drive down to the mysterious writer's secret hidey-hole the same night, where he is confronted by a loaded pistol and an unmistakably female Amos Klein (*played with splendidly offbeat gusto by Sylvia Syms*).

But that's just the start of the role-playing. A couple of members of the local plod turn up, responding to a report of gunshots coming from Amos' abode. Simon pegs them as imposters, but it's too late and before you know it he and Amos have been sedated and bundled off into the night.

It's only the next day that the enormity of the pickle they are in is revealed. They are being held by a bunch of megalomaniacs who have modelled themselves exactly on S.W.O.R.D. (Secret World Organisation for Retribution and Destruction), the SMERSH-like dastardly organisation of Klein's books. Can the world's greatest crime writer fulfil their criminal dreams?

Original press ads for The Fiction-Makers

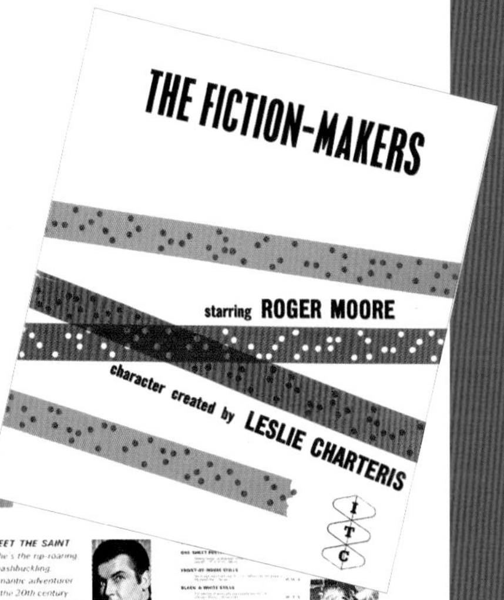
THE FICTION-MAKERS
starring ROGER MOORE
character created by LESLIE CHARTERIS
ITC

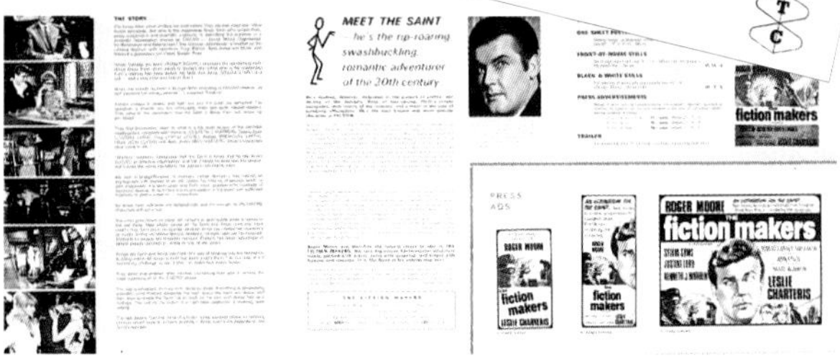
PRESS ADS
fiction makers
MICHAEL GREEN ENTERPRISES LTD
MEET THE SAINT

VENDETTA FOR THE SAINT
(1969)

CAST

The Saint	ROGER MOORE
Allessandro Destamio	IAN HENDRY
Gina Destamio	ROSEMARY DEXTER
Lily	AIMI MACDONALD
Marco Ponti	GEORGE PASTELL
Donna Maria	MARIE BURKE
Don Pasquale	FINLAY CURRIE
Euston	FULTON MACKAY
The Major	ALEX SCOTT
Lo Zio	PETER MADDEN
The Doctor	ANTHONY NEWLANDS
Maresciallo	GUY DEGHY
The Bank Manager	EDWARD EVANS
Cirano	STEVE PLYTAS
The Maid	EILEEN WAY
Giorgio	PETER KRISTOF
Doorman	AGATH ANGELOS
Barman	GABOR BARAKER
Bertoli	STEVEN BERKOFF
Bus Driver	HAL GALILI
Hotel Reception Clerk	CHARLES HOUSTON
Renato	GERTAIN KLAUBER
Nino	RICHARD MONTEZ
Woman Clerk	MALYA NAPPI
Airline Clerk	SALMAAN PEER
Maitre D'	DEREK SYDNEY
First Policeman	ERNST WALDER

Directed by JIM O'CONNOLLY

Produced by ROBERT S. BAKER

Screenplay by HARRY W. JUNKIN and JOHN KRUSE
From the original Saint story by **LESLIE CHARTERIS**

Music composed and conducted by **EDWIN ASTLEY**
Saint music theme by **LESLIE CHARTERIS**

Director of Photography **BRENDAN J. STAFFORD**

Recording Director **A.W. LUMKIN**
Associate Producer **JOHNNY GOODMAN**
Production Supervisor **VICTOR PECK**
Art Director **IVAN KING**
Editor **BERT RULE**

First Assistant Director **GINO MAROTTA**
Camera Operator **JACK LOWIN**
Camera Assistant **MIKE TOMLIN**
Casting Director **JUDITH JOURD**
Set Dresser **PAMELA CORNELL**
Continuity **JOSIE FULFORD**

Fight Arranger **LESLIE CRAWFORD**
Dubbing Editor **WILF THOMPSON**
Recordists **BILLY ROWE LEN ABBOTT**
Make-Up Supervisor **GEORGE BLACKLER**
Hairdresser **ELSIE ALDER**
Wardrobe **MASADA WILMOT**
Titles by **CHAMBERS & PARTNERS**

POLYGRAM VIDEO

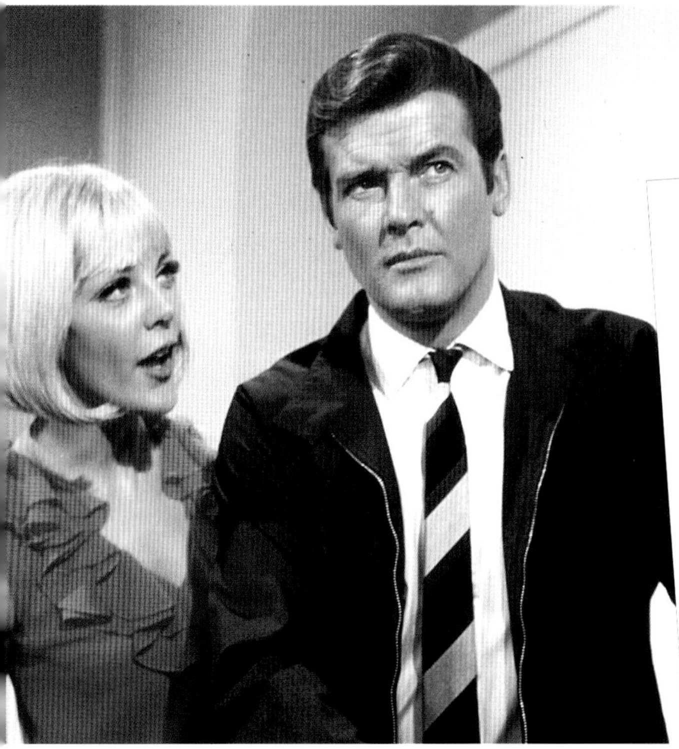

Aimi MacDonald assists as Mafia moll, Lily, in *Vendetta for the Saint*

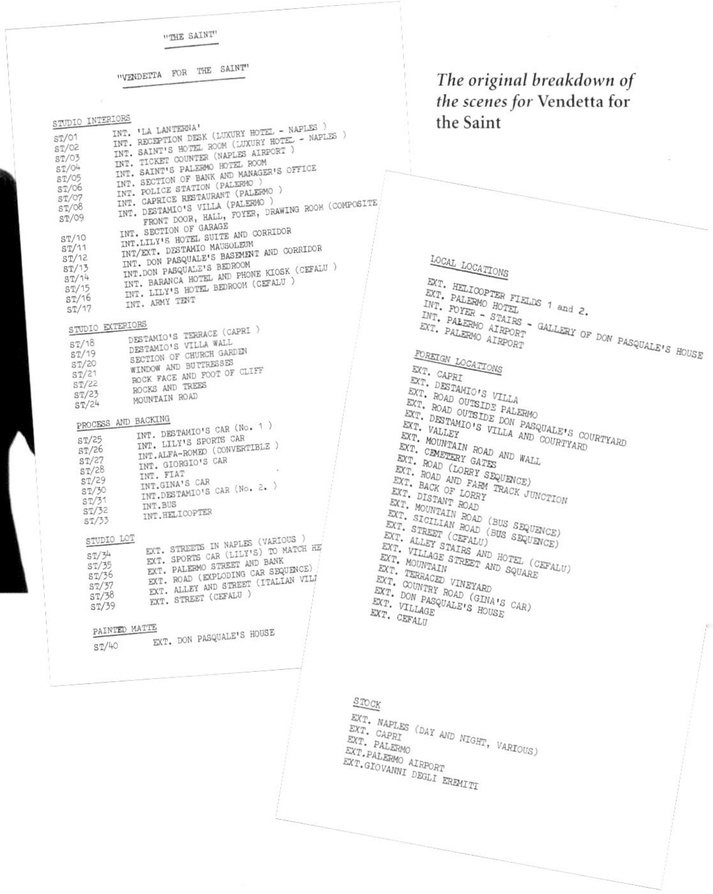

"THE SAINT"

"VENDETTA FOR THE SAINT"

STUDIO INTERIORS

ST/01 INT. 'LA LANTERNA'
ST/02 INT. RECEPTION DESK (LUXURY HOTEL - NAPLES)
ST/03 INT. SAINT'S HOTEL ROOM (LUXURY HOTEL - NAPLES)
ST/04 INT. TICKET COUNTER (NAPLES AIRPORT)
ST/05 INT. SAINT'S PALERMO HOTEL ROOM
ST/06 INT. SECTION OF BANK AND MANAGER'S OFFICE
ST/07 INT. POLICE STATION (PALERMO)
ST/08 INT. CAPRICE RESTAURANT (PALERMO)
ST/09 INT. DESTAMIO'S VILLA (PALERMO) FRONT DOOR, HALL, FOYER, DRAWING ROOM (COMPOSITE
ST/10 INT. SECTION OF GARAGE
ST/11 INT.LILY'S HOTEL SUITE AND CORRIDOR
ST/12 INT/EXT. DESTAMIO MAUSOLEUM
ST/13 INT. DON PASQUALE'S BASEMENT AND CORRIDOR
ST/14 INT.DON PASQUALE'S BEDROOM
ST/15 INT. BARANCA HOTEL AND PHONE KIOSK (CEFALU)
ST/16 INT. LILY'S HOTEL BEDROOM (CEFALU)
ST/17 INT. ARMY TENT

STUDIO EXTERIORS

ST/18 DESTAMIO'S TERRACE (CAPRI)
ST/19 DESTAMIO'S VILLA WALL
ST/20 SECTION OF CHURCH GARDEN
ST/21 WINDOW AND BUTTRESSES
ST/22 ROCK FACE AND FOOT OF CLIFF
ST/23 ROCKS AND TREES
ST/24 MOUNTAIN ROAD

PROCESS AND BACKING

ST/25 INT. DESTAMIO'S CAR (No. 1)
ST/26 INT. LILY'S SPORTS CAR
ST/27 INT.ALFA-ROMEO (CONVERTIBLE)
ST/28 INT. GIORGIO'S CAR
ST/29 INT. FIAT
ST/30 INT.GINA'S CAR
ST/31 INT.DESTAMIO'S CAR (No. 2.)
ST/32 INT.BUS
ST/33 INT.HELICOPTER

STUDIO LOT

ST/34 EXT. STREETS IN NAPLES (VARIOUS)
ST/35 EXT. SPORTS CAR (LILY'S) TO MATCH HE
ST/36 EXT. PALERMO STREET AND BANK
ST/37 EXT. ROAD (EXPLODING CAR SEQUENCE)
ST/38 EXT. ALLEY AND STREET (ITALIAN VILL
ST/39 EXT. STREET (CEFALU)

PAINTED MATTE

ST/40 EXT. DON PASQUALE'S HOUSE

LOCAL LOCATIONS

EXT. HELICOPTER FIELDS 1 and 2.
EXT. PALERMO HOTEL
INT. FOYER - STAIRS - GALLERY OF DON PASQUALE'S HOUSE
INT. PALERMO AIRPORT
EXT. PALERMO AIRPORT

FOREIGN LOCATIONS

EXT. CAPRI
EXT. DESTAMIO'S VILLA
EXT. ROAD OUTSIDE PALERMO
EXT. ROAD OUTSIDE DON PASQUALE'S COURTYARD
EXT. DESTAMIO'S VILLA AND COURTYARD
EXT. VALLEY
EXT. MOUNTAIN ROAD AND WALL
EXT. CEMETERY GATES
EXT. ROAD (LORRY SEQUENCE)
EXT. ROAD AND FARM TRACK JUNCTION
EXT. BACK OF LORRY
EXT. DISTANT ROAD
EXT. MOUNTAIN ROAD (BUS SEQUENCE)
EXT. SICILIAN ROAD (BUS SEQUENCE)
EXT. STREET (CEFALU)
EXT. ALLEY STAIRS AND HOTEL (CEFALU)
EXT. VILLAGE STREET AND SQUARE
EXT. MOUNTAIN
EXT. TERRACED VINEYARD
EXT. COUNTRY ROAD (GINA'S CAR)
EXT. DON PASQUALE'S HOUSE
EXT. VILLAGE
EXT. CEFALU

STOCK

EXT. NAPLES (DAY AND NIGHT, VARIOUS)
EXT. CAPRI
EXT. PALERMO
EXT.PALERMO AIRPORT
EXT.GIOVANNI DEGLI EREMITI

The original breakdown of the scenes for Vendetta for the Saint

'Okay, wise guy. Make like a private eye on television. Tell 'em my life story like you figure it all out in your head'

It may sound like another dry John Kruse wisecrack at the expense of the stereotypical TV detective, but in fact this line, delivered by the villain to Simon Templar, is from the book of *Vendetta for the Saint* not the screenplay. And the Saint's mocking reply is another example of the simpatico spirit that existed between Charteris and his favourite screen adaptor.

'All right, since you ask for it,' said the Saint agreeably. 'I've always rather liked those scenes myself, and wondered if anyone could really be so brilliant at reconstructing everything from all the way back, without a lot of help from the author who dreamed it up.'

In the case of *Vendetta for the Saint*, John Kruse had a good deal of help from the author. The story first appeared in *The Saint Mystery Magazine* in 1963 and Kruse stuck most faithfully to the original text when he came to adapt it five years later, proving he was equally adept at capturing Charteris' character whether working from source or from scratch. In fact, there is at least one scene where Kruse could even be said (oh, blasphemy of blasphemies), to enhance the original.

The story of *Vendetta* is straightforward enough. The Saint witnesses a scene in a Naples restaurant where an English banker, James Euston, recognises an old friend, Dino Cartelli, (played by a baleful Ian Hendry) only to be blanked and later killed by two of the henchmen of the same man, who now insists on calling himself Allessandro Destamio. Determined to avenge the innocent Euston's death and solve the puzzle of this double identity, the Saint begins to make a perfect nuisance of himself, getting involved with both Al's floozie (a very young and typically squeaky Aimi MacDonald) and his niece (newcomer Rosemary Dexter), while stirring up a hornet's nest in the ranks of the local Cosa Nostra.

After the self-referential plotting of *The Fiction-Makers* this is much more traditional fare, but the dialogue is reassuringly witty. ('Goodbye Mr Templar, we will never meet again,' says the dying Mafia don played by Finlay Currie. 'I know. I'm going *that* way,' says the Saintly One raising his eyebrows heavenwards.) There is a well-staged knife fight and an excellent early confrontation between Moore and Hendry where the former needles the latter by repeatedly calling him 'Dino'. With suitable Kruse embellishments it fair crackles, providing a tension which was less apparent in the original novel.

All that, and some genuine Italian locations, give the production an extra vitality, and in deference to its new big screen audience the Saint even gets to blow away a couple of Mafia dons with a shotgun. Now that's progress.

Screen fighting

POLYGRAM VIDEO

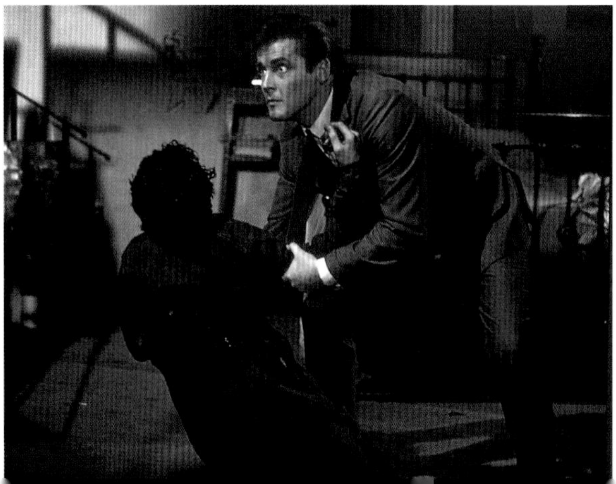

5: THE DIRECTORS

'I was fed up with these pictures where the director is showing the script to the actor, who blithely ignores him. I said to Roger, "You be the stooge for a change." This was the result.' - Roy ignores Roger, while script girl Marjorie Lavelly looks on (PHOTO: ROY WARD BAKER. PRIVATE COLLECTION)

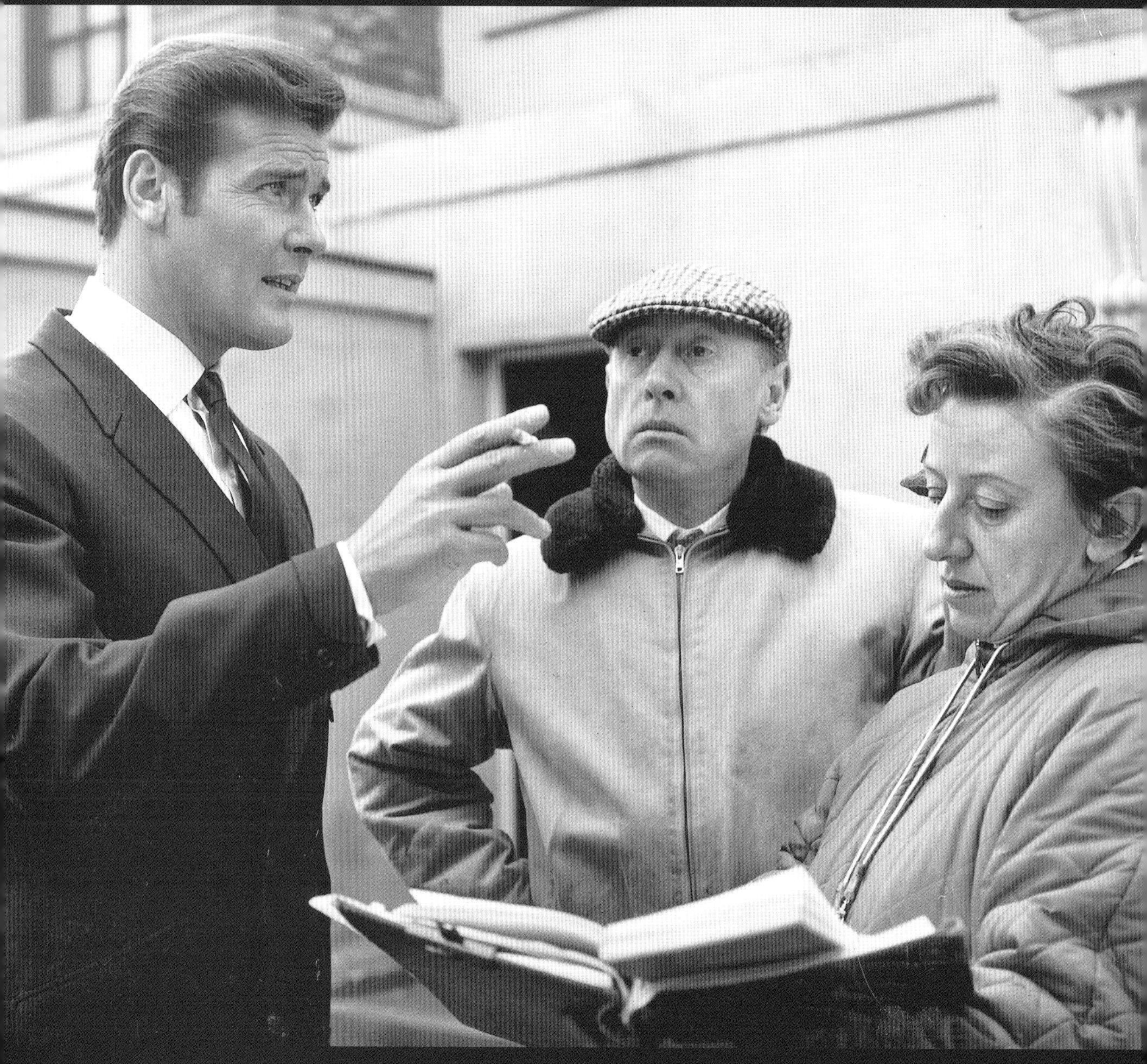

'Why don't you just listen to what the other person's saying?'

Roy Ward Baker, directing

These were the words of advice Roy Ward Baker would give to many a young actor he caught staring blankly into the middle distance, as they waited for their next line. From his early days in apprenticeship at Gainsborough, and working for Hitchcock to his seafaring pictures and later Hammer Horror films (including two personal favourites, *The Vampire Lovers* and *Dr Jekyll & Sister Hyde*), Roy always referred to himself as 'an actor's director'.

So when he came to his first *Saint* episode, in the middle of 1963, he was able to bring 20 years of experience that proved invaluable in helping to coax strong performances from many a nervous young actress. In all, he directed 17 episodes (including the two-parter *The Fiction-Makers*) in a broad range of styles from atmospheric thrillers (*The Scorpion, The Frightened Inn-Keeper*) and macabre dramas (*The Time to Die*) to romantic comedy capers (*The Queen's Ransom*) and even a screwball comedy (*Luella*).

Now in his 81st year, Roy reluctantly admits to be 'approaching old age'. But his only concession to the passing years is a dissatisfaction with most of the TV programmes he watches since he gave up going to the cinema.

THE SAINT DIRECTORS

Michael Truman
John Gilling
John Ainsworth
Jeremy Summers
David Greene
John Paddy Carstairs
Anthony Bushell
Robert S. Baker
Peter Yates
James Hill
Robert Lynn
Roy (Ward) Baker
John Moxey
John Krish
Roger Moore
Ernest Morris
Leslie Norman
Pat Jackson
David Eady
Robert Tronson
Gordon Fleming
Robert Asher
Jim O'Connolly
Freddie Francis
Ray Austin
Alvin Rakoff

Could you start by talking a little about how you got into the film business?
When I was at school I decided that working in the film business was what I wanted to do. My first interest, oddly enough, was sound recording. I was very keen on the wireless, as we called it in those days, because it was really – along with the gramophone – the most fascinating source of entertainment and instruction. So I built a shortwave radio and that sort of thing. But I just wanted any job within the industry and in the end I became a production runner – a gofer. This was at Gainsborough Pictures. And I've never done anything else really. I'm still a gofer, of a sort.

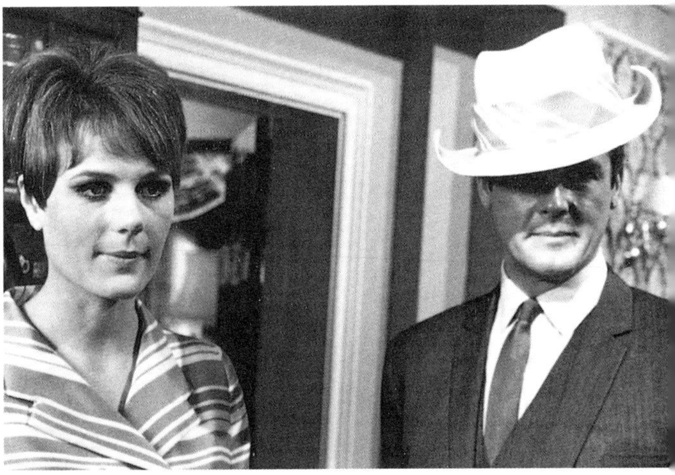
POPPERFOTO

Roger Moore replaces his halo with something a little more flamboyant

Roger Moore says you were an assistant to Hitchcock. How many of his pictures did you work on?
One – *The Lady Vanishes*. A very good picture.

Was there anything you particularly learnt from him?
Oh yes, the idea of working out the whole concept of the project, in detail, before shooting. He used to say that if he sat down quietly for half an hour he could review the whole picture in his mind before he even started to direct the production. He was a bit of a show-off of

ROY WARD BAKER FILMOGRAPHY

PRE-SAINT

1934-39 **apprenticeship at Gainsborough pictures**
Then War service
1947 **The October Man**
1948 **The Weaker Sex**
1950 **Morning Departure**
1951 **I'll Never Forget You**
1952 **Inferno, Don't Bother to Knock**
1954 **Passage Home**
1956 **Jacqueline, Tiger In The Smoke**
1957 **The One That Got Away**
1958 **A Night To Remember**
1960 **The Singer Not The Song** *(also producer)*
1961 **Flame in the Streets** *(also producer)*, **The Valiant**
1964 **Two Left Feet**
1967 **Quatermass and the Pit**
1968 **The Anniversary** *(with Bette Davis)*
1969 **Moon Zero Two**
1970 **The Vampire Lovers, Scars of Dracula**
1971 **Dr Jekyll and Sister Hyde**

EPISODES OF THE SAINT AS DIRECTOR

Teresa
Luella
The Good Medicine
The Scorpion
The Set-Up
The Inescapable Word
The Frightened Inn-Keeper
The Queen's Ransom
The Helpful Pirate
Little Girl Lost
Flight Plan
The Persistent Patriots
The Art Collectors
Simon and Delilah
Legacy for the Saint
The Time to Die
The Fiction-Makers

course, but he claimed that the shooting process was a bit of a bore because he'd already seen the finished film in his head.

But I agreed with his method absolutely. I've never been able to work any other way. I don't know how anybody else does. A lot of people do start with scene one, shoot that and then see how they progress – Chaplin would often re-shoot whole sequences two or three times as he had a skeleton crew on pay 52 weeks of the year – but it's not for me.

For *The Lady Vanishes* I was the Second Assistant, so I was the office man. One of my jobs was to go to his office first thing each morning, having obtained from the art department the plans for the sets that were to be shot the following day. I would leave them on his desk – straightforward plans, very bare and simple. Then after he'd lunched in his office – he would usually have a hamper or something – I'd collect them. Now they would be all marked up by him – the scene number, the lens to be used, possibly an indication if a tracking shot or a crane was required. So everybody knew exactly what was to be done the next day.

The most obvious place where this way of working shows up extremely well is in long sequences on trains, because you're working with people in very set positions. Unless this is all pre-planned – who's going which way and who's sitting where – you can get into terrible muddles. I've had a private laugh about it when I've seen the mess that some directors get into. There's too much arrogance about with some of the younger ones. They get halfway through a sequence and suddenly want to move an actor, and they can't.

Was Hitchcock really as dismissive of actors as he professed to be? For someone who said he had little time for them he generally got excellent performances.

Yes, I've never quite understood that. If you look at most of my stuff you will see that really I'm an actor's director, and I'm very popular with actors. I love them. I enjoy them. They can be very distracting at times and downright boring, but to me they are the tools of the trade. They are what the public's going to see. They are the ones telling the story and the audience has to believe in them. The public are not going to see me or the cameraman. The audience doesn't need to know how it's done and all that sort of nonsense. They shouldn't even be aware of that.

So I don't know why Hitch claimed to hate actors. A lot of what he did was affectation. He was a great showman and a master of his craft, so I'm not criticising him. But he'd openly say he despised actors and yet he got on extremely well with Cary Grant, Ingrid Bergman and James Stewart. I suspect if you'd said to him, 'Well, how do you feel about them?' he'd have said, 'Well, one doesn't need to. They're all very good actors so you can trust them to get on with it. It's the other people that are just rabble.'

Presumably, if someone wasn't quite right in the part then they were messing up the picture in his head?

Yes, that's perfectly true. It would disturb the decision he had already made. And once he had worked a scene out then it had to be that way – come hell or high water.

Did Hitchcock's method of pre-planning stand you in good stead when you were working on very small sets on *The Saint*?

The Saint was all shot in the conventional film studio method, in those days. You had built sets which had to be changed every week. They were most ingenious in the way they did it. Some of the art directors were very, very clever. They would start out the series with whatever standing sets were required for the first episode, but once you knew what was to come in the following episodes you could have other standing sets for later. You always had to have the Saint's flat – there would always be a scene or two there – so you could keep that for all 13 episodes. Of course they would be re-dressed a bit. But if you look closely you will see various sets – a pub, an office, a restaurant – which are used again and again.

So I made no change whatsoever in my methods. I just shot it as a movie. A short movie. A B-movie. Straightforward studio movie with very little location work. A little bit on the back lot and a few car run-bys on the roads round Elstree and Borehamwood.

Were you given a brief as to how the show should look and play?

Well, it was obvious that the tone would derive from the leading character. Roger Moore playing the Saint was Roger Moore playing the Saint. So that was alright. That was the linchpin. You didn't have to tell him anything about how to play the part, for heaven's sake. He was a great help. He had all sorts of good ideas. He's a very bright man. I developed the highest respect for him. I think he was unique as an actor. The first thing he always says is, 'Don't call me an actor, I'm not an actor,' which is nonsense, but nevertheless I know what he means by that and to some extent I think he's on the right track. People who 'act' in front of the camera usually look rather false. You can see them acting, whilst with Roger the process was invisible – which is as it should be.

Roger was always the first man in the studio in the morning and the last one out at night. He was buzzing around all the time – but not interfering. He would often have good ideas for staging the fight. That was something they had every week. There was always a fight and always a new girl. In fact this became quite a popular thing among the young actresses – 'I've done my first Saint' – and it was good experience for them.

Stephanie Beacham (in *Legacy for the Saint*) was quite remarkable. She was obviously going to be a very good actress. I loved working with all these fresh, young actors. I loved bringing new people in and pointing them in what I thought was the right direction. What they did with it after that was another matter.

'There was always a fight and always a new girl'

Roy Ward Baker on the magic *Saint* formula

Did you have a *Saint* bible to refer to?

Yes, there was a four or five-page document laying out the Saint can do this, the Saint cannot do that and so on. One of the most interesting bibles – or premises – was the one Brian Clemens did for *The Avengers*. The concept was that *The Avengers* was a constructed myth, a constructed fable – it all happened in limbo. In the end it was an idea that couldn't quite be followed through, but we certainly stuck to it in the early days of filming.

One of the principles was that you could have Emma Peel and Steed walking past Buckingham Palace or wherever – fictional characters in a recognisable setting – but there would be nobody else in the shot. It would have to be filmed at dawn on Sunday, or some such time. You'd clear the streets and stop the traffic for two minutes while you grabbed the shot. The effect was to make everything surreal.

So you could then invent the most unlikely storylines while still placing them in a commonplace setting...

Yes. Somebody would deliver a parcel at Steed's flat. The doorbell would ring. He'd say thank you very much and take the parcel, but you never saw who delivered it. It would come from nowhere.

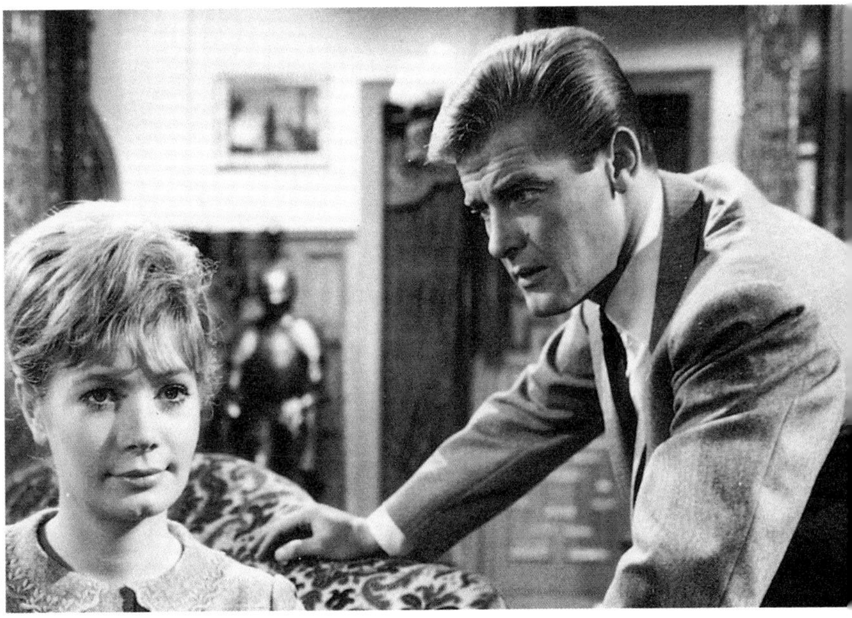

POPPERFOTO

First man in the studio in the morning, last one out at night – Roger waits for Ann Bell to finish up in The Inescapable Word

In contrast to *The Avengers, The Saint* does not really have a particular setting. Did you make many specific decisions about the look of the series?

Well, for the black and white episodes the lighting is all about trying to achieve the greatest possible contrasts – in order to give it a stereoscopic feel, as there's no depth in photography. I mean I've done a picture in 3-D, but basically it's a fact that people look at things with two eyes not one.

So black and white photography is basically very heavily backlit and crosslit. When colour came in that all changed, because colour is much better with flat front light.

That is not to say you have them facing the sun – you still have their backs to the sun – but you give them some front light as well. When you balance the two you get a very good result and it's much more flattering – irons out the wrinkles and so on.

But you're quite right. *The Saint* never had any more character than the Saint himself. That concept of the man who rights wrongs without reference to the police force – except contempt. In many ways the series was a continuation of the B movie *Saints* that had preceded it. There was no more that needed to be done to it.

I still think it's an excellent series with an appeal to a very wide audience.

One of the black and whites you directed, *The Scorpion*, is almost entirely shot at night. It's very atmospheric and you've got a great collection of villains in Geoffrey Bayldon, Dudley Sutton...

And Nyree (Dawn Porter)... Geoffrey Bayldon was a good actor who I liked very much. A charming man. A good egg generally. Dudley Sutton was a marvellous, eccentric character. Wonderful quirky delivery – you never quite knew what he was going to say next. He still does

'That's one of the most important things about actors – you musn't be afraid of them. A lot of directors are absolutely paralysed with fear working with them'

it in that series about antiques (*Lovejoy*). And, like Stephanie Beacham, you could tell Nyree was going to go a long way.

When Nyree Dawn Porter's all beat up in hospital she looks like Bette Davis in *Whatever Happened To Baby Jane*. How did you approach directing Bette Davis in *The Anniversary*? Would she try to direct herself like John Wayne did?

Oh no, no. She listened. I knew her very well. It so happened that when I went to America in the first place, in November 1951, we met in New York and travelled out on the same train to Los Angeles. You could do it by train in those days and neither of our families wanted to fly. We became fast friends – three and a half days in that enclosed space and you were either going to become friends or sworn enemies.

After that we were in and out of each other's houses all the time we were in Hollywood. She was very kind to me. And insanely pro-British, by the way. She adored England. Of course she was outrageous and frightened the wits out of people, but she and I got on extremely well.

I wasn't the original director assigned to *The Anniversay* but she couldn't get along with the first choice, so I was hired. Never a cross word. We talked about it and got on with it. In fact, her conception of her part and how she would play it was so clear cut that there was very little to discuss.

Were the other actors very much in awe of her?

They were. But they were most worried that because the whole piece revolved round her character they were going to get pushed to one side. But when they saw the finished film it wasn't so. They all got their break.

You very often have to say to an actor, 'Look, don't do your nut in this scene because it isn't your scene. It's his or hers. Yours comes later. Just hold your fire, do what's necessary and that's it.' They'd say, 'OK, I see, well tell me if I go over the top,' and I'd say, 'I will do – don't worry!' That's one of the most important things about actors – you musn't be afraid of them. A lot of directors are absolutely paralysed with fear about them.

Certainly David Lean. We were actually great friends for a time when he was doing *Great Expectations* and things like that, and he confided this to me. He said, 'I'm absolutely petrified of Alec Guinness.' I said, 'Don't be ridiculous'. He'd already made four pictures while I was on my first, but he couldn't deal with it. And to cover up this fear he would be very rude to them. Hitchcock too. It was their own insecurity.

After your first *Saint, Teresa*, which is quite a dark little tale, you went right to the other end of the spectrum with *Luella,* which gets cranked so hysterically – particularly the shouting between Hedison and Suzanne Lloyd – that it's almost a farce.

I had met David Hedison, oddly enough, when I was in Hollywood in the late 1950s. He'd had some short career as a kind of ringer for Tyrone Power, whom I directed in another film.

Suzanne Lloyd was a real find. She reminds me of the sort of dangerous females you'd get in screwball comedies. There's a scene where she and Hedison tussle over a black brassiere, she chucks a teapot, he bars her way and she smartly walks through the other door. Was she like that?

Actually she was terribly nervous. Very, very nervous. It got in the way of a lot of her work, I think, but she gradually settled down. I remember the first one we did I had to reassure her and calm her – 'Don't worry, it's only a movie'. We'd do each scene in bits and pieces. She had a temperament, she was sensitive and she wanted to succeed. These were all good points. But it's no good shouting at somebody like that. You have to get behind them.

In the end she was worth the trouble, because despite being fragile she was full of energy.

Do you recall a rather outrageous moment when Hedison knocks a dessert onto a large woman's blouse and then tries eating it off with a spoon ?

No, I don't. What I do remember is a very very old joke about some people dining at the Ritz. One woman has got a very low décolletage and the waiter drops some ice-cream down it. So he does his best to fish it out, but the head waiter comes rushing over, pulls him off and says (in a very grand voice): 'At The Ritz we do that sort of thing with a warmed dessert spoon!' Schoolboy stuff really. There was a lot of that at Elstree. It was a tremendous lark. That was another thing that Roger brought to every episode – 'We're never going to get serious about this. Come on! This is entertainment. This has got to be fun. And if it's fun for us then it'll be fun for the audience.'

A lot of people *try* to do that sort of thing, and of course they're having a ball and the audience is left thinking 'What on earth do they think they're doing?' So it doesn't always come off.

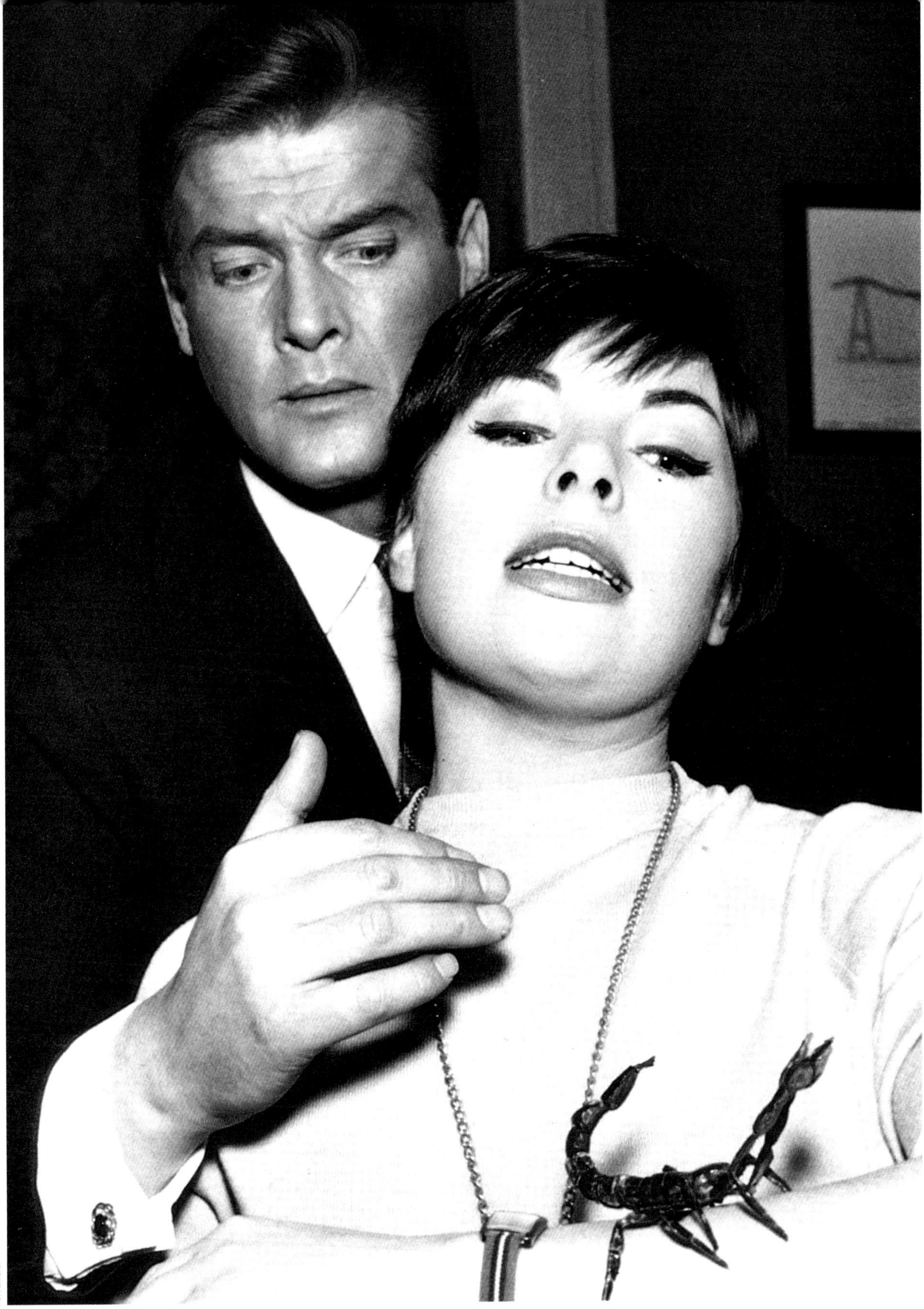
POPPERFOTO

A very dangerous game to play? Roger and Catherine Woodville, as Karen Bates, combat a none-too-deadly plastic scorpion in, er, The Scorpion

It's a very dangerous game to play, but provided you've got responsible, professional people you can crack jokes and lark about. There used to be great battles with soda siphons on the floor. One of the cameramen, a lovely fellow called Frankie Watts, was always stalking around trying to catch Roger out with a soda siphon, but he always got the worst of it.

But despite all the fun, Roger was an incredible worker. He claimed he never had to learn the lines and I think there's a certain amount of truth in it. He said to me once, 'I just listen to the other actors'. Now this is the key to acting. You look at most of the stuff on television now and you can see the actors are not listening to each other. All they're doing is waiting there till it's their turn to speak. Yak, yak, yak, yak, yak and then they just switch off again.

POPPERFOTO

Roger listens most intently to June Ritchie, as Mildred, in Little Girl Lost

It's one of the things on which I often picked up actors – 'Why don't you just listen to what he's saying.' 'Oh.'

Roger was an artist at that. He said, 'If I listen to what the other person is saying, then I know more or less what the answer is!'

But it breaks my heart most of the stuff you see on television today. Half the time they don't know where to point the camera. That's crucial. They play scenes with the camera on the back of someone's head, when it's a vital plotline. Elementary mistakes. Some of the time it's done deliberately as an affectation. That's fair enough – it might work for that scene. But most of the time they just don't know what they're doing.

In the late 1960s you became identified much more with horror movies, but seemed equally at home working on the more light-hearted *Saint* episodes. Did you have a preference?

I don't know. I have been criticised for being, apparently, a Jack-of-all-trades, which is to some extent true. I have been far too eager to try my hand at almost anything which came along. That was very foolish, because there was open to me in the 1950s a chance to specialise in stories about the sea. I'd had a roaring success with *Morning Departure*, which was set on a submarine, and *A Night To Remember*. Twentieth Century-Fox wanted me to go back and do another but I was tied up and perhaps that was a turning point for me.

I think the best thing I do is realism, films like *The One That Got Away* and *A Night To Remember*.

Did you enjoy your time in Hollywood

Oh yes, immensely. I was very grateful for it. Unfortunately, when I arrived the studio system was coming to an end and really all that people were worrying about was how to compete with television.

So was this when all the gimmicks like Cinemascope came in?

Yes. Cinemascope – that was a disaster. It was useless. It's alright having this enormous wide screen, but it was too narrow. It was like a letterbox. You don't see any pictures on walls by great artists like that. They said it would be quicker and cheaper. And of course it wasn't. None of these panaceas ever work. Chasing their own tails.

Did you approach *The Fiction-Makers* differently, knowing it was a two-parter and in view of the satirical nature of the script?

It was very ambitious in its production values and, I'm afraid, was far too rushed. It was shot in about 18 days. There really wasn't time to think and the coverage (*of different shots for a scene*) wasn't as full as it should have been. I have actually seen it quite recently.

Was there any debate as to the tone of the film? On the one hand you have a henchman like Phillip Locke who plays it very straight, while on the other you have Kenneth J. Warren rather camping it up.

Quite honestly, I don't think I did a particularly good job on that one. I don't think I brought out the satirical line at all well. To me it looked like an imitation *Bond* picture rather than a send-up. But there was also always a limit as to how far you could do a send-up in *The Saint* series.

The Saint was always light-hearted entertainment. But it never sent itself up. There was an element of drama in it – always – which had to be preserved. But certainly the original idea in John Kruse's script was extremely good. I don't think the cast was as good as it could have been. There were one or two deficiencies. Not enough personality.

The most enjoyable scenes are the ones between Roger and Sylvia Syms, particularly their first encounter at her cottage which plays for about six minutes and is a joy from start to finish.

Well, there you are. I mean Sylvia is a gem and we were lucky to get her. We'd made a movie together before, *Flame in the Streets*. Her sheer presence, her charisma would bring the film alive.

You see, it's no good complaining about actors because this is exactly the element that you do depend on. I used to describe it as if you take the whole crew – the writer, the producer, the director, the lighting cameramen, art director and so on – all of them together make about 95 per cent of the movie, but the other 5 per cent, which is the actors, is the per cent that impacts on the audience. And it's the audience that I want to come and see my film – the more the better. If you work in films you're working to a mass audience – not to play to your four friends in Kensington.

That's the satisfaction that I get. I don't get the money anyway. In very, very few cases did you get any royalties in my day. We were all underpaid and overtaxed. That's why none of the directors from my generation are rich.

You directed Vladek Sheybal in *The Helpful Pirate*. Again, as a young lad watching *The Saint* he was someone who made a big impression with his huge, hooded eyes. Can you tell us something about him?
He was one of those actors who had a wonderful presence. And whatever he did you thought – there's something else going on here. (*Chuckles.*) He was a delight playing devious spies because when he spoke you could never quite tell whether he meant it or not. I liked him.

But all the episodes were fun to do, because there was not the same responsibility that you would have with a film. A film could take a year-and-a-half of your life, while with *The Saint*s I think, one time, I did 13 hour-long episodes in a year. I must have been half dead by the end of it. Terrifying when you think about it.

Did you have many dealings with Lord Grade?
Never met him.

The one thing that was admirable with Bob Baker, Monty Berman until he left the series, and Harry Junkin was the way they managed the production of the scripts. They came rolling off – every nine days there would be a new one. And they would be immaculately timed and laid out and all the action would be carefully plotted to climax at each commercial break. Much, much later when I worked on *Minder*, people had become much more slovenly with things like this. The breaks would be indicated but not in nearly so precise a way. Sometimes the first act would run for half an episode.

Bob Baker says his favourite *Saint* episode is one you directed with Dawn Addams, *The Queen's Ransom*. There's a lot of great banter between Roger and his leading lady. Everything he does in it is done to antagonise her.
Yes, she was sweet. Funny girl though. Whenever she was doing a close-up I would have to sit right next to the camera and hold her hand. I don't know why. But she didn't have a very happy life.

It's interesting that that kind of relationship doesn't really seem to exist in movies now. It was very sexy, but nobody took their clothes off or started barging about on sofas. I find that all very unbelievable now. And if you do believe it then it's not very pleasant. I can't see the point of it. It's nothing to do with me but I think they're on the wrong track because it's a dead end. In fact they've already gone beyond the dead end and there's really no more they can do.

But instead, if you have this kind of feeling between two people where you think this might come to something, might not, it's interesting. You can play that for the whole episode.

The only time your films became more overtly sexual was with something like *The Vampire Lovers*, with Ingrid Pitt, Madeline Smith and Kate O'Mara.
Yes, that was a different thing altogether. They were supposed to be lesbians. That started out as being a sensational exploitation picture. I got a lot of stick from the producers, Harry Fine and Michael Style, because they wanted it laid on with a trowel. I wasn't having it. I said, 'You're crazy. I refuse to treat lesbians as figures of fun.'

Who would you cast as the Saint now?
That's a hard question now that I don't go to the cinema. Hugh Grant has some of the qualities, but he doesn't have the stature. George Sanders and Roger were both big men. Roger also had that perfect face to photograph and he was very deft. It may sound strange, but he was very good (*to film*) driving. A stillness.

The actor that Roger was a great admirer of was Errol Flynn. He would often refer to him, so I asked him what it was he so like about him as an actor. 'His cheek,' he said.

'If you're working in films you're working to a mass audience – not to play to your four friends in Kensington'

Roy Ward Baker

'I used to get a lot of funny actors in my movies'

Freddie Francis on his unusual repertory company

LOGER WHO?

Best wishes,

Freddie

As a twice Oscar-winning cinematographer (for *Sons and Lovers* and *Glory*) and director of countless Hammer and Amicus horror movies, Freddie Francis has enjoyed a double life.

Revered for his beautiful, haunting camera work on *Room At The Top* and *The Innocents*, he is equally lauded by gore-fest fans for shockers like *The Skull* and *Dracula Has Risen From The Grave*.

An added bonus to any Freddie Francis project is the repertory of supporting actors he brings with him. It was no surprise, then, that when he came to film his two *Saint*s, the name of Michael Ripper was in the cast list...

FREDDIE FRANCIS FILMOGRAPHY

PRE-SAINT
As Director of photography:
1947 **Mine Own Executioner**
1957 **Time Without Pity**
1959 **Room At The Top**
1960 **Sons And Lovers** (*for which he received an Oscar*)
1961 **The Innocents**

As Director only:
1961 **Two and Two Make Six**
1962 **Vengeance**
1963 **Paranoiac, Nightmare**
1964 **The Evil of Frankenstein**
1965 **Traitor's Gate, The Skull**
1966 **The Deadly Bees, They Came From Beyond Space**
1967 **The Torture Garden**
1968 **Dracula Has Risen From The Grave**
1969 **Mumsy Nanny Sonny and Girlie**

EPISODES OF THE SAINT AS DIRECTOR
The Gadic Collection
The Man Who Gambled With Life

How did you come to do your two *Saint* episodes?
I think what happened was, after I got my first Academy Award I started to get all these offers to direct. In this country you got paid more money for directing than being a cameraman, so that's what I started to do. I drifted off into all these horror films which have almost become my life. (*Chuckles.*) I'm always going to festivals with all these mad fans.

After I'd done about 25 of these I thought, 'this is crazy,' so I stepped outside of it and began to prepare a few things of my own. And while I was doing that I got offered odd television things like *The Saint, The Champions* and *Man In A Suitcase* and as I like making films, I did them. Unfortunately, one had so little freedom on them that I didn't like them very much. I'm afraid dear old Roger wasn't keen on experimenting.

Was Peter Wyngarde fun to work with on *The Gadic Collection*. He has this most extraordinary Arab make-up on. He looks like a cross between a zombie and Sammy Davis Jr.
Really! I had worked with Peter before on *The Innocents* and actually he and Georgia Brown were tremendous fun. Georgia Brown was a great girl – couldn't care less about anybody or anything. So anything in the scene we fancied playing about with we did, which I'm sure annoyed Berman and Baker no end.

Georgia Brown didn't do much film or television work did she?
No, she didn't. I think she was very disappointed not to play the part that she created on the stage of Nancy in *Oliver!* when they made the film. I thought she was very talented.

Another one to get in on the act, with some entertaining scenes, is Michael Ripper.
Oh yes. (*Chuckles.*) Another one of my repertory company. I usually found a part for Michael. In fact he was in a number of my so-called features. The reason you used the same people again was that we were on such tight schedules that one couldn't devote a great deal of time to directing everybody, so with those actors you could just say get on with it and you knew they could do it.

Howard Hawks did the same thing with actors like Walter Brennan, didn't he? He knew he could make an entertaining scene if someone like Brennan was involved.
Absolutely. Of course, these days with the tremendous budgets and schedules you have to

concentrate on directing every line from everybody. But back in the 1960s you needed a stock company you could rely on to carry the smaller parts.

Didn't you used to work with John Kruse in the days before he became a screenplay writer?

Oh yes. I knew John just after the war, when we were all in the camera department at Shepperton. I was a camera operator and Johnny was a focus puller and clapper boy. I had a spell in Ceylon with Johnny after that, when we did a Carol Reed picture, *Outcast of the Islands*.

One thing that is quite unusual about *The Gadic Collection* is the very high quality of the, presumably stock, location footage of Istanbul. There's a beautiful shot of the ferry at sunset, bathed in a deep orange glow.

After my first film, *A Hill in Korea*, there were plans to do a war film in Istanbul. The film was to be produced by Lord Brabourne, the son-in-law of Lord Mountbatten, who was head of the navy then. The only way we could get into Turkey, then, was on a warship pretending we were sailors on leave, so I did shoot a lot of stuff out there. I think probably I suggested they use some of that for *The Saint*.

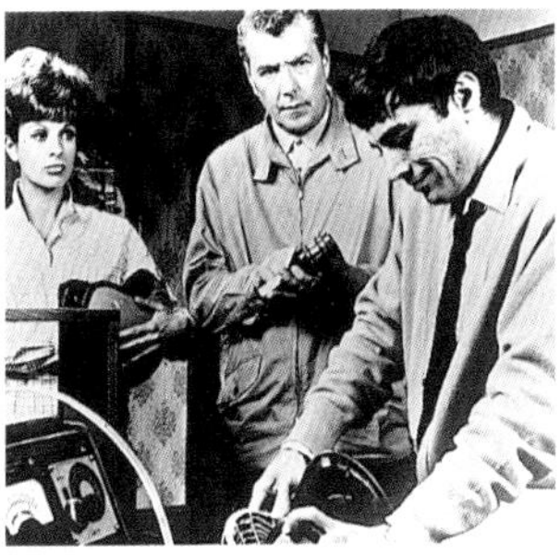

BFI

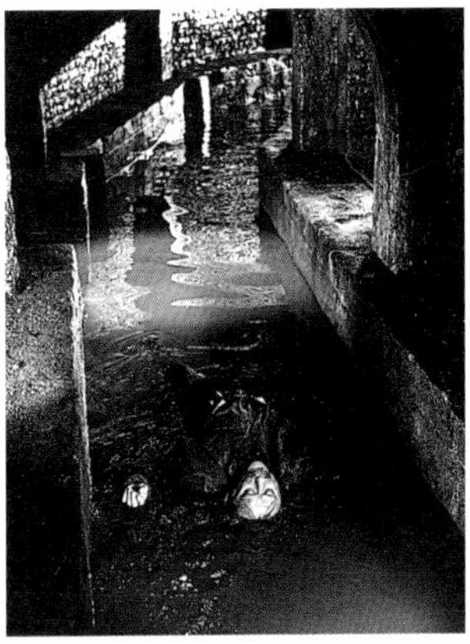

BFI

Buddy of an ex-President Robert Hutton (centre), in They Came From Beyond Space *(top)*

Michael Ripper lands another great Freddie Francis part as a victim of The Legend of the Werewolf *(above)*

What are your memories of *The Man Who Gambled With Life*? It has a nice, morbid beginning, with Veronica Carlson and four undertakers getting out of a van and presenting Roger Moore with a mouse in a box.

Well, I'd given Veronica one of her first parts in *Dracula Has Risen From The Grave*. The one actor I really remember from that was Steven Berkoff. Steven was terribly dedicated and (*chuckles*) I think he thought we were making *The Life of Christ*. In those days he was a very penniless actor. I'm not sure how I came across him, but I thought he had a good face. He did tend to play things in the script that weren't necessarily there.

Another actor I used was Robert Hutton (*The Contract* and *Invitation to Danger*). I discovered Bob after he left Hollywood and was struggling over here, and he became another of my stock players. He'd done very well in the early years in Warner Bros B pictures, then when that sort of actor went out of fashion he came over here and found it very hard to get work. He was very tall and quite good looking, so I cast him in this science fiction film we were making for Amicus, *They Came From Beyond Space*.

Poor old Bob. I used him a lot, but he went from bad to worse. It was a strange story. He went back to America and was in a really bad way living in this dingey tenement. One night, I don't know whether he'd been drinking or what, but he fell down the stairs and broke his back. So he was dropped off in this hospital, pretty much left to die. But there was this Sister who took an interest in him and worried about him. He kept saying, 'Get my friend, the President,' which sounded like mad talk. Anyway, she followed this up and they got in touch with Reagan. Sure enough, he'd been a mate of Bob's in their Hollywood days – because they were both B picture people – and he got him transferred to a military hospital and then a military home. I used to speak to him occasionally, but I think he later died.

Yes, I used to get a lot of funny actors in my movies. Fortunately, if one wants to get on a higher plane, I can refer to my other career as a Director of Photography and go and work with people like Martin Scorsese. In fact, we have still got something we're trying to set up which I will direct and he will produce, but I don't know when that will happen.

'Oi! Scorsese, no!' Freddie Francis directs from the only place he knows how – the studio floor

Presumably Martin Scorsese was a big fan of your work from Hammer and Amicus days, when he hired you to be Director of Photography on *Cape Fear*?

He loved all those stories. The thing with production these days is that directors tend to have a television (*monitor*) on the floor – which I hate. Scorsese has it because he does not like coming down on to the set. So I'd be sat up there with him and he'd just talk about the old days. I'd obviously been sold to him by Mickey Powell. But I enjoyed working with him.

If I'm directing though, I like to be right up beside the actors. I'd sit in their pockets if I could.

FREDDIE FRANCIS PRIVATE COLLECTION

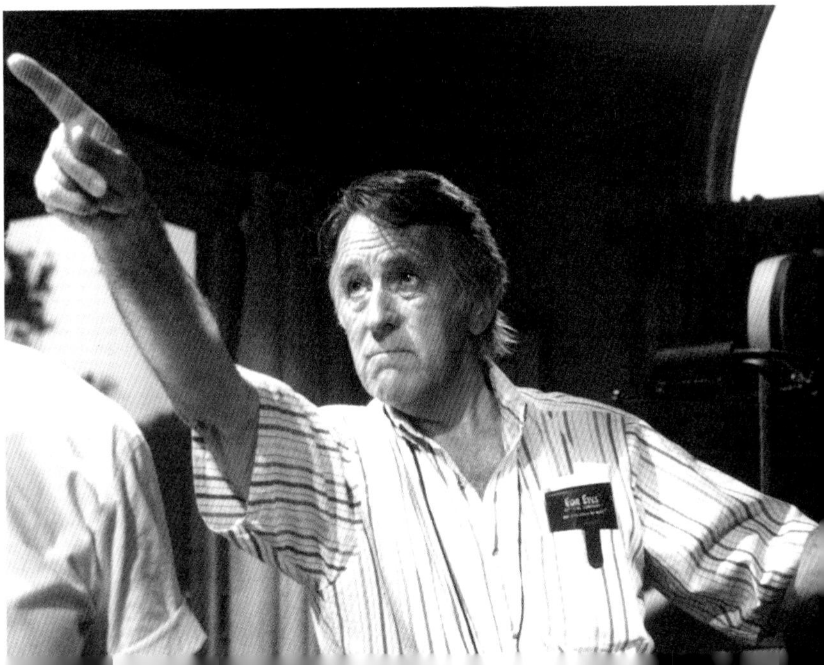

6: IN PRODUCTION

ROGER
LUISA MOORE
BILLY DEAN
Ex-boxer and
film stunt man
BILLY HERLIHY
Looked after
group casting
JOSIE FULFORD
Continuity girl
Camera focus puller
from South Africa
LIONEL BANES
Director of photography
(ie, lighting cameraman)
JEREMY
SUMMERS
The director
Sound mixer
Camera grip
LEN HARRIS
Camera operator
Worked in wardrobe
(a former film extra)
A stand-in who sadly
committed suicide a
year or so later
Patricia Donahue who
starred in this episode,
The Charitable Countess
(1962)
Prop man
Camera assistant
(clapper loader)
J.G. (still single!!)
BRUCE SHARMAN
First assistant to the
director

Johnny Goodman recalls his almost joint 35th birthday with Roger, in 1962, on the set of The Charitable Countess *at Elstree*
(PHOTO: JOHNNY GOODMAN. PRIVATE COLLECTION)

'I can't believe the farting about on television productions these days'

Malcolm Christopher on changing production values

In the 1960s, British television shows like *The Saint* were considered to be some of the best and most successful in the world. They were glossy 35 mm productions packed with glamour, action and adventure.

And where did these stylish tales take place? On the Côte D'Azur? Morocco? Amongst the glorious bustle of Paris in the spring, or Rome?

Nope, it was in a studio and its wintry back lot near Borehamwood. In the whole 118 episodes Roger Moore made it out of the country to some exotic destination just once.

And if the locations were limited, so were the budget and the time. Allowing for inflation, *The Saint* would cost about a tenth of the price of a standard TV cop show today and be shot in considerably less time. So how the hell did they do it?

***The Saint*'s one-time production supervisor (and later associate producer), Johnny Goodman, and location manager and production supervisor Malcolm Christopher, explain the amazing tricks of what now seems to be an almost extinct trade...**

A JOHNNY GOODMAN PRODUCTION

Over the past 35 years **Johnny Goodman** has been production manager/supervisor on *The Saint* (72 episodes); *The Baron* (30 episodes); associate producer on further *Saints* and 18 *Champions*; in charge of production on *The Persuaders*; executive director of production for Euston Films for *Minder*, *Out*, *Fox*, *Widows*, *Reilly Ace of Spies*, *Flame Trees of Thika* and many others; co-executive producer at HTV International on TV films like *Maigret* and *Indiscreet* and recently finished as executive-in-charge of production at Carlton.

MALCOLM CHRISTOPHER LOCATION MANAGER & PRODUCTION SUPERVISOR

Over the past 35 years **Malcolm Christopher** has been production manager/supervisor on 60 episodes of *The Saint*; 26 episodes of *The Persuaders* and *The Protectors*; 13 episodes of *Randall & Hopkirk (deceased)* and six episodes and a Christmas Special of *Minder*. Feature films as location manager are *That Lucky Touch*, *Rollerball* and *The Man Who Would Be King*. And as production supervisor, *Barry Lyndon*, *Voyage of the Damned*, *Raise the Titanic*, *Ragtime*, *Never Say Never Again*, *Death Wish III*, *Superman IV*, *Robin Hood -Prince of Thieves*, *Patriot Games* and many others.

He is currently working on the $50 million Laurence Fishburne/Sam Neill picture *Event Horizon*.

Johnny Goodman: I started off as a third assistant on some of Bob Baker and Monty Berman's 1950s B movies – *Barbados Quest* and *Tiger by the Tail* – going up the scale to second assistant, first assistant and finally production manager. One day they called me and said they were going to make a series on *The Saint*. So I went up to their offices in Jermyn Street and for the first time met this guy Roger Moore. Now, Roger Moore is one day older than me, but at that time I'd never heard of him. I had never seen *Ivanhoe*. Anyway, this tall, good looking boy's there and he says to me, 'Do you enjoy a joke?' I said, 'Yeah'. He said, 'Oh, we'll get on fine together then.' So I was in on *The Saint* from the word go.

He was stunningly good looking then. We were both in our early thirties and it made you sick. It seemed unfair that the Almighty had given one person all the good looks! The only thing he had trouble with a bit was his weight. But he used to work out and that generally took care of that.

I think Roger is probably more popular with crews than any other actor I've ever worked with. If you work with Roger he is professional, kind and – his most important quality – he wants to be loved. Not just by the chairman but by the guy who brings him his call sheet and cup of coffee.

Johnny Goodman

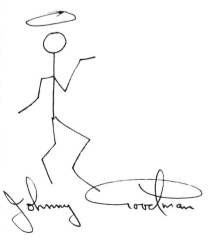

PRODUCTION STORIES

SCOUTING LOCATIONS WITH ROGER

MC: I remember taking Roger out a couple of times looking for locations. We were always looking for gates for him to crash through and walls for him to jump over. That's why Grimsdyke House in *The Fiction-Makers* was good. It had nice gates there. What we'd do every time was take the iron gates off and replace them with balsawood. So we were hoping to use this other place at Routham Park in Barnet owned by Lady Byng, the widow of Admiral Byng. Nowadays it's used by film companies all the time, but in those days never. Somehow I'd managed to persuade Lady Byng to let us just film the gates which were wonderful, very tall gates. Anyway, the morning we were due to shoot, Lady Byng phones up and says, 'I've decided against it'. This was 7.30am, the crew were just about to leave. I rushed out and spoke to Roger, who was directing this particular episode. He said, 'Let me speak to her'. I passed him the phone.

He said, 'Hello, Lady Byng, it's Roger Moore here. I understand you don't want us to film there anymore?' She said, 'No, I've changed my mind.' And he said, 'Well, we didn't bloody well want to come anyway!' and put the phone down.

MOBBED IN MALTA

JG: Filming *Vendetta for the Saint* in Malta was an incredible experience. I'd never seen hero worship like it. The fans used to surround the hotel at night and howl for Roger. In the mornings we used to have to form a phalanx like the Romans and rush with him to the car. It wasn't just girls – we pulled one guy off who was kissing and hugging him. Everywhere we went the cars were mobbed and besieged and the local ladies, married to various top dignitaries, were so overwhelmed when I arranged for Roger to meet them over coffee in his hotel suite, that they practically climaxed when he came in the room. At the end of the meeting they came to me and dropped the keys to a beautiful Mercedes sports convertible in my hand – 'While you're here, please have this car.' Just because I was associated with him!

Vendetta should have been shot of course in Sicily. But the prospect of shooting a film about the Mafia in Sicily didn't seem a very good idea.

Malcolm Christopher: I was working on *The Baron* with Ken Baker and I was desperate to get on to *The Saint*. That was like getting on to a James Bond film in those days.

I wonder if you could start by explaining what the production supervisor does?

JG: The production manager is the guy who from the beginning of shooting each episode literally sets up the whole production, under the supervision of the producers. The production manager starts to engage the crew; he does all the contracts, he negotiates what all the technicians will get paid, he books all the catering facilities, he organises the equipment hire. He then employs a location manager to go out and find all the locations which are approved by him, the producers and the director. He then breaks down all the scripts and schedules the picture.

How are the scripts broken down?

JG: Basically, when you first get the script it goes from Scene One straight through to Scene 250 or whatever. In the breakdown, what you do is go through the script and all the scenes that take place in Roger's bedroom go on to one sheet of paper; all the scenes that take place in the garage on another sheet of paper etc. So you end up with a booklet that shows all the various sets and all the various scene numbers as they relate to particular sets. That's how you then schedule the shooting of the picture. You couldn't start by doing two scenes in Roger's bedroom then going to the garage, then somewhere else, then five days later back to the bedroom. That'd be lovely for the director and the actors because it's much easier to follow, but it would be very time-consuming and expensive.

What actually happens is that they may have to film two of the very last scenes of the production right at the beginning. So that's what the production manager does in the pre-production stage.

With scheduling you'd also work out, 'OK, we've got to average filming three pages a day'. But while nowadays that might be a rough estimate, Bob Baker would actually time the action in each scene with a stop watch. Bob would sit there in pre-production with the script, working it out: 'OK, the Saint gets in the car, goes down the road, two shots ring out, he pulls up... click.' And he'd write on the script the time of the scene – 1 minute 38 seconds.

MC: Shooting Barry Lyndon with Stanley Kubrick, on the other hand it was one line – 'The Irish army advances' – and three weeks later we were still shooting it!

JG: Once the filming starts the job of the production manager is then to supervise it in terms of getting a progress report every day. That report will tell him how many scenes have been shot, how much film has been used; he keeps an eye on the budget so if the production

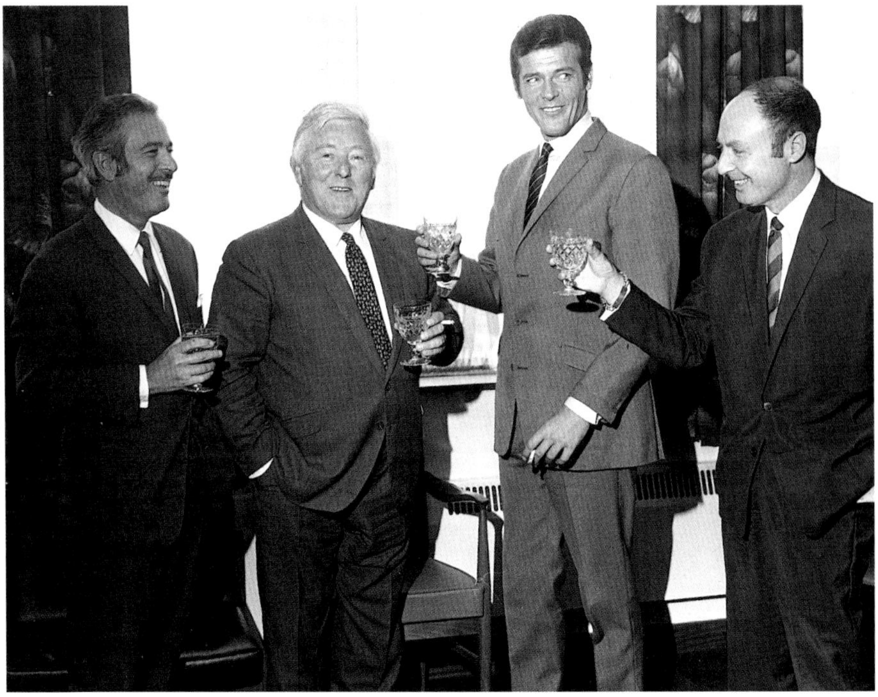

JOHNNY GOODMAN: PRIVATE COLLECTION

Tribune production company colleagues Robert S. Baker, Jim Wallace, Roger Moore and Johnny Goodman look to the future – and a refill

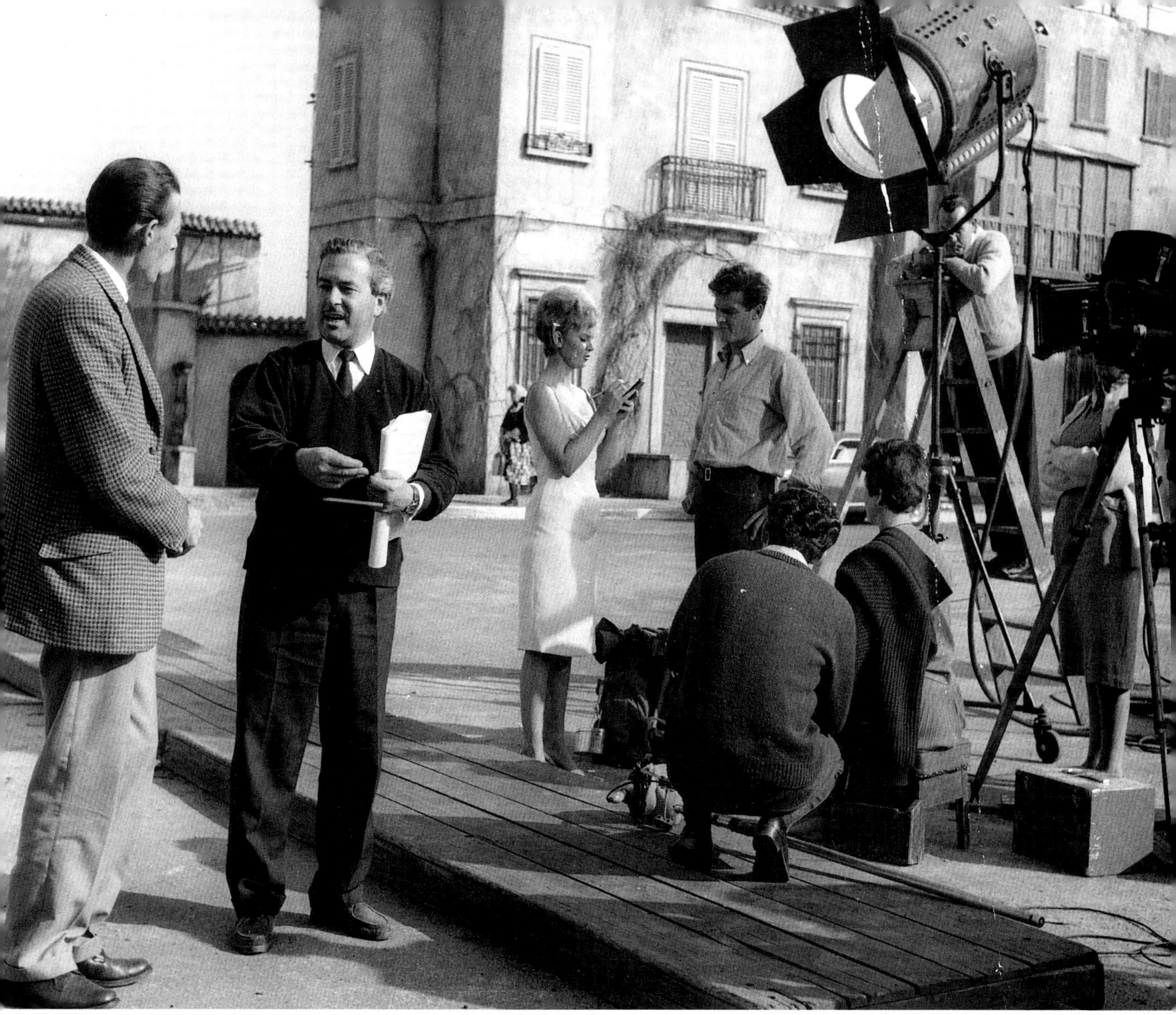

ROBERT S. BAKER. PRIVATE COLLECTION

'The back-lot would double as everything from Berlin to Hong Kong to Spain. You just changed the shutters,' recalls Johnny Goodman. Here Robert S. Baker, script under arm, prepares for a shot

accountant comes in and says we're getting a bit tight on wardrobe, he'll sort that out...

What sort of problems were there with wardrobe?

JG: One example I had was when the wardrobe department was buying silk shirts and stuff like that for a guy playing the part of a police inspector. I went down and said, 'I have to tell you my father-in-law is a CID Commander and he doesn't spend that on a fucking suit, let alone a shirt!'

Sometimes wardrobe departments get carried away by how wonderful things look in the flesh when, quite frankly, from the public's point of view you can't tell the difference when it's up there on the screen. It's like watches. We had a director who insisted on seeing 25 or 30 different watches to pick out a Rolex for a guy to wear in a scene. Half the time you can't even see the watch and if you can it could still be a cheap imitation. You don't want to castrate people and take away their creative endeavours. But you do have to balance between what is sensible, with the amount of money you've got to spend, and what they'd really like to put up there.

Malcolm knows when he worked for me that I'd say to the crew beforehand, 'I don't want the best film you can make. But I do want the best film you can make for the money the company's got to spend'. I do believe that there are investors, people who put up money to make a programme, and they are entitled to have their money respected. You should spend what they want to put up, not what you think you'd like to get through.

So when you had your first meeting with Bob Baker and Monty Berman did they have certain stipulations about the look and design of the series?

JG: Not really. I think the only stipulation was how much they were going to pay me, which I think was about £50 a week. Each episode cost about £25,000 then for 52 minutes of screen time. By the time we got to *The Persuaders* that figure was up to £80,000 and today a one-hour cop show, running round the streets of London, would be not less than £450,000 an hour, maybe going up to £600,000.

'You should spend what they want to put up, not what you think you'd like to get through'

Johnny Goodman, on honouring *The Saint*'s financiers

'I've got an old chalk stripe suit of Arthur Daley's upstairs'

Johnny Goodman on wardrobe perks

Did you experiment with different types of film for shooting *The Saint*?

MC: Yes. It was all shot on 35mm (*the same film as your average movie*). But we experimented with Super 16mm. In those days the quality wasn't good enough, but many good series are shot on 16mm these days and you can hardly tell the difference.

JG: The other reason it was shot on 35mm was that it was being sold to America and the companies over there wouldn't accept anything else. One thing we did to cut costs was shoot day for night because night shoots were too expensive. There were two ways of doing that. One, you can pre-fog the film. It's a system where the cameraman runs the film through the camera and exposes it slightly to daylight, which pre-fogs it. You then rewind it and shoot it so that it already has a dark texture before you begin.

The other way is you have a graduated filter so that the top half of the screen is darker than the bottom half. So the filter darkens the sky but keeps the bottom half a little lighter. It never looked very good.

MC: I don't know. I think the ones that Jimmy Allen photographed looked pretty good. When I first started on *The Saint* and we were doing day-for-night in town I used to have to hold up a sign to traffic, 'Filming – Please Put Your Headlights On'.

JG: It was funny because even when we went into colour Monty Berman said the rushes should still be in black and white to save money. What that meant was if it was a night scene and you were watching the finished episode in colour you could have the Saint slipping by the villain in the shadows, no problem. But when you were watching that back in black and white at the rushes stage there was the Saint completely visible to the other actor who was doing his damnedest to pretend he couldn't see him!

MC: In actual fact it was a very good money-saving idea of Monty's, and I've used it in a lot of movies since.

JG: Malcolm was actually originally in the camera department and I remembered him from the days when I was an assistant director. So I brought him in as location manager on *The Baron*, and from that it was on to *The Saint* as production manager – what they now call the line producer. Anyway, whatever title you give it Malcolm was, and is, still one of the top guys.

To cut costs, could you have any product placement in *The Saint*?

JG: No, it wasn't allowed in television at all.

MC: You could do it in a very subtle way sometimes.

JG: Sure. If a guy's going to hire a car and he goes past a showroom and you can see from a distance that it happens to be Hertz, then that's OK. What you can't do is start on a close up of the sign and pan down to him going through the door. Now in America, sponsors will pay hundreds of thousands of pounds to get their advertisement on a hoarding which the hero drives by in an episode. You'd also get cases of the beer that was being featured being delivered to the props room.

MC: Or production supervisor.

JG: And quite right, too!

Malcolm Christopher's son Giles in suitable stick-related product.

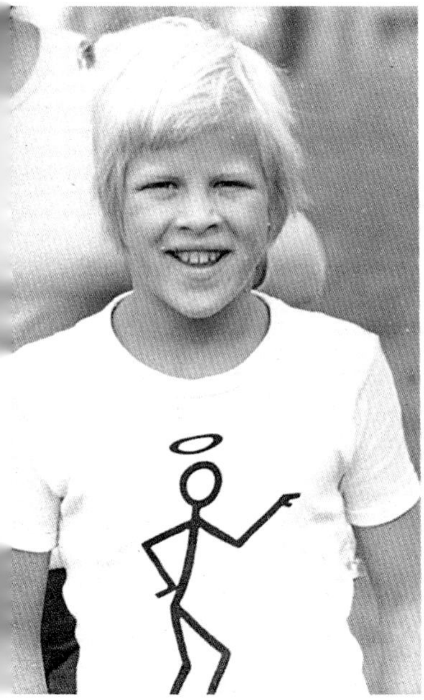

MALCOLM CHRISTOPHER

Was there a props department at Elstree?

JG: Oh yes. Enormous.

MC: In fact, when ITC closed down they had a couple of soundstages full of furniture collected from all the series.

JG: That was in the Harry Saltzman building. What happened when we started *The Saint* was we bought tons of furniture from G-Plan. That was the modern furniture in the 1960s – when I married my wife Andrea we got 40 per cent discount on G-Plan. But when you start collecting all this stuff it just piles up in a warehouse and finally you can't get at anything, so the art directors can't be bothered to scramble through it and instead they just phone up Old Times Furnishings or whoever and order it that way.

MC: We used to re-paint the furniture. You'd see the same blue settee so many times – blues and greys were always good – that in the end we had to change the colour. And then at the end of the series we'd sell off all the wardrobe. I've got a few of Roger's old shirts and a raincoat, because we're about the same size. They were quite good. Laura Nightingale's husband, who worked in Austin's in Charing Cross Road, used to design them for the doubles and for Ken Nash and Les Crawford – who died recently – who did all the stunts.

JG: And I've got an old chalk stripe suit of Arthur Daley's upstairs from when I was executive producer on *Minder*. I still wear it out occasionally.

What were the particular do's and don'ts for selling to America?

'Roger decided his belly was a little big, so he took the scissors to this. I said, "If you're doing that, then I'm giving myself some hair".' More honeymoon snaps in Majorca with Johnny, Andrea and Roger

JOHNNY GOODMAN PRIVATE COLLECTION

MC: You couldn't fire a gun towards camera. In the early episodes you could, but then the Code of Practice came along and changed all that.

JG: What you also had to really avoid were any heavy accents. The Americans would actually jump at the excuse to say they didn't understand us. If you had a heavy Scottish or Welsh accent they'd reject it.

MC: Personally, I don't understand the Americans. I've been listening to that tape of Bob Evans reading *The Kid Stays In The Picture*, and I'm having to run it again because of all the bits I can't make out. They're so fast-talking.

JG: That's my tape.

MC: You gave it to me.

JG: Did I? Oh.

MC: But yes, on *The Saint* the accents were all very clipped, Standard British.

How long would it take to shoot each *Saint* episode?

MC: Ten days. Scheduling was something you had to learn. You pick it up as an AD (assistant director) and as a location manager, working up to a production manager. You discover, for instance, that you never schedule love scenes in the first two or three days as the actors have not had time to get to know each other. You would also always try to finish in the Saint's standing set so you could always start the next episode in the same set. So Roger would go off mid-morning and change, a new co-star would come in and you could start filming the next episode the same day. That way it might take nine and a half days.

JG: It was assembly line filming. Nothing stopped for anything. In the middle of filming *The Saint* I went in to see Bob Baker and Monty Berman and asked if I could have tomorrow off. They said, 'Well, what for?' I said, 'Well, actually I'm getting married.' Monty said, 'Hm. Well could you be back for the 2.30pm production meeting?'

So I was married to Andrea at 10a.m., had lunch at the Savoy and was back at 2pm to attend the meeting.

How many standing sets would there be?

MC: Usually there would be one standing set, which would be the Saint's apartment. And

PRODUCTION STORIES

TRIBUNE

JG: Bob Baker, Roger and I formed Tribune, and I'm still a director of the company with them. Roger and Bob bought it as a tax loss and they asked me if I'd like to become a partner. They offered me ten per cent of the shares, but at the time I hadn't got the £550 needed to buy in. So Roger and Bob both lent me £225. Over the years, as our fortunes improved, I paid them back. I've still got Roger's letter. He said, at a time when he was earning millions as Bond, it was really his lucky day when he opened his post to find a Johnny Goodman cheque for £225!

JACKIE COLLINS

JG: Jim Hill directed her in *Starring the Saint*. He said, 'Don't try to act, dear, just lie there and do as you're told!'

RICKY GREENE

MC: One time Ricky Greene, who was the location manager and used to be a roadie for Herman's Hermits, said to Roger, 'Look I'm bringing a girlfriend in for lunch tomorrow. Could you just stop by the table and say hello? It'd really impress her.' So Ricky's there having lunch and Roger comes up. 'Hi, Ricky, how are you? Is this your girlfriend?' Ricky says, 'Yes, Roger. Look I'm having lunch with her at the moment. I'll see you afterwards.'! Now you couldn't do that with every star.

THE WEDDING GIFT

JG: When Roger got married I was, at that time, a 10 per cent partner in the company. On my wedding invitation Roger wrote: 'Johnny Darling, even in marriage you're in for 10 per cent of the action. See you in bed. Love Roger.'!

LES CRAWFORD

JG: When we were shooting *Vendetta* in Malta Les Crawford, who was Roger's stunt double, was romancing a local lady and arranged to take care of her in one of the hotel bedrooms. What she didn't know was that he had already secreted myself, Roger and the director Jim O'Connolly in the wardrobe. There was the three of us all squeezed in this wardrobe with the door just half an inch ajar, while Les did what he had to do. Every now and then he'd get off the bed, walk past the wardrobe and give us all a little wink. We were in hysterics.

PRODUCTION STORIES

PRIMED SUSPECTS

JG: There's a scene at the end of *The Arrow of God* where all the various suspects are gathered together in a semicircle and Roger is going through their alibis trying to find out which one is the murderer. There was an actor called John Carson, who was dressed up as an Indian guru. So Roger goes through his list and finally gets to him. He says 'Ram Singh,' – or whatever – 'You were deported from so-and-so for being a phoney.' John Carson replies, 'Yes, Mr Templar, it is not I that is out of step with the world, but the world that is out of step with me.' And Roger said, 'Well, that may well be true, but show us your cock!'

MC: Monty used to send Roger a bill at the end of each week for all the ruined takes!

GARY MILLER

JG: Gary Miller was a singing star of the 1960s that I was totally besotted with. Very good looking guy with a cleft chin, a bit Kirk Douglas. Blond hair. He was the voice on *Robin Hood* and *Aqua Marina*'. I was so in love with his voice that we went to see him in cabaret at The Hungarian Shardash in Lower Regent Street. I sent my card backstage and he came out and we met. I was totally impressed by him and became determined to get him into movies. I was punting him so much that I think people were beginning to wonder if I'd gone the other way. And I got him a part in *The People Importers* as the blond villain Slater. At the same time he was appearing on the stage with Danny La Rue in *Come Spy With Me*. So he was working night and day. After a week of shooting I said goodbye to him on the Friday night, and over the weekend he dropped dead of a heart attack. We had to finish the episode with a double with his back to camera.

FINLAY CURRIE

JG: Poor love, he was gone towards the end of filming. There was a scene in *Vendetta for the Saint* where he was dying and Roger was leaning over him, pretending to be a doctor or something. Anyway, poor old Finlay decided that Roger actually was a doctor and started telling him about all his ailments and showing him where he had various pains. It was all very embarrassing.

there would be another set that we would re-vamp.

JG: And the back lot which would double as everything from Berlin to Hong Kong, just changing the signs and shutters on the cafes and garages etc.

MC: I had a Volkswagen at the time and it was always featured in the scenes in Borehamwood High Street. A black cloth would be put over the left-hand drive steering wheel, it would have Swiss number plates on if it was meant to be Switzerland and in the background you'd just be able to see F.W. Woolworth! Sometimes we'd have to flip the shots to make the cars drive on the right side of the road.

JG: And we'd do car shots with the Saint driving the car and we hadn't even shot the moving background plates at that time. So when they were eventually shot it would sometimes happen that when he turned the wheel to go round a corner one way, the shots behind him would have the road twisting in the other direction. Quite ridiculous, but nobody ever noticed.

Other times we'd do a scene that was supposed to be Nice airport. We'd shoot through the leaves of a potted plant. There would be two wretched girls standing in bikinis, their tits frozen stiff in the middle of winter, outside what was, in fact, the camera room, with a sign above them saying Nice Airport.

MC: There was also a water tank on the back lot where we shot all the scenes that were done at sea. This tank had a great big backdrop that was probably 60 feet high and about 120 feet wide, painted grey or blue depending on the scene. And there was a lip to this tank where the water was pumped in and would overflow, and that made your horizon. The boats on the sea would all be fixed to the bottom of the tank and made to bob up and down with hydraulic rams.

There was also a reservoir from which they'd pump in all the millions of gallons of water they needed. This was just a straight square reservoir with sloping concrete sides, and that doubled as everything – from the Bahamas to the Far East. We'd have to bring sand and palm trees in. We couldn't really afford more than three or four yards of sand, but it was actually quite effective.

JG: What would sell it for the public then was the stock shots you would buy of world locations. Elstree had a huge library of footage, which might have been shot years before. So if you wanted to establish Roger Moore in a hotel bedroom just off the Croisette in Cannes, you'd buy this stock shot of the main street of Cannes with the cars going by, and the camera would just pan up to the window of a hotel. Once you've shown that you can cut – bang! – inside to the hotel room with Roger having a cocktail, and the audience was convinced they were in a hotel in the South of France.

MC: We are fiction-makers. I had a saying, 'You don't have to go to the moon to make a moon movie.' The trouble is, nowadays in feature films they want to go to the moon to make a moon movie and the cost of it is just phenomenal.

I remember that Cannes shot. We'd asked the library for a shot of a white car driving through the Croisette with the camera then panning up to the hotel window. But we hadn't stated what make of car we wanted so when the shot came in, I then had to match that car – which was a white Peugeot – with another shot of the supposedly same car on the set with someone sitting in it. It took me forever to get hold of a real white Peugeot.

JG: I used to pull Bob Baker's leg about one shot they used for all the black and whites. They'd bought this stock shot of a Ford V8 Pilot that comes tearing round the corner, crashes, bursts into flames and three guys stagger out. Every episode they did after that – it didn't matter if it was a Mercedes chasing a Ferrari – you'd hear a bang and cut to this same piece of film with the guys, whose faces you couldn't see, staggering out.

MC: OK, cut. We're now shooting in colour with Johnny Huff who was the second unit director. They would have to go out shooting the white Volvo round the roads of Borehamwood with two extras as Roger and the girl – they could have been monkeys with pipes for all you could see of them. But we'd have this one day per episode of what you called Run Bys. First you film the Volvo whizzing by right-to-left, then the baddies' car etc. At first, Johnny would come back with these in the afternoon and it was great. But Johnny was a bit of a movie buff, so he'd start going through different movies. Now we go up to town to shoot the Saint's car going round Trafalgar Square and suddenly we're shooting hours and hours and miles and miles of film of pigeons walking through puddles.

JG: So I fired him. And the funny thing was, about two days after I fired him *The Avengers* hired him as a first director. He always told people, 'If you want to get on in this business get Johnny Goodman to fire you!'

For years and years I remember the trick shot was to pull back from a close up on a coffee percolator. This was meant to have some deep significance.

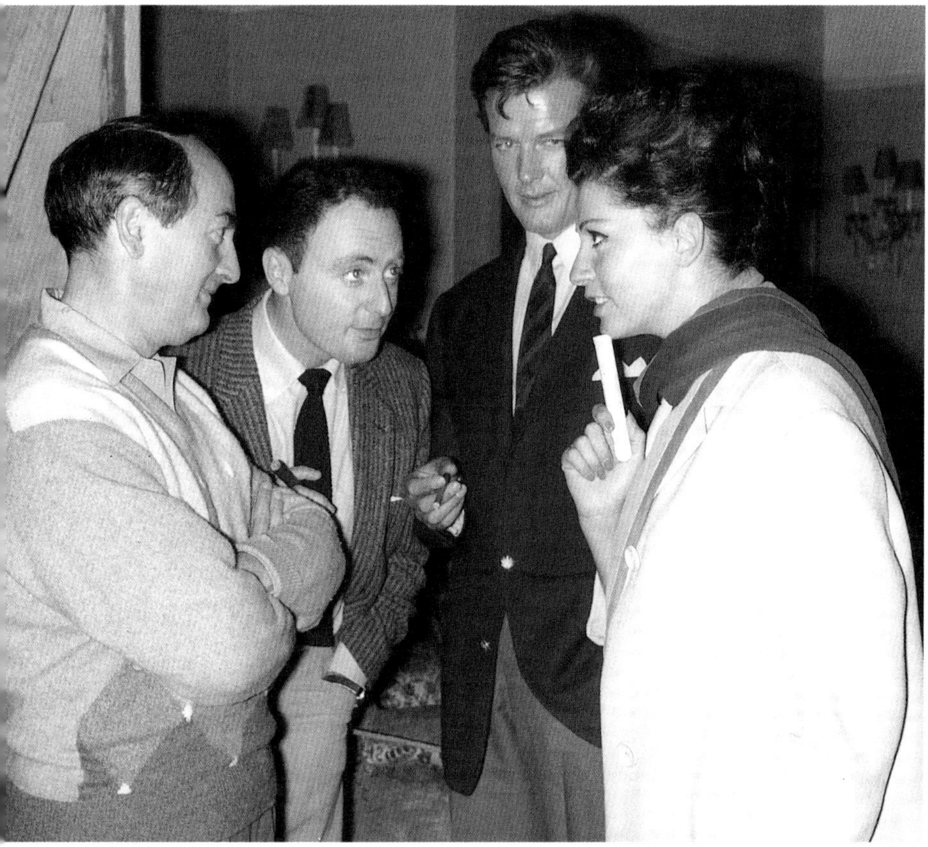

JOHNNY GOODMAN PRIVATE COLLECTION

Monty Berman, Johnny Goodman and Roger Moore wait for the punchline as Luisa relates one of the many quite unrepeatable jokes she used to innocently pick up off the crew

There weren't really many extras used in crowd scenes were there? I think there are about four running behind Roger in the neo-Nazi riot scenes at Trafalgar Square, in *The Saint Plays With Fire*.
MC: No, you couldn't go over your limit. And if you'd used them all in one scene you couldn't really use them again in another.
JG: Malcolm and I once worked on a *Robin Hood* pilot together and we were so short of extras that we named it *Robin Hood and his Merry Man*.
MC: I had a superb bow and arrow which I'd brought back from making *The Man Who Would Be King* in Morocco, so we used that. But we only had the one arrow, so every time Robin fired it someone had to run and get it back.

Was Monty Berman more involved with the money side of things?
MC: He did look after that, but I remember Monty would be on the set at 8.30am and if Frankie Watts, the cameraman, hadn't turned up on time Monty would light the set himself. That was the great thing. He had been a cameraman and so had Bob Baker. They'd both directed. They were technicians in their own right. You couldn't pull the wool over their eyes. That was where Bob and Monty were great. They were proper producers. Producers nowadays don't know the technicalities. Working on series nowadays with inexperienced producers is horrendous.

We made those *Saint* shows in nine-and-a-half to ten-and-a-half days, Monday to Friday – very rarely Saturday or Sunday, except for some second unit stuff in town.

We would have an 8a.m. call. At 8.30am the cameras would start turning over. We would finish at 5.20pm – the time till 5.30pm then being allocated by the unions as the time for them to wash their hands. An Emergency Hour would extend the day to 6.20pm and you had to call that by 4pm that afternoon.

With an Extended Day you could work till 9.20pm But Bob always reckoned that the work you would get through the next morning after an Extended Day would be less than you'd taken the night before, because the crew were tired.

Nowadays Johnny's son and my sons start their day at 5am for 7.30am-8am calls, which will then go on shooting till eight, nine, ten, eleven o'clock at night.

PRODUCTION STORIES

IVOR DEAN
MC: Ivor Dean, who played Chief Inspector Teal, was a terribly nice man. He read palms and would read your cards. And later he also wrote the pilot script to *Return to Treasure Island*.

OLIVER REED
JG: That was very funny in *The King of the Beggars*. We had a scene where he gets shot and Ollie at that time was heavily into the method acting – I'm a teapot and all that. So we did the scene, the shot rings out and Oliver Reed hurls himself backwards, as he's supposed to do to die. The director, John Gilling, says cut and we go to do the next set up. Then we hear this snoring noise. We look round and there's Oliver Reed spark out unconscious on the floor. Trying to be realistic, he'd given himself mild concussion. We had to carry him up to the dressing room and call for the doctor.

IAN OGILVY
MC: We were shooting *The Return of the Saint* in Rome and one day I bumped into Roger coming out of this incredible toy shop. He didn't know we were out there filming. Roger and Luisa had a villa near Grosetto, which was round about where we were, so he said he'd come over to our hotel.

We were all in the bar – Ian Ogilvy, Frankie Watts the cameraman and everyone – and in walks Roger. Of course everybody gathers round Roger and poor old Ian was left on his own. I mean, Roger said hello and everything but it was hard for Ian to follow in his footsteps. He may have been the better actor but he certainly didn't have Roger's charisma.

THE BEST OF BRITISH
JG: We all did very well filming the first episode, *The Talented Husband*. There was a big location scene in this butcher's shop in Cookham and all the meat was left lying around. At the end of the shot all the crew went out the door with legs of lamb and sides of beef.

ROY WARD BAKER
JG: He was basically a very kind man, a very nice man, a very intelligent man. But when he blew he'd go bananas. I think he'd just get a bit frustrated. There was a lot of pressure. I remember he used to drive a Porsche.

JOHNNY GOODMAN, PRIVATE COLLECTION

Halfway up a mountain in Malta was one of the few places Roger Moore could escape the fan hysteria whilst filming Vendetta for the Saint. *Johnny Goodman and Robert S. Baker lend an ear*

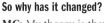

So why has it changed?

MC: My theory is that Bob and Monty were film-makers and they had a formula for making a show. There was no waste. Les Norman and Roy Baker used to cut in the camera. Les would cut an actor in the middle of a line: 'OK, cut. Right, go into the close up, put a 50 (*lens*) on here.' So you weren't wasting any film.

It was a team working together. Nowadays the directors come from film school. They'll shoot the Master – say, of six people sitting round a table – and they'll shoot that 16 times till they get the perfect Master. And it's not necessary. If you shoot a Master and someone fluffs his line it doesn't matter, because you're going to go in and do close-ups anyway.

On *The Saint* we had a very tight budget of film. Nowadays they shoot tons of it and go over budget.

JG: It's not quite as simple as that. The reason that the hours changed is because in those days we were much more studio-orientated, which meant you had more control over the shooting. It's much quicker and much easier if you're shooting in a room on the set. You say, 'Right, take that wall out,' and the wall's taken out. If you're shooting on location, in natural locations, you have to manoeuvre the camera, you've got travelling time – all these problems.

In the days of *The Saint* overtime was paid, so people would earn ridiculous money if you worked long hours. As producers you therefore restrained the hours as much as possible. Now the unions have been more or less broken and everyone works on all-in deals. They can earn quite good money, but when you take a guy like Malcolm on you pay them £2000 a week or whatever, but that's it. You can then work them round the clock.

Did some directors tend to run over time?

JG: Peter Yates did. I liked working with Peter, except I'd ask him what time he'd be finished on the set and he'd say, 'Don't worry, I'll be off by 5.30pm' Then you'd get down there and he'd still be shooting away. When I reminded him what he'd said he just said, 'Oh, don't take any notice of what I tell you!'.

MC: That used to create terrible problems.

JG: Anyway, cut to a few years later when he was doing a big movie at Pinewood, Krull. So someone asked me down to have a look, and as I walked onto this huge set a disembodied voice from way up on top of a crane somewhere shouted, 'I promise you, Johnny, I'll be off by 6p.m!'

MC: I always put my watch back two minutes, because if you had to take the quarter at lunchtime you could waste a precious 10 minutes of the day. What the quarter was, was if you were coming up to 1pm and you were still doing a shot, you wanted, if possible, to get that shot finished and be set up on the next shot when you broke for lunch. You didn't want to pay any overtime and the crew would stop dead on one. Not one minute past. One. So the actors would get nervous and be fluffing their lines and it would all get very tense.

At that point, if you still hadn't got the scene, you could call the quarter. That meant you could go on for another 15 minutes, to 1.15pm But if you did that and then you got the shot within, say, three minutes you'd have wasted those other 12 minutes because the crew would still take the quarter and come back at 2.15pm That could be a whole extra shot wasted, which you just couldn't afford.

JG: An added catch to calling the quarter was you couldn't call it unless you already had one take of that scene in the can. So what would happen was, it would be about 18 minutes past five, you would have an actor who was on £50 a day and if you didn't get this very last shot of him you'd have to pay him for a whole extra day tomorrow. Just to do one more shot. So even if you weren't ready – even if the bloody set wasn't lit properly – Monty Berman would say, 'Turn over, Johnny'. We'd shoot something and as soon as that was done – whatever it looked

Malcolm Christopher

like – we could call the quarter and then re-light and shoot the thing properly. You couldn't use that time to get anything apart from that one shot, but it was at least a union perk that we could take advantage of.
MC: I still reckon that's the way to make movies. When we finished shooting *The Saint* at 5.20pm the director, the cameraman, the first AD, the prop man and the gaffer would then go and line up the shot for the following day. So after a final bit of lighting and set dressing the next morning, usually we would be shooting by 8.45am Sometimes on television shows these days – even well-organised shows – they don't start shooting till 10 or 11am I can't believe the farting around.
JG: To illustrate the help Bob and Monty would give as producers, I remember we had finished shooting one day and were going to do the line-up on the next set. So I went through with the director to look at it and he started complaining, 'I can't shoot this – the set doesn't work.' I thought what the hell am I gonna do. So after he'd gone I went up to see Bob and Monty and told them I had a problem. Up they got, went down onto the floor and Bob Baker said, 'Right, I'd bring the actors in over there and pan to here.' Monty said, ' I'd put a 10k lamp in here and light it over this way. Right, fine. It works perfectly. And if the director doesn't want to shoot it we'll do it ourselves.' Of course he came in the next day and shot the bloody thing. Now how would that happen today?

So what's replaced the old way of working?

JG: I don't know. Nowadays nobody seems prepared to exercise authority or be concerned about the amount of money that is sometimes wasted. Directors have become powerhouses today with very little control over them. In my day the producer was the supreme boss and under him was the production manager/supervisor. Between the two of you, you could keep an eye on things.

Obviously, if you were working with someone like David Lean you knew what you were buying in the first place – you knew that he had carte blanche to wait for the right clouds to be in the right place. But otherwise, I could go on the floor and say to the director, 'Look, I'm sorry. I've got problems. This actor has got to finish tonight. He can't come back tomorrow. So you either get this shot in the can or we cut the scene out of the film.'

I finished filming at Carlton last year and our way of working is now considered passé. It's old hat.

Mrs Harvey,
Conway Furnished Flats Ltd.,
154, Peckham Rye,
London,S.E.22.

25th March, 1966.

Dear Mrs Harvey,

This is to confirm that we would like to film the outside of your house at 8, Lees Place on Sunday 3rd ~~March~~ April.
We are only concerned with the outside of your house although we would like access through the front door for our actors.

For this facility we are prepared to pay forty guineas, and would be responsible for any damaged property etc., caused during our filming.

We are a small film unit of approximately fifteen people engaged on making the 'Saint' and 'Baron' television series'.

Yours sincerely,

p.p.Malcolm J.Christopher
Unit/Loc: Manager

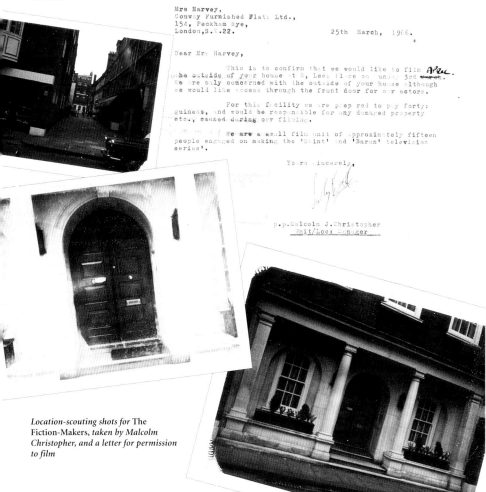

Location-scouting shots for The Fiction-Makers, *taken by Malcolm Christopher, and a letter for permission to film*

PRODUCTION STORIES

LESLIE NORMAN

JG: I worked with Leslie on quite a few of the early black and white *Saints*, and he was always a bit worried that he wasn't going to get any more work. So I'd reassure him, 'No, you're doing fine.' Years and years later he unfortunately had cancer of the throat and was going in for this terrible operation to remove his voice box. Before he went in for the operation Bob Baker said to him, 'You're going to come out of this OK. And when you do I will ensure that you have an episode of *The Return of the Saint* to direct.' Bob kept his word.
MC: Unfortunately, the episode was in Rome, which must be the noisiest place in the world, so it was very hard for him to make himself heard with his voice box. It became a very difficult episode. He was then going to do another one, but I think the strain on Les was pretty tough.

THE MISSING HANDLES

JG: When Leslie was healthy, though, he was good to work with. He did explode a couple of times, though. One was on an episode with Roger that was meant to be set in Italy. At that time Rome taxis were black Fiats, or something. There was one company who supplied us with all the cars. They used to get them from a lot of the American forces bases, at places like Ruislip.

For this particular episode Roger had to rush up to the car, jump in it and it would drive off. So the car arrived and had his number plates put on, only for us to find that it only had door handles on one side. It was in the process of being resprayed and they hadn't fitted them back on. Les went absolutely ape, so of course the shot had to be done from the other side and it didn't quite work with the action.

RAY AUSTIN

JG: Before directing episodes of *The Saint* Ray had been a stunt man, then a stunt director. He was an enormous cocksman – anything that wasn't bolted down. Then he went off to Hollywood to work and the last I heard he'd married again and has now bought a title. If you get a letter from him, it says Baron De Beauville De Austin or something on the top of the headed paper.

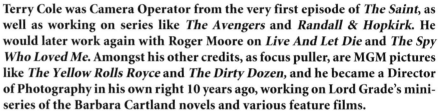

'On the floor, my God, it was murder...'

Terry Cole on Roger Moore's on-set mischievousness

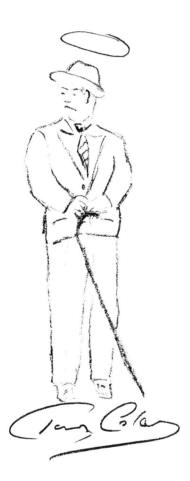

Terry Cole was Camera Operator from the very first episode of *The Saint*, as well as working on series like *The Avengers* and *Randall & Hopkirk.* He would later work again with Roger Moore on *Live And Let Die* and *The Spy Who Loved Me.* Amongst his other credits, as focus puller, are MGM pictures like *The Yellow Rolls Royce* and *The Dirty Dozen,* and he became a Director of Photography in his own right 10 years ago, working on Lord Grade's mini-series of the Barbara Cartland novels and various feature films.

Terry was also one of the main participants in the many practical jokes played on, and by, Roger Moore during the *Saint* series...

'**The Saint was** one of my first jobs. I was 17 when I became the clapper boy to Ken Baker, who was the assistant director. On the floor, God, it was murder because Roger would unzip my fly just as I was standing ready to put the clapperboard in. He'd get me every time. But we got our own back. One day they were rehearsing this scene where Roger had to pack two cases. He'd already got one packed on the bed, so while he wasn't looking we put a 56lb stage weight inside it. What we hadn't expected was that Les Norman, the director, suddenly decided to shoot so we couldn't get it out again. Of course Roger, as ever, was overplaying his part, so he took ages to do up the other bag then came rushing into the room, grabbed the handle of the case which was on the bed and nearly pulled his arm off. The case didn't budge an inch and the handle snapped off in his hand. Silly boyish pranks.

'There was another terrible situation. Ken Baker had managed to get hold of Roger's dressing room key, which was taboo in those days. So we crept up there very quickly, while Roger was rehearsing on the stage, and started to attach this cup of water above the door. While I was up on this chair Ken whispered to me, "God, have you seen the state of this room." We turned round and his dressing room had been absolutely wrecked – his suits had been ripped, the mirror had been smashed, his bed was torn to pieces. We thought, "Christ, they're gonna blame us for all this," so we ran out as fast as we could. Roger was living with Luisa by now. What we didn't know was that Roger had been having a few problems with a former partner and she had got into the studio and devastated his room.

'We used to push these terrible pictures of Roger, from when he used to model knitting patterns, under his dressing room door. We'd find as many as we could and slip them under. That used to drive him mad. Another time when he lived at Denham, he used to go on about this big garden he'd got so the whole unit tried to buy a goat to send to his house. But we couldn't do it because the *Exchange & Mart* wouldn't accept it. In the end we sent him three bags of chicken droppings instead.

'The whole unit tried to buy a goat to send to Roger's house'

Terry Cole on pranks-a-plenty

'It was an incredible time because, thanks to Monty and Bob Baker, we were making these great looking series in an amazingly short time and yet on a Friday night, when the last shot was over, I can still recall climbyng up into the gantry, waiting over the door where Roger was going to go out – because he used to make a quick getaway on a Friday night – and tipping a bucket of water over him. He would chase me all round the studio. People wouldn't believe it.

'Roger would have water pistols in his pocket when he was filming so he could squirt us whenever he wanted. I tell you, the person who always used to come off worst was cameraman

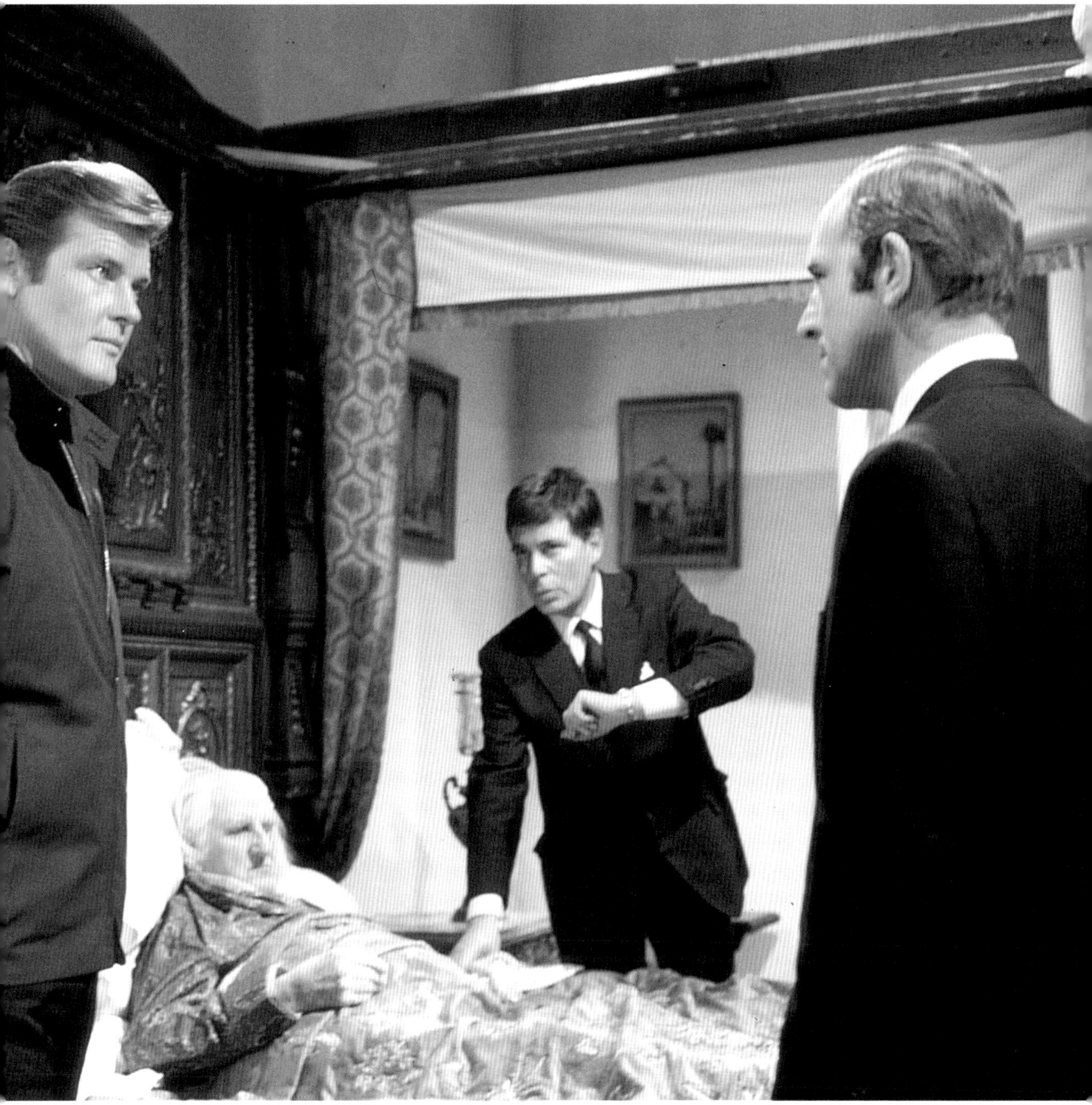

POLYGRAM FILMED ENTERTAINMENT

The genuinely none-too-well Finlay Currie awaits the verdict from Dr Moore, while Ian Hendry (far right) recommends some rather more violent treatment in Vendetta for the Saint

dear old Frankie Watts. If anybody was going to get soaked by Roger it was Frank. I remember one day Roger had had my new Del-boy three-wheeler van towed away after a prank I'd played on him, and while I was looking around for it Frank pulled up in this new white sports car. Just as he beckoned me over to speak something passed between us and completely soaked Frank in his open-topped car. It was Roger. He'd just tipped a bucket of water out of the top window of his dressing room and poor Frank had to drive all the way home to Fulham completely drenched.

'There were all these pranks being played, but I don't think it caused any great anxiety to Monty Berman and Bob Baker. They were funny because they seemed to be total opposites. Bob Baker always looked like he was enjoying himself while Monty pretended he never had a sense of humour about it all, but I'm sure he did. He had this great deadpan face. You could have had Tommy Cooper on the set, or somebody actually dying, and he'd have had the same expression. He must have been a nightmare to have in the audience if you were a comedian. He'd have just sat there, almost, "Come on, entertain me". Of course, to Roger that was like throwing down the gauntlet.'

7: CASTING

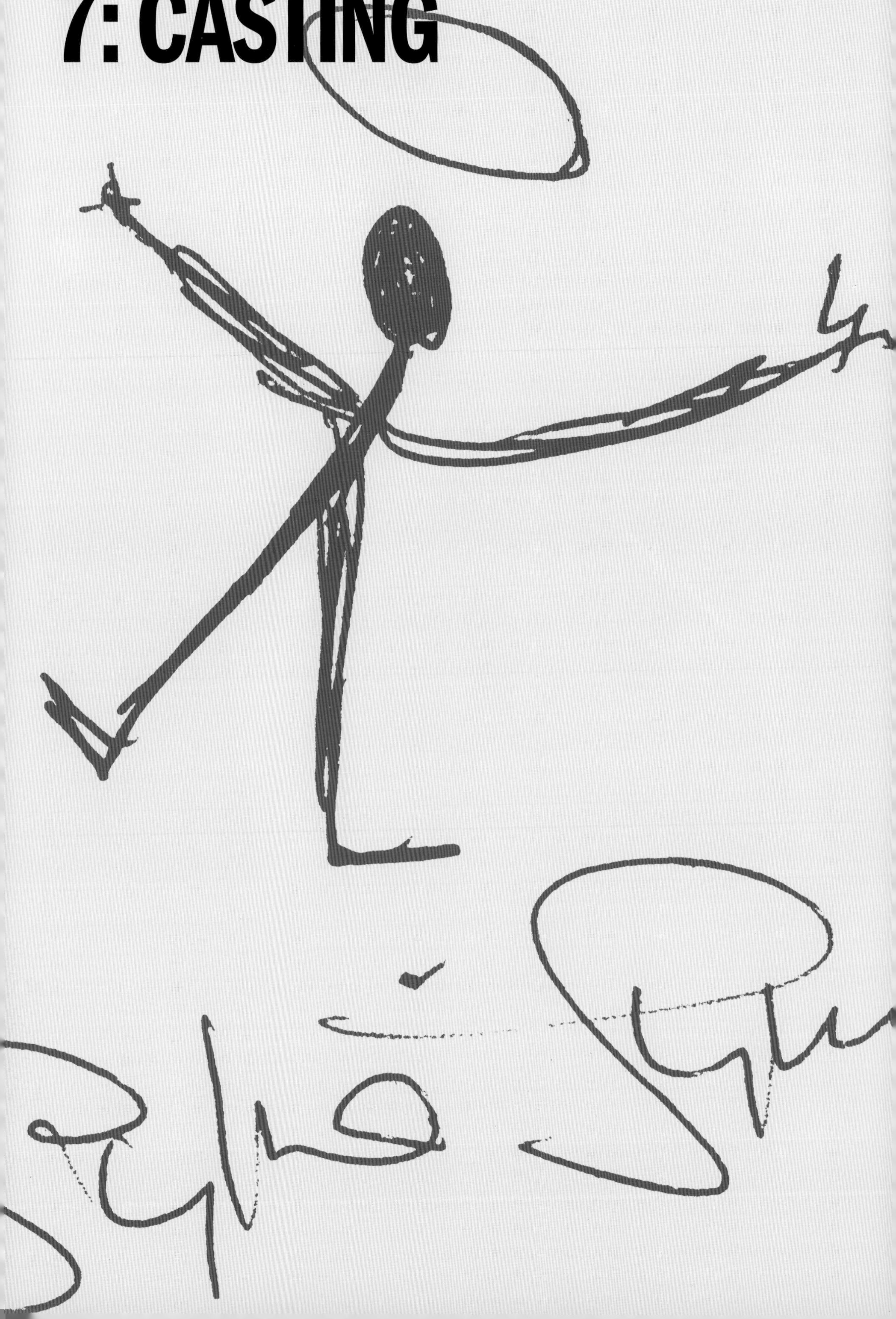

The 'How Not To Run A Career' Girl

When Sylvia Syms came to *The Saint* she was already one of Britain's most popular and respected actresses. She'd enjoyed hit movies with *Ice Cold in Alex, Expresso Bongo* and *Suzie Wong* and balanced her more commercial work with powerful, ground-breaking dramas like *Victim*, with Dirk Bogarde as her husband in the first British film to deal with homosexuality, and *Flame in the Streets*, which tackled racism in Notting Hill.

Forty years on, she's still one of our very best actors with a wicked sense of humour and a sharpness that probably keeps her agent awake at nights. A real one-off, she gave some of the most entertaining peformances in the whole *Saint* series, culminating in her portrayal of the offbeat thriller writer Amos Klein, in *The Fiction-Makers.*

To paint a picture of the young Sylvia Syms from early 1960s press clippings, you had been under contract to Associated British and had, by 1963, made about 20 pictures including *My Teenage Daughter* – your big film break with Anna Neagle, *Ice Cold in Alex, Suzie Wong, Victim, No Trees In The Street* and *Woman in a Dressing Gown*...

I did something very stupid, actually. I signed a contract after I'd made my first film, *My Teenage Daughter*, which was actually not made for them – it was made at Shepperton. Then Associated British offered me £30 a week and like an idiot I signed a contract before the film came out. I was a huge hit in the film (*roars with laughter*) and I'd just signed the next seven years away. When it came to stupidity, I had a degree almost.

In the last three years of my contract they also gave me 50 per cent of what I earned when they hired me out to other studios. So sometimes I did alright. But if a film by another company was shot at ABC studios, like *Woman in a Dressing Gown*, the company who made it had to pay for my services. I was told ABC were paid £1000 a week for me, while in my contract I got £30 a week because this was counted as an ABC film. I had the crappiest contract it was almost possible to imagine.

That same company had Audrey Hepburn under contract, and they never knew what to do with her. So she bunked off to America and never came back to England in case they tried to hold her to it. Years later, when I met her, she was still full of venom about them. She disliked them intensely.

So presumably you were very happy to go independent?

Yes, and I had children by that time and the whole studio thing was crumbling and changing. It was television things like *The Saint* that were taking over.

The thing you have to understand is, I've always led these two very different lives. One is this desperately ordinary woman who has always had a couple of kids and a husband for 33 years. Although the latter is all finished now. But career-wise, if you want to know how not to run a career but at least to laugh – look at mine!

Reading interviews from that time, you seemed to be engaged in a private battle with yourself. Whether you should be trying to forge ahead for international stardom or quietly building up a solid body of work, with the hope that the really meaty character parts would come your way in about 10 years time.

Yes. But nobody can say I didn't have the chances. I had a lot of chances. In the end though, I suppose you have to be what you are. I was ambitious, but I was never that ambitious. I didn't see myself out there alone

SYLVIA SYMS

EPISODES AS GUEST STAR:

The Noble Sportsman. As the adulterous Lady Anne Yearley, opposite Anthony Quayle: 'Nice frocks. I was somebody posh in that one.'

Jeannine. In the title role of a devious jewel thief.

The Best Laid Schemes. As Arlene, the wife who, it seems, is being terrified out of her wits by phone calls from her 'dead' husband.

The Fiction-Makers. As the highly unorthodox crime writer hiding behind nom de plume Amos Klein.

Chemistry a-go-go with Sylvia and Roger Moore in their opening scene in The Fiction-Makers

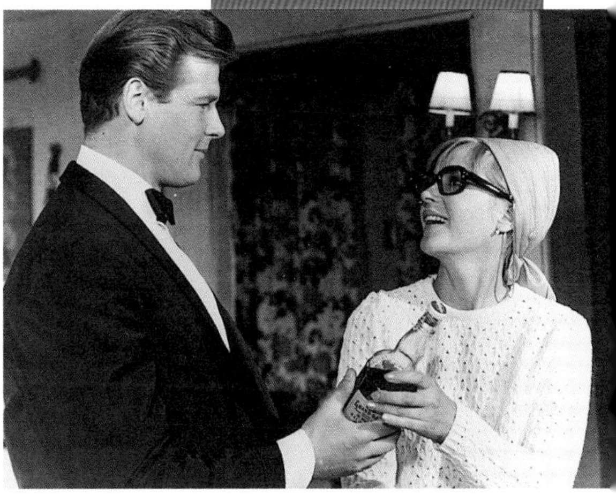

POLYGRAM VIDEO

in Hollywood and I knew my ex-husband would never have gone there, because he wasn't terribly interested. To him, acting was just something his wife did.

And having the children and not having been looked after as a child myself – I was a war child – I wanted to be protected and be with my family. But although I'd been tied to that studio, I did always get to go away and do a play every year. I'd already worked with a young lad called Peter O'Toole by the time I was 28. We did a dreadful play called *The Holiday*, which was where he met Sian Phillips. My films, like I*ce Cold In Alex*, were filling the cinemas, and we were emptying the theatres! But it was a bit of Art, you see. We were very big on Art.

So what was the particular appeal of *The Saint*?

How can I explain this? By this stage I'd had these children, both of whom had been a considerable effort to get. Ben is adopted and Beattie (*Edney*) was the result of three pregnancies. So the jobs that came along were jobs that I wanted to enjoy, and Roger and I were kind of mates.

I remember once he came over with Luisa to my very ordinary house in Barnes, and we had an hysterical night with them and Clive Dunn and his wife. Clive and Roger were exchanging memories of times when they had both played the straight man to comics. We had this big dining table and I remember thinking, 'If I laugh any more I'm going to throw up the dinner we've just eaten!'

Roger's one of the funniest men I've ever met. I know that he was good looking and a lot of women found him very sexy – I don't know that I did really – but he made me laugh hysterically. And I adored Luisa. I believe she became very grand later – I never see any of them now – but in those days she was this enchanting young Italian. We were pregnant together. She couldn't speak much English then. 'Ma Roger! Ma Roger!' She would tell rather dirty stories that she'd heard on the set, without really realising what she'd said.

There's certainly a wonderful chemistry between you and Roger. Particularly in *The Fiction-Makers*. You have a long scene together at the beginning which plays beautifully.

I've only ever seen bits of it. I'd probably do a lot of crying if I saw it now, because I didn't even know I was beautiful. I realise now I was rather stunning then. But comedy was Roger's forté. He was always a light comedian rather than an action man. I think Roy (*Baker*) directed that one. I liked working with him, but he was quite fierce, you know.

He was very nice to me, but don't forget a lot of the women they had in *The Saint* were not known, shall we say, for their histrionic ability. They just had nice tits, or whatever. So I think Roy probably got frustrated with some of them. Roy was always very meticulous about making things look as good as possible, and when you realise how quickly things were shot I think the results were fairly nice.

I spoke to Paul Marcus, who produced your daughter Beattie in one of the *Prime Suspects* films, and he was amazed by how short *The Saint*'s shooting schedules were. Almost three days less than *Prime Suspect*.

Yes. I don't really know about Paul Marcus. I know he does all this brilliant work, but you have to remember that very few of the young directors nowadays know about a fingernail as much as Roy Ward Baker does, technically. They may fart about discussing scenes, but Roy would have it all plotted out before he came on the set.

He was technically so well trained, while nowadays you don't have the same way in. It's very hard for people now. You can't just hang around a film set and learn your trade. Going to film school won't do it. Half the directors I worked with in the early days would have worked first as focus pullers, clapper boys, third assistants – they had the experience. So when it was rush, rush, rush, they could get it all done.

I'd actually worked with Roy before on a film called *Flame in the Streets,* with Johnny Seka and Johnny Mills. Good movie. Nice little movie. It was a brave film to make then. Johnny Mills played this trade unionist who believed in equality and made speeches about it, but when it came to his own daughter wanting to marry an African it was a different matter. The mother was a bigoted pillock played by a woman I absolutely loathed, Brenda De Banzie. Everyone said she was a good actress, I thought she was crap. She did a couple of Hollywood movies and thought she was.... oh, dreadful.

The truth of the matter with something like *The Saint* was that if they cast you in one of the leads – except for saying where to move and how they were going to photograph you – they didn't give you a lot of directions. They'd cast you because you were right and because you were good enough. There wasn't time for Christ's sake. You learned your lines, went on the set and you did it.

'I didn't even know I was beautiful. I realise now I was rather stunning then'

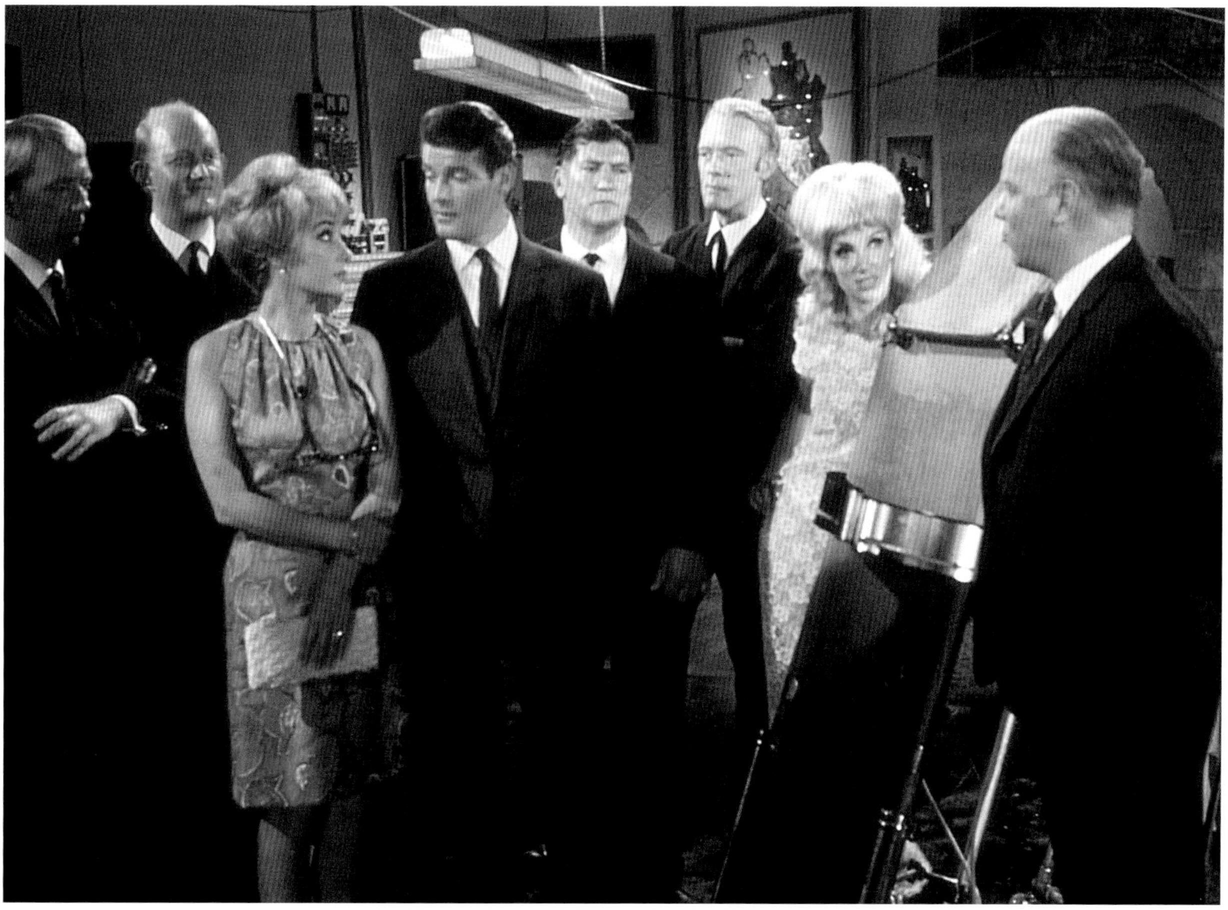

POLYGRAM VIDEO

The creations of Amos Klein: (l-r) Nero Jones (Roy Hanlon), Bishop (Nicholas Smith), Monk (Tom Clegg), Frug (Philip Locke), Galaxy Rose (Justine Lord) and Warlock (Kenneth J. Warren)

Do you prefer that way of working to sitting around for ages between takes on a feature film?
No, I quite like those long periods when you sit around. I do my embroidery or read a book. Mainly I fall asleep. (*Chuckles.*)

Because of your range you seemed to get a lot of the best parts in *The Saint* series. In *The Best Laid Schemes*, Godfrey Quigley is trying to send you round the bend phoning you pretending to be your dead husband. It's almost a *Tales of the Unexpected*, with you coming downstairs to discover your dead husband's raincoat dripping wet on the chair and his pipe left smoking on the table.
Yes, I did get some fun parts. I adored John Moxey, who directed that one. I tell you who was very clever, was Johnny Goodman. He realised that the money was to be made behind the camera, not in front of it. Of course, there are some rich actors like Roger, but Johnny always knew where the best jobs were. He was a businessman who understood the business better than anyone I've ever known. Clever clogs.

Did you ever fall victim to any of Roger's practical jokes?
No, I don't think so. Not the big practical jokes. He once asked me if I liked them and I said I didn't, so he didn't do them on me. He was very, very, very kind to me. When we did one of the John Moxey ones I had just lost a baby, had a baby or been seriously ill – I can't remember which – but he looked after me. And of course we had a lot of disgusting laughs – disgusting! Some that I couldn't possibly tell you. Things down trousers. Somebody embraces you, and presses up against you, and you think, 'Christ, they're having an erection,' and they've shoved a hairdryer down there. Then they look at you all innocently...!!

I would say Roger was one of the nicest people, but nice is such a boring word – and Roger was never boring.

Did you have many dealings with Lew Grade, as he was then?
Not on *The Saint*. But later I did a series for ABC called *My Good Woman* with Leslie Crowther, which Leslie Grade – Michael's dad – set up. And Lew was involved. But I see Lew occasionally. I just think that they were phenomena of the showbusiness world. A couple of years ago dear Ted Willis died (*Lord Willis, creator of* Dixon of Dock Green, *46 plays and films like* Woman in A Dressing Gown *and* Flame in the Streets *with Sylvia*) and Lew stood up to give a eulogy.

> **'I'm sure these days they think I'm an arrogant cow, because although I'm known to the public I'm hardly world famous. I'm just one of those names that people vaguely know'**
>
> **Sylvia Syms on the 'joys' of reading for casting directors**

Lew must have been in his mid-eighties then, and he got up and spoke without notes and I thought, 'There aren't many people of 40 who could be doing this'. He spoke clearly, he was witty, he was very warm, because he and Ted were such old friends. Just amazing.

One of the things I remember about Michael Grade on *My Good Woman*, which we did for about three years, was that as Leslie Crowther's agent he came to every single one of the recordings. My agent came to none. That sums up the Grade attitude to what is their job – it's a full-time job and they love it!

Do you enjoy working in television now, as much?

Well, I'll have to be careful what I say here or I'll never work again. I've just done a PD James *Inspector Dalglish* with Roy Marsden, which was fun because it was quite an old, experienced crowd.

But it's certainly different now. I'm not used to reading for people. In the past someone would ask you to do a job and you'd do it. I'm sure these days they think I'm an arrogant cow, because although I'm known to the public I'm hardly world famous. I'm just one of those names that people vaguely know. But anyway, I went for this interview for a part and there was this young lad in there who had seen me in a short called *Dancing*, which was at the Edinburgh Festival. I played a 70-year-old dying of cancer. It was terribly short but it was a wonderful part and fun to do.

So he'd seen this and suddenly the casting woman said, 'You do know that you're reading don't you?' And my face, which I've never learnt to organise particularly, must have given her the idea that I wasn't too mad about this. It's a bit late to read for parts, isn't it, when you're 63 and you've been doing it for 40-something years.

The director said, 'Do you mind?'

I said, 'No, but I get paid for reading.'

He said, 'I'm sorry?'

I said, 'Well, I've got these friends who write plays. You know Pinter, John Osborne… and sometimes they ask me to come round and do a reading. "Buy yourself some champagne," they'll say. So I know I read reasonably well…' He didn't get the joke at all.

He said, 'Well, your CV is very impressive.'

I said, 'Ah. And what have you done?' I don't think anyone had asked him that before, because here he was all ready to do this long series for Granada.

He'd done two *Thief-Takers*.

I thought well, that kind of answers my question. I didn't get the job, of course! (*Roars.*) And the casting woman rang up and complained to my agent. She said, 'She can't go around behaving like that.' I said 'Well, I'm giving up the business anyway.' My agent said 'That's unfortunate, because you're starting in a film with Steven Poliakoff on Monday.' He didn't want me to audition and didn't ask me to read!

If you were casting a new Saint, who would you pick?

Well, it's a combination of charm and having a good sense of humour. Roger wasn't such a wonderful actor – and he never claimed to be – but he was very charming and he had a great sense of fun. And classy. Roger had class. I mean, his accent was slightly suspect because it was an acquired posh accent, but he still carried it off. From a looks point of view I'd say someone like Ralph Fiennes, but he doesn't make me laugh. I thought the same about Ian Ogilvy.

The one that would have been good, but now is too old for it, is Simon Ward (*Young Winston*). You might not have been aware of it, but Simon Ward has a delicious sense of humour. And he has class.

Pierce Brosnan is the one that Bob Baker spoke to a few years back.

I worked with Pierce in the very early days, before he'd done *Remmington Steele*, in a thing about Nancy Astor for the BBC. Pierce Brosnan played this painter and I remember somebody said, 'I don't know that he's such a good actor.' We had a lot of posh actors in it, like James Fox. But I said, 'All I know is that the camera loves him'. I happened to have seen some rushes and it was just obvious. He was also one of the sweetest men I've ever met.

Hugh Grant?

I'm sorry. Hugh Grant would then do the same kind of acting that he does in the other things. I don't know. I suppose he wasn't bad in that thriller that his girlfriend produced. But has he got the… The thing with both Pierce and Rog is that they could be soppy and funny, but underneath it you knew that if you pushed them too far they'd black your eye. I don't feel that with Hugh, and I knew him quite well when he was younger. He hasn't got their balls.

The 'Doris Day of ABPC' Girl

Annette André has no illusions about the scope of her roles in *The Saint.* 'I was the standard pretty girl with smart clothes and nice legs,' she says. But despite this careful stereotyping a little of her Italian-Australian feistiness still crept in, and not being one to take the giant ants and plaster of paris rocks all too too seriously she was a popular choice both with Roger and *The Saint*'s producers.

She followed this with another big ABPC hit, *Randall & Hopkirk (deceased)* and after a decade in, then a couple out, of the headlines she's now beginning to act again.

ANNETTE ANDRÉ

EPISODES AS GUEST STAR

The Saint Steps In. As the daughter of an industrial scientist who asks S.T. for help in the bar of a swanky London hotel.

The Loving Brothers. As a district nurse in Australia.

The Abductors. As an innocent English girl who's won a competition to Paris but gets kidnapped.

To Kill a Saint. Disguised as an assassin who tries to gun down S.T., but is actually using blanks.

The House on Dragon's Rock. As assistant to a mad scientist. Nice work if you can get it.

When you were starting off doing radio and television plays in your native Australia you were given encouragement by Leslie Norman (the British film and TV director, and dad of Bazza Norman). How did you meet and what advice did he give you?

Leslie was out making a movie in Australia and he tested me for it. Apparently, he wanted me to play the part but the other powers-that-be wanted this girl (*laughs*) who had once been Miss New South Wales or something. He was rather disappointed but said , 'When you come to England make sure you get in touch with me.'

Can you remember your first day's shooting on *The Saint*?

Yes, I remember it vividly because John Gilling was not very nice to me. He was just difficult with actresses apparently. It was a bit hard on me, because already you had the pressure on you of being told to do everything in one take. (*Laughs.*) I wasn't really used to working that way and my first scene was very wordy. (*Her character, Madeine Gray, collars S.T. in a hotel bar with a plea for help. He thinks she's winding him up.*) I was getting more and more nervous and he was being abrupt and curt and not making me feel at all good about anything. I got very scared and was standing there waiting for the take when Roger walked up to me, took my hand and said, 'Don't let him bother you. He's like that with all the actresses.' He said, 'Hold my hand. Everything will be fine,' and literally took me through the whole episode, which was wonderful. He was very attentive and sweet and we became good friends.

You have a scene in *The House on Dragon's Rock* where you're being crushed behind a big fake rock by a giant ant. Wasn't it hard not to get the giggles?

Those rocks were made out of polystyrene, I think. Yeah sure, it was all we could do not to giggle when we were doing a take. There were giant bloody spiders coming at you and rocks falling which you

POPPERFOTO

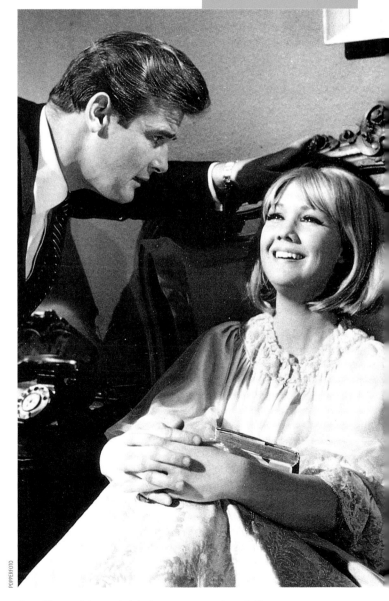

Roger Moore and Annette André enjoy some on-screen japery in The Abductors. *But where's the condom?*

'There were giant bloody spiders coming at you and rocks falling which you could fend off with one finger'

Annette André on the 'perils' of filming *The Saint*

could fend off with one finger. All the parts I played were fairly similar. I'd just have a different name and a different hairstyle. Apart from the giant ant, the thing I remember mainly from *The Saint* is just looking forward to going to work with Roger, because we had the best time. Apparently, he used to like having me work because he'd get a bit bored and I'd always tell him jokes. I remember one day I said to him, 'Betcha can't tell jokes through the alphabet,' and he did it. I can't remember if we got all the way through, but I chucked him a 'z' at one point and he came up with something. He taught me you've got to have a good sense of humour when you're working on a long series.

Wasn't there an incident in the studio's restaurant with a condom?

Yes, that was me. I was on *Randall & Hopkirk,* but Roger was still on *The Saint.* Kenny Cope had put this terrible self-lubricating condom in my script, as a page-marker. When I saw it I must have gone scarlet, because that sort of thing really wasn't done in those days. Anyway, I thought this was quite funny.

At lunchtime Roger was sitting at a table with a couple of grey-suited men having a very serious conversation. So I got a bread roll, stuck the condom in the middle of it, put it on a platter with a silver cover and asked for it to be delivered to Mr Moore. It arrived, Roger took the cover off and there was just this bread roll sat there. So he picked it up, opened the roll... well, I've never seen anyone put a bread roll back together so quickly. The two men he was with nearly fell off their chairs. Roger stared round, saw me in absolute hysterics and the next thing I get this silver platter back, except now he's filled it with water and it's actually flapping around on the plate.

Of course, after that it got passed through the whole restaurant. It ended up with Peter Wyngarde, I think.

Did you have any say in what you wore on *The Saint*?

Oh yes, we were always consulted about clothes. They didn't just bung us into anything. And I knew Laura Nightingale, who was wardrobe mistress, very well. She'd always bring two or three things for you to try on. If you ran out of time then you'd just have to make the best of what you'd got, but she was always accommodating.

In *Dragon's Rock* you have some particularly alluring long, black eyelashes.

Oh, I always used to have my own long black eyelashes! In those days they were very popular, so the lashes tended to come with the actress – they were part and parcel of the package. Once they got to know me they actually let me get on with my own make-up. We'd all be working together on so many different series that there was a great degree of trust.

Did you find it frustrating that you seemed to always get the standard leading girl parts, while the likes of Justine Lord and Dawn Addams could get their teeth into the bad girl roles?

Yes, I always wanted to play the bad girls. But I never got cast as bad or vampy, which was really off. I was always the little do-goody – the Doris Day of ABPC (Associated British Picture Corporation).

What do you think made shows like *The Saint* and *Randall & Hopkirk* so special?

There was a sense of glamour. It was the lighting, the make-up, the hairstyle – you never wore your hair hanging round your face. And the clothes. I was very particular about the way I dressed and I still get letters from fans about what I wore.

Were you very aware of being part of this 'happening' London scene?

Yes, but not in terms of the work we were doing. That didn't seem to be anything special. It was just what you did. In fact you could have knocked me down with a feather if you'd said these series would still be successful 30 years on.

My daughter and her friends groan now when she hears me raving on about 'what we did in the Sixties'. But it was a special time. I remember before that being a teenager in the mid-1950s. We all wore clothes and make-up that Dior models were wearing, which was all styled for women who were in their forties. With the Sixties that all changed. Suddenly, it was very youthful.

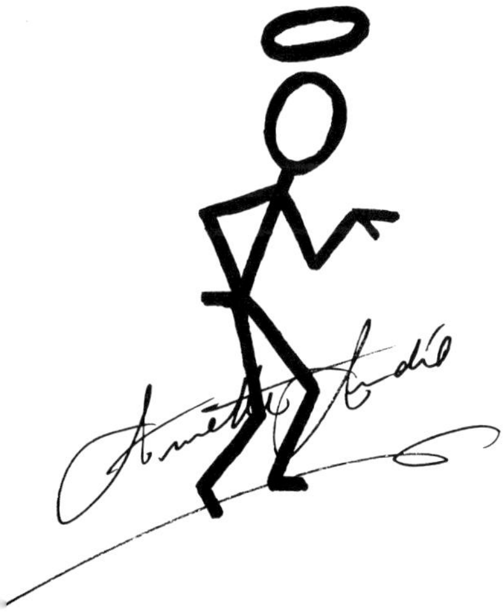

Do you keep in touch with Roger?

On and off. I'd like to have worked with him more because we had such a good time. I mean, the scripts weren't something you could get terribly involved in working on your character.

The Oomph! Girl

Shirley Eaton had already enjoyed a decade of movies, radio, TV, variety and stagework when she was hired to co-star in the very first *Saint* episode in 1962. One of the great British 1960s sirens, immortality in the shape of a re-spray by Mr Goldfinger was still two years away.

At 32, deciding there were no half measures, she turned her back on acting to devote herself to her husband and two sons. Since the death of her husband Colin, she's now returned from their home in France to London where she's still busy answering fan mail from around the globe, fielding questions at various *Bond* conventions about kissing Sean Connery and writing her autobiography.

SHIRLEY EATON

EPISODES AS GUEST STAR

The Talented Husband. As an under-cover insurance investigator.
The Effete Angler. As the devious wife of a smuggler in Florida.
Invitation to Danger. As a very self-assured blonde that S.T. follows out of a London casino – with extremely painful repercussions.

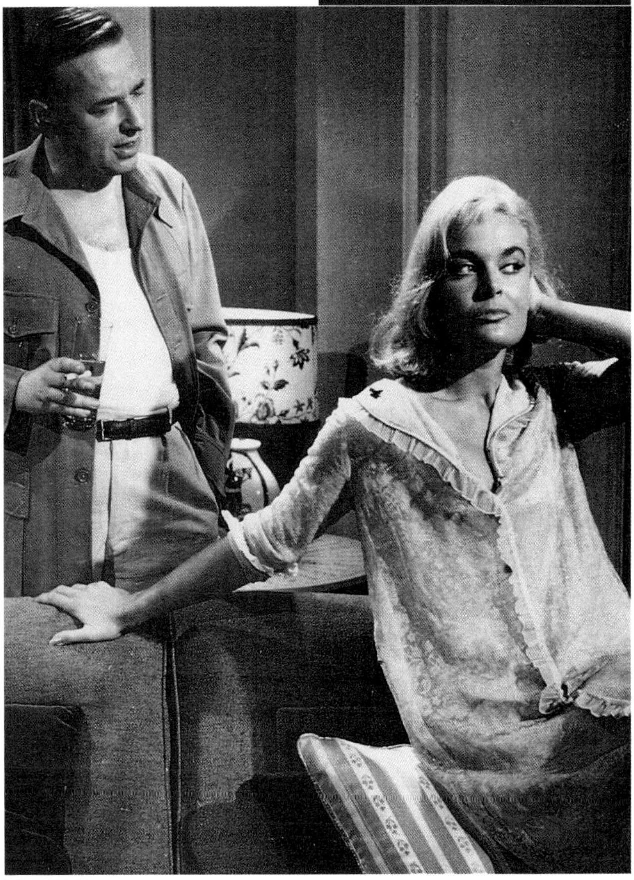

Shirley Eaton, as the duplicitous Gloria Uckrose in The Effete Angler, *shows George Pravda a bit of oomph*

POPPERFOTO

Can you paint a picture of the 25-year-old Shirley Eaton in 1962? I believe you'd been a dancer and singer, on and off, since you were three and as well as numerous stage and TV appearances had made a number of comedy films including the horror spoof *What A Carve Up* for Bob Baker and Monty Berman, and *Carry Ons Sergeant, Constable* and *Nurse*.

What A Carve Up was a jolly good spooky film with Sid James and Kenneth Connor. I played the nurse to the old man who dies, and it was a bit like Agatha Christie's *Ten Little Indians,* which I also did. In fact, the young writer Jonathan Coe, who is helping me with the research of my autobiography, wrote a bestseller with that title two years ago. He features me in the book because of the impression I made on him at the cinema when he saw *What A Carve Up*. His parents walked out in the scene where I began to take my clothes off.

At the beginning of the 1960s I'd just taken a break while I had my first son Grant. I'm a black and white, 100 per cent girl and I realised you couldn't do both jobs well. I was born in 1937 and when my father was away for six years in the Second World War that left a desperate impression on me. I didn't want to put my children through the same thing, so I took a break.

In an interview with Ramsden Greig of the *Evening Standard,* in 1960, you are quoted as saying 'short of being sawn in half, I had done everything in showbusiness'. Was there any fresh challenge, then, in being in the first ever episode of *The Saint*, or was it just another job?

Another job. When you're young – and I was so lucky (*pause*) and pretty (*chuckles*) – that once I'd done my two cameo scenes with Dirk Bogarde in *Doctor in the House* I never really stopped making films. So I did *The Saint* because it was offered to me.

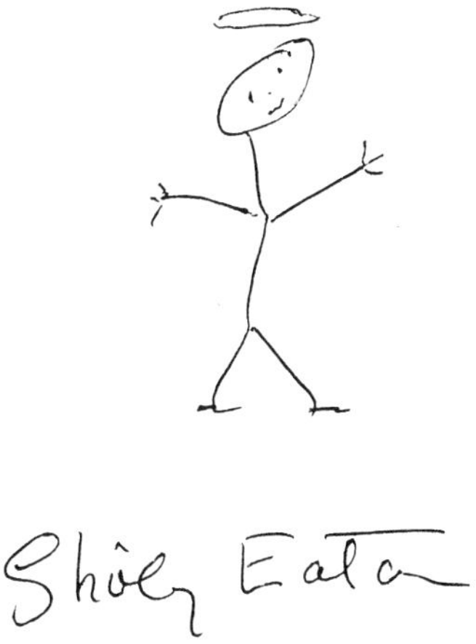

What were your first impressions of Roger Moore?

Oh, he was a sweetie. Until he split up from Luisa I remained in close contact with him. Our families would get together in the South of France in the summer. Roger and Luisa had actually just met at the beginning of those *Saints*. They'd been together for as long as Colin and I, so it was terribly sad when it all came to an end. Funnily enough though, I did see Roger very recently at the Cubby Broccoli Memorial (*at the Odeon Leicester Square*) which was an amazing morning. Very special. (*Along with tributes from Tim Dalton, Pierce Brosnan, Roger himself and many others, Shirley read a poem onstage, which she had written for her husband when he died.*)

THE SAINT MEETS 007

Dastardly master criminals, glamorous gals and disposable henchmen were bread and butter for the 1960s' two great sagas of international intrigue, the *James Bond* movies and *The Saint* TV series. No big surprise, then, that some familiar faces should turn up in both.

Check the exclusive roll-call of actors that got to meet both the famous Simon Templar and Meester Bond...

Shirley Eaton

In *Goldfinger* she was the gold-plated Jill Masterson. In *The Saint* she was insurance tec' Adrienne Halberd (*The Talented Husband*); the devious Gloria Uckrose (*The Effete Angler*) and the double-crossing Reb Denning (*Invitation to Danger*).

Honor Blackman

In *Goldfinger* she was Miss Pussy Galore. In *The Saint* she was Miss Pauline Stone, high society glam (*The Arrow of God*).

Anthony Dawson

In *Dr No* he was the slimy and ill-fated Professor Dent. ('That's a Smith & Wesson – and you've had your six.') In *The Saint* he was the equally slimy and equally ill-fated (arrow through the heart) gossip columnist Floyd Vosper (*The Arrow of God*).

David Bauer

In *Diamonds Are Forever* he was the splendidly unctuous funeral parlour director Morton Slumber. In *The Saint*, devious lawyer Carlton Rood (*The Element of Doubt*); industrial billionaire Burth Northwade (*Judith*); extortion's his game as Rick Lansing (*Iris*); blackmailer Vern Balton (*The Ever Loving Spouse*); misguided scientist Dr Charles Krayford (*Island of Chance*).

Paul Stassino

In *Thunderball* he was Mr Angelo/Derval, the pilot who swipes the atomic warheads. In *The Saint*, the thuggish Vincent Innutio (*The Effete Angler*); Italian thug Ricco (*The Rough Diamonds*); crime syndicate boss Abdul Osman (*The Death Penalty*); Col Rakos (*The Ex-King of Diamonds*).

I understand the schedule was quite pressurised. Were you ever one to fluff your lines ?

Actually, I did. It's my most vivid memory of working on the series. When I was filming *The Effete Angler* I had this longish speech and I kept getting it wrong. Roger was so sweet. I mean you get to a stage where you just have to get up from the set and walk about, have a cup of tea, do something to get over the damn word or sentence that you keep stumbling on. I felt such a fool, but Roger was adorable. He helped me through it. Both he and the director (*Anthony Bushell*) were terribly patient.

What would you say are the pros and cons of filming for TV, as opposed to the movies?

It's just quicker. Much, much quicker. But *The Saint* was the only TV series I did. The only other thing was a singing and dancing comedy half hour called *Great Scott, it's Maynard!* with Bill Maynard and Terry Scott.

What made you come back to *The Saint* three times then?

Because they asked me! You always have a flavour of the month. At the moment it's *EastEnders* isn't it? So at that time, with the *Doctor in the House* and *Carry On*s, I was the girl who was being asked to do everything. Mostly comedy. I was the flavour of the time for glamour, for comedy, for freshness.

In *The Talented Husband* you're still quite the typical, clean-living English sex symbol. But by *The Effete Angler* later that year, you'd developed into something much more fruity which seemed to then point the way to your femme fatale opposite Mickey Spillane in the movie *The Girl Hunters*. Had it been hard convincing casting directors that you could make this change?

Yes, it was. Apart from the comedies there weren't really many directors that knew what to do with me in England. That's why the last few films I did were American. A peer of mine was Sylvia Syms, who went into a couple of really good English dramas and carried on in that vein, while Shirley came from a variety background and got all the comedies. You do get typecast. So I'm pleased I did *The Girl Hunters*, which was more dramatic. And *Goldfinger*, which was funny but dramatic in its own way.

Did the incredible success of *Goldfinger* actually typecast you even more? Your final *Saint* appearance in 1968 is again as a 'cool blonde'.

Well, a natural sexy blonde is what I am, really! There's very few actors who actually become someone else. Most people, especially fans, love actors because of their personality. When you see someone photogenic who's got this – as the Americans say – 'charisma', someone who's got this oomph on screen – and I had it – that's why they like you. They don't write you fan letters for your acting. (*Chuckles*.) It's that inner something that comes across when you see that person on the screen.

If you think about Sean, he's an excellent actor but to me he's still got that quality that he had when he was young. It's Sean that the public love, not his acting. And it's absolutely the same with Roger. Some people won't like what I'm saying, but it's that whoosh of personality. That's what makes people stars.

Who do you think would make a good *Saint* for the 1990s?

They're all so funny-looking now, aren't they? I think Pierce is absolutely gorgeous. I met him at the restaurant after the Cubby Broccoli memorial, and he was such a sweetie. I just walked up to him and asked if I could have my picture taken with him, like a fan.

Of course, you'd already made a big impression on him. *Goldfinger* had been the first movie the 11-year-old Pierce saw when he moved to London.

Yes, with that and him losing his wife as well, and the fact that I have some Irish in me, we could have talked for hours – but sadly there wasn't time. But Pierce is Bond. It's a shame there isn't another Roger, really.

Do you ever regret not making more movies or TV series?

The only thing I really miss is not the stardom, but the comradeship. I loved all the backroom boys – the people in hair and make-up and wardrobe. All those people supporting you.

I gave my career up at the height of it, when I was 32, for my husband and kids and I've never regretted it. I've got a strange situation now, because my husband's died and my children have got families. So I'm alone. But don't feel sorry for me – I'm Shirley again. Much older, but still good looking! It's all come full circle.

'The women have got to be more pretty – every time!'

US network directive to *The Saint*'s casting director, Tony Arnell

'WHEN I FIRST worked as a casting director there were only about 30 of us in the whole country. My way in, if you like, was by doing weekly rep in Bristol when I was 16. After seven years of that I went to *Spotlight*.

ITV had only been going for two or three years and they were looking for casting directors. Because I had knowledge of actors, through my time at *Spotlight*, I went in as an assistant. I worked with a lady called Dodo Watts who was a very famous film star back in the 1930s. It was just she and I doing the whole output of ABC Television at Teddington (*which is now Thames*).

TONY ARNELL PRIVATE COLLECTION

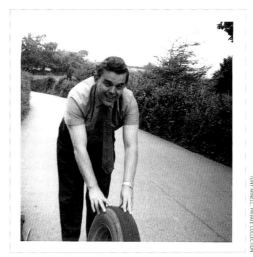

Tony Arnell, guardian of the Saint's spare tyre.

My first job was casting *The Avengers* and a science fiction series with, would you believe it, Boris Karloff. In television then they would film everything live – once the cameras were rolling you couldn't stop for anything – and he would come in and introduce each play with a sinister speech. His one stipulation was that he would only do it so long as he was allowed to watch the cricket first on the Saturday afternoon.

I then worked at Associated British Picture Corporation (ABPC), which was the parent company of ABC, on *The Baron* and in 1966 moved onto *The Saint*.

The main difference between *The Avengers* and *The Saint* was that *The Saint* was shot on film. This was for the benefit of the American market. The only problem I found with catering for that was that you tended to get more typecasting. The beautiful thing with casting for television in those days, doing shows like *Armchair Theatre*, was that you were out going round the reps and the fringes finding new talent and the directors you worked with were often prepared to take a few risks with new faces. But not so for America.

Another problem I found with casting for *The Saint*, was that although English women are certainly beautiful they're sometimes afraid of showing their sexuality. You go to America and of course it's all tits and bums, but English girls are not so confident with their body language. So by the time you'd found someone who was attractive and was willing to be attractive, *and* had the sort of personality to be a fun foil to Roger, there were surprisingly few choices. And when you did find them, of course they went round all the different series and they'd get tired and decide they wanted to do some serious acting instead. And so the hunt began all over again. Meanwhile, I'm getting these directives from America.

THE SAINT MEETS 007

Marne Maitland
In *The Man With The Golden Gun* he was the toady weapons manufacturer Lazar. ('Speak now or forever hold your piece,' warns Rog's 007, aiming a gun at his vitals.)
In *The Saint*, the malevolent hitman Borota (*Teresa*).

Robert Brown
In *Octopussy, A View To A Kill, The Living Daylights* and *Licence To Kill* as 'M'.
In *The Saint* as newspaper editor and old friend 'Jacko' Jackman (*The Saint Plays With Fire*); Atkins (*The Miracle Tea Party*).

Joseph Furst
In *Diamonds Are Forever* as Dr Metz. ('Get out you irr-itating man!')
In *The Saint* as Nazi Industrialist Kane Luker (*The Saint Plays With Fire*); Dr Zellerman (*The Saint Sees It Through*).

Joe Robinson
In *Diamonds Are Forever* as smuggler Peter Franks. ('Third floor, come on up.')
In *The Saint* as head neo-Nazi thug Austin (*The Saint Plays With Fire*).

David Hedison
In *Live And Let Die* and *Licence To Kill* as Felix Leiter.
In *The Saint* as randy newly-wed Bill Harvey (*Luella*).

Julian Glover
In *For Your Eyes Only* as the duplicitous Kristatos.
In *The Saint* as catburgling sidekick Hilloram (*The Lawless Lady*); ill-fated henchman Ramon Falconi (*Invitation to Danger*).

Eunice Gayson
In *Dr No* and *From Russia With Love* as games player Sylvia Trent.
In *The Saint* as stabbed-in-the-back Nora Prescott (*The Invisible Millionaire*); diamond thief's wife Christine Graner (*The Saint Bids Diamonds*).

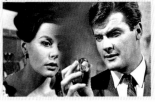

POPPERFOTO

THE SAINT MEETS 007

Geoffrey Keen
In *The Spy Who Loved Me*, *Moonraker* and *For Your Eyes Only* as Minister of Defence Frederick Gray.

In *The Saint* as greedy tycoon Hobart Quennel.

Walter Gotell
In *From Russia With Love* as SPECTRE agent Morzeny and in *The Spy Who Loved Me*, *For Your Eyes Only* and *Octopussy* as General Gogol.

In *The Saint* as heister Hans Lasser (*The Hi-Jackers*).

Burt Kwouk
In *Goldfinger* as Red Chinese agent Mr Ling and SPECTRE 3 in *You Only Live Twice*.

In *The Saint* as villain Tawau (*The Sign of the Claw*); Colonel Wing (*The Gadget Lovers*); Mr Ching (*The Master Plan*).

Peter Madden
In *From Russia With Love* as the losing chess player McAddams. ('A brilliant coup'.)

In *The Saint* the devious Colonel Faied (*The Queen's Ransom*).

Lois Maxwell
In *Dr No* and all the *Bonds* thereafter, up to and including *A View To A Kill* as the very wonderful Miss Moneypenny.

In *The Saint* as stepmother-in-distress Helen (*Interlude in Venice*); movie PR Beth (*Simon and Delilah*).

Vladek Sheybal
In *From Russia With Love* as scary-eyed Kronsteen.

In *The Saint* as equally scary-eyed Nikita Roskin (*The Helpful Pirate*).

Valerie Leon
In *The Spy Who Loved Me* as blousy hotel receptionist.

In *The Saint* as Paris Symphony Orchestra member Theresa (*To Kill A Saint*).

Vernon Dobtcheff
In *The Spy Who Loved Me* as Mojave club owner and *Jaws*-victim Max Kalba.

In *The Saint* as assassin Vogel (*The Gadget Lovers*).

TONY ARNELL ON...

ROGER MOORE (as an actor) It's hard to put your finger on it really. He had a charisma. I mean, no one's going to say he was the world's best actor, but he was certainly the most charming. His voice was attractive. He had a physical presence. He had a sparkle – everyone likes a bit of a sparkle in their leading man.

ROGER MOORE (as a director) He was very nice, very open to suggestions with casting. There is one story that is rather against me, really. I'd seen this girl one day for a certain part. She'd had her coat on as it was a cold winter's day, but she seemed OK. She was pretty and she got the part. Roger came to do the scene with her a few days later at Elstree. The part was of a girl who owns this rather swish antique shop, and he had one line as he was looking at her bosom where he had to say something like, 'Yes, my gosh, you have got some nice pieces here, haven't you,' and of course when he looked down she was totally flat-chested. Did he pull my leg after that!

Thereafter at castings, I would always instruct the actors to come into the office with their coat over their arm.

Roger was also very good at keeping the atmosphere very light. There were one or two directors from the Old School who were used to barking orders on feature films and taking a long time setting up each shot. You couldn't really have that in television. You had to be much faster and you had to be pleasant and willing and sort of win over the confidence of the artist, who was probably a lot less experienced than the stars they'd previously worked with. You had quite a lot of unknown people playing fairly large parts.

ROY BAKER (director) He always had a little sparkle about him, did Roy. I remember we had a casting session at my office, which was in Lower St James Street, Golden Square, and afterwards he suggested we go for some lunch. But before we did he had to collect his top hat from one of those hatters that existed then. It was amazing. Then he said, 'I must also get a trowel because I'm building myself a little wall'.

You could just picture him in this marvellous hat building the little wall.

LESLIE NORMAN (director) We didn't see eye to eye originally, over casting. He'd tend to say, 'So what rubbish have you got for us this week?' which got a bit wearing. But he'd been doing great big films before and I guess he might have seen doing TV as a bit of a comedown. He wasn't a young man – like many of those big old British feature film directors who were suddenly then working in television – while I was more Roger's age. So we had a few disagreements, but then he had some heart trouble and his whole attitude changed. I'd never seen such a transformation in a person. After that I became his blue-eyed boy. He let our kids ride in the Saint's Volvo, he wanted to come over for tea and everything.

HONOR BLACKMAN (classy society woman in *The Arrow of God*) I didn't cast Honor in *The Saint*, but I did cast her as Cathy Gale in *The Avengers*. What happened was Ian Hendry left *The Avengers* to do films. Patrick Macnee was just the sidekick originally, so they suggested re-casting the part with a woman. I drew up lists of more than 100 names of leading actresses, and I put Honor's name forward simply because when I was at *Spotlight* I remember she used to come and see a colleague of mine for help and advice. She was way down on her luck. I think her health wasn't good, her father had died, her marriage was up the creek –she was way down on her uppers, but she still looked amazing. She might not have been a superb actress in the Judi Dench league, but nevertheless she had great stamina and I thought could probably do this part. Some people worried that her accent was 'too Kensington', but I didn't think that mattered at all.

DAVID BAUER (as assorted *Saint* villains and the foolish professor in *Island of Chance*) Wonderful man and an excellent actor. He'd come over to Britain from America following the McCarthy witch hunt. He could play anything from a powerful executive to a real nasty, wicked villain. He died too early, sadly. Back in the 1970s.

OLIVER REED (Italian henchman in *The King of the Beggars*, Greek villain in *Sophia*) He'd been used before my time. My only Oliver Reed story was when I was casting at LWT for a series, *Enemy at the Door,* (about the German occupation of the Channel Islands). I'd advertised in the local press over there for extras. I thought there'd be about 20 local people to see but when I

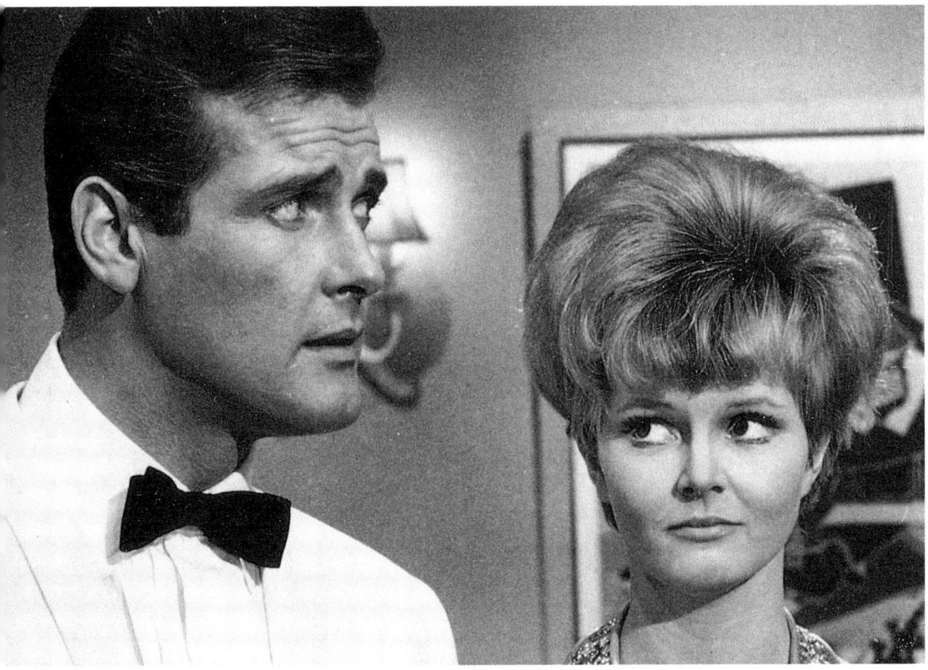

POPPERFOTO

'Everyone likes a bit of sparkle in their leading man.'
'Fun foil' Erica Rogers sizes up the Moore charisma in Lida

got to the hotel there was a huge, huge queue of hopefuls. I hadn't even taken a secretary with me. So I was sat there, head down, taking all their details. The next thing – before I knew it – this great big bloke had taken my face in his hands and given me the most revolting wet kiss I've ever had. Of course it was Oliver Reed – wanting to be an extra. Like hell he did, he was just living out there!

DUDLEY SUTTON (*The Scorpion* - babyface killer) He got very fed up with playing villains in the end. I think I offered him another one when I was at London Weekend and he turned it down. And I think he was quite right. Believe it or not, the buzz when you're a casting director and you're doing your job right, is trying to cast people differently. But you were up against it because Bob Baker and Monty Berman liked people being fairly obvious – probably for the Americans. You have to remember that these were the early days of actually getting a series from England over to the States. That was unknown up to that time.

One strange thing I remember, in nearly every script it would always say about the villain: 'He is very narcissistic.' Always!'

ANNETTE ANDRE (The Girl) In fact she only contacted me two or three years ago to see about getting back into the business. She was always good value. Being Australian she was a little more relaxed – not so uptight as some actresses – so she was very good. I liked her.

VLADEK SHEYBAL (in *The Helpful Pirate*) Very good actor and ideal for casting. He was a visually good casting straight away, whether he was a sympathetic man or a real vicious killer. It was that sort of look you kept your eye out for, rather than something bland. If you saw Vladek you thought, 'Hallo, there's gonna be something going on here!' I'd have him in everything I could get.

GLYNN EDWARDS (as a Russian bodyguard in *The Gadget Lovers*) Once again I'd used him a lot at Teddington. He was very good value. I actually thought he'd go on to be a very prolific character actor, but instead he went into *Minder* and we haven't seen much of him since that. Nice guy.

STEVEN BERKOFF (a tiny part in *Vendetta* and also in *The Man Who Gambled With Life*) Yes, well, as an actor he hasn't changed a lot. He was dead right as a sort of very acid villain. Vicious, sadistic. A definite presence.

A PERFECT SAINT FOR THE 1990s... I instantly think of Nigel Havers, but he's a bit too old now. Of course, Pierce Brosnan is another name that comes to mind, but he's Bond. But someone along the lines of those two. I'll have to have a quick flick through *Spotlight*...

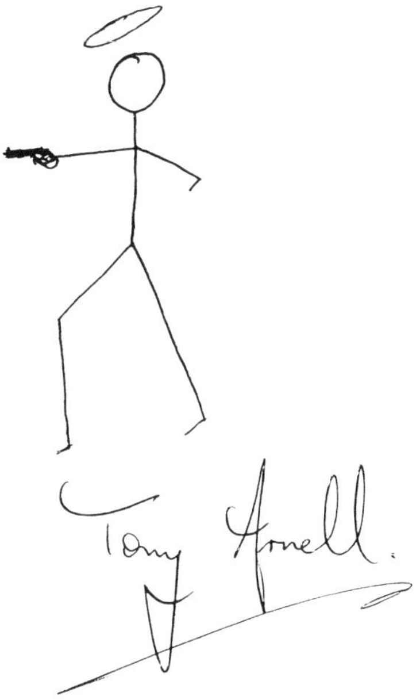

'Very nice people, very nice car.'
Roger and his Volvo
(PHOTO: TONY GALE/PICTORIAL PRESS)

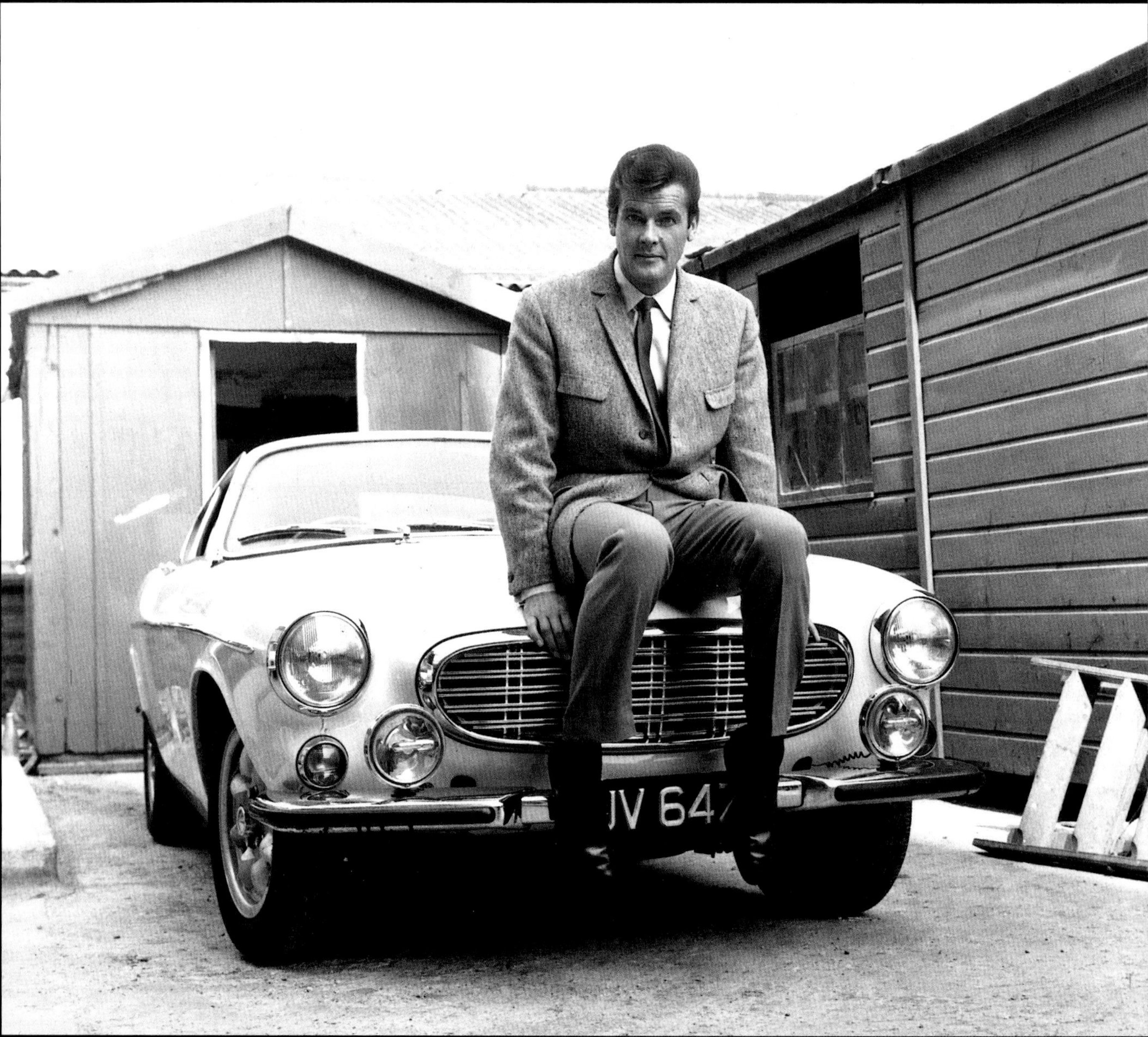

'Doh!'

Just like the A&R man who turned down The Beatles, the story of Jaguar informing the producers of a new 1960s series called *The Saint* that no, they could not supply them with a car for their hero, is legendary.

Johnny Goodman, whose job it was as Production Supervisor to find an appropriate car, recalls the day *The Saint* went Swedish...

'I WENT THROUGH every car company that you can imagine, and they all turned us down. If you think what it costs today to get 10 seconds of exposure on television, here we were offering week after week of this bloody car on screen! I think Mercedes offered us one day's use, and it all got pretty ridiculous. Eventually, we had a meeting and Roger said, "Look, I'm going to be living here for a while now, so I'll buy a car and we'll use that in *The Saint*". He said, "I don't want an E-type, because an E-type will be a bit difficult to get in and out of when you're filming. There's a very nice new car called the Mk 10 Jaguar, I'll get one of those."

'I said, "Alright, it pains me to have to pay to do this, but so be it." So I rang up Jaguar and said, "Mr Moore's decided to buy a car, so can we have a Jaguar?" The chap said, "My dear fellow, we can't give you any priority on delivery". We couldn't even get priority! I was devastated. Then a policeman friend of mine in Special Branch said, "I saw a new car going round town the other day – a very sleek-looking sports car called a Volvo or something". I sent Roger to have a look and when he came back he said: "Very nice people, very nice car. They're going to get one ready immediately in white, and they're going to give us a complete extra cockpit and everything for shooting in the studio". And that's how we got it. Volvo never looked back after that. Wherever Roger went around the world in the 1960s there would always be a Volvo waiting for him.'

Airfix E-type Jaguar featured on the shelf of the race track bar in The Chequered Flag. *Property of Mike Jones*

SAINT CAR MINUTIAE THROUGH THE AGES

In Leslie Charteris' novels *The Saint* gets through a number of different autos. A Furillac. A Desurio and, most memorably, a Hirondel which was described as an eight-cylindered, 5000-pound cream and red opulent monster, that gobbled a gallon of petrol every four miles and was capable of roaring along at top speed from here to kingdom come.

There was only one snag with the fabulous Hirondel – it was a figment of Charteris' feverish imagination and as such, not a lot of use to Bob Baker and Monty Berman when shopping for the TV series.

During the course of filming The Saint *in the 1960s, four P1800s were used. The first, which was a 71DXC built by Jensen in the UK, was blown up in the episode* The Frightened Inn-Keeper. *The second model, the 77 GYL, had large bumper-mounted fog lamps and in a number of episodes, car lovers will be able to spot the Volvo undergoing lightning transformations of design even as it whistles down the road.*

When *The Saint* went into colour in September 1966, two more up-to-date P1800s were provided – the NUV 648E was for filming and the NUV 647E for Mr Moore's personal motoring pleasures.

Not everyone thought it was big and clever for the Saint to hare round bends in his Volvo. In February 1968, 60 schoolchildren, from Stoke-on-Trent's junior Accident Prevention Council, sent a letter to the then Transport Minister Barbara Castle, complaining about the bad example the Saint and Simon Dee set with their driving on TV.

Seventeen-year-old Kathleen Dulson said, 'The Saint usually seems to be driving around at break-neck speed, with one hand on the steering wheel and the other arm round a pretty girl.' The villain of the hour, Roger Moore, took note saying, 'I think the children are splendid, taking this amount of trouble over road safety. When we shoot the film, it's usually on a specially controlled road where there's no danger to other road users.' The children also had a go at June Whitfield for an episode of Beggar my Neighbour, *where she fell off her bicycle 'while carrying an umbrella'.*

In the 1970s, for *The Return of the Saint*, Jaguar had had time to mull over their earlier mistake, so were first out the gate to offer Ian Ogilvy two Jaguar XJS for the series to use. One was automatic and one manual. As an added refinement, production supervisor, Malcolm Christopher, had them fitted with sunroofs, 'Because it's very good when you're filming from outside the car to have a light source coming in'.

Ian Ogilvy liked the XJS so much that at the end of filming in Rome, he asked if he could drive one of the cars back to England. Bob Baker okayed it, so he took the manual. He got as far as Florence and burnt the clutch out.

When the Volvo C70 coupé, which Val Kilmer drives in the new Paramount *Saint* movie, was still in the design stage, the project leader, Mr Hakan Abrahamsson, had only one thing to say to his team: 'Just give it four seats and an overdose of hormones'. With a top speed of 150mph and a 0-60 acceleration in 6.9 seconds, it certainly has that.

9: THE SAINT AT THE CINEMA

Caddish Sanders rubs noses with Sally Gray in The Saint In London

BFI

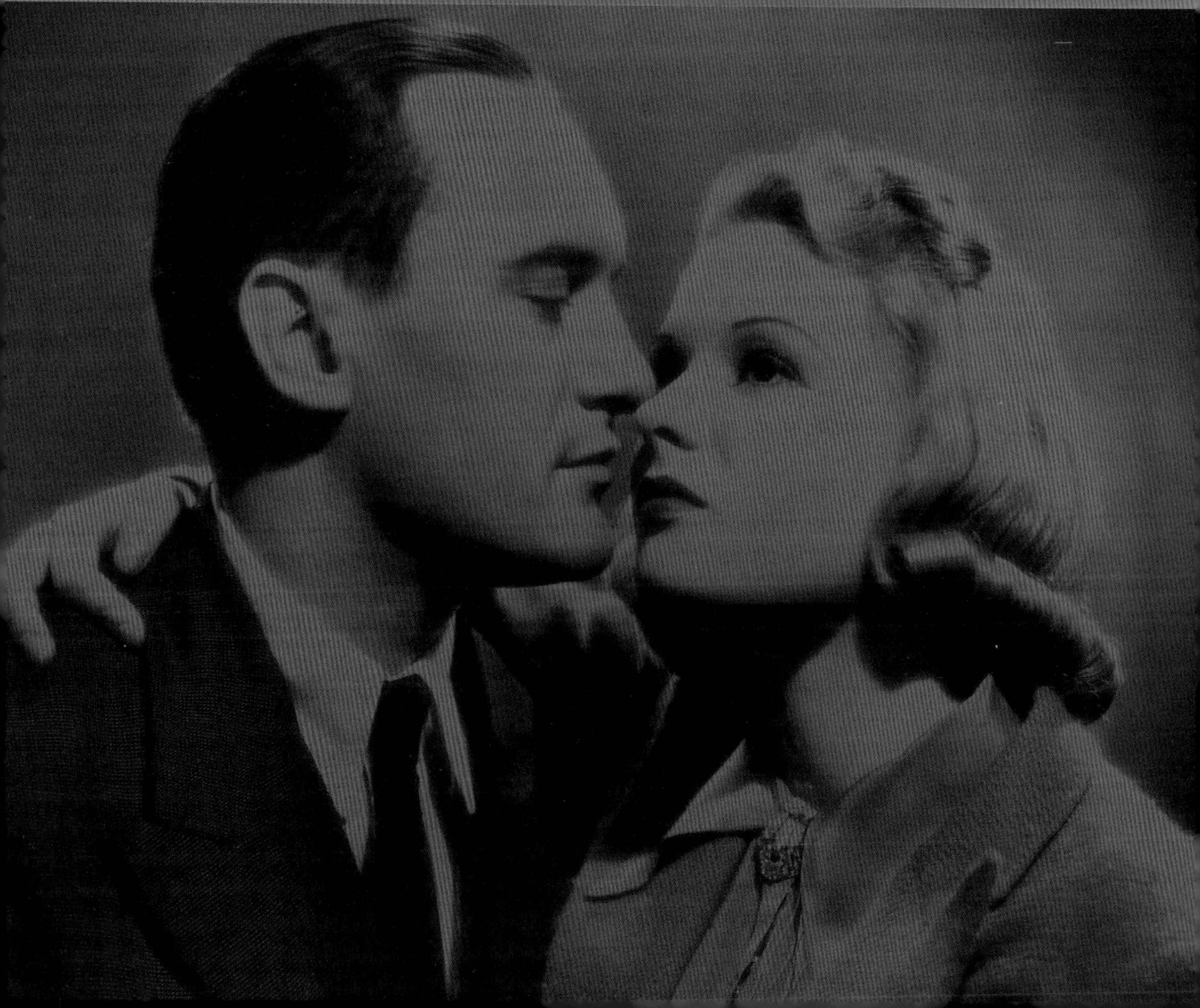

'Blondes, bullets and blackmail...'

From the days when Louis Hayward ran about at breakneck speed, rubbing out all the top gangsters in *The Saint in New York*, through the oily and downright aggressive seduction techniques of George Sanders ('I'm very sorry, but under certain conditions I just can't resist the temptation to be a cad'), the moustachioed pipe cleaner pose of Hugh Sinclair, the bantering wit of Roger Moore in *The Fiction-Makers*, up to Val Kilmer's present little boy lost, *The Saint* has had a varied and not altogether satisfying – particularly in the late Leslie Charteris' eyes – screen career...

THE SAINT IN NEW YORK *(RKO, 1938)*

Almost 60 years on and the jury is still out on Louis Hayward's Saint. Played as an almost psychotic exterminator, hired by the New York police to do a Travis Bickle and wash all the scum off the streets, he goes about it like there's no tomorrow, aided by Kay Sutton's gangster's moll whose attitude to death and destruction is even more morally ambiguous than his.

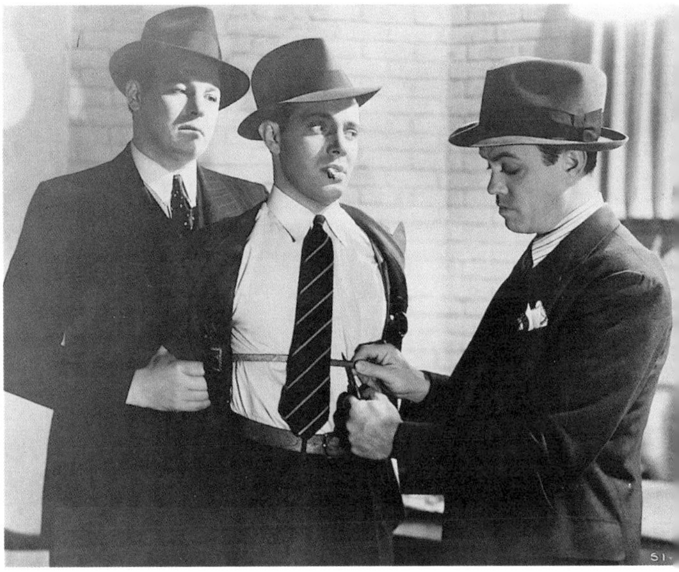

BFI

Louis Hayward shows off his nice shirt in The Saint in New York

THE SAINT STRIKES BACK *(RKO, 1938)*

After the frenetic dash of Louis Hayward it takes a while to get acclimatised to the oh-so-smug lounge lizard that is new Saint, George Sanders. ('Not the man who knows everything. But just the man who knows the important things.') Set in San Francisco, the Saint rather mean-spiritedly guns down gangster Tommy Voss, then spends the rest of the tale mixing it with Voss' associates and uncovering judicial corruption. Directed by Mia's dad, John Farrow, there's some surreal violence with Templar striking one villain with a tennis ball and an extraordinary indigestion-induced dream sequence with a lobster driving a fire engine. (Hitchcock's *Spellbound* has nothing on this!)

THE SAINT IN LONDON *(RKO, 1939)*

Acknowledged by Leslie Charteris to be the best of the RKO films, this is directed by John Paddy Carstairs, who would later direct Roger Moore in two early episodes of the TV series. Like an American film noir, the Saint is plunged into deeper and deeper trouble when he comes to the rescue of a wounded man. Chiaroscuro lighting, the obligatory pea-souper and glamour, in the shape of Sally Gray, are served up for George Sanders.

THE SAINT'S DOUBLE TROUBLE *(RKO, 1940)*

This one is very silly indeed. There are two George Sanders walking around Philadelphia, one the Saint, the other a notorious gangster called Duke Bates. To add a touch of the exotic, the story starts in Cairo with a white panama-ed Bela Lugosi sending a coffin by freight to one Professor Horatio T. Bitts. A headline in *The Transvaal News* sums up the minuscule plot – 'International Smugglers at Work. Diamond Stealing BAFFLES The Authorities'.

'Dreadful,' Charteris called it. And unless you have an overpowering curiosity to see what George Sanders looks like dressed as a woman, wearing a black veil (pretty much Charles Gray in *Diamonds Are Forever* but not nearly as much fun), then don't waste an hour of your time.

THE SAINT TAKES OVER *(RKO, 1940)*

A lot of fun, with George Sanders again using his verbal dexterity to compensate for the fact that he moves with all the sensuality and lithe athleticism of a box of Frosties. A consortium of hoods have bumped off a stool pigeon and framed Detective Fernack. Directed by Jack Hively, it plays as a fast-moving black comedy, with most of the gallows humour stemming from the unfortunate Fernack's habit of being caught with a smoking gun in his hand, every time another hood bites the dust. Character actor, Paul Guilfoyle, almost steals the show as the dopey sidekick Clarence 'Pearly' Gates, who reads *Dick Tracy* in the funny papers and worries about his diet of milk. ('They tell me you ought to chew this stuff. Now I ask you, how's a guy gonna chew milk?')

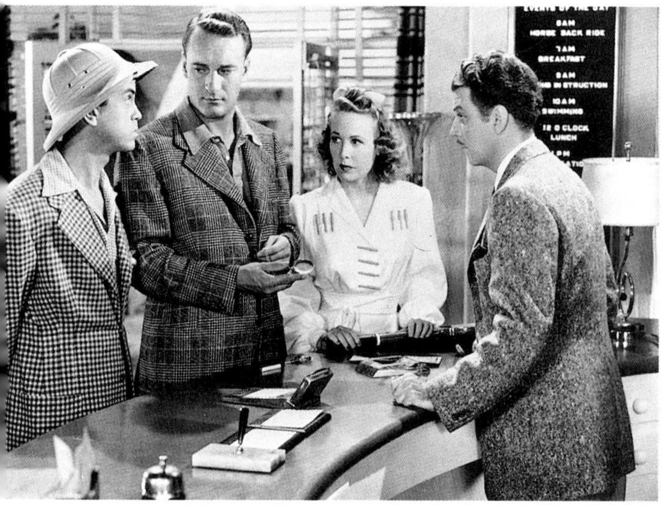

BFI

Are you taking the pith? George Sanders and Wendy Barrie appalled by Paul Guilfoyle's ludicrous hat, in The Saint in Palm Springs *(above)*

THE SAINT IN PALM SPRINGS *(RKO, 1941)*

The whole gang's back together for this excursion. Not only Jonathan Hale as Fernack and Wendy Barrie as another femme (though not so fatale), but Paul Guilfoyle as 'Pearly' Gates. ('Not Pearly any more – Clarence Gates, house detective.') The Saint has to deliver some valuable merchandise ('three newly discovered Guyana penny stamps of 1856, worth £200,000'), to the niece of a recently bumped-off friend of Fernack's in Palm Springs.

Again directed by Jack Hively, it's an entertaining romp with good work from the supporting crew. Guilfoyle, as ever, does a pretty neat job of stealing the show; first parading in a succession of ludicrous hats (everything from a bowler to a jauntily arranged ice-pack), then performing an astonishing trick where he gets a cigarette to spring from its case into his mouth, somehow already lit.

THE SAINT'S VACATION *(RKO, 1942)*

After the solid shape of Sanders, Hugh Sinclair could hardly have provided a greater contrast. Looking like a Ronald Searle cartoon, he has jug ears, a nose that could open envelopes and a moustache that Leslie Charteris strongly objected to.The skulduggery over a box and its mysterious contents is splendidly perpetrated by Cecil Parker, who would appear some 25 years later as Lord Gillingham in the TV episode *A Double in Diamonds*. Sally Gray returns, proving to be one of the feistiest females of the RKO films, and the flighty music score sets the tempo for one of those battle-of-the-sexes movies, so popular at that time. Sadly, Sinclair has the charisma of a codfish and only ever really looks the part when he's clambering about Cecil Parker's castle like some deadly spider.

THE SAINT MEETS THE TIGER *(RKO, 1943)*

A surprisingly enjoyable *Saint* adventure, with Hugh Sinclair relaxing into the role and having a fine old time on the gold bullion trail. Jean Gillie provides the banter as Patricia Holm.

THE SAINT'S GIRL FRIDAY *(Royal, 1954)*

A welcome second bite at the cherry for a 20 years wiser Louis Hayward. Produced by Anthony Hinds, who would be the creative force behind Hammer, later employing *Saint* directors like Freddie Francis and Roy Ward Baker, this is almost a prototype for the series. Pacey, tight and atmospheric. 'Blondes...bullets and blackmail...can't stop him!', screamed the poster. Indeed.

THE SAINT *(Paramount, 1997)*

Perhaps doomed from the second Kilmer was cast, this is a veritable monument of missed opportunities. The *Oliver!*-style prologue adds no resonance, there's no thrilling title sequence using Orbital's version of the Astley theme, the set pieces are almost non-existent, Kilmer's accents are sub-Clouseau, Alun Armstrong's Inspector Teal is not even identified and the climax is the two villains being handcuffed. Only consolation for Saint fans is Roger Moore's newscaster voice-over namechecking the Red Cross, Salvation Army and his beloved UNICEF.

'At least the author of this novelisation knew The Saint...'

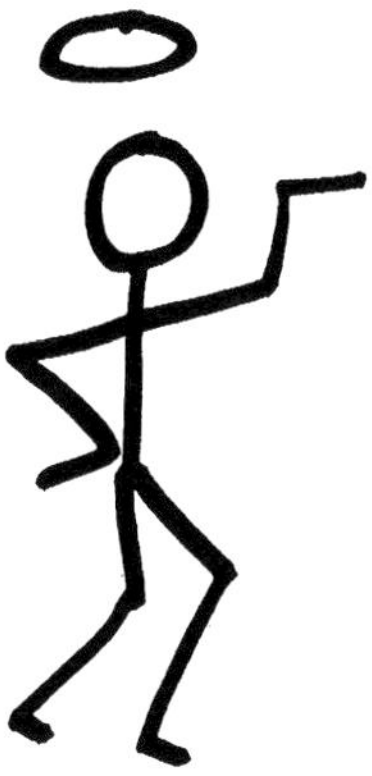

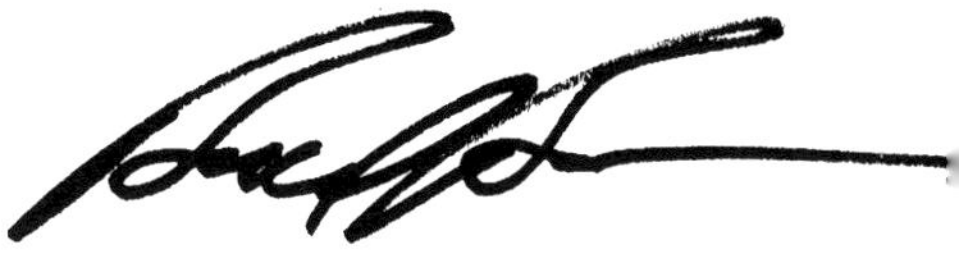

Burl Barer is the author of the most astonishing study of *The Saint* ever compiled: *The Saint: A Complete History in Print, Radio, Film and Television.* Unlike so many analyses of artists, it's both detailed and witty, capturing perfectly the sprightly wit of Charteris and his hero. It was no surprise, therefore, that when Paramount needed someone to write a novelisation of the new movie, they turned to the man from Walla Walla.

Here he talks about the writing process, the many embellishments he made to turn the film back into something which would at least be vaguely recognisable to Saint fans, and the forthcoming publication of his own *Saint* novel, *Capture the Saint,* which has been approved by Leslie Charteris' widow, Audrey.

What was your first introduction to *The Saint*?

That was when I was in high school in the 1960s. My friend David Benefiel loaned me a *Saint* book - *The Saint in New York*, I think - and said, 'Here, read this. It's great fun'. I followed that with the Saint's *Getaway* and I was off and running. Everything was happening then at the same time. The Roger Moore TV series – the black and white episodes – came on 10pm Sunday nights here in Walla Walla, Washington. The old George Sanders movies were running during the day, *The Saint Mystery Magazine* was on the news-stands and all these *Saint* books were coming out through a fiction publishing company. With the magazines, I wasn't actually so much interested in the stories as in the editorial Charteris would write at the beginning of each issue. I wanted to know his slant on things. I just became this huge *Saint* fan.

How did the TV series fit into your *Saint* obsession as a 16-year-old? Were the books always your maln love?

Well, the TV series used to make me a bit crazy because there was always high quality in the productions, but inconsistency in the scripts and the characterisations. Harry Junkin was script supervisor and even though he and Charteris didn't always get along, when I was 16 if it said, 'Script by Harry Junkin' at the beginning of the episode, I knew the characterisation was going to be fun. Moore wouldn't be scowling, he'd be smiling. Some weeks he'd say, 'There's been a murder', and he'd raise his eyebrow and have that cute little look on his face. While other weeks when he said 'murder' his brow would knit and I'd go, 'Aw, give me a break!'

Of course, by the colour episodes John Kruse just wrote marvellous, marvellous stuff.

John Kruse says he thought 16 was the perfect age to start reading *The Saint*. That buccaneering spirit just captures the imagination of a young lad.

Yes, I think it does. Charteris wrote an introduction to *The Saint versus Scotland Yard*, called *Between Ourselves*, where he talks about the whole thing of vowing never to grow up and lose that youthful exuberance, which is just great. That whole philosophy of approaching life as if it were an adventure – which it is. It certainly keeps you from being dreary. (*Laughs.*)

'We will go out and find more and more adventures. We will swagger and swashbuckle and laugh at the half-hearted. We will boast and sing and throw our weight about. We will put the paltry little things to derision, and dare to be angry about the things that are truly evil. And we shall refuse to grow old'

From Burl's favourite Charteris introduction, 'Between Ourselves' , The Saint versus Scotland Yard.

'I always knew it would make me feel like some kind of moss-covered monument, and it does'

Letter from Leslie Charteris to Burl Barer, thanking him for his magnum opus on *The Saint*

Charteris said there were never really any new plots. The idea is just to entertain the audience – some fun and some witty dialogue.

When did you first contact Leslie Charteris?

When I got the go-ahead from McFarland to write *A Complete History*. I wrote to him and he said that he didn't give interviews anymore – I'm sure he'd been approached by many people over the years – but he politely finished, 'If you really do it, let me know'.

So I wrote him a longer letter asking him if I could have the copyright, not just to a couple of quotes but to everything – his correspondence, bills, the books, the lot, which is all housed at Boston University – and when he saw it was actually going ahead he gave permission.

Why do you think he decided that you were the right person to entrust all this to?

I think the fact that no one had actually gone that far, and the contract from McFarland, swayed it. So he said for me to do it, 'But please don't write me unless you have to'. And when the book was done he said he would review it for any errors of fact, which only he could correct. So I sent him the page proofs and, bless his heart, he even corrected the typos (*missing punctuation,etc.*) The only thing was, he didn't say whether he liked it .

Anyway, the book came out and I was really happy. You know, to see *The Saint* and my name together on the same cover was pretty cool. So I sent him an autographed copy and then he wrote this wonderful note back:

'Dear Mr Barer,

Many, many thanks for my personal copy of your long-awaited magnum opus and the inscription therein. I always knew it would make me feel like some kind of moss-covered monument, and it does. I have now conscientiously read it from cover to cover and I can only say that I'm awed and humbled by the scope of your research, which I feel could hardly have been merited by any lesser subject than the works of Homer, Shakespeare or Walt Disney. Certainly not ordinary reading for someone who is still at least clinically alive.

If I had been behind this project myself – and you may have a hell of a job convincing a lot of cynics that I wasn't – I couldn't have hoped for a more profound and sympathetic appraisal of everything I tried to do with *The Saint*...'

It brought tears to my eyes.

So did you then meet him soon after?

Yes. The timing was perfect. There was an event called something like Action 93, a celebration of ITC projects, so I ended up on a panel about *The Saint* with Robert S. Baker and Johnny Goodman. And then my wife and I had lunch with Leslie and Audrey Charteris in a coffee shop in Surrey. We sat side by side and he held my hand. His voice was very soft then, because he'd had a series of strokes, but he spoke right into my one good ear and told me stories of Hollywood, and he was very funny.

His opening line to me was, 'How can Bill Macdonald concentrate on my *Saint* movie when he has Sharon Stone in his bed?' (*Macdonald was at that stage one of the producers and originators of the Val Kilmer movie as well as La Stone's beau.*) He was such a sweet man, with a real twinkle in his eye. Just wonderful.

I'm trying to get a star for him on Palm Springs Canyon, like the one on Hollywood Boulevard. I think he definitely deserves his own star.

Which is your favourite RKO *Saint* film?

Well, it's not regarded as the best, but visually I love *The Saint Strikes Back*. It's a beautiful-looking film. I've also finally seen *The Saint's Girl Friday*, which I had not been able to get a copy of when I wrote the book. It's shot in England and what it resembles stylistically is some of the early *Saint* TV shows. The ones which are shot with a real nice, tight economy of field. American TV shows at that time, like *Perry Mason*, had a similar feel. Added to that, the dialogue's pretty good.

So how did the novelisation come about?

Well, I'd written this new *Saint* novel, *Capture the Saint* (or *The Saint in Seattle* depending on my mood), and while I'd been writing it I'd become friendly with a bunch of people in Robert Evans' office (*producer of the new* Saint *movie and 1970s hits like* The Godfather *and* Chinatown). I never met Evans personally, but there was a real nice guy called Paul Sauer in development there. I'd go over for bagels and coffee just to yak for half and hour, and having done a book on the filming of *Maverick (with Mel Gibson, Jodie Foster and James Garner)*, they decided I was the man for the job.

AND THIS IS ME

Is Val Kilmer's Saint the new Mike Yarwood? In the course of the movie he goes through any number of ludicrous disguises, including...

A grungey-looking Russian peasant

A dopey and extremely hairy tourist

An improbable Spaniard by the name of Martin De Porres

A geek with Dick Emery's vicar's teeth

An Aussie gentleman called Vincent Ferrer, 'The Saint who betrayed his best friend'

An old babushka

The Italian-accented Mr Orseolo, named after a Venetian Saint 'who left his family for a life of solitary contemplation'

On his e-mail, various foreign totty know him as Dominic, Francis and Patrick and Peter Damian

A latter-day Byronic poet and artist (good for mingling amongst the dons and doctors at Oxford University)

The bearded Ivan Tretiak

August Christopher, different glasses

Edmund Campion, a Kremlin guard, 'named for a Saint who was tried on falsified charges of treason'

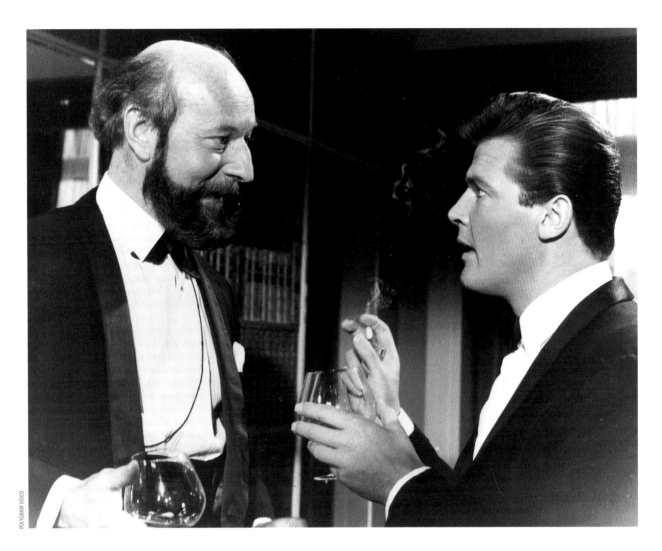

POLYGRAM VIDEO

'I'm a capitalist. I'm through with publishing so-called important books. I don't want to educate people. I just want to be a millionaire.'
The Fiction-Makers' *publisher Finlay Hugoson wonders if it's time to try his hand at this novelisation lark*

As far as the new novel goes, it's a real *Saint* novel. (*Burl also has rights from the Charteris estate to write three more.*) In it the Saint is older – we don't exactly say how old and in some ways it's a sequel to *The Saint in New York*. If you remember little Viola Inselheim was kidnapped.

Well, in this one the Saint is in Seattle to promote a movie version of his own book, *The Pirate*. Barney Malone, who used to write for *The Clarion* in the old *Saint* novels, is now a movie producer and, according to my book, he spent a year on his knees and several hours in a bar convincing Simon Templar to sell him the movie rights (*which is what Robert Evans has said he did to acquire the worldwide movie rights to all 56 Charteris books*).

So the Saint has to go to all these media receptions. While he's at one of these in Seattle, this woman walks up to him and points at his logo and says, 'Do you remember when you gave me one of these?' It turns out she is Viola Inselheim, now all grown up and married, and she's called Viola Inselheim-Berkman. And she has a request of the Saint: just as he rescued her as a child, now she wants him to rescue some other kids from a predatory paedophile in Seattle.

How did you then go about turning the Wesley Strick/Jonathan Hensleigh screenplay of *The Saint* into a novel?
Well, first you have to expand it. I mean, a 120-page screenplay is not enough for a novel. But it wasn't so hard. I'm basically easy to work with. I'm not one of these authors who thinks he's writing plays. I'd change anything they wanted me to, and as the script kept changing I did.

Could you then embellish the story?
Oh yes. I got a real kick out of that. Simon and Schuster (*the publishers*) said they wanted even more of a back-story than there is in the movie. They wanted to know who his parents were. If you recall in all the old *Saint* books of the 1930s, there was always this running joke where the Saint would say, 'As the actress said to the bishop...' So I made his mother an accomplished British actress and his father a former Anglican Bishop-turned-entrepreneur. I even made him half-Asian. (*A nod to Charteris' Chinese origins. He was actually born Leslie Charles Bowyer Yin*

on 12 May 1907, but changed his name by deed poll when he was 20 to Leslie Charteris-Ian. This became further abbreviated on his British passport.) In fact, I said the play the Saint's mother made her name in was a revival of Homer Quarterstone's *Love The Redeemer*, which was this horrible play mentioned in the old *Saint* story *The Star Producers*. So throughout the novelisation there are references and sub-references to *Saint* stories, old *Saint* characters and so on. In fact, I even changed the opening line of *Saint* dialogue from the movie, when he's an adult.

Ilya says, 'Who the hell are you?' or something, to the Saint and I changed the reply to 'Saint Uniatz the Inebriate, Patron Saint of the Fashion Impaired.' (*Hoppy Uniatz was Simon Templar's boozy sidekick from the novels, who would also appear in the early TV episode* The Careful Terrorist.)

And when the Saint sneaks back into England, on his passport, instead of saying Martin De Porres, it says Ian Dickerson (*see Chapter 10: Fans*). And when he goes to his hotel instead of just being named Orsoleo – after the Saint who spent a life in contemplation – I've given him the last name of Orsoleo Bodenheimer, named after the Saint at Santa Cruz bibliophile who left his family for a life of contemplation. (*Dan Bodenheimer is the Internet author of* The Saintly Bible, *which deals with everything connected with the halo-ed one*)

I even managed to get in a dear friend of mine, James Westlake, who passed away at a very early age from bone marrow cancer. James owned the Volvo 1800 which is featured in my book. At the end of the book, when the Saint takes off for the airport in his Volvo C70, I say that the car is registered in the name of James Westlake. I thought James would like to own the Saint's Volvo!

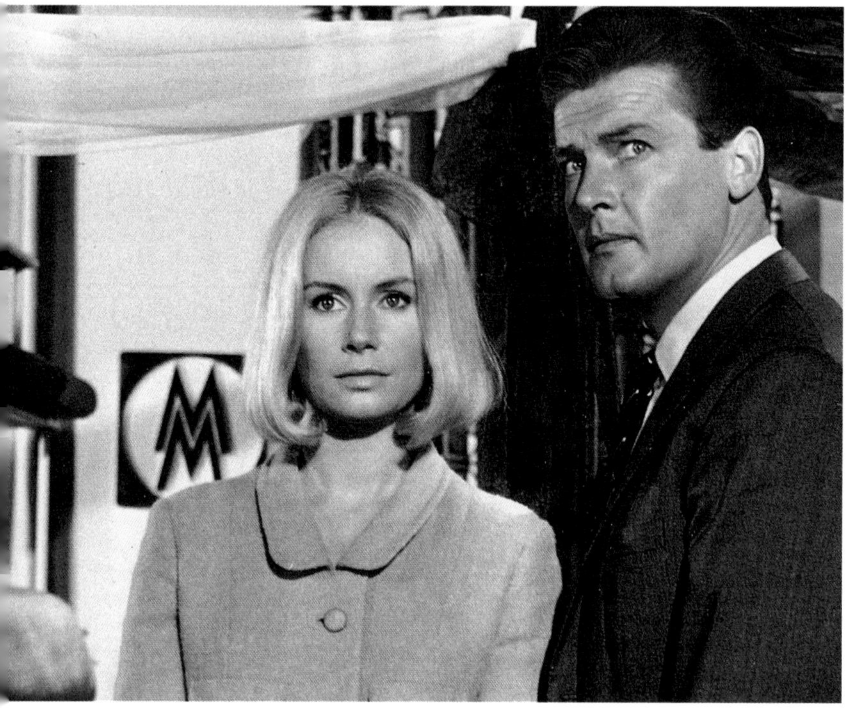

POPPERFOTO

'Murder.' Roger and Penelope Horner test Burl Barer's patience with their serious dispositions in Paper Chase

I also talk about all the Saint's different houses, because there's a scene where the Saint meets the Elisabeth Shue character, Emma, at a farmhouse that he owns. So I mention that he also owns all these other houses under the names of Hugh Sinclair, George Sanders, Louis Hayward. I left off Roger Moore because I thought that was a bit too obvious.

And did the publishers mind all these Saintly in-jokes?

No, just the opposite. They thought it was just dandy. They said it works on all levels. For people who don't know it doesn't interfere with their reading of the book, but if you do it's a nice little bonus. For that minority who remember the literary Saint, when they read this and query all the background stuff about his being in an orphanage they'll know that at least the author of this novelisation knew *The Saint*. I certainly tried to stay completely faithful to the screenplay because millions and millions of people are going to see this film, and hopefully love this film, who have never read a *Saint* book and I want them to be able to read it and enjoy it, even if they have no prior knowledge of the character.

That said, I even worked in an entire sub-plot about George Sanders! There's a scene in the film when the Saint gets back to England and he's flicking through the channels on his TV. In the script it says he flicks through 57 channels in 30 seconds or something. And I just have him stop when he sees this old black and white movie on the screen. There's George Sanders cracking a safe. The Saint goes, 'Ah, this must be the educational channel.' So he carries on watching Sanders do this. Well, that becomes a metaphor for what he's going to do with Emma. The Saint uses a mechanical safe-cracking device at the beginning of the movie, to get into Tretiak Industries, but to break into her heart he's going to have to use the George Sanders method. It's gonna have to be touch. It's gonna have to be sensitivity... So at various times throughout the novelisation he makes reference to George Sanders.

At the end of the book – which was originally the middle but they changed the ending, so I had to rewrite it – they're in bed together and the Saint talks to Emma about how much he and George Sanders have in common. I don't mean liking Zsa Zsa Gabor and her sister, but

Sanders was born in Russia. He was born in St Petersburg. In fact, Sanders left Russia, at Finlandia Station, the day that Stalin arrived and they saw each other at the train station. So now, in the movie, you have the Saint interacting with the equivalent of a modern-day Stalin. While in real life Stalin confiscated all of Sanders' family's wealth. George kept these resentments with him always and eventually they killed him – he committed suicide. So in the book the Saint says, 'That's what's going to happen to me.' So he decides he's all done with resentments, he's done with Russian gangsters, 'and I'm madly in love with Dr Emma Russell.'

So you've basically managed to inject back into the novelisation everything that is missing from the movie!
Well, everything from the movie is in there, and this other stuff was approved. The only thing they made me change back was that in the movie he doesn't come up with the *Saint* logo – she does. In the book I'd had her come up with the stickpin only after he'd drawn it in the sketchbook.

And the line of dialogue, the joke, that they made me change, was when Emma is being shown all these pictures of the Saint in various clever disguises by Chief Inspector Teal. It's basically shots of The Saint Around the World, which was of course one of the book titles.

I have the pictures labelled and Emma (*Elisabeth Shue*) is reading them off. So it's *The Saint in New York*, *The Saint in Miami*, *The Saint on the Spanish Main*... Then she comes to this one, *The Saint in Hollywood*, and she stops. She says, 'I don't see the resemblance here at all!' But they took that out. Now it just goes, 'I don't see the resemblance here,' and it's a picture of him at Heathrow or something.

Oh yes, there was one thing I changed from the script, which I felt I had to. In the screenplay Emma has heart problems and takes heart medication. She also drinks a lot of wine. So I went to a pharmacist and asked what would be the drug interaction between someone taking Interol and drinking. He said, 'The drug will negate the Interol'. So, as her character is a chemist, I didn't have her drink when the Saint orders a bottle at dinner. I felt a moral obligation to do that.

Are there any characters in the first script you received that have now disappeared from the film?
Well, I think the character of Frankie, who helps the Saint in Russia, has now been greatly reduced in the final film. But that often happens. You want the film to be tight, you want it to move fast and certain things end up being discarded.

So what happened to the whole thing with *The Saint* logo? I thought the original producer on the new movie, Robert Evans, was set on using the original stick figure? It seemed the perfect bus stop teaser in the *Batman* and *Ghostbusters* movie promo tradition.
I think it's now being used in Britain. But the reason they weren't using it over here in America was for the same concern they always run in to, which is whether the positioning of the Stick Man's hand looks effeminate. Anyway, for the new version which Paramount is using, they've just turned the hand round so the thumb is pointing up and it looks like he's waving.

And do you think the scriptwriters solved the problem of having to revive Elisabeth Shue's character, who had been killed off, when it tested badly with audiences in America?
I think they actually did a very clever job on that. I've gotta give them credit where credit is due. I mean, I guess it would have been much easier for them to have resolved that problem while they were still writing the screenplay. But as Paul Sauer said, 'Why do that when you can spend $2 million on a reshoot!'

They've actually solved the problem by using some existing footage and doing some restructuring. That's the nice thing about doing a test screening of the film. Not only do you find out what doesn't work, you also find out what does work. And in early screenings the audience apparently absolutely loved it when Kilmer puts on this particular disguise where he plays a real dork. He has a fake bald head and buck teeth.

So they had Kilmer do this again at the end of the movie, where he now has this whole cat-and-mouse chase with Teal. Now it's this real upbeat ending. A real crowd-pleaser.

Finally, if you were to cast a movie of your *Saint* novel, who would you have as the Saint?
You know, this might sound heretical, but I think Ian Ogilvy is perfect now. He's 53 and he thinks he's too old, but he doesn't look that old. He's a very good actor and he's kind of got that ruggedness to him now that he didn't have in the seventies.

'The audience apparently absolutely loved it when Kilmer put on this particular disguise, where he plays a real dork'

Burl Barer on one of the plus points to come from the infamous early screenings of the new movie

R.I.P
TERRY NATION
(8 August 1930 - 9 March 1997)
Apart from creating those gliding pepper pots of menace, the Daleks, Terry also contributed a number of *Saint* screenplays: *The Revolution Racket*, *Jeannine*, *Lida*, *The Contract*, *The Inescapable Word*, *The Sign of the Claw*, *The Crime of the Century*, *The Man Who Could Not Die*, *Invitation to Danger*, *The Desperate Diplomat*, *The Time to Die*, *Where the Money Is* and the very wonderful *Sibao*.

10: FANS

I think the real 'Saint' is the guy in the middle!! - all the very best my friend

Johnny Goodman

To Mike Best Wishes Bob Baker

Anyone for a warm, nourishing pint? Mike Jones gets the bevvies in with TV Saint main-men Johnny Goodman and Robert S. Baker

Disciples of the famous Simon Templar

Without fans to applaud their work, heroes wouldn't be heroes and stars wouldn't be stars. In the 1960s, when the Internet might have been something you used to cover your strawberries, being a fan of *The Saint* TV series was a pretty simple pastime. You wrote letters, joined the fan club (receiving, if you were lucky, a signed photo and various bits of info), bought the tie-in Corgi car and taped episodes off your black and white with your hand-held Grundig tape recorder and microphone, simultaneously trying to stop the rest of your family from eating, talking or breathing.

Now, in 1997, with the opening of the new *Saint* movie and the return of the Roger Moore series to terrestrial television, a whole new generation is beginning to repeat the happy process all over again.

Below, Ian Dickerson and Mike Jones recall 30 years of devotion to *The Saint* and what it's meant to them...

THE SAINT IT AIN'T

FOR ALMOST A DECADE Ian Dickerson has run The Saint Club, the Charteris-endorsed organisation which publishes the official *Saint* magazine, *The Epistle*. In a nutshell, he's the leading expert on all things *Saint*, keeping in close contact, from his base in Paris, with Leslie Charteris' widow Audrey and generally standing guard over the flame of the twentieth century's brightest buccaneer.

At present he has any number of *Saint* projects coming out of his ears, including the authorised Charteris biography, *A Saint I Ain't*, due for publication this summer, and a proposed *Saint* novel from *The Return of the Saint*, an old Charteris outline sent to Paramount which tells a tale of how the Saint got to meet his son.

When did you first become aware of *The Saint*?
I have always watched television and I used to love *The Return of the Saint* when I was eight years old. I watched it every week religiously – that's an interesting word to use – and then I discovered that my elder brother had a *Saint* book called *Saint Errant*, which appeared to be about the same guy. So I read it, and as you can imagine if you've ever read a *Saint* book, I was hooked. I discovered he had another one. And another... So I went round collecting them over a period of years and one day I decided I wanted to know more, so I wrote to The Saint Club at the address in the back of one of the *Saint* books. Much to my astonishment, I got a reply a few weeks later from the guy who ran it, Norman Turner.

So everything was great, then Norman passed away in the late 1980s and the club passed into the hands of someone who wasn't really that interested in it. I suggested doing a newsletter, as the Simon Dutton series was on at that time, and one day I was at home from college, the phone rang and it was Leslie Charteris. Once I'd picked the phone up off the floor we had a chat and hit it off. I became good friends with him and Audrey.

Reading his memos to Bob Baker, and the editorials in the *Saint Mystery Magazine*s, he seemed to have a wonderfully dry sense of humour.
But I don't think it was just his sense of humour. It was his command of the language. Even in the shortest letter he would concoct these beautiful phrases. There is a curious dichotomy

THREE FAVOURITE EPISODES BY IAN DICKERSON

THE BETTER MOUSETRAP

It's a light-hearted story, as only the Saint could do it. A wonderful tongue-in-cheek, eyebrow-raising performance from its star and a delightful comedic turn from Ronnie Barker as the bumbling Alphonse. Quite simply, an episode that leaves you wanting to see more - more comedy from Roger, the return of Alphonse and more of Alexandra Stewart!

THE FICTION-MAKERS

With the somewhat *Saint*-inspired *Bond* movie phenomenon in full swing, *The Fiction-Makers* provided the Saint, aided and abetted by John Kruse, with the opportunity to poke fun at the whole genre. An ingenious plot with crisp, sparkling dialogue, alongside top notch performances from Roger Moore and Sylvia Syms, make a thoroughly entertaining movie.

THE SAINT PLAYS WITH FIRE

Alongside the light comedy of *The Better Mousetrap*, the straight thriller is also something I think the show did well. And there's probably no better example than this. Tight direction, an excellent script and spot-on casting make for an outstanding 50 minutes, and it's also an excellent adaptation and updating of the original novel.

because he always said he wrote for money – he made no bones about the fact. But he loved writing. In reply to a letter from Michael Avelone, asking him to contribute to an anthology of his, he wrote, 'Apart from my addiction to eating and many other indulgences, my distaste for writing increases in geometrical proportion with every job I do. It has now reached such magnitude that my output has dwindled to close to microscopic proportions.'

That was it, you see. He did like writing, but his flippant laziness over-rode it, so he didn't write much in his later years. Also, he'd wanted to retire since 1948. There were various projects that then persuaded him otherwise. He spent a lot of the 1950s trying to get *The Saint* on TV, and then when Bob Baker and Monty Berman came on the scene, it finally happened.

When Leslie then fell ill (he died on April 15 1993, aged 85), did you feel that you were then becoming curator to *The Saint*, with a responsibility to guard his memory?

Well, I wouldn't do this if I didn't enjoy it. People frown that they've updated *The Saint* again, but although the Saint belongs in his own time, I also believe that somebody with the Saint's philosophies and attitudes – always looking for adventure in life – can exist nowadays. Having spent the last 20 years reading these books, I guess I've even adopted those philosophies myself.

So has your opinion of the Paramount movie, from the early scripts to the final product, changed ?

No. It was fairly obvious all along that they weren't going to make a Charteris Saint. I've got to be honest, once they ditched Charteris' four page proposal – his outline called *The Return of the Saint* – I hadn't a lot of faith. All I would say about the final product is that it's a darn sight better than some of the early scripts that I read.

I share what I think is Bob Baker's view of it, which is that it's a very good action adventure movie, if a bit too *Bond*-like. I guess it has to be that to compete. But *The Saint*, it ain't.

Who would you cast as a Saint for the 1990s?

Pierce Brosnan. I don't think he's physical enough to be Bond, but he'd make a perfect Saint.

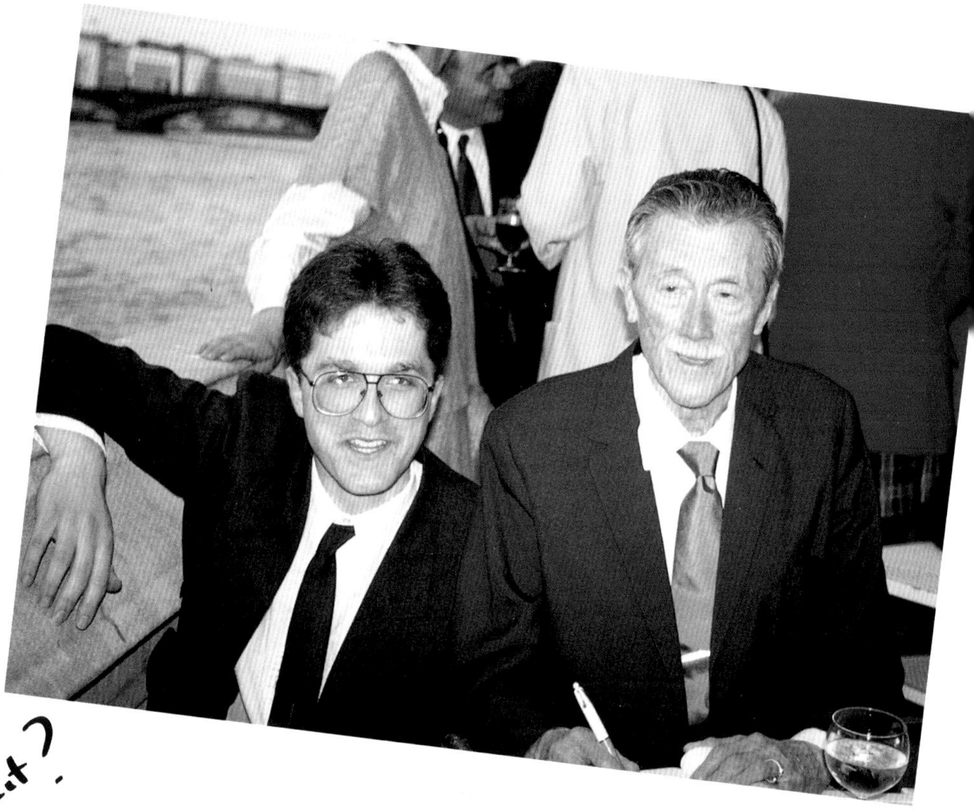

Most noble fellow drinkers... Ian Dickerson with the man himself, Leslie Charteris, creator of the halo-ed hero and founder of The Saint Club

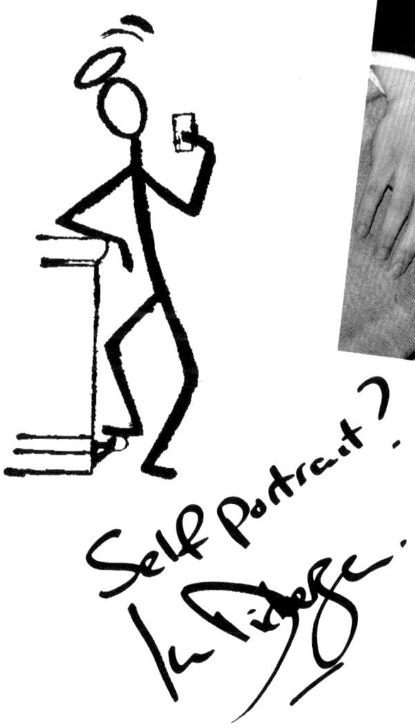
Self Portrait?

NO DIRTY VEST HERO

Owner of perhaps the largest *Saint* and Roger Moore collection in Britain, Mike Jones can quite rightly polish his halo and declare himself a devoted fan. What started with a pre-signed black and white photo in the mid-1960s has now taken over a whole extra wing of his house in the Wirral, where he lives with his most tolerant wife of 16 years and two children. And when you've got a Volvo P1800 in the garage, there's no doubt as to who's got the classiest toys...

Let's begin at the beginning. What are your first memories of *The Saint*?

Well, I was born in 1960 so I was about five at the time, but I still remember vividly a moment from *Little Girl Lost* where the Saint fixes a tin of paint, with a hole in the bottom, on the back of the VW. He's trying to find out where the kidnappers are holding the hostage girl, so Rog sneaks round, puts a tin of paint on the back bumper, pulls the little sticky bit off and then follows the white line it leaves, all the way to where she is. It wouldn't work in practice, but that's one thing that I've never, ever forgotten.

Was it like a bolt from the blue when you saw *The Saint* for the first time?

Remembering that I was so young, he was the hero figure for that time. All boys look to heroes, and Roger was it. He was the cool, well-dressed, suave, sophisticated action man. Whereas today the average action man has got a dirty vest on, he was immaculate. To me, growing up in Liverpool, he was everything that you could look up to. Wow! If only...

And presumably, for you then, it was the Saint rather than Bond, because you were really too young to go and see the Bond movies..

Yes, and the first thing I ever got was a small, black and white, pre-signed printed photograph. My mum wrote to Elstree studios for me and a standard Saint photo came in an envelope: 'Best wishes, Roger Moore'. That began a 25-year collection.

I remember it arrived in the morning before I went to school and I wouldn't take it with me in case it got damaged. I couldn't think of anything else for the rest of the day. I was just dying to get home and see it again.

At the other extreme, what's the most you've ever spent on a Saint item?

There are things I would love to have bought but couldn't afford. One of his Volvos came up for sale about seven or eight years ago, but you were looking at £30-40,000. Luckily, I now know the person who owns it, Peter Nelson. He runs the Star Cars Museum so I've seen it, I've sat in it, I've got photographs of me with it.

But I'm not in it for the money. It becomes annoying when things become so expensive that I can't get them. It's just the love of it. I've got everything from theatre programmes to early toothpaste adverts that Roger did.

So what contact have you had with Roger over the years?

I speak to Doris (Spriggs, his PA) about once a fortnight. I'm doing his life story at the moment, using my collection and a friend's collection, and when it's finished Doris is going to forward it on to Roger. I would love him to say, 'Thanks very much and let's meet,' and just have a photograph taken with him.

Aren't you surprised that he's not written his own autobiography?

Yes, I'm sure he'd be offered a lot of money and he seems to love writing. (*As witnessed by his excellent Bond diary book for* Live And Let Die *in 1973,* Roger Moore as James Bond 007, *now sadly out of print*). But Doris says he just isn't interested in doing it. I hoped he might have been spurred on to do it when Michael Caine published his.

If you were casting a new Saint who would be your choice?

If it couldn't be Roger – and when you think of something like *The Equaliser* it could be – then I would go for Lewis Collins. They'd have to teach him how to speak and that kind of thing, but I think he'd do it justice.

I tell you what I've always thought would be a great idea, for *The Persuaders* to be re-done, with Roger's son Geoffrey as the son of Lord Brett Sinclair and Jamie Lee Curtis as the daughter of Danny Wilde. From a publicist's point of view that would be a dream. And Geoffrey has his dad's looks.

THREE FAVOURITE EPISODES BY MIKE JONES

THE FRIGHTENED INN-KEEPER

The crucial thing in that episode is that his original Volvo gets blown up, and so the new Volvo is brought on for the first time. Of course, you don't actually see the car being blown up. I'm sure they weren't going to waste it, but the great thing is that he's so happy with the Volvo that he doesn't change make, he just gets a new one.

STARRING THE SAINT

I love this one for many reasons, but most of all because you've got this view of Elstree. Rog pulls up in the Volvo, gets out and walks into the administration building - something which he would, of course, have done many, many times. It's like 'Wow, that's what it must have looked like!' The other good thing about that episode is that you've got Ivor Dean in a non-Teal role. He plays this sleazy assistant.

THE MAN WHO WAS LUCKY

Because it's a much more gritty episode. You see more of the genuinely evil side of *Saint* baddies - or as much as they could show in those days. It's gangsters in Soho, with Eddie Byrne as this money-lender who you didn't cross because he'd come round and beat you up. Best of all is the opening scene, where Lucky Joe's henchmen trash the office of the people who owe him money. You think, 'God, this is quite strong for 1962!'

SO YOU THINK YOU KNOW THE FAMOUS SIMON TEMPLAR?

Been a fan of the series since you were knee-high to a halo? Then try this quiz of *Saint* TV minutiae...

1 Where do we first encounter the Saint in the TV series? Is it a) collapsed on the frozen Arctic tundra after a plane crash b) in a theatre bar, recovering from the first two acts of a dreadful play c) relaxing on the tiny island of Phuket being served drinks by a pistol-toting midget ?

2 What type of theatre does the Saint prefer? Is it a) the sweat and grunt school of acting b) fun, laffs and excitement c) the very best that strip joint owner Paul Raymond has to offer?

3 As a daytime pub tipple, what does the Saint prefer? Is it a) a Manhattan b) a vodka martini, shaken not stirred c) a warm, flat pint from the barrel ?

4 How does Simon Templar describe Rome? As a) one of the most thrilling and beautiful places in the world b) the city of yells, bells and smells c) a city of tremendous contrasts?

5 The phrase 'Homo sequendo' gets the Saintly one out of a very nasty jam in *The Latin Touch*. Does it mean a) a man who must be followed b) a man who must be squeezed c) a man who should be treated with dignity and respect and not just tossed to one side like an old pair of tights?

6 Saint sidekick Hoppy Uniatz is most impressed by the prospect of S.T. going on TV. Which of the following great TV stars does he say the Saint could be another of? Is it a) Jack Benny b) Bob Hope c) Mr Jelly Wobbly?

7 In *The Careful Terrorist* corrupt union boss Nat Grindel reckons the Saint talks like a) a mixed-up boy scout b) a honky who should be wasted c) the son of a south London policeman?

8 In *The Covetous Headsman*, how does the Saint know Georges Olivent couldn't have stayed last week at The Royale in Brussels? Because a) it's too expensive b) it burnt down three months ago c) they don't take bookings from ex-Nazis?

9 How does feisty old landlady Madame Duras describe the French police? Like a) a glistening baton of hope in an unsure world b) a school of whales at the Folies Bergére c) firm but fair?

10 If you take a guy with a well-developed sense of suspicion and give him a five-year course in how to make people blush what, in the opinion of Simon Templar, do you end up with? Is it a) a priest b) a lingerie salesperson c) a customs inspector?

11 In *The Loaded Tourist* why does the doomed Alfredo not consider New York to be civilised? Is it because of a) the booths on 42nd Street b) the hamburgers and chewing gum c) Milton Berle?

12 In *The Loaded Tourist* why does the double-crossing Carlo tell Helena Ravenna he doesn't want to go away with her? Is it a) because they'll live to regret it, not now, but one day and for the rest of their lives b) because she's old, she's dull and she's ugly c) because he's decided to walk the earth alone, like Caine in Kung Fu?

13 In *The Arrow of God* how does wealthy Lucy Wexall introduce her sister Janet Blaise to the Saint? Is it as a) 'Good for a few bob' b) 'A mistake from my parents' middle years' c) 'Not much up top, but the compensations speak for themselves'?

14 What does Ronald Leigh-Hunt's character tell Honor Blackman poverty is? Is it a) 'Only being able to afford one mistress' b) 'The smell of cabbage water and the despair of peeling wallpaper' c) 'A very cheap little shop just off Portobello'?

15 Again in *The Arrow of God*, where does the Indian mystic Astron tell S.T. he was at the time of the murder? Was he a) 'Having a quiet stroll along the beach with my trusty bow and arrow' b) 'In the smallest room in the house' c) 'Working in my mind, but geographically I was in my room'?

16 In *The Golden Journey* what does the local woodsman do when he hears Simon spanking Belinda? Does he a) rush to her aid b) clap along to the rhythm of her spanking c) go for a bit of a lie down?

17 When she's looking at him all cow-eyed at the end of the same episode, Simon says Belinda must go back to her fiancé, Jack, 'because he's your life'. But how does S.T. describe himself? Is it as a) 'Just a walk by the shore' b) 'A quick paddle in the pool' c) 'Hung like an Arabian stallion'?

18 In *The Gentle Ladies,* when S.T.'s car is pranged in an empty car park, who does he put it down to? Is it a) a sea serpent b) an irate yachtsman c) the ghost of King Knut?

19 In *The Saint Sees It Through* S.T. admits to having done some pretty crazy things in his time. Which of the following has he done? a) packed his bags for a journey, even though he doesn't even know where he's going b) rolled his eyes heavenwards, to an imaginary halo c) advertised knitwear in women's magazines?

20 In *The King of the Beggars* when the Saint goes undercover as a blind beggar, what does he manage to sell in the course of one day's work? Is it a) three lovely bunches of chrysanthemums b) ten Topo Gigio dolls c) a pencil?

21 In *The Benevolent Burglary* how does the Saint describe Monte Carlo? As a) 'A marvellous masquerade of marble, mink, music and millionaires' b) 'A marvellous masquerade of muff, mink and millionairesses' c) 'A bit fancy but fun'?

22 At the beginning of *The Fellow Traveller* what news has depressed the Saint terribly? Is it a) the death of his Aunt Prudence b) the placings in the 3.30 at Kempton Park c) the fact that birds don't sing because they're happy, but because they're warning all the other birds to stay the heck off their branch?

23 The Saint describes English cricket as 'Let's kill time with another cup of tea', and American baseball as 'Let's kill the umpire!' How does he describe Canadian ice hockey?

24 In *The Ellusive Ellshaw* why is the Saint joining 'the unspeakables'? Is it a) because he's visiting a monastery b) because he's going pheasant shooting c) because he's going on a fact-finding mission to Amsterdam's red-light district?

25 **In *Starring the Saint* why is Simon's chance of becoming a movie star brought to an abrupt end? Is it a) because he keeps forgetting his lines b) because the producer is murdered c) because the producer decides to go with Patrick McGoohan instead?**

26 In *Teresa* how does the Saint describe Mexico? As a) the land of the proud and the profane b) the land of adobe walls and skyscrapers c) the land of limousines and donkeys d) sunny?

27 **In *Iris* how does S.T. describe the producer of the appalling play he is watching? Is he a) 'A fellow who can turn wine into water' b) 'A fellow who would take his grandmother's scalp and then sell it for a toupé' c) 'The new Cameron Macintosh'?**

31 **In *Luella*, S.T. states that 'man may have evolved from the trees but...' a) 'his eyes still swing from limb to limb' b) 'there's still many a good tune played on an old vine' c) 'it doesn't stop him from playing with his nuts.'?**

32 In *The Lawless Lady* how does S.T. define 'a good red-blooded lion-hearted English female'? Is it a) a woman who kills what she wears b) a woman who makes a right signal and then turns left c) a woman who laughs when she trumps?

33 **Where is the secret rendezvous for *The High Fence*? Is it a) a suite at Claridges b) a caff called the Cosy Corner c) Chiswick roundabout?**

34 What is it in *The Saint Steps In* that S.T. says isn't true about him. Is it a) his Casanova image b) his hairline c) his ability to mimic a selection of migratory birds?

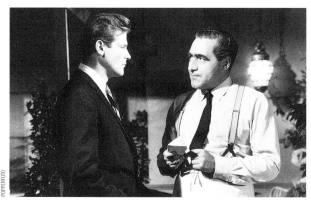

POPPERFOTO

Roger asks Leslie Sands for the answer to question 28

28 What happens to *The Well Meaning Mayor*? Is he a) elected b) found dead on the beach c) found guilty of gross indecency in a Brighton florist's?

29 **In *The Sporting Chance* what does S.T. say the fairer sex are always telling men to do? Is it a) comb their hair b) put on a tie c) stop adjusting themselves?**

30 Which whizz in the kitchen made her first guest appearance in *The Noble Sportsman*. Was it a) Fern Britton b) Jane Asher c) Susan Brookes?

35 **In *The Death Penalty* what is it that causes the Saint to set a while in Marseilles? Is it because he's a) picked up a French nail in his English tyre b) picked up a French bird in his Swedish car c) stopped to see where they filmed French Connection 2?**

36 True or false: in *The Unkind Philanthropist* the Saint impersonates a woman?

37 **How does the mystic Sibao find out the Saint's name? Does she a) spell it out in the sand she tips from her bottle b) call upon the wandering spirit of a man with a very small head who lost a fight with a chicken c) call Directory Enquiries?**

38 In the episode *Sibao*, CIA agent Tony Kreiger is operating under a phoney name. Is it a) Jeffrey Daniels b) David Grant c) Phil Fearon?

39 **In *The Loving Brothers* what is the title of the handy little book the Saint thinks he might get around to writing? Is it a) *How to Be Happy in the Australian Outback with a Broken Feed Pipe* b) *How to Be Happy in the Australian Outback with a Pair of Platforms and a Fabulous Array of Dresses* c) *Quip While You're Ahead*?**

40 According to the ever knowledgeable Saint, what special properties were emeralds supposed to possess back in Cleopatra's day? Did they a) prevent epilepsy and preserve chastity if worn at the throat b) do wonders for the eyesight if swallowed c) cure chronic diarrhoea if sensitively administered?

41 **How does Simon Templar compliment Chief Inspector Teal's police work in *The Smart Detective*? Is it a) 'Incompetent, yes. Forgetful, never' b) 'Flat-footed but fortunate' c) 'As brilliant as a very, very dull stone'?**

42 How does the TV episode *The Persistent Parasites* differ fundamentally from the original Leslie Charteris story?

43 **In *The Man Who Could Not Die* what does Simon Templar reckon the game of polo provides? Is it a) an exclusive and expensive way of breaking a leg b) as much high class crumpet as you can swing a mallet at c) a horse?**

44 How does the Saint describe Wales? Is it as a) a land of mountains and scudding clouds b) a land of brooding mysteries, steeped in the past c) a land of song and sorcery d) the home of Merlin and unpronounceable names e) all of the above?

45 **In *The House on Dragon's Rock* what terrible fury turns over a two-ton tractor, demolishes a stable, kills horses and cows and tears up trees by the roots? Is it a) a tornado b) a dragon c) an ant?**

46 According to the local Welsh folk in *The House on Dragon's Rock*, what can Llewellyn Scofield do when he's 'covered himself with ointment made from a dead cat'? Is it a) win the heart of any fair maiden who crosses his path b) turn into a werewolf c) catch mice?

47 **True or false? In *The Gadget Lovers* the Swiss cuckoo clock plays a few notes of the Adam Ant smash hit *Prince Charming*.**

48 In *The Master Plan* what fashion change is the Saint thinking of making? Is it a) a new cravat b) a pair of the latest figure-hugging hipsters c) abandoning clothes altogether in favour of baked-on striped paint and a small loincloth?

49 **In *The Scorpion* which of the following does Rog dress up as? Is it a a) 'Bent all the way' thief called Long Harry, wearing a åshabby old raincoat and shooting cap b) 'Bent all the way' gentleman's fitter called Camp Freddie, wearing a ruffle and platforms c) 'Skid kid' called Eddy, wearing tight motorcycle leathers and goggles?**

50 In *Island of Chance* what does the baddie answer when S.T. asks where the gold bullion came from? Is it a) 'Francisco Scaramanga gave it to me. He got it from Nick Nack's.' b) 'Goldfinger gave it to me. He got it from Fort Knox.' c) 'Jimmy the Gent gave it me. Don't ask'?

And the answers...

1. b) **2.** b) **3.** c) **4.** all three **5.** a) **6.** all three **7.** a) **8.** b) **9.** b) **10.** c) **11.** b) **12.** b) **13.** b) **14.** b) **15.** c) **16.** b) **17.** c) only kidding, it's a) **18.** all three **19.** a) **20.** c) **21.** a) **22.** c) **23.** 'Kill everybody' **24.** b) **25.** b) **26.** all four **27.** b) **28.** b) **29.** a) and b) **30.** b) **31.** a) **32.** b) **33.** b) **34.** a) **35.** a) **36.** true **37.** a) **38.** b) **39.** a) **40.** a) and b) **41.** a) **42.** it's no longer a nudist colony **43.** a) **44.** e) **45.** c) **46.** b) **47.** false, but damn similar **48.** c) **49.** a) and c) **50.** b)

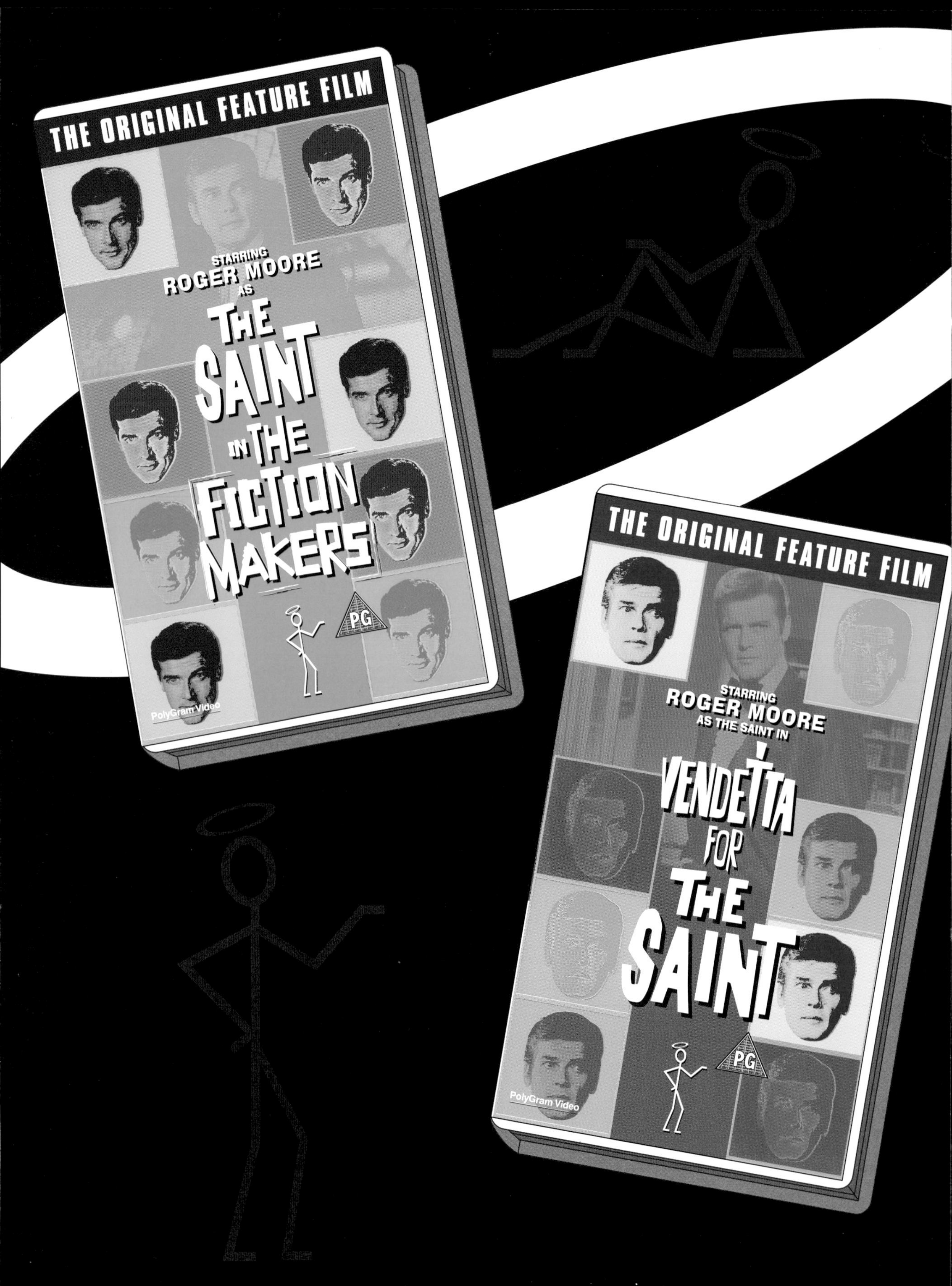
THE ORIGINAL FEATURE FILM
STARRING
ROGER MOORE
AS
THE SAINT IN THE FICTION MAKERS
PG
PolyGram Video
THE ORIGINAL FEATURE FILM
STARRING
ROGER MOORE
AS THE SAINT IN
VENDETTA FOR THE SAINT
PG
PolyGram Video